I0684948

The Winds of Battle

The Journey of James Addington

John Schork

This book is an original publication of Jupiter Pixel Publishing
http://jupiterpixel.com/schork.htm
18380 SE Lakeside Drive
Jupiter, FL 33469

TABLE OF CONTENTS

PART ONE

1770-1775

Chapter One

A New World

The journey from Albany had taken the better part of a week. Traveling parallel to the Hudson River, the small group on horseback had enjoyed mild spring weather following a particularly harsh winter. On the stretches where the post road was clearly defined, they had made good time, the spring rains not heavy enough to create the quagmire that would certainly come within the month. Rear Admiral David Addington, formerly of the Royal Navy, had decided not to take his coach, knowing the potential the heavy rig had for getting stuck anytime it wasn't on solid ground.

Joined by his young son James, the admiral was making the journey to New York City for a very specific purpose. Just as he had done when he had reached his twelfth birthday, leaving his home in Exeter and traveling to Portsmouth to join his first ship as a midshipman in the Royal Navy, James was now doing the same.

From a seafaring family, the decision for David Addington to follow his father had been made for him, just as he was making the same decision for James. As a second son, James would not inherit the large tract of land that David Addington had been granted by King George for his lifetime of service to England. However, when Rear Admiral Sir David Addington requested that his son join the Royal Navy, the Admiralty was only too happy to oblige. His wife's illness and the difficulty of communicating with the Admiralty had delayed the admiral's plans for over two years. He knew that his son was getting a late start at age fifteen, but it couldn't be helped.

Addington's request was even more unique as he was now living full time in the Colony of New York and there had been very few colonials voluntarily joining the Royal Navy. The colonists who did go to sea were normally in the service of the many small shipping companies that lined the eastern seaboard from Maine to the Carolinas.

However the English colonies did supply manpower to the fleet through impressments of non-volunteers into service aboard the many men-of-war that patrolled the Atlantic. A very unpopular practice with the colonists, the Admiralty felt that the protection provided to the colony's commerce and territories justified the commandeering of able-bodied men to keep the fleet fully manned.

"In the distance, James, you can see the ferry landing to the city."

David Addington had reined in his horse as they crested a small knoll to see the northern end of Manhattan Island, the smoke from the city visible to the south. A fresh wind blew from the east, rolling the occasional cloud across the bright blue April sky.

"How much further?" his son asked.

The young man was tall for his age. His dark brown hair and deep green eyes making him appear older than his years.

"I should think we will be in the city for supper."

James turned to ask his father a question, then thought better of it. His mind raced with questions about the navy and what it would be like. All he could get from his father was that the navy was "a good start for any young man."

The young man had asked his father's coxswain, Tom Faircloth, who had been at sea with the admiral for over twenty years and was now his trusted servant. A veteran of many ships and battles, Faircloth had given James brief glances into the life of "young gentlemen" on a ship in the Royal Navy. He had also taught the youngster how to use a navy cutlass, their mock battles lasting for hours in the fields near the house. A poacher in Kent before being pressed into the king's service, the old sailor had shown James the ways of the forest also. In time, James became as comfortable in the deep woods as any young man in Albany. Now he was to leave that world for the strange realm of the sea.

Expected to learn every aspect of how to sail and fight a ship, James's duties would take him from high in the rigging to the lower gun decks. His primary goal during those first formative years was to prepare himself for the lieutenant's examination which would mark his progression to the commissioned ranks.

James found himself expectant and hesitant at the same time. Leaving his home and everything he knew would be difficult. But it couldn't be harder than losing his mother last year after a long illness. James and his mother had been very close. Even now when he thought of her his eyes would mist over.

Rowena McKenna had been strikingly beautiful, the daughter of a prosperous farmer near Albany. She had met David Addington only six months after the death of his first wife of sixteen years, Abigail. Despite the difference in ages, Rowena and David had fallen in love and married just one year after Abigail's death. James's birth only one year later brought them both a sense of joy they would share until her death.

Rowena had been very protective of her only child and that often frustrated her husband who felt that boys should be boys. Introducing him to books at an early age, she had taught him to read, do figures and even speak French.

His father, knowing James future would lie at sea, had taught him of battles, tactics and war. It was an unusual education to be sure, but James was an intelligent young man and seemed to absorb his lessons well.

Francis Addington, James's older half-brother had always resented the arrival of Rowena in the household. The subsequent birth of James had only deepened the boy's anger. While the admiral tried to treat both sons alike, Francis always felt that James received favor. Consequently the two boys had never gotten along, their dislike only growing stronger as they both matured.

James thought of their last argument which had ended when Francis punched James hard in the stomach, doubling him over in pain. The malevolent look in those dark eyes had scared James more than ever before. Perhaps the best prospect for his future did indeed lie at sea. Tomorrow he would find out.

It had taken two trips for the men and their horses to be ferried across to Manhattan on the small wooden ferry. Operated by an old man and young boy, the crossing had taken almost thirty minutes each way.

Once ashore, the men rode south toward the city and harbor. The number of buildings surprised the young man. The largest town he had ever seen was Albany, which had a population of 3,000. His father told him that over 20,000 people lived in the city of New York. The second largest city in the colonies, it had become a center of commerce and government. Along with Boston and Halifax, the large harbor at the southern end of Manhattan provided a secure haven for the navy's Atlantic Squadron.

As they moved farther into the city, James found the smell repugnant. The mixed odor of manure, wood smoke and sewage made him queasy. He felt his stomach roll over as they turned down a wide road that led between several wooden buildings. Perhaps his original excitement about his new adventure had been premature.

"You've been a mite quiet."

James turned as Tom Faircloth pulled up beside him, the two horses naturally matching the slow gait. It was hard to imagine leaving the man who had been at his side for his entire life. He was closer to the old sailor than he would ever be to his brother. Faircloth had always been there for him, offering encouragement, teaching him the ways of a man. Now he could see the concern in Tom's eyes.

"Truth be known, I'm a little scared." James would have only admitted that to one man in the world and now it helped to share his burden.

Faircloth seemed to consider James statement for a long minute then said, "Only natural. Any man going to sea for the first time should be scared. But that fear will help you be a better seaman and officer."

James reined his horse to a stop.

"But how do I do that?"

Faircloth smiled. "You watch and learn. Don't be afraid to ask questions. And find someone you respect and always ask yourself, what would that man do? And listen to the old hands. A man who's spent twenty or thirty years before the mast has a knowledge that will take you a long time to gain, so use their experience. Trust your men and treat them fair. That'll make you better than most."

James wished the old coxswain was going with him, but Faircloth would always be with the admiral, until one of them was gone.

Ahead he could see a green sign over the roadway which identified the large two story building as "Hunter's Inn." As if she could sense the journey ending, his black mare began to toss her head and whinny.

An elderly negro took the reins of their horses from them and led the animals around behind the inn. Picking up their saddle bags, the men entered a low wide room which smelled of lilac.

Behind a large table the inn's clerk sat carving a piece of wood.

"I require four rooms for my company," the admiral said, his voice rather imperious.

Looking up from his carving, the young man squinted at them. "Four, you say?" The man's face was scarred by the pox and he was missing his right ear.

"That is what I said, is there a problem?"

The man stood up, looking slightly perplexed. "Most folks put everyone in the same room, dogs too."

David Addington said flatly, "Of that, I am quite sure."

"Sign the book," the man said, sliding a loosely bound journal toward Addington.

The admiral took a pen from the man, dipped it into the inkwell and signed the book.

"You Addington," the man asked?

"If you care to read the book, you would know that."

"Can't read," the man said in a matter of fact tone. "Bleedin' navy man was asking for you. Said he'd come back."

"Admiral Addington, Julian Powell, second leftenant in *Andromeda,* at your service. Captain Fletcher's compliments and he would like to invite you aboard for dinner tomorrow night at eight bells."

"You say Captain Fletcher? I thought Hiram Percy commanded *Andromeda.*"

"Quite right, sir. But he was taken ill and had to go ashore. Captain Fletcher took command six months ago."

"Could that be Stephen Fletcher?"

"Why yes, sir, it is."

"Well damn my eyes," the admiral laughed. "Your captain was a midshipman of mine in *Resolution*. And now he's a post captain with his own ship. Good for him. But I would tell you that when your midshipmen become captains, you are indeed getting old. Please pass my compliments to your captain and I would be most pleased to accept his kind invitation. Now, what can you tell me of the arrangements for my son to join the ship?"

Powell looked momentarily surprised, but replied directly, "I am directed to collect him at your earliest convenience, sir, and repair onboard."

Sir David frowned slightly and cleared his throat. "Ah, yes. No reason to drag this out. That will be quite acceptable."

James looked at the tall man in the blue uniform, his white lapels and bright brass buttons in stark contrast to the drab surroundings of the room. It seemed to the young man that everything was happening much too fast. He had thought there would be time to get acquainted with this strange new world before leaving his father. Perhaps that was the way in the navy.

"I've ordered his uniforms from Lipscomb Brothers and will have them delivered to the ship tomorrow."

The lieutenant nodded. "Very well, sir. We can make do from ship's stores until then." He turned to look at James. "Mr. Addington, it's time we shoved off. The tide is turning and it will be a hard pull back to *Andromeda*. Admiral, I will take my leave." He nodded formally and turned for the door. "Come along, young man," he said over his shoulder.

James looked at his father, seeing a look he had not seen before. His very controlled and unemotional father looked concerned, as if the reality of their parting had just struck home.

Sir David seemed to come alive, standing up and putting his hand on James's shoulder. "Off with you now. I'll have Faircloth bring your new chest to you in the morning." He paused and looked at his young son, about to enter the harsh and demanding life of the sea. "Remember what we discussed. Above all things do your duty. Now that you're a sea officer, your loyalty must be to your captain, your ship and your king. You must put everything else out of your mind."

James nodded and said with as much confidence as he could muster, "Yes, father."

"And son, you will be busy, but a letter now and again would be welcome."

Following the young officer down the stairs, James realized he had never written a letter to his father.

A sharp wind cut across the darkening harbor as the ship's cutter, manned by eight oarsmen, pulled toward the anchored frigate. James sat in the stern, next to another midshipman named Culley who had been waiting with the boat and crew at the wharf. Culley appeared to James to be a year older, with a six inch height advantage. He even had a light beard. The young man had acted neither friendly nor hostile, but intent on carrying out his duties. James looked across the dark water, interrupted only by the few lights of anchored ships. It seemed a strange and hostile world he was entering.

A man had been waiting for them in the street that Powell had addressed as "Petty Officer Adams." The burly man was beside a small wagon drawn by two tired horses and driven by a man who appeared to be one step away from death.

Since leaving the inn, Lieutenant Powell had acted distinctly different than when in the presence of Sir David. During the fifteen minute trip to the pier, Powell had only said, "I expect your attention and obedience at all times, is that clear?"

James realized that his notions of what the navy might be like could very well be quite wrong.

"Ahoy," came the cry from the side of the ship as the boat pulled under the lee.

"Aye, aye," the boat's coxswain replied, telling the watch that the boat carried an officer.

The jet black hull glistened in the light of several lanterns hanging above the ship's side. Confused waves washed along the side, jostling the cutter smartly as the bowman hooked onto the main chains. Almost instantly the lieutenant stood and grasped rope hand rails that hung down over the side. Quickly turning his sword to allow his legs freedom, he climbed up the side and through the entry port.

"Let's go and be quick about it," Culley said to James, grabbing his arm and pushing him toward the ropes.

James's shoe slipped as he stepped toward the side and he pitched toward the massive black hull.

"Take care, young sir," one of the oarsmen called as he caught James and kept him from falling between the cutter and the ship's hull. "Remember, one hand for the ship, one hand for the man." The sailor held James by the waist and helped him grab hold of the rope. "Take it steady, one step at a time," the man said quietly, as James pulled himself up the side.

He realized there were small steps cut into the heavy planks and James planted his toes in each one as he climbed.

"He's got to learn, Stevens," Culley snapped at the man.

"Aye, sir," the man named Stevens replied, averting his eyes.

Scrambling through the entry port, James found himself standing on the main deck, its length lit by a series of lanterns spaced fore and aft. Even in the reduced light, he could see the big cannons which lined each side, their massive barrels visible behind the closed gun ports. Forward of what James knew was the main mast, two large boats sat one on top of the other. Everywhere there were ropes and pulleys forming a massive spider web above his head.

"Follow me," Midshipman Culley said sharply as he brushed past James and headed forward.

Descending the steep wooden ladder, James was struck by the pungent smell of unwashed bodies and tobacco. The murmur of quiet conversations rose up to meet him and he heard a flute being played somewhere forward.

Culley ducked below a wooden beam and turned aft. "Watch your head," he said sharply.

9

They descended one more ladder and turned into a partitioned area where a square wooden table sat with a bench on each side.

"This is the gunroom, where we mess and sleep," he said, his voice now indifferent. "They are now four of us, John Paine is the senior and Lucas Brown is second. I'm third, my name is Paul Culley."

Two small lanterns hanging from iron ring bolts in the overhead swung gently, casting a pale light over the table.

"You can put your sea chest against that bulkhead when it arrives. We sling our hammocks from those hooks on the overhead."

James's head was swimming. The foreign smells coupled with the pale light from the lanterns and the rocking motion of the ship made him feel very queasy. Everything was quite overwhelming.

A short, wiry man entered the gunroom. He wore a faded blue shirt with dingy white pants. His hair was tied at the nape of his neck with a small piece of cord. The man's small eyes darted between the two young men.

James thought the man resembled a mouse with his hands in front of him as if ready to reach for a morsel of cheese.

"Small, this is Mr. Addington, just joining," Culley said, his tone showing feigned indifference. "A chest can be expected from ashore some time tomorrow. For the present he shall require a basic rig from the slop chest to tide him over."

"I'll see to it, sir," Small said and ducked back into the passageway.

"An odd duck. Small takes care of the gunroom. He used to be a gunner, but one day he was observed in conversation with a twelve pounder on the gun deck. They said we didn't need a daft man working around gunpowder." The older boy sat down heavily. "Typical of the cretins they expect us to work with," he went on, "Half are criminals and the rest are dunces of the highest degree."

James looked hard at Paul Culley to see if he was serious.

"And don't ever trust any of them," Culley continued. "Now sit down. Small will get us food when he returns."

This is not at all what I expected, James thought.

One hour later, James found himself wearing a pair of white britches that were big for him and a long sleeved white shirt with two buttons missing. While he didn't feel like a midshipmen, he at least looked like one.

The summons from the captain came after he had finished a nondescript meal of cheese, stale bread and watery beer. It would take some getting used to the strange fare aboard a king's ship.

A wooden screen which ran the full width of the ship sectioned off the area reserved for the captain. Mr. Culley had left to stand his watch on deck directly after the meal and the second midshipmen, Lucas Brown offered to escort him aft to the big cabin.

Brown, probably two years older than James, had a friendly face under tousled blonde hair. He smiled constantly and seemed to be thoroughly enjoying himself.

"Captain Fletcher is a good captain, but a bit stiff if you know what I mean," he said climbing the steps to the main deck.

James wanted to ask questions, but his father had always told him to listen first and talk second.

"But be on your toes around the first leftenant," Brown said with a quiet, cautionary tone. "He's exceedingly precise, cross him and you'll find yourself bent over a twelve pounder."

"I haven't met him as yet. Mr. Powell collected me at the inn."

"Leftenant Powell's a mean one too. Many of the crew have tasted the cat because of it," Brown said quietly.

"The cat?"

"Flogged, young James. The cat of nine tails. It takes a man's back and turns it into raw meat."

James's trepidation about his new situation increased greatly as the two worked their way aft toward the big cabin.

"The third leftenant is a bit of all right. He joined in Portsmouth just before we left, his name is Carlyle. We also have a Marine, his name is Haydon. But he has no time for mids, so stay out of his way. Normally we would have a fourth leftenant, but Mr. Sterling became ill when we left England. He took fever and died a week out of New York."

They approached a Marine sentry standing guard next to a door in the screen. The man watched them approach, his eyes indicating that he expected the newest ship's officer.

Without warning the man slammed the butt of his musket into the deck and called, "Midshipman Addington, sir!"

How did he know my name, James wondered, I just arrived.

Before he could consider the possibilities, the door opened and an older man with stringy grey hair and wearing spectacles beckoned James into the cabin.

"I'll leave you with Mr. Murray, the captain's clerk," Brown said and ducked back forward.

Entering the cabin James was surprised to see the large open space, very much in contrast to the crowded conditions in the gunroom or on the main deck where the crew berthed.

"Over here, Mr. Addington."

In the light from several lanterns, James saw Captain Stephen Fletcher sitting at a small desk, a quill in his hand. A lean man, his dark black hair was pulled back into a tight que that rested on his open collar. James was struck by the deep tan on his face, like leather almost, the result of over twenty five years at sea.

"Get our newest midshipman a chair, Murray." He turned to James without smiling or changing his demeanor in the slightest. "Sit down while I finish this dispatch."

Using only four inches of the chair, James sat with his back straight and his hands in his lap. Able to study the man behind the desk, he saw a hardness in his manner, as if he was ready to go into battle.

His clerk moved next to Fletcher as if knowing what his captain would want.

Turning, Captain Fletcher handed the letter to Murray. "Make sure that is on the first boat in the morning."

"Aye, sir."

The captain now looked at James, his deep blue eyes narrowing just slightly. "Did you know I was one of your father's midshipmen?"

12

"Yes, sir."

"It was in *Resolution,* I was about your age. But that was a ship of the line, seventy four guns and a dozen midshipmen. It was easy to blend into the background with almost seven hundred in the crew."

On deck a shrill boatswain's pipe called the oncoming watch to muster. The captain's eyes registered the sound as he continued, "But this is a frigate, Mr. Addington. Every man and officer must do their job and do it well. And you will learn your trade well aboard *Andromeda.* The navy does not have enough frigates and we spend most of our time at sea."

James found himself feeling excitement for the first time since leaving Albany. Perhaps this was going to be a great adventure after all.

"Your charge for now is to learn everything you can about this ship. You will train in navigation, gunnery and ship handling. Teaching you will not only be the ship's officers, but also the master and his mates. They know the sea and from them you will acquaint yourself with the many mysteries of the deep. You will also learn from the surgeon, the carpenter, the gunner and the sail maker. It takes many skills to keep a ship at sea and fighting, thousands of miles from home. You're starting late. Most midshipmen your age have two or three years at sea already. It will require extra work and diligence on your part."

The captain sat back in his chair and looked at the young man sitting expectantly in front of him.

"And finally, you must learn about yourself. As time passes you will discover what it takes to earn the respect of your seniors and juniors alike. You'll find out about courage and sacrifice. It's a tough and demanding road you're taking, but I know your father understands that. If he feels you have the makings of a sea officer, I will do all I can to make sure you become one."

"Thank you, sir," James heard himself say before he realized he'd spoken.

Stephen Fletcher chuckled. "I hope you will say the same thing a year from now. Murray?"

The small man appeared from behind a screen.

"Aye, sir."

"Please escort Mr. Addington back to the gunroom. I believe he has duties to attend to."

Chapter Two

A Terrible Reality

Andromeda encountered the first hint of the storm one day out of New York. Bound for Antigua, the ship began to heave in response to the deepening swells running up from the south. The deep blue sea turned a frothy gray green as the breeze turned into a stiff blow, throwing spray across the rolling wave tops.

Those days before leaving port had been just a blur to James. He never seemed to be in the right place at the right time. The whistles and calls that everyone else reacted to without thinking left him confused and wondering if he would ever get used to shipboard life. But one incident would never leave his memory. It was the second day when Tom Faircloth delivered his midshipmen's chest with supplies and uniforms. When they returned to the deck for Faircloth to catch the small boat he had rented, the old sailor raised his hand to his forehead, the traditional mark of respect by sailors to their officers. In James entire life, he had never done that, nor had James ever seen him "knuckle" the admiral. It was as if Tom was acknowledging James transition to the sea. It made the young man proud.

By the next morning, the wind had risen to a full gale, the frigate now carrying only a reefed forecourse to maintain steerage as she rode out the storm. Below decks, the inevitable result of constant buffeting had taken a heavy toll on the new hands. The wild swaying became more violent as the day wore on and many men were too ill to go on deck. The old hands were available if the captain needed to make sail, but for the present, manning the pumps and checking the rigging were the only requirements of the crew.

"A nasty blow," Lucas Brown commented, his foot jammed hard against the table to counter the lurching of the hull. The sounds of working wood and pounding waves provided an unsettling background to the small cramped gunroom.

"Is it always like this?" James asked, his voice unsteady.

"Sometimes worse," John Paine, the senior midshipman, said with little emotion. A tall lean young man, Paine came from a wealthy London family with strong political connections. Almost nineteen years old, he had been at sea for over six years, but last year had failed his lieutenant's examination.

"You certainly got your sea legs quickly," Brown said to James. "Most new snotties would be curled up in a puddle of their own puke."

James didn't understand why he wasn't seasick, but judging by how miserable the other new hands were, he considered himself lucky.

"That's a small fact in your favor, Mr. Addington," Paine said. "And why are you joining the ship in New York?"

"I'm from Albany, Mr. Paine."

The tall man narrowed his eyes at James. "A colonial?"

James felt confused. The vehemence of Paine's comment made his colonial background sound as if had the pox.

"I may have been born in New York, sir. But I am British," James said defensively.

Paul Culley came through the door, water dripping from his oilskin parka. Pulling off the soaked garment he hung it on a wood peg jutting from the bulkhead.

"Leftenant Powell sent me down early," he said turning to his three messmates. "And I wasn't going to argue with him."

"Well, James," Lucas said, "Time to get ready for your first watch. The first leftenant has the deck and it doesn't pay to be late."

His observations so far of Lieutenant Judson Shaw told James that his friend was certainly correct. Since coming back aboard just before sailing, Shaw had made it very clear he was not a man to be taken lightly. James had watched him keenly as the ship got underway, marveling at how the man seemed to be aware of everything happening on deck. Armed with a brass speaking trumpet, he was quick to provide acerbic orders or comments to anyone he felt was not performing up to his standards. How would he be on watch?

James pulled on an oilskin and followed Lucas Brown up the first ladder heading topside.

"Another bloody colonial," Paine said quietly to no one in particular as if he was thinking aloud.

The two midshipmen struggled against the pitching, rolling deck as they made their way from the companionway to the quarterdeck ladder. The full force of wind and sea now hit the young gentlemen, making them stagger like drunks as they reached the ladder.

James looked up to see Lieutenant Shaw speaking with the second lieutenant who was pointing to the mainmast rigging. Behind the two officers, two helmsmen were braced on each side of the large wheel, holding the rudder against the surge of the sea. Sheets of spray lashed across the deck as the ship fought into the heavy waves.

"The wind has slackened," Powell said in a loud voice. "She seems to be holding well and Mr. Bagley thinks we're through the worst of it."

"The master has a nose for it. I hope he's right, Mr. Powell." Judson Shaw turned and saw the two midshipmen as they crossed the quarterdeck. "MR. BROWN," he yelled across the deck.

James followed his friend across the slanting deck, pulling up short of the first lieutenant who glared at them. His hawk-like nose accentuated his stern look and James felt extremely uncomfortable under his gaze.

"I don't expect the junior officers of my watch to arrive on deck after I do. Mr. Addington, you are certainly off to a poor start."

The ship hit a large wave and they all lunged forward, catching themselves against the heave.

"No, sir," Brown said.

A tall man, Judson Shaw stood a good foot above the two boys. He looked up in the rigging where the masthead pendant whipped in the wind.

"Before the end of the watch, Mr. Brown, I expect you to teach our newest officer the names of all lines associated with the mainmast. Do I make myself clear?"

Brown nodded. "Yes, sir."

Shaw looked at James, his gray eyes betraying nothing. "Now be about your duties."

Four hours later the boatswain of the watch struck four bells and the two young gentlemen went below, relieved by John Paine. As James moved down the ladder he felt as if the ship was receiving him into a place of warmth and safety.

He and Lucas Brown had studied the myriad of lines, all with different names while the wind had continued to buffet *Andromeda* without mercy. But in the final thirty minutes of the watch, the violent gusts had dropped off significantly.

Now sitting down at the gunroom table, Lucas Brown wiped his face with a piece of cloth.

"A word of wisdom. Now that Leftenant Shaw has told you to know the lines on the mainmast, we must teach you the differences on the fore and mizzen masts. He'll ask you, mark my words. And heaven help you if your answer is wrong."

Everything was a bit overwhelming, James thought. So much to learn and apparently in a very short time.

Brown grinned. "Don't worry, you'll catch on. Besides, we men of the colonies have to stick together in the midst of these proper Englishmen."

"You're from the colonies?"

"Boston, born and bred, my good fellow. And we New Englanders can sail as well as any bloody Englishman."

Lucas Brown's conspiratorial smile suddenly made James feel very good.

The last remnants of the storm were finally left in the ship's wake three days later. The crew of HMS *Andromeda* was sore and tired but oddly content. The ship had escaped any major damage from the rough weather and all hands were safe. For the first time since leaving New York, the on coming watch saw the sun as it broke through the clouds, turning the sea bright blue.

James watched Hiram Bagley, the *Andromeda's* sailing master, as he surveyed first, the horizon, then the ship's rigging. The rotund Bagley was perhaps the oldest man aboard, having spent his entire life at sea. Tasked with executing the captain's sailing instructions, he also oversaw the ship's navigation including teaching the young midshipmen the complexities of that most crucial science. His face looked like leather, the result of years exposed to the elements in every ocean of the world. In what seemed like a permanent squint, his bright blue eyes always seemed to have a twinkle.

"Mr. Bagley," the Captain said, catching the master's attention.

"Aye, sir."

"Do you see the wind continuing to veer to the west?"

The old man nodded.

"I want to make up for time we lost in the storm. Set the t'gallants and the royals, if you please."

"As you say, captain. Mr. Slocum, call the hands."

The master's mate ran to the quarterdeck ladder, and announced, "All hands on deck. Set t'gallants and royals."

Immediately the boatswain's whistles sounded their shrill calls which were answered by the pounding of bare feet as the crew raced on deck.

"Mr. Addington," the first lieutenant called in his most forceful voice.

James realized he had been watching the master and not paying attention to events on the quarterdeck.

"Sir!"

"Time to continue your education. Report to Mr. Carlyle for sail drill."

Raising his hand in a salute of acknowledgment, *Andromeda's* youngest midshipmen ran forward to the mainmast.

Hands were running on deck, the topmen leading the way to the shroud lines which ran from the deck up to each of the three masts. To an outside observer the scene looked like total bedlam, but each man knew his assignment and could carry it out in darkness or the stormiest night. Today the bright sun made the trip up the mast seem like child's play to the experienced hands.

Seeing the third lieutenant standing with a speaking trumpet by the lee braces, James ran up and said breathlessly, "Sir, Mr. Shaw told me to take part in sail drill."

"Did he now?" Carlyle looked around at the men scrambling on to the tarred standing rigging. "Stevens," he called to a big man about to climb onto the mainmast shrouds.

"Sir," Stevens said as he raised his hand to his forehead as a mark of respect for the officer.

"Take charge of our young gentleman. This will be his first time aloft."

Stevens grinned at the lieutenant. "Aye, sir." He turned to James. "Remember what I told you in the boat, one hand for the ship, one hand for the man. Take it slow and do just what I tells ya."

Suddenly James felt a pang of fear. He looked up at the men climbing onto the footropes that hung under each of the big yards.

"No higher than the main yard," Carlyle said as they moved to the shrouds.

James knew from his study that the main yard was the first large horizontal spar from which the main course hung. And while it might be the lowest yard, it was still forty feet above the ship's deck.

"You'll do fine," Stevens said. "Now you go first and I'll be right behind you. Slow and steady. One hand always holding on to a ratline."

Listening to the steady tone of Steven's voice, James felt reassured, and grasping the heavily tarred manila line, he pulled himself onto the shrouds and began to carefully climb.

Stephen Fletcher watched from the quarterdeck. He knew the first time a man went aloft things could go very wrong.

"Do you remember your first time?"

Captain Fletcher turned to see Hiram Bagley also watching the young midshipman.

"I do indeed. And his father was standing where I am now."

The older man chuckled and said quietly to himself, "And he was probably worrying just like you are."

The roll of the ship became more pronounced the farther James climbed. He had never imagined it would be like this, the wind, flapping canvas, cursing men and the lunging ship forty feet below him. His heart was pounding as he came even with the main yard.

"Now you're going to step to the yard, using the handhold and the footrope," Stevens called over the sound of the wind as he climbed even with James. "I'll go first. Do what I do. Reach for the handhold then smartly step on the footrope and pull yourself onto the yard. Pay attention to where you puts yer foot. Now watch me."

James found he was holding the tarred lines with all his strength, a feeling of panic starting to rise up inside him. The powerful wind held him in its grip, adding to his fear.

Stevens leaned across to the yard, and pulled himself onto the footrope. He turned to face James.

"Sees what I mean? All right, young sir, tis yer turn."

The young boy looked down briefly, the fear now starting to take control of him.

"I....I....I...."

"Don't look down and remember I'm right here."

James forced himself to look across to the young sailor. The man seemed so comfortable standing on the swaying footrope. Slowly he released his left hand and slid his body to the edge of the shroud lines. Reaching across to the main yard, James grabbed the handhold and stepped toward the footrope. His foot slid just slightly as he reached with his other hand to grasp the hand line and found himself standing next to Stevens.

His heart still pounding, he turned to see the man grinning at him.

"See? Nothing to it."

"Quite…right."

"Now watch as they release the buntlines on the royals and t'gallants. Then you'll see this old girl really fly."

James looked up watching the topmen releasing the upper banks of sails. The cracks as the wind took the strain

21

and lines seized tight made his heart pound. The winds blew his hair wildly and he found himself hollering, "huzzah......huzzah."

Able Seaman Richard Stevens, 'Dick' to his mess mates, smiled and knew the *Andromeda's* newest officer would do fine.

Standing on deck later, James looked up at the main yard and felt good. He had taken an important step. As he watched the blue sky and white clouds, it suddenly struck him that these men had to go up the mast in all types of weather and at night.   The thought made his stomach queasy, but he knew he would do it too when his time came.

The ship's surgeon, Jim Goodrum, was one of the better doctors in the Atlantic Squadron. While many of his colleagues had gone to sea to escape debt or family problems, Goodrum had always wanted to see the world and couldn't think of a better way to do it than shipping out as a naval surgeon. At the same time, he found a particular challenge keeping a crew of over two hundred men alive and well in both dangerous and isolated conditions.

Educated at the Royal Medical College in London, Doctor Goodrum had turned down several offers to join established physicians in London. Instead he'd embarked in his first frigate and with the exception of one year ashore, had been at sea ever since. Now in his forties, he had treated every type of battle injury and dealt with diseases that most of his colleagues could only imagine.

"Good day, Mr. Addington   What brings you to my study?"

Working in a small space off the wardroom, Goodrum was always available to any crewmember who might need his ministrations.

"Sir, Mr. Powell asked that you examine my finger."

"Very well, come in and sit down on that stool."

The doctor moved a lantern to the table said, "Which finger, pray tell?"

James held his right hand up to the light.

"Ah, yes," he said, gently taking James's arm and turning it over. He pulled up the midshipman's sleeve and looked at both sides of the arm.

"Does that produce any level of pain or inconvenience?" he asked as he squeezed the arm from wrist to elbow.

"A little," he said with a wince.

His attention returned to the boy's index finger.

"A splinter, would be my initial diagnosis" he pronounced.

"Yes, sir."

Goodrum pressed on the finger.

"Ouch!"

"Yes, I do believe we have the narrowed it down to a piece of foreign matter within the digit."

He continued to examine James's finger.

"That will have to come out or there is a chance of mortification."

"Yes, sir."

"I will meet you on deck in twenty minutes. The light is better and it will offer the crew some entertainment."

He chuckled as James's eyes opened wide.

"And Mr. Addington, I see your hands need a good washing. We do have soap aboard *Andromeda.* I insist that a superior level of cleanliness be maintained at all times. Better for the crew, better for the ship. Now off with you."

Used to holding down men while their limbs were amputated, Leadbetter, the surgeon's assistant, had only brought two instruments and a small wooden table on deck. Standing with his legs balanced against the roll of the ship, he held James's arm in a vise-like grip.

Goodrum took one last look at the swollen finger. He pulled the cork from a small bottle and poured the contents into a cup.

"Here, my boy, drink this down."

The fiery burn of strong rum made James cough violently.

"A touch of spirits always makes the surgeon's task easier on the patient. And there are times when it allows the surgeon a modicum of respite from the more difficult work."

"Aye, sir" James said hoarsely.

"Now this will just take a just moment, try not to move."

With the assistant holding his arm and the doctor gripping his finger, James felt incapable of moving in the slightest.

The midshipmen felt a sharp pain and then heard Goodrum say, "There we have it. Nasty little piece."

The doctor held the small piece of wood to his nose for a moment. "Quite good, no sign of mortification. Now a liberal application of vinegar and you'll be ship shape in no time."

Chapter Three

The Sound of Battle

The mood of the ship improved as *Andromeda* moved south into warmer waters. While the tropics held just as many challenges, most sailors preferred the sun and blue waters of the Caribbean to the frigid wind-swept Atlantic.

Enroute to Antigua, the frigate would join Rear Admiral Sir Roger Kinsey's Leeward Squadron. Protection of commerce and English investments were just as important as maintaining a political presence in the Caribbean. The clear waters and numerous islands had long been the home to men who made their life as pirates on the high seas and attacks on British merchant ships had been increasing each year. The lords of the admiralty were not convinced this was by chance.

There had been major political adjustments following the Seven Year's War and France's influence in the new world had been remarkably reduced. Did that provide reason for this increase in attacks on the English? While many of the cutthroats who preyed on honest commerce were acting alone, there were also brigands who appeared more like privateers than pirates, although the distinction sometimes was very blurred.

"No, no, Mr. Addington. You must be more precise as you swing your arc to accurately mark the horizon."

James stood with his legs apart trying to compensate for the ship's movement while at the same time peering through a brass sextant at the far horizon.

Hiram Bagley, standing behind James, continued, "There are those who will try to tell you navigation is a science. But I'm telling you it is an art if you want to do it well. Now try it again and work on striking an arc that averages the pitch and roll of the ship."

Watching Lucas Brown as he took his sighting, James brought the sextant back up to his eye, the horizon's motion accelerating as he watched through the lens.

"This is the devil," he said under his breath to Lucas.

"John Paine told me you have to handle a sextant like a woman," Brown whispered back.

James laughed, followed by Lucas, not sure what naughty thing the older boy might actually be talking about. However, the mysteries of the opposite sex were becoming clearer each day as he listened to the senior midshipmen discuss lurid subjects James found both titillating and hard to fathom.

"And what do our two young gentlemen find so amusing with your noon sight, Mr. Bagley."

They all turned to see the captain standing at the lee rail.

The master said nothing, but his stern look left no doubt of his displeasure.

"Perhaps a little exercise will curtail the skylarking, gentlemen. To the top of the mainmast, both of you."

James felt his face reddening.

"You heard the captain," Bagley said, "Off with you."

As James pulled himself up the tarred shrouds he knew the captain would talk to him later. Several times after making a mistake, Stephen Fletcher had called James aside to provide advice and guidance. Unaware that it was very unusual for a ship's captain to regularly interact with his young midshipman, James felt that his tutelage was very intense compared to his counterparts.

From above them they heard the masthead lookout calling down to the watch.

"Deck there, two sail on the horizon, three points off the larboard bow!"

The two young men stopped their climb and looked across the bow. Just visible on the horizon was the top of a triangular sail.

Over the sound of the sea, they could hear a rumble in the direction of the strange sail. But the sky was clear of the cumulous clouds which normally brought thunder in these waters.

Judson Shaw had come on deck and was standing next to Fletcher.

The two men listened to the distant rumble, saying nothing for a moment.

"Cannon fire, no question," the captain said.

"Aye, sir, someone's up to mischief," the first lieutenant agreed.

"Bring her two points into the wind, Mr. Bagley. We shall close and determine what is afoot. Mr. Shaw, have Leftenant Powell take a glass aloft and see if he can identify the ships."

Shaw touched his hat and walked forward to the main hatchway.

Now seated in the maintop next to Seaman Harmon, the mast head lookout, James waited for Lucas to finish using the big glass.

"Harmon, what think you," the older boy said without taking the glass from his eye.

"Judging by the rig, it looks like a brig and a schooner. Can't tell much more than that from here."

Lucas handed the telescope to James who steadied it against one of the top shrouds. Through lens the sails of two ships were now plainly visible.

"What's happening," James asked, handing the glass back to Harmon.

Brown's reply was interrupted by the second lieutenant pulling himself onto the platform. Without a word he raised his long glass and surveyed the distant ships.

Lowering the glass, Powell shouted down to the deck, "Appears to be a running battle.....brig chasing a schooner....must be using bow chasers."

He turned to the two midshipmen. "Down you go, smartly now."

"Beat to quarters, Mr. Shaw," Captain Fletcher said, his voice very forceful. "Run up the colors, if you please."

"Aye aye, sir."

Two hours had elapsed while the frigate worked the weather gauge to run down on the two smaller ships. Mr. Powell's earlier analysis of a running battle appeared accurate although the pursuer seemed unable to close with her prey.

"No flags flying from either," the captain noted with the glass still raised.

Mr. Bagley lowered his glass. "They don't have the look of working craft, neither fish nor cargo," he opined.

"Deck there, land fine on the starboard bow," came the call from the masthead lookout.

"I expect that'll be the Spider's Legs," the master offered. "Not shown on most charts, but well used by pirates looking for shelter from storms."

"Or men-of-war?" the captain wondered.

James stood aft of the mainmast at his station on the main deck between the nine pound cannons which now pointed outboard through their ports. With his blue jacket and cap he looked all the part of a young gentleman, although he felt totally intimidated by his duties. Tasked to pass orders from the quarterdeck to the main battery of guns, he felt comfortable he was up to that task. But he was also expected to take over if Lieutenant Powell or Mr. Paine fell in battle. When the second lieutenant had talked about actual death, he'd been shocked. But if it was his duty and he would do his best.

The guns crews stood alongside the long barrels, three men on a side. Controlled by a gun captain, they had been drilled to load, run out, fire, sponge out and reload twice a minute until their gun was either disabled or the order to cease fire received. Here and there, ship's boys stood ready to run down to the magazine if more charges were needed. The deck had been sanded to provide traction on the deck which could become slick from sea water or blood.

Practiced until their hands were raw from hauling the heavy weapons in and out on the trucks, the gun crews knew the very survival of the ship would depend on them in a fight. While the cannons would often be fired in a broadside, the individual gun captains could also expertly lay the gunline using handspikes. Compensating for roll of the ship, they took pride in their ability to hit a floating keg at half a mile.

"Have the gunner put a shot between the two of them. We'll take control of this situation or I'll sink them both." Fletcher walked to the lee side sounding irritated.

"Mr. Dalgleish," the first lieutenant called to the bow-legged ship's gunner standing next to James.

"Sir?"

"A shot between the two, if you please."

"Aye, sir," the gunner called as he ran to the port bow chaser, a nine pound long cannon.

James watched in fascination as the crew manhandled the heavy gun's line of sight in response to small adjustments from Mr. Dalgleish.

The gunner turned and raised his hand over his head, signifying his readiness to fire.

"At your command, Mr. Dalgleish, fire when she bears," Judson Shaw called from the quarterdeck.

Taking the quickmatch from his gun captain, the heavy-set gunner's mate crouched down, aligning his sightline with the cannon's long barrel. As the ship began to rise on a wave, he moved the quickmatch to the touch hole. Instantly the gun fired, the big weapons hurled back against its tackle, a cloud of acrid smoke blowing back over the main deck.

On the quarterdeck, two long glasses were raised to follow the flight of shot. In the distance a large plume erupted fifty yards in front of the pursuing brig.

"Damnation! Closer than I'd like, but it'll do the job," Fletcher said. "Reload, standby to fire," he ordered Shaw.

"She's veering off, captain," the first lieutenant called.

James ran to the rail, watching the sleek brig turn starboard, away from the schooner and toward the low lying island to the west. This was real action he thought excitedly, just like he imagined, the glory of battle.

"Return to your station, Mr. Addington," he heard Lieutenant Powell say, his tone icy. "This is not for your entertainment, damn you."

"He's running for the reef, captain," the master called, "He knows we risk tearing our bottom out if we follow close inshore."

Fletcher knew the master was right, but he wasn't happy about it. "Very well. Let her drop off two points, Mr. Bagley. Mr. Shaw, have the starboard guns run out. We shall exercise the main battery."

The captain walked to the quarterdeck rail and looked down at his gun crews. "A gold guinea to the crew that puts a shot into her," he called down to them. "And an extra ration of rum for every shot through her sails."

The men cheered as they heaved on tackles to pull the cannon barrels into the open gun ports. Blocks squealed as each gun was worked into position, the gun captains all making final adjustments in their sightline as the ship swung around to place the brig under her guns.

"Mr. Addington," Powell snapped, "Position yourself behind each gun as they fire. But mind the recoil. We don't want you losing a leg this early in your career."

Running forward to the first gun on the starboard side, James saw Hitchens, the gun captain, kneeling on deck, the quickmatch held in his left hand, his right arm extended over his head.

"Fire as you bear, Mr. Powell," the captain ordered sharply.

"Fire as you bear," Judson Shaw called to the gun deck.

"Fire as you bear," the second lieutenant echoed.

James could see the brig through the gun port and was trying to estimate the distance when Hitchens fired.

The massive roar was followed by the gun carriage recoiling inboard, the massive weight caught by the ropes and pulleys of the gun tackle, squealing in response to the violent force.

"Sponge out," Hitchens bellowed and his crew jumped to ensure there were no burning remnants of powder in the barrel. Shoving a powder charge into a barrel that had not been cleaned would almost certainly result in a premature explosion, killing or maiming the gun crew.

Stunned by the violence of the discharge only feet from him, James staggered briefly then moved from gun to gun, following the rippling fire of the starboard cannons.

Heavy smoke obscured the target and he focused on watching the crews preparing their guns for the next shot. His ears rang and he shook his head trying to stop the strange noise. He didn't notice the second lieutenant smiling to himself.

"Well done, by God," Fletcher called as they watched the brig's upper works crumple, the top of the mainmast severed by the last ball from *Andromeda*.

"That'll slow the bugger down," Bagley exclaimed. "But we'd still be risking all to follow her into those reefs."

"I have no intention of doing so, Mr. Bagley. Mr. Shaw, were you able to read her name?"

"Aye, sir. *Revanche*."

"Perhaps a Frenchy?"

"Reload, but don't run out," Powell called to the main deck gun crews.

The flurry of activity was in direct opposition to the larboard crews, who stood by their guns waiting for orders. One by one the gun captains raised their hands signaling readiness.

"All guns re-loaded, sir."

"Very well, Mr. Powell," Lieutenant Shaw responded, "Tell the crews to stand easy."

"Now, let's catch the other one, Mr. Bagley. She's past the point where she can tack into shallow water and I shall have her." Fletcher walked to the quarterdeck rail. "Mr. Dalgleish, stand by your bow chaser. And Lacy," he called down the last gun crew on the starboard side."

A tall skinny man, bare to the chest with a kerchief tied around his head stood up and knuckled his forehead.

"Aye, Captain."

"Damned fine shooting, damned fine, by God. A guinea for the crew and an extra ration of rum to boot."

Lacy grinned from ear to ear, displaying several missing teeth.

"Thankee, sir."

His gun crew gathered around him, slapping him on the back.

James had watched the exchange and it struck him that the captain didn't have to do what he had just done.

31

But he saw the look in the men's eyes. It was pride. For men who had almost nothing to their names, had not been off the ship in some cases for years and could probably look forward to an early death from disease or injury, they were proud of their skills.

From forward, the roar of the bow chaser brought James back to reality.

"She's wearing ship, Captain," Judson Shaw said as the schooner dropped her jib and turned to spill the wind from her mainsail.

"Now we'll find out what we have here," Fletcher said. "Mr. Shaw, prepare to lower the cutter, if you please. Take some experienced hands and find out what that ship is about."

"I can just make out her name, Captain," the master said, "*Petrel.*"

Chapter Four

A Lesson Learned

Sitting in the stern next to the first lieutenant, James felt his heart pounding as the cutter pulled alongside the schooner. Armed with a boarding cutlass and a pistol stuck in his waistband, he felt very much a warrior who wasn't entirely sure how to fight. Schooled in use of firearms since the age of eight, he'd spent many hours in sword drill with Faircloth. But this was not practice and now he felt very unsure of himself. Thankfully he was expected only to watch and learn, not to take charge.

Because the schooner had run from a king's ship, there was reason to board and inspect her papers. If there were any irregularities the ship would be taken to the nearest port for adjudication.

The bow man reached out with a boat hook and pulled the cutter alongside the fixed wooden boarding ladder that ran up the low side to the rail.

"In the King's name, prepare to be boarded," Crider, the sergeant of Marines called as he pulled himself up the side, disappearing through the entry port. His four Royal Marines followed in quick succession, their weapons slung from their shoulders.

When James reached the deck, the Marines were standing in a semi-circle, their muskets now at the ready with bayonets attached.

Two men in dirty clothes stood on the deck, the rest of the crew hanging back on the far rail. The older of the two was missing his left hand and bore a large scar on the left side of his face. His eyes burned black with anger and he fixed his stare on James.

"What's this, a boy? They send a boy to board my ship?"

"Shut your mouth, damn you," Judson Shaw said as he cleared the entry port. "And I'll remind you a king's officer is just that, regardless of age."

The man simply glared at Shaw.

"I am the first leftenant of His Britannic Majesty's ship *Andromeda.* And you are?"

"Harry Thigpen, master of the *Petrel.*"

"Where bound?"

"Saint Nevis."

"Cargo?"

The man hesitated.

"Riding empty. I hope to pick up a load of sugar cane on the island."

Shaw surveyed the deck. There were four small four pound cannons on the rail and a large swivel gun on the foc'sle.

"Mr. Thigpen, your armament seems excessive for an island trader."

"As you saw, leftenant, these are dangerous waters," his tone sarcastic.

James counted fourteen men of the schooner's crew on deck. Several of them wore large knives at their waist. From *Andromeda* there were eleven on deck and four men still in the cutter. They were outnumbered. But less than two cables away, the *Andromeda* lay with her gun ports open, the black muzzles of the cannons looking very menacing.

Turning to a master's mate, Shaw said, "Mr. Harvey escort the master down below and bring me his log. I also want to see any bills of lading from recent trips."

The master led Harvey below.

"Do you speak English," Shaw asked the second man.

"Not your kind of English," the man said with a thick Irish brogue.

"I will require the individual papers for your crew."

The man stared back at Shaw. "And why would you be wanting to do that?" he said, his anger obvious.

"Sergeant, line them up on the starboard rail. Mr. Addington accompany Karlsen below and inspect for any contraband."

Typical of most ships in the Royal Navy, the crew contained many nationalities, Karlsen hailed from Sweden. He now moved to James's side without a word. Over six feet tall, the big powerful sailor carried a cutlass and also had pistol in his other hand.

"Follow me," James said as he walked to the main hatch and headed down the ladder.

Karlsen, aware the schooner's crew was listening, answered smartly, "Aye, sir," and knuckled his forehead.

When James reappeared on deck twenty minutes latter, he saw Judson Shaw finishing his inspection of the crew.

"Anything to report, Mr. Addington?"

"Several arms chests, sir. Enough to equip two crews, in Karlsen's opinion."

The master stood next to the wheel, the master's mate Harvey by his side holding a handful of papers in a leather folder. His dejected expression indicated his displeasure at the results of Shaw's inquiries.

"Sergeant, show me that man's back," the first lieutenant said, pointing to an average looking man wearing a brown long sleeved jerkin.

"You heard 'im," the sergeant said to the man. "Strip to the waist or my lads will do it for you."

The man looked trapped, but there was no way to run. He slowly pulled the shirt over his head revealing a fouled anchor tattoo on his left breast.

"Now turn around," Shaw ordered.

When the man turned his back, James couldn't believe what he saw. Covered by scars on top of scars, the man's back bore no resemblance to normal flesh. The ugly welts had turned dark in the sun, but still had a reddish tinge. It was worse than James could have ever imagined.

"A deserter, if I'm any judge," Shaw said. "Sergeant, take that man in custody. The man's eyes flashed fear, knowing the punishment for desertion from the Royal Navy was death by hanging, with few exceptions.

"Mr. Thigpen, you are not what you claim. I'm seizing this ship in the name of the king. Take him back to the ship."

The fat man started to struggle as Mr. Harvey grabbed his arm forcefully. A marine moved to his other side, his musket ready to administer obedience.

"You'll regret this," Thigpen spat out.

"I think not," Judson Shaw replied calmly and the two prisoners were manhandled over the side to the waiting cutter.

Chapter Five

From Boy to Man

Adam Carlyle checked the schooner's mainsail as she moved steady into a choppy sea. *Andromeda's* third lieutenant had been assigned the task of sailing what Captain Fletcher hoped would turn out to be a prize to Antigua.

James had been left aboard to assist Mr. Carlyle who now commanded a small prize crew which consisted of the master's mate, John Harvey, eight seamen and four marines.

"Steer north by west, Kelly. We'll maintain this tack for the next watch."

"Aye, sir."

"Mr. Addington, you'll stand watch with Mr. Harvey. I will alternate. I expect a two day transit to Antigua, but will lay off and enter on the morning tide."

Taking it all in, James was still stunned to be assigned to the prize crew. Looking at the opportunity to learn more about his craft, he felt lucky the captain had given him the chance ahead of the other midshipmen. He would've been crushed to know that Stephen Fletcher, already short one lieutenant and concerned about the *Revanche*, had decided that Lieutenant Carlyle and Midshipman Addington were the two officers he could most easily do without.

"Mr. Addington," Carlyle said quietly, "Walk with me."

"You are very new to the service to be second in command of a prize crew."

James answered quietly, "Yes, sir, I know."

"Well, that's the way of the sea, Mr. Addington. By virtue of your position, you will be given responsibilities that would seem exceptional by a landsman. But you will learn by doing and the men expect no less. Don't let them down or the captain. Do you understand what I am saying?"

Suddenly the reality of his responsibility hit James.

"Aye sir, I won't let you down."

Several of the men from James's division were aboard, including the gun captain, Lacy and Stevens from the mainmast. Although new to the ship, his familiarity with the men made him feel part of the crew. But now he knew that his job was much more than just to watch what happened around him or follow normal routine. He had to rise to the challenge that all sea officers faced throughout time. He knew he could.

Corporal Abernathy led the small Marine contingent, their primary duty to maintain control over the schooner's crew. Six of those men had been taken back to *Andromeda* to be locked below decks. But the remaining six were needed to sail the ship and it had been Mr. Harvey who decided those to stay behind.

"Mr. Addington. While your experience at sea is limited, I count on you to use your head and diligently apply common sense to all activities. Rely on the experienced hands, especially Mr. Harvey."

"Aye, sir." James knew that this was Lieutenant Carlyle's first assignment following his promotion to lieutenant. But he seemed so confident and sure of himself. Will I ever be like that, he wondered?

One day later, with the wind still steady, James realized that there was nothing glorious about the monotony of watch standing around the clock. Mr. Harvey had been a wealth of information and James knew his comfort with the ocean and sails would be increased greatly when he returned to *Andromeda.* But after hours on the same tack, plunging into the oncoming sea, he felt sore and tired. Gratefully the temperature remained moderate, even at night the constant spray became only an inconvenience, and not a threat to life.

Mr. Carlyle saw this transit as an opportunity for James to expand his knowledge of the diverse world of sail. While very different from the traditional square rig of the frigate, this schooner's sails and tackle were a good example of the fore and aft style used by half of the world's vessels.

"Get a feel for this rig. Easy to handle, the mainsail allows you to turn as quick as you might. A well-handled schooner can best any frigate when it comes to handling."

"A nifty rig," Stevens had said later when they began to go over each line and piece of hardware.

The big topman always wore a serious expression, but his manner was friendly and generous.

"Under a good crew, she can sail within a point of the wind. But her real beauty is with a following wind. Running full before the wind with spankers flying, she'll put over two hundred miles on the log from noon to noon."

"Sail off the starboard bow," came the call from the forward lookout interrupting their discussion.

James joined Lieutenant Carlyle at the weather rail.

The young officer already had a long glass up to his eye.

John Harvey joined them at the rail.

Carlyle handed him the glass.

"What say you, Mr. Harvey?"

The master's mate lowered the glass and looked at Carlyle.

"It's the brig, sir."

Carlyle nodded. "Agreed."

He raised the glass. "It looks like they've jury rigged the mast. In these winds it will most likely hold."

"Get that tall negro up here. Perhaps he might tell us why that brig is after this ship."

"What's your name?"
"Cantu."
"Where from?"
"Sant-Domingue."

The man stood well over six feet, his powerful frame leaving no doubt that he could be a deadly opponent.

"Do you know that ship," Carlyle asked pointing to the brig, now visible from the deck.

His eyes moved to the horizon. He looked back to Carlyle and nodded. "The captain is Truffant, Emile Truffant."

"Who is Truffant?"

"A man who will kill you, English. He will kill all of us."

"Tell me everything you know about this man. Your life may depend on it."

"It makes no difference."

"You will let me be the judge of that," the anger rising in his voice. "Now who is he?"

Taking a deep breath, Cantu said, "He preys on ships in these waters. Some say he works for the French. I do not know. But he is a butcher who kills without mercy. He and our captain argued and they vowed to kill each other."

Suddenly James was scared. He could hear the tone in Cantu's voice and see the concern on John Harvey's face.

"Very well, return to your duties. Mr. Addington, Mr. Harvey please join me at the lee rail." The young lieutenant strode across the deck as if he were on a stroll in the park.

"This will likely come to a fight. We have the weather gauge, but the brig is between us and Antigua. If we can break her line, we might just be able to out run her. Getting past her will not come easy, but we must try."

"What's your plan, sir"

"We've enough men for two gun crews. We'll try to add to the damage in their rigging if we get that close."

James remembered the big negro. "Sir, what about the old crew?"

"Quite so, Mr. Addington. I'll make a proposition to them which will be hard for them to turn down."

"We must avoid is grappling with them, sir," Harvey added. "They'd overwhelm us in short order."

Carlyle nodded. "I agree, Mr. Harvey, and they know that only too well. So we must do the unexpected. They outgun us and have a larger crew. But we'll use that to our advantage. They'll be overconfident. Mr. Addington, you will take over our gun battery. Prepare the guns for action and report back to me. Mr. Harvey, check the weapons lockers and break out everything we can use. A cutlass for each man and as many pistols as we have."

"The original crew?" the mate questioned.

"Get them all up here on deck."

"You wanted to see me, sir?" Lacy knuckled his forehead to James.

"Yes, Lacy. We're in a situation that will require use of these cannons. I'm making you the ship's gunner."

The older man's eyes opened wide.

"Me, sir? The gunner?"

"You're one of the best gun captains in the navy. You can certainly do this job, don't you think?"

Lacy smiled broadly. "You can count on me, sir."

"Pick two crews, break out powder and shot for the cannon and swivel."

"The swivel, sir?"

"Load them all, Mr. Lacy"

"Aye, aye, sir."

"The *Revanche* is closing us. We find ourselves in much the same situation that you were in two days prior. According to Cantu, this Truffant intends to kill all of us, you included. But you're thinking that a hangman's noose waits for you in Antigua, what difference does it make?"

The men were now listening very carefully.

"If we're to survive, I need every man. If you'll fight with us I'll make a promise to you as a king's officer. Once in sight of Antigua, I'll put whoever desires into a boat and you can go your own way. So you now have a choice, Truffant or fight and go free."

"Why should we believe you?" a short man in front asked.

"Because my proposal gives you a chance. If we're taken by Truffant there will be no chance."

Cantu spoke up. "I will fight with you."

The other men saw the big negro walk over to the weapons on the deck. He picked up an unusual blade which looked like a cutlass but without a hand guard.

His companions followed him, the short man turning back to Carlyle to say, "All right. We'll trust you."

"We're ready as we're likely to be," Lacy said surveying the shot charges and round shot now laying on deck near the guns. "I wish we had chain shot to go after their rigging."

41

James thought for a moment. "I saw an entire chest of iron manacles below. What would happen if we loaded those?"

Lacy looked at him with a look of surprise then grinned. "It might just work, sir. Leave it to me."

Adam Carlyle stood next to the helmsman, his cap squarely on his head, the white lapels of his coat standing out in contrast the weather-worn wood on the deck. The *Revanche* had been closing on a constant bearing for the last hour. Now the test would come, he thought. A lieutenant for only six months, he knew that he must show confidence to his small crew. He only wished he felt confident. Half of the crew were pirates, his midshipmen was only a boy and he had no one to fall back on. But the last six years had prepared him for this and he would do his duty.

"The wind is rising, sir."

He turned to see John Harvey looking up at the mainmast.

"He'll be on us in twenty minutes, if we hold this tack."

"I agree, Mr. Harvey. Have the weapons been handed out?"

"Aye, sir."

James rushed up to the two men.

"Walk, Mr. Addington. You are a king's officer and running is unseemly. And where is your hat?"

Stunned at Carlyle's notice of such trivial matters, he blurted out, "Down on the foc'sle, I think, sir."

"I expect you to be in full uniform when we engage, the men will expect it. Now, how are the guns?"

"Cleared for action, sir, two crews will alternate on the main deck guns and two marines on the swivel."

"Very well."

Carlyle looked at the brig bearing down on them, now less than two miles away on the starboard bow.

"Take your stations, gentlemen."

Blue green water burst over the bow of the *Revanche,* the increasing wind blowing spray across the wave tops.

"Standby to tack," Harvey yelled from next to the wheel.

The two ships were closing fast. If they maintained course, the brig would crash into the schooner's starboard side. Adam Carlyle had been in several sea engagements and knew he must anticipate what Truffant would do. With a stronger main battery, the Frenchman would likely fall off, allowing his starboard battery to rake the smaller ship. But Adam would not allow that to happen.

"NOW!"

"Shift your rudder," Harvey yelled.

The deck crew flew into action as the big mainsail swung on its yard. As the stern came around, *Petrel* veered sharply to starboard, the initiative having now shifted to the schooner.

"Standby on your guns, Mr. Addington."

James glanced forward over the swinging bow and saw *Revanche*'s bow swinging toward them.

"Port guns, man the port guns," he yelled and the crews swarmed over the two small cannon on what was now the lee rail.

Adam Carlyle could hear shouted orders on the brig's deck, knowing he had fooled the Frenchman once. Could he do it again?

Petrel accelerated, now running directly before the wind.

Her bow now turning larboard, the *Revanche* was trying desperately to close the schooner.

"Fire as your guns bear, Mr. Addington," Carlyle called.

"Fire as your guns bear!"

Lacy sighted down the shotline and fired the touch hole.

The weapon's report seemed very different to James. He looked to Lacy, but smoke obscured the gun and its crew.

Careening crazily, *Revanche* steadied momentarily as one of her bow chasers spit an orange tongue of fire.

James heard a sharp rip as a hole suddenly appeared in the jib along with the report of the enemy gun. With terrified fascination, he realized that men could die on either vessel.

Another blast from Lacy's second gun was followed by the old gunner yelling in exultation.

"What? What is it?" James yelled as the crews reacted to Lacy's orders to re-load.

"That last chain hit their foremast! Come on lads, run out, run out."

On the brig, crewmen were struggling with lines and the forecourse that now drooped from the end of the main yard.

"Marines, musket fire if you please," Carlyle yelled at the four men manning the swivel. They immediately turned and began to sight their long muskets on the rail commencing individual fire.

Now only separated by a cable, men on both ships had begun to fire small arms. James ducked involuntarily as a five foot section of the larboard rail exploded, throwing deadly splinters across the deck, cutting down two men from the original crew. He moved toward where they lay writhing on the deck but he froze at the sight of Karlsen's body on the worn planking. The ball which destroyed the rail had torn the man in half, his entrails now spread in a bloody circle around him.

"Mr. Addington!"

Staring at the Swede's body, James was aware of Lieutenant Carlyle's voice.

"MR. ADDINGTON!"

Looking away from the horror on the deck he turned to focus on Carlyle.

"Sir?" he said, slightly bewildered.

Carlyle rushed up to him.

"Listen man. Shake yourself out of it. Prepare to repel boarders. That brig is trying to tie up with us and it will be a close thing. Now DO YOUR DUTY."

Turning to Lacy and his gun crews James now called, "Stand by to repel boarders," his voice shrill. He pulled the cutlass from his belt and saw the brig's bowsprit coming over the rail. Before he could move, the two vessels collided in a grinding tearing motion, throwing many of the crew to the deck.

Not sure what to do, James ran toward the point of collision hearing guttural yells coming from the other ship.

Slipping on the deck, he saw a group of men from the other ship jumping down to the *Petrel's* deck.

A loud crash from the swivel tore into the packed enemy taking the fury out of their charge. Only five men made it unhurt to the schooner's deck and they began to rush aft.

Seeing a wiry little man running toward him carrying a small axe in his hand, James remembered what Faircloth had taught him, let a running opponent defeat himself. The enemy raised the ax high to strike down as James ducked to the right and thrust out with the cutlass. He felt the blade hit the man's side cutting through flesh and muscle. Pitching forward to the deck his opponent dropped the ax and reached for the wound in his side.

Staring at what he had done, James didn't see a large man who appeared from behind the main cargo hatch.

"Behind you," Stevens called and ran toward James's assailant with a boarding pike.

Seeing the enemy blade coming down at him, James desperately raised his blade to parry the thrust. The two blades collided as Stevens drove the pike deep into the man's back, taking some of the force away from his blow at James.

Never hit by a blade swung with such force, James fell backwards, the swinging steel tip of the man's cutlass ripping a jagged cut in the boy's shoulder.

Kneeling on the deck, James watched as Stevens pulled out a large knife and slashed the man's throat, blood spurting on the deck like a flood.

In what now seemed like a dream, James stood unsteadily. Forward, he was aware that the brig's bowsprit was not longer over the *Petrel's* bow.

"She's falling away," someone called as one of Lacy's guns fired at the *Revanche,* now moving down the schooner's port side.

James turned to see the big negro Cantu locked in battle with a giant of a man wearing a large red waistband. The clash of steel from their powerful swings rang across the deck. But the larger man doubled his effort and attacked Cantu with a frenzy that James could have never imagined.

Staggering back toward the starboard rail, Cantu slipped and sprawled backward on the canted deck.

James watched in horror as the giant raised the huge cutlass over his head for the killing blow. Without thinking James yelled, "Stop!"

Perhaps it was the high pitch of the command that made the giant turn and look at James. The huge man's initial curiosity was replaced by contempt and he lunged at the young midshipman, smashing the hilt guard hard into James's face.

Cantu desperately swung his blade at the giant, slashing into the man's thigh.

Roaring with pain and anger the pirate turned back to Cantu. Holding his wounded leg with one hand, he raised the curved blade.

A shot rang out, making the giant stop and turn again to face James, who stood unsteadily, blood running from his face. Slowly the man fell to his knees, the ball from James's pistol now lodged in his heart. Pitching forward, the pirate collapsed on the deck, blood running from underneath his body.

Suddenly the deck was quiet. Cantu's attacker had been the last boarder still standing and now the *Revanche* was rolling out of command as *Petrel* stood before the wind, opening the distance between the two.

Walking forward James heard Carlyle yell, "Loose the topsail if you please, Mr. Harvey. That bugger will be after us quick as you will if my guess is correct."

Absent the mayhem of battle, James found himself sitting on the edge of the cargo hold, feeling very shaky. The pain in his shoulder was muted compared to the numbness in his face. Slowly James brought his hand up to his face, wincing as he explored the torn flesh. Through watering eyes he saw his hand was covered in blood. Suddenly the horror of the last few minutes and his own injuries grabbed him and he threw up violently on the bloody deck planking.

"Lacy, see to Mr. Addington," came the call from Carlyle.

As the old gunner moved toward James, Cantu knelt down and said, "I will look after him."

The look in Cantu's eyes was something that Lacy would never forget. It was if the young man's act had touched the big man at his very soul.

"Aye. I know you will."

Chapter Six

The Measure of a Man

Captain Stephen Fletcher sat quietly as the third lieutenant completed his report. *Andromeda* moved gently to a following sea, the lantern hanging above the desk swaying accordingly.

The two vessels had come within visual range two days following the action with the brig, *Revanche.* Now sailing in company, they were only a day's sailing from Antigua barring a change in weather.

Pouring a glass of claret for himself, the first lieutenant and Adam Carlyle the older man raised his glass.

"To your health, sir. A fine job of seamanship if ever I saw one."

"Thank you, sir," Carlyle replied.

"Damn bad luck with young Addington. You say he stuck one with his cutlass and shot another of the boarders?"

"He did, sir. It was after he'd been wounded that he worked his way forward and shot the last boarder, truly one of the largest men I've ever encountered."

"Quite the tiger," Judson Shaw offered.

"We can only hope the good doctor can encourage his wounds to heal. His face is none too pretty just now."

"The doctor assures me he should live." The captain looked down at the chart on his desk. "One more thing, Mr. Carlyle. Your promise to those men that they would go free was not yours to make. They are possibly pirates and it will be up to a court to decide their fate."

Carlyle put down his glass.

"Sir, if they had not thrown in with us, the schooner would have likely been lost and we would all be dead. When I gave my word as a king's officer I did so with the utmost commitment."

Fletcher's eyes narrowed. "Damn you, sir. You put me in an entirely awkward position. Either I violate king's regulations or I dishonor one of my officers."

The young lieutenant did not flinch.

"Perhaps we have an alternative, captain."

"Pray tell, Mr. Shaw?"

"Mr. Carlyle states that the six men he had on the *Petrel* were good seamen and sturdy in a fight. Particularly the big negro, Cantu."

"Go on."

"We remain twenty hands short of our full compliment. If these men volunteered for service, we would not only prevent them from doing any mischief, we would gain six experienced hands."

Fletcher nodded. "A worthy proposal. I shall give it some thought."

"Sir, if I might add?" Carlyle asked.

"Yes."

"After the action, the man Cantu took care of Mr. Addington constantly until we returned aboard. While both Lacy and Stevens tried to assist, he acted like a mother lion protecting her cub. He used a poultice on the wound that the doctor said has brought great relief."

"Most interesting. It seems our young midshipman already has a remarkable tale to tell."

"Now get on about your duties, I have work to do."

Doctor Goodrum wiped the sweat off James's brow and sat back against the hull. Situated on the orlop deck, the sick quarters were empty save for the wounded midshipman. Knowing these things could always turn bad very quickly, the doctor felt encouraged that the fever was slight and the boy seemed to be resting well. But he also knew he was not out of the woods by any means.

I must find out more about that poultice, he thought to himself. The black man called it "curcuma" and remarkably, the wound had none of the red swelling that sets in after the initial blow. Goodrum's encounters with local cures throughout the world had generally proven to be positive and he now used many of those techniques as part of his practice.

James slowly opened his eyes, confusion rising in his slowly awakening mind. Feeling the ship's motion, he knew that he was somewhere within a vessel. But which one?

Turning his head he saw in the lantern light a man who appeared to be sleeping, his chin resting on his chest.

Yes, he thought with the happiness of recognition, it is Doctor Goodrum. And this must be *Andromeda.* But something was wrong, his head felt swollen and then the realization of the bandages hit James.

"Doctor!"

"What? Oh my, you're awake, young man." The doctor rose and moved to the side of James's cot. "Now don't get excited, I'll explain everything shortly." He called to his surgeon's mate. "Grimsby, my compliments to the captain and please pass that Mr. Addington is awake. And fetch some breakfast.....soup only."

"Aye, sir."

"How long have I been here?" James asked as he raised his hand to the bandages on his face.

"A little over a day. Now don't fuss with the wrappings. That is most important. And you've been here since a very large negro carried you over from the schooner."

"Cantu. Where is he?"

"My understanding is that they are all in irons on the foc'sle."

"What'll happen to them?" James asked, his voice urgent.

"That's not something for you to be concerned with, young sir."

James thought back to that moment on the deck when he had pulled the trigger and seen the look on Cantu's face. Over the next two days the big man had hardly left his side. But the several times James had attempted to converse with him, the man had remained mute. But there was something about him and James meant to find out.

The doctor continued, "Your shoulder is healing quite well. I did add a butterfly closure when you came aboard, but I think the time with the poultice was sufficient for draining. Now, you shall spend several days with me as the wound closes itself and we apply a prophylaxis of vinegar. You shan't be using that arm for some time, and certainly will not be going aloft for at least a month."

"Doctor, what about my face?"

Goodrum smiled and brought the stool next to James's cot.

"You took a nasty blow, James. The work of that man Cantu thankfully left the wounds clean and I was able to place bandages in place to start the healing process. Now it's up to you to follow my instructions to the letter and I mean exactly to the letter if we want you to heal correctly."

James nodded, the unusually serious tone in Goodrum's voice convincing him that it was not the time to protest.

"I've treated many midshipmen in my time and it was more often the case that failure to heed my instructions resulted in a longer period away from duty. That is certainly not something you would want?"

"Oh no, sir, of course not," James said earnestly.

Doctor Goodrum turned away, his eyes betraying the concern he was feeling. The wounds would certainly heal, but how would the boy handle his disfigurement?

The watches were changing on deck as James finished his breakfast, a warm bowl of burgoo. The oats and molasses mixture, a staple of shipboard cuisine, often was not a favorite of the crew. But in his short career, James had found it nourishing and palatable. He felt much better after his meal and looked forward to getting out of the sick quarters.

"There you are, Mr. Addington," Captain Fletcher said as he ducked his head under a beam.

"Sir."

"I wanted to see how you were getting on. The report seems positive, eh, doctor?"

Goodrum nodded. "Always tricky when you have a wound like that, but it appears to be healing nicely."

"You did a fine job, Mr. Addington. Mr Carlyle has made a full report and I will include your name in my dispatch to the Admiralty. Quite a thing, for sure. A sea battle and repelling boarders with less than two weeks in service. Your father will be mightily impressed."

"Sir, might I add that Seaman Lacy performed in a most exemplary manner, laying guns and supervising the crews."

Fletcher chuckled. "I do believe you surprise me, Mr. Addington. Most midshipmen wouldn't take the effort to note such a thing."

"But, sir, without him who could guess what might have happened?"

"Quite right you are. I'll make a note that we consider him for the next gunner's mate opening."

Feeling happy, James lay back but then the expression on his face changed.

"Sir, they tell me the crewmembers from the *Petrel* are under guard on the foc's'le."

"Quite true, they'll hang, that I'm sure of," Fletcher said, his tone losing much of its friendliness.

"We could have never bested the Frenchy without their help and Mr. Carlyle promised they could go on their way."

Fletcher frowned. "Let that be a lesson to you. Don't give your oath when it's something over which you have no control."

Feeling crestfallen, James said, "No, sir."

"But Mr. Carlyle has expressed a similar sentiment and I'm inclined to find some way to work this matter out to everyone's satisfaction."

"Yes, sir."

"Now, get your rest." He turned to leave then said to Goodrum, "Doctor, I want this officer back on watch at the earliest possible time."

The doctor watched the captain leave and grinned.

"Well said, Mr. Addington. I believe you made quite a good impression."

The bright sun hurt James's eyes as he came on deck for the first time since returning to *Andromeda*. Wearing a newly washed shirt and britches, he had also endured a thorough washing at the hands of the doctor as one of the requirements for leaving sick quarters. He remembered the doctor's words, "Next to doing our duty, cleanliness is our next greatest challenge."

In the distance the green hills of Antigua stood in stark contrast to the brilliant blue sky. Already the heat of the day was making its effect known, the crew locating shade wherever they could.

James's right arm remained in a sling, the orders of Doctor Goodrum very specific that "...immobilization is key, don't forget that in your youthful enthusiasm." The circular bandages on his face had been in place except for regular changing and Goodrum had told him it would be at least ten more days before they could come off permanently.

It felt good to exercise his legs after several days of confinement and he worked his way forward past the ship's guns. Around the deck the crew was busy with a myriad of tasks necessary to maintain a man-of-war. Two boatswain mates supervised a small group of men re-reaving the large pulley on the starboard main course brace. A large coil of new manila line lay at their feet and they were beginning to unroll it. The smell of fresh paint mixed with fragrant tropical scents from the beach, only 500 yards on the larboard side.

A sense of belonging struck James. These men and I are part of the same crew and we accept each other for just that fact. For the first time in his young life, James began to understand his own individuality by recognizing his part in a larger group.

On the foc'sle a group was folding up canvas under the supervision of the old grizzled sailmaker, Mr. Crimmons.

"Ah, Mr. Addington, good to see you on deck," the wiry sailmaker said, his smile genuine.

"Thank you, Mr. Crimmons. I'd begun to think our good doctor would never allow me my freedom."

At the far side of the men, Cantu stood, arms at his side, his eyes on James. The captain had allowed the six seamen from the Petrel to sign onto the ship's company and they were now integrating into the crew.

"Might I have a word with Cantu?"

Crimmons nodded. "Our work is done here. Noon meal is almost on us, we'll resume at two bells."

The men dispersed leaving the tall black man standing alone. His eyes stayed on James, but he said nothing.

"I didn't have a chance to thank you properly for taking care of me on board the *Petrel*. According to the doctor, your medicine was most beneficial and he would like to learn more of it."

Cantu's expression changed from wariness to slight relaxation.

"You are well?" he finally asked quietly. Standing in front of the young midshipman, Cantu appeared to be searching for words. Finally, with his eyes still riveted on James, he said, "I owe you my life. I will not forget."

The man's solemnity told James that this was not a phrase lightly offered and he didn't know how to reply.

"I'm glad you're now part of this crew," he quickly said, still feeling awkward. "But I must confess, I'm most curious of your past. What can you tell me of yourself?"

The two stood at the rail while the tall heavily muscled negro talked of his youth on the island of Hispaniola. His full name was Armand Cantal Granville, but he had always been called Cantu. Descended from slaves imported to work the sugar and coffee plantations, his father had been a healer in the slave community. The boy had followed in his father's steps, but finally he had decided there was no future on the island. He shipped out on a small schooner and had worked on ships since. The life of a sailor in the islands had taught him how to survive the dangers of the sea, but his real lesson had come from discovering the dangers of the men who sailed that sea.

"Was the *Petrel* a pirate?"

Cantu shook his head. "We smuggled tobacco, rum and guns. But we were not pirates. Truffant, he is a pirate."

Despite his youth, James knew the big man was being truthful.

"Have they told you which division you're in?"

"Leftenant Powell's."

"Then we'll work together, I'm also in that division."

For the first time Cantu smiled "That is good."

As an afterthought, James asked, "On the *Petrel,* you were carrying a blade I've not seen before. What was it?"

Cantu nodded. "We call it a machete'. Many in the islands use it, some for work, others for killing."

James looked with surprise at Cantu, who smiled slightly, leaving the question of what he used his machete' for, unanswered.

Two days out of Antigua, the time had arrived for Doctor Goodrum to remove James's bandages. Rather than conduct the procedure in the dank and dark orlop deck, the doctor made the rather unusual request to the captain that he use the big cabin while removing the wraps. Having some experience with the shock that can accompany seeing a wound for the first time, he thought it would be most beneficial to have the relative comfort and privacy of the captain's cabin.

"Come over here by the gallery and sit yourself down."

James walked slowly to the doctor and sat down. While his bandages had been changed several times over the last week, he had not been given a chance to see his face. Following the last re-wrapping, Doctor Goodrum had pronounced that two more days would suffice for the bandaging. Now it was time to take the wraps off for the last time.

The doctor began to remove the dressings, unwinding the white muslin cloth which circled James's head like a turban. Grimsby stood to one side, holding a tray which contained several instruments, a small brown bottle and a stack of folded cloth pads.

"There we go," the doctor said to himself as he lifted the final circle of cloth clear of James's face. Dropping the wrap on the seat next to James, Goodrum reached up and carefully grasped each side of James's jaw and turned his head slowly to gain full illumination from the gallery windows.

"Doctor?" James asked hesitantly.

"Yes, yes indeed," the doctor said to himself as he continued to examine the patient.

"Sir?"

"Ah, yes, of course, you'd like to see for yourself. Grimsby, fetch that small mirror."

Without a word, the diminutive helper reached under the cloth pile and withdrew a small circular mirror in a wooden frame. He handed it to the doctor.

"Here you go, my boy."

James took the mirror and held it up at arm's length, the light from the sun flashing briefly as he turned the instrument to align its field of view.

The doctor and Grimsby said nothing for a long minute as James stared into the mirror which now told a young man that he would be marked for life with an ugly scar.

"As you can see, your lip has healed nicely, as well as we could have hoped.."

"Nicely?"

"Mr. Addington, there is only so much that the body can do to replenish itself. Your wounds were severe and I am thankful they have healed sufficiently for you to have normal use of your mouth. And the survival of all your teeth is also something that we must be pleased about. Now I know this has been hard, but you will get used to it. That is the way of the navy,"

James stood slowly and walked to the cabin door. Without looking back, he opened the door and left the cabin without a word.

H.M.S Andromeda 23rd of
July, 1770

Admiral,

I earnestly hope this letter finds you in good health and anxious for news of your son. Andromeda is at anchor in St. Nevis and I am assured that my letter will be dispatched for New York in short order.

Let me assure you that your son is well and progressing in a most handsome manner learning the ways of the navy. However, it distresses me that I must convey news of his injury in battle. His injuries were not life threatening and in fact his bravery during the battle earned him the respect of the crew.

Serving as the second in command of a prize schooner, his ship was attacked by a larger vessel which Andromeda herself was pursuing. The mysteries of the sea put the smaller vessel in harm's way, although I can't think of any action that might have presented a different outcome.

Taking command of the schooner's deck guns, James took the other ship under fire with good effect. When the ships closed hulls, he was instrumental in repelling boarders, killing one and wounding another. During that fight, he received a cutlass slash to his shoulder, which is healing nicely. Unfortunately, he also was hit with great force in the face and sustained wounds to his nose and mouth.

Sir, as you might expect, the scars to his face have had a most distressing effect on him and I have been concerned that this might prevent him from reassuming his duties in an effective manner. But I have hope that his strong constitution coupled with his natural affinity for the sea will prevail and in time he will put this behind him. As an aside, he has become friends with a sailor from the prize who has since joined Andromeda. Not something I would normally condone, but it reminds me of how that rascal Faircloth watched over you. I think this will help him in the future.

Your son has shown a remarkable ability as a leader for one so young and I know he will excel as a lieutenant when the time comes. For now, let me assure you that I and my officers will do our best to put James to right.

Your obedient servant,

S. Fletcher
Captain, commanding

Chapter Seven

The King's Justice

Six months service with Sir Rodney's squadron had turned the men and officers of *Andromeda* into well-tanned and healthy sailors. Two deaths from fever had been the only losses to the crew despite several violent storms and a bloody encounter with a slaver. Every ship develops a unique character over time and *Andromeda* could be described as a happy ship with a crew that felt they were fairly treated and respected.

Doctor Goodrum's insistence on large amounts of fresh fruit, clean water and regular inspections had made the ship a place that defied the expected shipboard conditions of a frigate long away from England. And while the conditions on a man of war could never be described as pleasant, the crew went about their duties without the undercurrent of discontent often evident on other ships in the fleet.

Holding the ship's salt pork and beef for emergencies, Captain Fletcher had been able to victual regularly from the many ports throughout the islands providing fresh meat and vegetable whenever possible.

While use of citrus juice to prevent scurvy was now an accepted practice within the service, Doctor Goodrum had begun using lime and lemon juice with the daily issue of rum which ensured the men received full doses of the required fluids and did so readily.

Involved in many boardings of suspected smugglers and slavers, the ship had only had to fire her guns on two occasions. Both times the threat of further bombardment had compelled the suspect vessel to lie to and await inspection.

Returned to full duty, James Addington found that he was not only accepted by the crew but enjoyed a friendly relationship with many of the men in his division. Cautioned by Mr. Carlyle to be careful of familiarity, James had learned to walk the fine line a leader must to get the most out of his men. His scars continued to heal, but in time he had come to accept that his face would always show the effects of that first battle at sea. The pain of his wounds and dealing with his disfigurement had helped him grow as a man and officer. His growing friendship with the big, quiet sailor also seemed to add an extra layer of strength to his personality. Unfortunately this maturation as a midshipman had also resulted in a schism within the gunroom.

"Are you not responsible for drawing our spirit ration from the purser, Mr. Addington?"

"Aye, sir, I am. Is there something amiss?"

James put down his navigation text and looked up at John Paine.

"Bless me, but don't you sound the innocent one."

"You have me confused, sir. Is there a problem?" James asked, his anger beginning to show.

"There should be seven bottles of rum in our spirit locker. I only count six."

"That can't be right," James said getting up from the gun room table and walking to the locked cupboard on the bulkhead. Looking inside he saw with dismay that the senior midshipman was correct. But that couldn't be.

"Well, Mr. Addington. What do you have to say for yourself?" Paul Culley chimed in.

"There were seven yesterday when I added the two for this week's ration."

"A very convenient story. But the evidence suggests something quite different. Perhaps you decided to share our ration with your big nigger."

Suddenly James found his anger turning to cold rage.

"Are you calling me a liar, sir?"

"Of course not," Paine retorted. "I would never accuse the son of an admiral of being anything but pure and chaste."

The sneer in Paine's voice prompted Lucas Brown to rise and move between the two midshipmen. "There's no need of this. From either of you," Brown said harshly.

Paine looked hard at James. "I shall be watching you, Mr. Addington, as disgusting as that might be." He turned to Lucas. "And you as well, you little shit."

Lieutenant Judson Shaw watched a large jolly boat approach the starboard side, its wake marking a direct path from the large jetty on the eastern side of the bay. Directed to make call in English Harbour, Antigua, the message received by the ship via mail schooner had provided no amplifying details.

"My respects, Mr. Brown and please tell the captain a boat is approaching. No honors."

In one minute Stephen Fletcher stood beside Shaw, the approaching boat having shipped oars and now secured to the main chains.

A middle-aged man wearing a loose fitting coat and open collar climbed nimbly through the entry port. Removing his hat he spoke to Fletcher without appearing to notice the first lieutenant.

"Captain Fletcher?"

"At your service, Mr.?"

"McPherson, Robert McPherson of the foreign office. I must talk with you in private."

This is very odd, Fletcher thought. "Very well. Please follow me. Mr. Shaw, please expedite getting the water lighter alongside. I want to be ready to weigh anchor as soon as possible."

The two men sat on opposite sides of the small dining table. Waiting for his servant to pour two glasses of wine and depart, Fletcher took a measure of the man who sat quietly. He seemed unremarkable in every way. But there was something about the way he carried himself that told the captain that this man was not an ordinary civil servant.

"Now, Mr. McPherson, what can I do for you?"

Reaching inside his coat, McPherson removed an envelope and handed it to Fletcher.

"This is a letter from Sir Rodney. I would ask you to read it before we talk."

Breaking the heavy wax seal, Fletcher pulled the one page letter from the envelope and unfolded it. Recognizing the admiral's signature, he scanned the contents and looked up at McPherson with some surprise.

"This is quite good news if it's true. What level of confidence do you have that this is accurate?"

"It is extremely accurate, Captain. I've been working on this for some months now. The vessel in question is most surely going to be in the area of Pigeon Island or I have misjudged Truffant terribly."

"The *Revanche* made her escape from me once. I don't intend for that to occur again. What can you tell me of this island?"

"From the ocean it can appear as an island, but is in fact connected to St. Lucia proper by a finger of land that gives whoever controls the heights on the island a very defensible position."

Fletcher knew a ship, even a well-armed frigate, stood no chance if there were emplaced gun batteries on the island.

"What do we know of their defenses?" the captain asked.

"There is a two gun position on the western heights. Truffant always anchors *Revanche* in the bay north of the island under the protection of those guns. Our agents on the island have told us they are French made artillery pieces, 12 pounders."

One of the best guns in the world, Fletcher thought. In the hands of trained gunners, those two guns, firing from the stability of land and from an elevation, could hold *Andromeda* off very effectively.

"Sir Rodney's orders are quite specific," Fletcher said. "Take *Revanche* and seize Truffant. However it appears the brigand possesses the ability to hold us stalemate with those guns. Unless I'm mistaken, this appears to need a land expedition."

McPherson watched Fletcher examine the chart of Pigeon Island.

"The admiral came to that same conclusion, captain."

Fletcher looked up in surprise at the tone of McPherson's voice.

"I have my Marines, but they're a small group and the lieutenant has little experience in battle ashore."

"That's why I'm here, sir. I have a great deal of knowledge of what would be required to silence the guns of Pigeon Island."

"But you said you were from the Foreign Office, I believe. I don't need diplomats for this expedition, sir."

"I am currently attached to the diplomatic service, Captain Fletcher. But let us just say, my activities do not involve anything remotely diplomatic."

"Anchor's aweigh, sir."

Andromeda, under fore course and jib, fell off as the wind filled the sails and pulled her bow toward the open ocean.

"Very well, Mr. Shaw. Main course, if you please."

Following a busy afternoon replenishing water, fresh fruits and vegetables, the frigate was now taking advantage of the offshore breeze and ebbing tide to start south for Pigeon Island.

Mr. McPherson had remained below decks, only the arrival of a small trunk indicating his intention to stay aboard for the voyage.

The presence of a mysterious passenger prompted a cascade of rumors that can only give birth within the confined quarters of a man of war.

Transfer of a vast quantity of gold currently enjoyed the greatest support among the lower deck gossips. Reference to Spanish wrecks and pirate hoards added to the excitement as the ship pushed south in clear weather.

Mr. McPherson had enjoyed the company of the wardroom, dining with the officers at each meal save the evening meal on the first night when he supped with Captain Fletcher.

The officers of *Andromeda* had found the Scotsman to be engaging and in no time they accepted him as a comrade, albeit in civilian clothes. It also was interesting that after the many hours of conversation, no one seemed to have gained any real knowledge of who Mr. Robert McPherson really was, except his conversation carried a military air about it.

"Good morning, Mr. Addington."

James turned to see Mr. McPherson, freshly shaved and taking in the morning air. The sun had only been above the horizon for the past hour and it was still passably cool on deck.

"Good morning, sir."

"Another fair day I see."

"Aye, sir. The storm season is just starting, but for now the glass is steady and winds only fresh."

The two stood in silence, the sounds of morning tasks echoing across the deck.

"I enjoyed our conversation last evening," McPherson said, breaking the silence. "It was interesting that of all the officers on the ship, you are one of the few with any real knowledge of the forest."

"It had never come up previously, but it does seem the rest joined the navy from the cities of England."

"The world is changing, James. There was a time when most Englishmen would be as comfortable in a wood as anywhere."

James had never considered how the world had become so modern. People living their entire lives in a city. It was difficult to grasp.

"The colonies are different. I guess the new world is still behind the progress of Europe."

Robert McPherson smiled to himself. A remarkable lad.

James reflected that he truly liked the crusty Scotsman, and realized that the man had never reacted to James's scars. It was if they didn't exist for Mr. McPherson.

Stevens approached James in the waist and quickly knuckled his forehead. "Sir, they've seized Cantu."

"What?"

"Aye, sir. Mr Paine has accused him of malingering and disrespect. Lieutenant Powell had the master at arms take him before the first lieutenant."

Cantu was quiet, but very aware of the rules and regulations aboard a King's ship, James thought. It made no sense that the man would fight authority.

"Where is he now?" James asked.

"Down in the hold. He'll taste the cat for sure, I just know it."

A single lantern provided only the weakest illumination and James stopped for his eyes to adjust to the darkness in the hold.

"Cantu?"

On the far side the big man sat with his back against the bulkhead, his legs outstretched and his manacled hands in his lap.

James knelt down.

"Stevens told me you were here. What happened?"

Cantu stared straight ahead, his jaw set.

"Tell me, man. I can't help you if I don't know what happened."

Slowly Cantu shook his head.

"Mister Paine said that I was not doing my work, that I was disrespectful of him. He told Lieutenant Powell."

"What did you say to Mr. Paine?"

"I said nothing to the man. I was working on one of the lee brace blocks and he just came up behind me."

James didn't understand what Cantu was saying.

"He didn't say anything to you, nor did you say anything to him."

"No, sir. He just began to yell and curse me."

"Who else heard him?"

"I was alone, there were no others near me."

Suddenly James realized the terrible truth.

"I know the man, sir. He would not show disrespect to Mr. Paine. It must have been a misunderstanding."

"Mr. Addington. When one of my officers comes before me accusing a seaman, I have no choice but to uphold the chain of command."

James could tell from the tone of Judson Shaw's voice that his mind was certain on the issue.

"If Mr. Paine withdrew his accusation, or decided there was some failure to understand events correctly, I would gladly not refer the man to the captain."

The gun room was empty save for John Paine when James entered and sat down opposite him.

"The first lieutenant is willing to keep the matter to itself if you would withdraw your accusation." James kept his voice steady, but his heart was pounding.

John Paine looked at James without speaking. He grasped a cup and took a long drink, wiping his mouth with the back of his hand.

"Piss off."

"He told me what happened," James said, the anger starting to rise within him.

"Oh did he now? And since when did an officer in the Royal Navy take the word of a common seaman over the word of a fellow officer." Paine's voice was low, but vicious.

"When that officer is a liar."

Paine stood up abruptly and grabbed James by the front of the shirt.

"You little piece of shit. Are you calling me a liar?"

James shoved the man's hands down hard, then straightened his shirt.

"Of course not, SIR! I would never accuse a man who almost passed his lieutenant's exam, anything but pure and chaste."

Paine came across the table as Lucas Brown and Paul Culley entered the gun room. The two newcomers grabbed James and his assailant, pulling them apart.

"Enough.......I said enough!" Brown yelled harshly.

Culley was holding John Paine, who looked at James with unbridled hatred.

"Get out of my sight," Paine spat out.

"With pleasure," James said as he left the room. His heart continued to pound as he climbed on deck.

Robert McPherson sat back from the small table and waited for the captain's reply.

A large scale chart lay between them, the legend on the bottom denoting it as "St. Lucia."

"You make a most unusual request, sir."

"I've considered every aspect of this raid and I don't make my request lightly," McPherson said, his gaze unflinching. "Captain, by the very nature of your position, you're isolated from the crew and your officers. I understand why that is the custom, but I didn't have the luxury of time. I had to decide which of your men might provide my best advantage for success."

Fletcher frowned. Not only was McPherson requesting that his youngest midshipman accompany him ashore to silence the batteries, but that he stay the punishment of the man Cantu. Very odd, very odd indeed.

"Mr. Addington is the only officer you have who is experienced in the woods, or jungle in this case. This raid must be clandestine if it is to have any chance of success. For that reason I'll be going at night. Put a city dweller in a jungle at night and he might as well be suckling on his mother's teat for all the good he'll do me. Cantu is not only from the islands and understands the jungle, but he speaks French, as does Mr. Addington. I quite expect we'll have to use that capability to move close to the battery."

Fletcher stood up and turned to the rear cabin windows. He knew this blunt Scotsman made a good argument, but naval tradition had always allowed the more senior officers to avail themselves of opportunities for recognition. It made advancement possible in a navy not currently at war. But the letter from Sir Rodney emphasized the importance of success.

The darkness of the hold was broken by the lantern James carried in front on him as he came down the wooden stairs.

"Cantu?"

"Aye."

His hands manacled, Cantu still sat with his back against the wood beams.

James put a small package on the deck and then set the lantern next to it.

"I brought you some bread and cheese. Here's a canteen with water and lime juice."

Handing the food and drink to Cantu, James sat down and crossed his legs.

"The captain has agreed to delay your punishment if you'll go ashore with Mr. McPherson on Pigeon Island."

"Pigeon Island? It was known as one of the places Truffant would hide."

"The captain thinks the *Revanche* will be anchored under the cliffs of the island. There's a gun battery that must be destroyed if we're to have any chance of taking the ship."

Cantu chewed in silence then said, "I would be punished after I returned?"

James couldn't mislead this man. "I believe...... yes."

"And you still expect me to go?" Cantu now looked at James.

"Mr. McPherson feels that we'll have a better chance of success if you're along."

The big man's expression changed. "You are going?"

"Of course, I thought you understood."

Cantu nodded. "If you go, I go."

Chapter Eight

A Test of Honor

Approaching from the north, *Andromeda* remained out of visual range of St. Lucia until darkness, tacking back and forth as the first dog watch turned over to the second. Then, taking advantage of an onshore wind, Captain Fletcher closed Pigeon Island while the preparations were completed for the landing party.

Mr. McPherson would lead the raid, with Lieutenant Powell as the senior naval officer. Accompanying Powell would be Midshipmen Paine and Addington. There would be, in addition to the boat's crew, six marines led by Corporal Abernathy. In deference to the heat and a desire to be as inconspicuous as possible, the bullocks as they were known, would wear the same warm weather rig as the sailors.

"We'll attempt to come ashore in this small cove," McPherson said pointing to a spot on the chart.

Around the table, the three other officers in the raiding party and the captain watched as the Scotsman laid out his plan to scale the hill to the gun battery.

"Do we know if *Revanche* is there?" Powell asked.

Captain Fletcher said, "We couldn't close the island enough to determine. Sunrise will tell the tale certainly and we shall hope you'll have taken the battery by then. My intent is to close the island from the east using the mainland to screen our approach. If the wind holds, we should be able to close for a broadside before they can make sail or slip her anchor."

"Sir, if we're unable to take the battery, what provision is there for our return to the ship," Paine asked.

"That is a problem, Mr. Paine," McPherson answered. "If we don't remove the battery, *Andromeda* will be sorely pressed to close the island to pick us up and we stand little chance of rowing out under the guns. Our best course of action would be to hide in the jungle until dark and then pull out to the ship."

"And hiding on the island may be quite the challenge if our presence is known," Mr. Paine said.

"If we don't silence the battery," James added in an even voice, "That would be a small problem, I'm thinking."

"Quite so, Mr. Addington," Fletcher said. "But I am assured by Mr. McPherson that it should not come to that. Am I right, sir?"

The Scotsman smiled. "That is my inclination, sir."

A quarter moon appeared periodically through the clouds and provided enough illumination that Lieutenant Powell had good reason to believe they might actually find the small cove which Mr. McPherson had described. The wind had remained steady, the choppy waves showing white in the pale light.

James watched the men straining at their oars. It had been a long hard pull from *Andromeda* and the men were beginning to tire. Thankful for the following wind, he wondered how they would hold up fighting that same wind on their return.

In the rear of the cutter, Petty Officer Adams held the tiller hard under his left arm, straining to make out the shoreline.

As the cutter neared the island, the sound of waves breaking on the rocky shore could be heard, the thundering sound covering the normal sounds of the cutter.

"Can you make out the cove, Mr. Powell?" The tone of Adam's voice betrayed his concern.

The tall lieutenant craned his neck, unwilling to try and stand up in the swaying boat.

"Nothing yet. Make for the highest point on the island."

"Aye, sir," he replied.

James held onto the wooden thwart with one hand, steadying himself against the constant rolling. He glanced over to John Paine who sat on the opposite side of the cutter next to Mr. McPherson. The older midshipman had ignored him during preparations for the raid and that was fine with James.

The choppy water and brisk wind had kept a steady spray coming over the bow and everyone in the cutter was wet through to the skin. Despite the tropical days, the evening temperature on the water was now cool, prompting several of the passengers to shiver.

"Christ," Paine muttered, his stomach unhappy that he had taken cheese and beer before boarding the cutter.

"Are you quite alright?" McPherson asked Paine.

"Aye, sir," he replied, but his voice lacked any conviction.

James began to feel the cutter heave in response to the surge of the surf as they neared the island. Looking forward, he could make out a low rock cliff on which the water was breaking hard, spray flying high over the glistening back wall. Peering into the darkness he couldn't see the opening that showed on the chart. Were they too far east? He suddenly felt uneasy, the cutter was accelerating toward disaster.

"Back your oars," Adams ordered desperately. "I don't see anything up there, sir," he hollered to Powell over the crash of the surf.

The cutter canted crazily in the maelstrom of heaving water as Adams fought the tiller to keep the bow into aligned with the waves.

Powell stood up, his hand on Adam's right shoulder.

"Steer over there, Mr. Adams." Powell was pointing toward the shore. "I think that's our entrance off to the starboard," he yelled, the roar of crashing water now filling the night.

"Give way all," Adams cried over the roar. "Put your backs into it or we'll all be swimming."

There were no replies as the ten oarsmen tried to pull their oars against the power of the rolling surf. Most of the crew couldn't swim and if the cutter swamped they knew they would die.

"Yes, I believe that's it," Powell yelled at McPherson, his voice now frantic.

The Scotsman didn't reply, but kept looking toward the dark island and foaming white water.

The moonlight broke out from behind a scudding cloud casting a pale light on a sight that would always haunt James.

"Sweet mother of God," Adams exclaimed as the cutter surged toward a rocky wall.

The force of the impact shook the cutter violently, the port side oars shattering as they slammed into the rocks. Men grabbed hold of whatever they could as the boat rose on the next wave and slid to the right, its stern slewing hard starboard.

James held on to the thwart for his life, the violent motion throwing him against McPherson, who crashed into Paine.

Petty Officer Adams struggled against the force of the following waves threatening to drive the cutter beam on to the crashing surf, swamping them. He grunted as he forced the tiller over hard right then back to the left as the stricken boat careened between two high rock walls which shattered the remaining oars.

Men now grabbed for any hand hold as the cutter accelerated into the small channel and crashed to a stop on a small rocky beach.

Without thinking, the oarsmen scrambled over the side and fought to work the damaged cutter farther up on the safety of solid land.

"Jesus," McPherson said as he pulled himself over the side, his feet landing in foaming water as it rushed back toward the sea.

James followed him, dropping into the waist deep water, feeling the water's surge around his legs. Turning, he fought his way toward the rocky beach. Struggling against the powerful undertow, he felt a strong arm grab him. Together he and Cantu stumbled forward to where Mr. McPherson lay on his side.

Petty Officer Adams and several men, fighting the rushing water were finally able to secure the cutter to a large rock using the two bow lines. For the moment they were safe.

Men now fell to their knees, their chests heaving as they tried to regain their wind.

James reached out to touch McPherson's arm.

"Are you all right, sir?"

McPherson nodded. "Wet, but apparently still whole."

Down the beach John Paine knelt in the sand, his hands resting on his thighs

Where was the lieutenant, James asked himself looking around the small cove?

"Cantu, did you see Mr. Powell?"

"Overboard when we hit the wall, sir."

"Has anyone seen Leftenant Powell?" James asked the men who were now huddled in a circle on the rocky sand. No one replied.

James got to his feet and moved down the rocky beach to the turbulent foaming water. Their first casualty.

"Damned bad luck."

Turning to see Mr. McPherson, he was surprised at the man's matter of fact tone.

"That will make Mr. Paine the senior man."

"Yes, sir," James replied, the thought making him uneasy.

"Very well, then," McPherson said to the group kneeling on the sand. "Cantu, you'll go first. Be watchful for anyone, anyone at all. There are only enemies on this island, remember that. Find the guns, then meet us at the top of the ravine. We'll wait there until you return. Do you understand?"

The big man nodded his answer.

"Now off with you, and quietly."

The raiding party remained kneeling as McPherson covered everyone's duties. The coxswain Adams would remain with his oarsmen to guard the boat and attempt to get it ready for sea. The Marines would make up the main party with the two midshipmen and McPherson.

"Keep quiet. No talking at all. Make sure muskets and pistols are unloaded. Single file, watch the man in front and pay attention to where you're stepping. It will be a hard climb up this ravine, but we have no choice. Once we reach the gun battery, we'll survey the position and deploy ourselves accordingly. Is that understood? "

The men said nothing, but they knew what was expected of them.

"Remember who's senior here, snottie," Paine said quietly to James. "I don't want you getting in the way up there, is that understood?"

Knowing he was trying to bait him, James ignored the remark, instead strode over to McPherson.

"Orders, sir?" James asked.

"I will want you up with me at the front of the column. Your French will likely come in to play if our ruse is to succeed."

"Aye, sir."

John Paine joined the two officers and asked, "Shall I lead, sir?"

"Actually I need you to cover the end of the party, make sure no one goes missing or lost."

"But, sir..."

"Please do as you're ordered, Mr. Paine. This is not the time to quibble over protocol. Do I make myself clear?"

The tall midshipman glared at McPherson.

The noise of the surf remained with the party as they moved single file up the steep ravine. James doubted any noise they made would be noticed against the constant crashing of waves below them. They climbed in silence, the men concentrating on maintaining their footing on the slippery path. What should have been a tiring climb seemed to go easily, the tension and anticipation masking their physical effort.

As they climbed higher, the vegetation became thicker. Men now used the tough bushes as handholds to make their climb easier, their breathing becoming more labored as they moved higher.

Clouds scudded above the small party, driven by the strong wind, the occasional break in the clouds bringing a welcome swath of moonlight.

Almost at the top of the cliff, James stepped up to mount a small knoll and felt his shoe slipping on a smoothly worn rock. Balanced precariously for a moment, James fought against the wind trying to regain his balance. For one moment his mind screamed he was falling.

"Easy does it, Mr. Addington."

Mr. McPherson had grabbed James's flailing arm and firmly pulled him over the top of the hill.

The two men knelt and peered into the darkness. Ahead small trees and bushes covered the rocky summit of Pigeon Island.

"A bit of a brisk climb, if I do say so," Corporal Abernathy said quietly as he knelt down.

"How are your men doing?" McPherson asked.

"No worries, sir. The lads are fine."

John Paine joined the three, breathing hard, but saying nothing.

"We'll give Cantu thirty minutes before we send anyone else out there. I don't want any confusion in the dark."

A single light winked in the darkness, the first sign of humans that Cantu had come across as he worked his way across the rocky spine of the island. He knew this had to be what McPherson was looking for. Slowly he moved forward in a crouch, his eyes scanning the darkness for any sentries.

The outline of a breastwork shone against the moonlit ocean. Jutting from behind the row of logs, Cantu saw the shape of at least four cannons. Moving closer he could now see there were six cannons pointing out over the bay where the brig *Revanche* tugged against its anchor. But it wasn't the ship that drew Cantu's attention. Instead it was several white tents on the wide strip of land connecting the main island. He could see fires on the beach and he realized there was a second ship anchored beyond the brig.

With the surf crashing below them on the rocks, McPherson listened to Cantu's report. A second ship with more men and guns was not something the Scot had anticipated. If the cutter were not so severely damaged, he would have put back to sea to warn the frigate. This development put *Andromeda* in a difficult situation. Assuming Captain Fletcher conducted his attack as planned, the captain would not know that the strength of the protective battery on the hill had trebled. If the guns fired only regular shot, it would be a very close thing. But there was also the possibility of heated shot. Even one hit by a red hot ball could turn the dry timbers and rigging of *Andromeda* into flaming wreckage in minutes.

The barest hint of dawn lit the eastern sky as the raiding party looked across the small clearing toward the revetted gun battery. A tent slightly down slope from the guns remained quiet with no sign of life from within. At the end of the gun emplacement a single sentry sat on a large box, his head down on his chest, asleep.

"This is our chance," McPherson said quietly. "If we can spike those guns and withdraw, our job is done."

"My men have the spikes," Corporal Abernathy offered, referring to the metal nails which would be driven into the touch holes to disable the cannons from firing.

"Mr. Paine, take two marines and work your way to the right. Watch the tent while we take care of the guns. If anyone comes out, shoot only if you have to. I don't want to alert the people down below."

"Aye, sir."

"Mr. Addington, you'll move forward with the corporal and his men after Cantu takes care of the sentry. Keep watch while the marines spike the guns. Corporal, be as quiet as you can."

Abernathy nodded.

"I'll send Cantu in five minutes, Mr. Paine. Please be so good as to take your position."

Two marines carrying muskets followed the midshipman, all crouching low to remain below the crest of the hill.

"Cantu."

The sailor looked at McPherson and moved next to him.

"I need you to kill that sentry and do it quietly."

"I understand."

James saw the marines replacing the flints in their muskets, removed to prevent an accidental discharge. Reaching into his britches pocket, he pulled out the flint for his pistol and did the same. Checking that the powder in the pan was dry, he tucked the weapon inside his belt, his anxiety giving way to a determination to do his duty.

The men now were ready. As they all watched Cantu move down the slope into the darkness, not a word was spoken. They all knew that they could soon be fighting desperately to save themselves and the ship.

Chapter Nine

Strike Hard, Strike Quick

Slowly the surroundings became more distinct, day now opening across the eastern sky. The wind of earlier had dropped and now did little to mask Cantu's approach.

James worked to follow the big man's progress down the slope. Slow and deliberate steps took him closer to the battery until he disappeared in the landscape. The sounds of early rising seabirds now broke the silence over the battery and James feared the noise might stir the enemy.

Below the guns a lantern cast a pale light from inside the tent. John Paine watched from behind a large rock as one of the marines moved his musket to the ready.

"Stand fast," Paine whispered.

In his right hand, Cantu carried a short machete' as he moved steadily down the hill. The blade of the weapon was the same length as a boarding cutlass, but much wider. Born in the islands, he had used the brutally sharp blade since he was a boy. Slowly he approached the sleeping sentry. Cantu saw the soldier wore a rough leather shirt over canvas britches. Next to the man a musketoon leaned against the dirt wall of the revetment. The lantern which Cantu had originally seen had burned out, but a rapidly lightening sky was all the illumination he needed.

As the sentry stirred slightly, then lifted his head slowly, Cantu's machete swung down and struck the man's neck, severing his windpipe and driving the blade deep into the spine.

Jerking hard, Cantu pulled the blade out of the flesh, blood pouring down the front of the sentry's shirt. The force of the almost severed head pulled the man to one side and he collapsed on the ground without making a sound.

"Forward," McPherson said sharply.

James broke cover and began to run toward the cannons, his cutlass held at the ready.

Next to McPherson, the stocky corporal ran with his bayonet tipped musket. The other marines flanked out to the right, their bayonets forward.

The line approached the guns, the men raising their muskets ready to plunge down into the battery. As if they had been given a silent order the men held up at the edge of the emplacement. The battery was deserted.

"Get about it, corporal," McPherson said quietly as he turned to survey the surrounding area.

The marines jumped down into the battery and leaned their muskets against the dirt wall. Pulling the long metal nails from their pockets, they moved to the guns, inserting a nail into each touchhole.

The sound of a shot shattered the morning quiet, freezing the marines.

James turned to see McPherson slowly fall sideways off the side of the battery wall. From down the slope there were shouts, which he recognized as French. Jumping down to the ground, James ran to McPherson who lay on his side, his sword under his body.

"Sir, sir.......are you all right?"

Robert McPherson only groaned at James's question.

"Cantu....... Cantu....over here," James called out.

James rolled the Scot on his back and saw a large black stain spreading across his shirt as blood pumped from the man's chest. A sense of panic began to engulf the young officer.

Cantu dropped to his knees and quickly examined McPherson.

"He will die," Cantu said quickly. "There is nothing to be done."

Another ball whined by them and hit the revetment.

Looking down at McPherson, James knew it was now up to him. He must take command.

"Back into the battery," James yelled as another ball ripped past them thudding into the dirt.

Two more shots echoed across the slope as James and Cantu jumped down next to Corporal Abernathy.

"McPherson's dead," James said quickly while he tried to see over the top toward the tent. Down the row of guns, four marines knelt, each now holding his musket.

More shouts from the tent told them that there were a number of men now firing at them.

"Your orders, sir?" Abernathy asked, falling back on his training.

"Mr. Paine should be firing on our flank." James thought about what he had learned on withdrawal from his father. "That will allow us to fall back."

"Right you are, sir," the corporal said, his grin visible in the early light. Right steady for a young gentleman, he thought. Maybe he's one of the good ones.

Two shots rang out on their right.

"Them's our lads, I'd know a Brown Bess anywhere."

The sounds were different, James thought, the pirates musketoons a much sharper report.

"Are the guns spiked?"

"Yes, sir. Those buggers won't be firing at anyone for a long time."

"Very well, corporal. Have your men fall back one at a time and take cover at the top of the hill."

"Aye, sir. Higgins, over you go. Run like hell and take position at the hill top."

Higgins rolled over the top of the back revetment and ran up the hill in a crouch.

Shots continued to be heard from where James guessed Paine and his two men were. A musket ball whined over the battery causing him to flinch.

"Parker, you're next. Shake a leg, man," Abernathy called to the skinny private at the end of the gun battery. The man scrambled over the log, grabbed his musket and ran hard up the hill.

Surveying the scene, James wondered what they should do next. He could see the heads of their two marines with muskets pointing down hill.

"Cantu, we need to find out what's on the southern side of the hill. I must know if there's a way down to the water or across to the mainland."

Corporal Abernathy gave the young midshipman a sideways glance before sending Private Grimes after his comrades.

Without a word, Cantu rolled over the top and sprinted for the southern side of the summit. Two shots range out from the pirates, the balls throwing up dirt behind him as he neared cover.

"All right, Private Little. Up and over. Keep your head down if you don't want to lose it!"

Bearing no resemblance to his name, the beefy private climbed over the dirt ledge and tripped as he started up the slope. His flaying left arm flew up in the air to balance the heavy musket in his right hand. Several shots rang out, a puff of dirt flying up next to the marine. The man staggered and lunged up the hill as a ball thudded into his lower back. Like a puppet doll, Little collapsed, dropping his musket and slamming hard into the slope.

"Bloody hell!" Abernathy spat out.

Private Little lay almost motionless, with only his left hand twitching erratically.

Looking to Abernathy, James knew he needed help to deal with this.

"Can we pull him back in here?"

The stocky corporal shook his head.

"Like as not, they'd get both of us."

The wounded private lay fifteen feet from the gun battery and at least four times that distance from the three marines at the summit.

"Private Little," the corporal yelled harshly.

There was no response from the prone figure, the twitching hand now still.

"I think he's done for, sir."

Think of your whole crew, his father used to say. Sometimes you will lose a man, but your job is to bring as many home as you can. Making a decision, James grabbed the corporal's arm.

"Your turn, corporal."

Abernathy looked at the midshipman, surprise evident in his face.

"You heard me. Get up the hill and take charge. Have the men ready to fire. I'll check the private."

Grabbing his musket, Abernathy looked at James.

"We'll be ready, sir." His voice had a tone of respect in it.

Shots rang out as Abernathy ran up the hill, disappearing over the top.

Looking down the empty gun battery, James thought he should feel lonely or scared, but he didn't. Taking a last look at Little, he saw that he would be sheltered if he took cover on the private's right side in a small depression. Checking his pistol primed, he rolled over the edge and ran toward the wounded marine.

Sliding to a stop next to the private, he heard one musket shot and nothing from the musketoons.

"Private Little....can you hear me."

He could smell the sickly sweet scent of blood and it took him back to the deck of the schooner. Remembering what he'd been taught by Faircloth, he grabbed Private Little's neck to see if he could feel the man's heart beat. The hot skin was sweaty and covered in dust. Squeezing hard, he felt nothing. Then he put his hand under Little's nose and mouth, but there was no breath that he could discern.

Another musketoon shot rang out and James felt the ball slam into Little's left side. Any hope for the private was now over. Shoving himself up James focused on the top of the slope and ran as hard as he could. The whine of balls going past seemed like a bizarre melody as he fought up the slope. Leaping the last several feet, he dove over Corporal Abernathy who ducked to avoid a collision.

Trying to catch his breath, James gasped, "Little's dead. Is anyone else hurt?"

The corporal shook his head.

"Not a scratch. Looks like you were mighty lucky, Mr. Addington."

"What?"

Abernathy stuck his index finger into a round hole in James's shirt, the edges black from powder.

"A souvenir of Pigeon Island. What do you think, corporal?"

Abernathy laughed.

"As you say, sir."

James turned serious.

"Take one man and see if you can contact Mr. Paine."

The sun rose higher as James waited for Cantu and Abernathy. It promised to be another warm and windy day, their lack of water and shade potentially deadly.

"Sir, here they come."

Abernathy led the small group, his musket at the ready. The Marines followed in single file with Cantu at the end of the column. In his arms lay Midshipman Paine.

"He's bad wounded, sir," Abernathy said, dropping to his knees and laying the musket against a rock.

Cantu gently laid Paine on the ground, the officer's left shoulder wrapped in a bloody bandage torn from a shirt.

James knelt next to Paine, noting the lack of color in his face.

"Mr. Paine."

Opening his eyes, John Paine grimaced with pain.

"Water......."

"Lie easy, we'll get you back to the ship in short order."

"Cantu wouldn't let us leave until he'd bandaged his shoulder," Abernathy said.

Cantu knelt down to adjust the bloody dressing.

Paine looked very weak lying in the dirt and James wondered if even Cantu's ministrations would save the man. He watched John Paine reach out and take Cantu's hand.

"You will be well," Cantu said, continuing to hold Paine's hand.

Another musketoon shot rang out to remind the men of their enemies down the hill.

James said, "We can't fall back or the pirates will be on us." He looked at the men around him. Dirty, sweaty and in a desperate situation, but he saw they didn't look dispirited in the least. These are remarkable men, he thought. He had to get them back to the ship. "Cantu, make your way down to the cutter and find out what's happening."

A slight grin came from Cantu. He shook his head. "I will stay with you."

In that moment James Addington learned about loyalty. It was a lesson he would never forget. He nodded and turned to Corporal Abernathy who had heard the exchange.

"Corporal."

"I understand, sir. I'll send Higgins, he'll make it there and back, don't you fret."

"Sir, look!"

Climbing to the top of the ridge, James carefully raised his head and saw a magnificent sight. Under full sail, *Andromeda* was closing the island, the sun rising behind her, painting the morning sky a vivid pink.

"I don't think the pirates have seen her yet," Abernathy said, now lying next to James.

"The lookouts may have seen her, but it appears they haven't alerted the brig."

"Sir, here's Higgins."

The stocky marine knelt.

"Report."

"Sir, Petty Officer Adams told me to tell you that the cutter is seaworthy. They've jury rigged four oars and he figures that they can double man those to get out through the surf."

Below them a trumpet began to blow on the brig and James could see men appearing on deck.

"All right, now is our chance. Corporal, take Mr. Paine and your men back to the cutter and tell Petty Officer Adams to be ready to shove off. And tell him to load the swivel gun if the powder warrants it."

Abernathy touched his forehead. "Aye, aye, sir."

"Cantu, you're with me."

The big man pulled the machete' from his belt and knelt next to James.

Captain Fletcher lowered the long glass as *Andromeda* cleared the headland. "Port battery, load with chain shot and run out!"

The first lieutenant echoed the command as did the officers on the gun decks.

"She waited too long, Mr. Shaw."

Judson Shaw understood that Fletcher wanted to hit the brig's rigging and cripple her. But he also knew they were soon going to be within range of the gun battery on the hill. Had McPherson done his job?

"By God, look at that, Mr. Shaw." Fletcher had the glass to his eye again. "A schooner anchored behind the *Revanche*."

Closing the anchored ships at almost nine knots, the men on the frigate could see crews from both ships swarming into the rigging, trying desperately to make sail. If they could get underway and slip their anchors, at least one would likely get away, if not both.

"Maximum elevation, fire as you bear."

The first cannon roared and recoiled inboard, the squeals of the gun truck blotted out by the next gun firing. Chain shot, designed to rip the sails and rigging of the target apart, crashed into the masts and yards of both vessels.

Fletcher and Shaw watched the carnage above the ships as men's bodies, lines and torn sails crashed down onto the decks of both ships.

A single shot from *Revanche* was the sole reply to the *Andromeda's* full broadside at less than four cables. The battle had been decided.

"They're going over the side, sir," Mr. Bagley exclaimed. "The sharks will have a feast today."

Fletcher didn't respond, instead his eyes were fixed on the two prizes and the men aboard that were still to die.

"There, on the right," James said as a single man moved up to take cover behind a rock.

From the left side of the gun battery a shot rang out, the bullet ricocheting over their heads.

It had been twenty minutes since Abernathy had left for the cutter. Had they been able to negotiate the steep cliff with the wounded midshipman?

"I believe they're going to attack," James said quietly to Cantu.

"Yes," he replied, the machete' ready in his right hand.

Both men had two pistols, left behind by the others, with a small supply of shot and powder.

"If they don't rush in the next ten minutes, we shall try to slip away. Hold your fire and if the buggers do come at us, let them get close enough that you can't miss."

Cantu nodded.

Another shot rang out followed by shouts. The pirates were forcing the issue.

"Steady," James said seeing six men struggling up the slope. His heart pounded seeing the hard looking men, heavily armed and yelling at the top of their lungs.

"Steady......steady.....NOW!"

Two simultaneous shots rang out catching the two men farthest up the slope in their chests, the heavy balls ripping flesh and throwing them backwards down the hill. Behind them the remaining men knelt down, one raising a musketoon and firing wildly at Cantu.

Below the gun battery at least a dozen men gathered, ready to add to the attack.

James fired at one of the kneeling men, hitting the rocks in front of him, the ball glancing up and hitting the man's leg. He screamed in pain and fell on the ground holding his wound. Two more men got up and began to run the final ten yards to the summit.

Cantu quickly aimed and fired his second pistol, but the ball missed its target. He dropped the pistol and stood, the machete' ready to meet the pirate's charge.

His cutlass at the ready, James knew the big man directly in front of him would be his attacker. The man wore a filthy overshirt, his bearded face sweating from the exertion.

Scrambling to the top of the ridge, James clawed at the sandy soil trying to gain the advantage before they met. Suddenly he knew what he would do. Grasping a handful of the soil, he stood up, raising his cutlass to the ready.

The big man yelled and raised his sword, the blade now high above his head.

James flung the handful of sand into the man's face, side-stepping and slashing hard across the man's stomach. The blade sliced through skin and muscle, the man's belly now opening like a melon.

The scream was not of this world and the pirate dropped his sword, both hands now clutching his belly, trying to hold the wound together.

Cantu struck down at his opponent, the machete' rasping off the man's cutlass. Quicker at the parry, Cantu brought his curved blade back in the horizontal before the man could set up his guard, slashing across an outstretched arm, severing it at the elbow.

James gasped for air, seeing the group of men below. They hadn't begun to climb the hill, but if they did, the matter would not be in doubt.

"Quick, down the hill, Cantu. Run, man, run!"

Breaking onto the beach, James and Cantu saw the Marines in a line with the cutter behind them. Each man held his musket at the ready, with Corporal Abernathy standing to the side. On the cutter's stern, the swivel gun was manned by two men, the rest of the crew standing ready on the oars, holding the cutter on the sand.

"Hold your fire!" Abernathy bellowed.

James ran toward the line, Cantu next to him.

"Standby to shove off," James yelled at Adams while pushing Cantu to the sand.

"PRESENT..........FIRE!"

The marine's volley crashed over James into the gaggle of men who had emerged from the ravine. Three men went down, their bodies collapsing on the rocky beach. The remaining pirates slowed their headlong rush.

"Fall back," Abernathy ordered and the marines ran to the cutter where a small group had gathered at the stern.

Up and sprinting toward the boat, James and Cantu reached it as the pirates surged onto the last stretch of beach.

The vicious explosion of the swivel gun tore into the remaining attackers. One man remained standing, but then he slowly fell headfirst into the sand.

"Back to the ship, lads."

"Deck there, boat off the port beam. Looks like the cutter."

Adam Carlyle grabbed a long glass from the rack and lay it atop the rail. In the distance he could see the cutter, with the small driver sail hoisted, closing the ship from the headland.

"My compliments to the captain and tell him we have the cutter in sight."

One hour later, with the frigate turned into the wind, James Addington brought the cutter alongside, the small sail now lowered and four makeshift oars driving the boat.

The captain and third lieutenant stood at the rail watching the approach. They could clearly see the damage to the cutter's hull and the lashings holding her oars together.

"Quite a story, I should think, Mr. Carlyle."

"Aye, sir. Young Addington seems to have a bent for it."

"Call the surgeon," Fletcher added, seeing the prone figure of Midshipman Paine in the bottom of the cutter. "It appears Mr. Powell is missing."

Continuing to watch the boat's crew secure the lines, Fletcher started for a moment then said aloud, "Damnation, McPherson's not there either." Then he realized who was in charge of the cutter.

Sitting opposite the Captain, James had felt sure of himself as he gave his report. Leaving no detail out, he described the night's events and their return to the ship.

"Corporal Abernathy is to be commended for his actions, sir. His marines acquitted themselves quite well in every phase of the raid."

"So it seems, Mr. Addington." Stephen Fletcher got up from his chair and walked to the sideboard. He poured two glasses of claret from a small jug, placing one on the table in front of James.

"I would say that you also acquitted yourself admirably in the circumstances. Your actions and those of your men allowed this ship to capture two rogue privateers with no loss of life. Well done, sir. Your father would be extremely proud of you, as I am."

Embarrassed by the praise, James took a drink and found the warmth of the wine comforting.

"And it sounds like that man Cantu is a true jack of all trades."

"Yes, sir. I would gladly have him with me anytime."

Fletcher chuckled. "I don't think he's going to allow you any choice in the matter, sir." The Andromeda's captain watched his young midshipman grin, the bright scar across his upper lip pulled tight. He is going to be just fine, Fletcher thought to himself, just fine.

Chapter Ten

Full Circle

Four days of repairs resulted in both prizes, *Revanche* and *Lila*, a gaff-rigged schooner being ready for the trip back to Antigua. Some of the crew had escaped into the jungle but over forty had been taken prisoner and now were locked below decks. No trace had ever been found of Emile Truffant.

Mr. Shaw would command *Revanche* while Lieutenant Carlyle commanded *Lila*. Spreading the thin crew across the two prizes, Mr. Brown and Mr. Culley would join the two lieutenants as their seconds in command leaving James Addington as the temporary first lieutenant in *Andromeda*.

Jim Goodrum stared down at the sweat-covered body of John Paine. The fever had appeared on the second day after the man's return to the ship. The doctor initially felt optimistic for Mr. Paine's eventual recovery after examining the bandage and herbal dressing applied by Cantu. But these things were often hard to anticipate. The deadly humours that infected these islands could take a healthy man and in two days he would be stitched in his hammock and plunging to the bottom, dead as a mackerel.

"I fear this is not going to be an easy battle," he said aloud.

"Doctor?"

Goodrum turned to see James Addington.

"May I come in?"

"Certainly."

The doctor smiled then sighed. "I'm afraid things are not going well for Mr. Paine. The fever has taken deep hold. I'm afraid the only chance is to bleed him."

James looked down at the hammock. Once this arrogant man had been antagonistic, but now he felt no animosity toward him. Paine had done his duty and would now likely die thousands of miles from his home and family. That fate might well be ahead for James and in his mind it bound all of the men aboard *Andromeda* together as comrades.

"Cantu was a healer before he went to sea. He knows these islands. Would you talk with him?

The doctor reacted with mild surprise. "I didn't think you and Mr. Paine were exactly friends."

"He's important to this ship, as is every man we have. Anything we can do is worth trying."

Goodrum looked at the young officer. Only fifteen and he sounds like a senior lieutenant. Perhaps we have a future admiral here, he thought. "Very well then, have the heathen come see me. Let it never be said that Jim Goodrum left any stone unturned in his quest for knowledge."

"Will this help restore his balance?" Goodrum asked.

"Balance, what is this balance?" Cantu responded.

The doctor seemed exasperated.

"Everyone knows that a fever is the result of an imbalance in bodily fluids. I am simply trying to understand if this potion will help to restore that balance. I have already begun the rebalance by bleeding him this morning."

Cantu shook his head, handing Goodrum a glass of brown liquid.

"This will allow him to rest and help the fever to leave his body. Of that I'm sure.

"Tell me again what's in it."

Report of the Admiralty Examining Board
Antigua
February 4, 1774

May it please the Lords, be it known that serving Midshipman James Addington appeared before the board consisting of Captain David Williams, Captain Gregory Wood and Captain Lawrence Yarham.

It was the unanimous judgment of the board that Mr. Addington does indeed possess the requisite knowledge to assume the duties of Lieutenant on active service with the fleet.

His service to this date has been exemplary in Andromeda according to Captain Fletcher. During that time he has demonstrated leadership and bravery during numerous actions with hostile forces throughout Caribbean waters and into the Atlantic.

In keeping with Admiralty policy, a transfer for Mr. Addington from Andromeda should be accomplished as soon as a new billet can be arranged.

PART TWO

1775-1777

Chapter Eleven

A Cutting Out Expedition

The low wooden cutter moved steadily across the darkened bay, the muffled oars beating a smooth rhythm as the sailors pulled in unison to the quiet cadence of the coxswain. Sitting in the stern, Lieutenant James Addington searched the far shore where he could see a single flickering light.

"There's the brig, two points starboard," he said quietly to Kelly, the coxswain.

"Aye, sir,"

Subconsciously, Addington checked the pistol tucked into his sword belt. The metal was cold despite the warm humidity of the night. He adjusted his sword as he shifted on the hard wooden seat.

"I doubt if they have a guard boat, Mr. Enright, but keep a sharp watch in any case."

"Aye, sir," came the reply from David Enright, one of the eight midshipmen currently serving in H.M.S. *Challenger*. Almost fifteen years old, Enright had been with the ship for over two years which had included an extended period as part of the Mediterranean Squadron.

Now on independent duty, the 28 gun frigate was operating off the northwest coast of Africa in search of slavers and pirates. Lines of commerce had become the lifeblood of the British Empire and crushing the recent growth of piracy off the African coast had become a priority for the Admiralty.

Forward in the bow, a dozen Royal Marines sat holding boarding pikes. Lieutenant Archie Tatnall, the second in command of the Marines aboard *Challenger,* stared attentively ahead at what was now clearly visible as their intended target.

Thirty yards in the cutter's wake, the ship's second cutter followed, commanded by the ship's third lieutenant, Andy Thorton. Normally a cutting out party would have been led by the ship's first lieutenant, his best friend, Will

Thorpe. But the feisty Cornishman lay in his small cabin, his body wracked by one of the many fevers that took so many sailors in these waters.

The twin masts of the brig rocked slightly in the offshore swell, the sails now furled and the crew probably below or perhaps ashore searching for provisions. The *Challenger* had been searching for this particular vessel for over a month. Only a chance encounter with a small native fishing boat had led them to the anchorage the cutter was now approaching. The *Serpentine,* originally a Portuguese trader, had been captured two years ago by a pirate known as Speir. Mounting several six pound cannons, the little ship was more than a match for most coastal traffic. Her shallow draft also allowed her to slip away from the larger frigates of the Royal Navy, often using the rivers and estuaries that flowed into the Atlantic as a sanctuary. Over the last six months, seven vessels were have thought to have fallen prey to this ship, their cargoes stolen and their crews put to death or sold into slavery.

James listened intently for any sign of activity as they closed under a cable's length from the brig. The watch is probably sleeping on deck, he thought. They'll regret that.

"Be ready with the grapnel," he said loud enough for the seaman in the bow to hear.

The skinny man nodded and held up the three-pronged metal device secured to a hemp rope and ready to secure the cutter to the ship's side.

"Take her along the port side, we'll make up amidships," he whispered to Kelly.

"Aye, sir," the coxswain replied in a hoarse whisper. Standing up to his full height, the big Irishman gauged the distance and speed, waiting one long count he said, "Up oars......easy, now."

Dripping blades rose above the cutter as the bow closed the *Serpentine's* side, the bump barely audible over the quiet lapping of waves.

"Up you go, marines," James said quickly, the redcoats and white cross buckles moving up the side as if they were rising from the depths of hell.

A shout came from on deck, followed by frantic calls from the foc'sle.

"At 'em, now," Archie yelled as he climbed on the brig's deck, his sword held at the ready.

"Let's go," James called to Cantu, who followed him up the boarding ladder to the ship's entry port.

A shot rang out, the bright flash coming from forward, throwing one marine backwards, his pike clattering to the deck. Confusion broke out as men climbed out of the main hatch, weapons in their hands.

The clash of steel, grunts of men engaged in death struggles and more shouts from below added to the bedlam as small vicious fights broke out across the deck between the marines and the brig's crew.

James saw a man pull himself on deck, looking around wildly, a cutlass in one hand. Lunging forward, he drove his sword into the man's side, the blade plunging deep into his bowels. Pulling hard, James was able to yank the sword free as the man cried and fell backwards into the hatch.

A pistol fired behind James, the explosion ringing in his ears. Turning quickly he saw a squat man rushing from the darkness toward Cantu, an axe held high for the killing blow. The man appeared not to see James, who slashed hard with his sword catching the man on the side of the head, laying his scalp open and cracking the skull. Dropping the axe, the pirate staggered forward, his hands reaching slowly toward his head.

Cantu caught the movement as James yelled his name. With practiced ease, the big man continued around, his machete' held horizontal and it caught the man across his forearms, severing one and breaking the other.

Several shots rang out and suddenly the deck seemed to go quiet. James knew there would be no formal surrender or request for quarter, these men knew they already carried death sentences. But it seemed the pirates on deck had been killed or wounded and the remainder must be below decks.

"Archie, to me," James called and in a moment the lieutenant stood next to him holding a cutlass covered with blood.

"Aye."

"Have we taken the deck?"

Archie nodded, his breathing still labored.

"Most fell back to the foc'sle. We cut them down where they stood."

"There must be more below, have your men guard the hatch while we take count. Cantu, have Kelly send up some men and throw those bodies over the side."

"Several of them are wounded up forward," Archie said.

"Dump them all over the side, we can't be bothered," James said. "How about your men?"

"Two dead and one man wounded. Not sure he could survive a boat trip back to *Challenger*."

"Cantu, see what you can do."

From the foc'sle the sound of bodies hitting the water could be heard over the wash of water against the hull.

"Fast and furious, what?"

James could see Andy Thorton in the lantern light.

"I suspect they were mostly drunk," James replied. "I want the bullocks to guard the hatch until we can determine what we have down below. Once we've secured the crew, We'll make sail and take advantage of this wind. We should be able to rendezvous with *Challenger* by day break.

"Back in time for breakfast by God," Thorton chuckled.

Despite serving as Captain Robert Pelham's second lieutenant for two years, James still found the livid scar that ran across the man's face from ear to mouth hard to look at. Wounded in a fight off the west coast of Africa, Pelham's wound had healed badly and now the shiny white skin looked like make up painted on at the theater. In contrast, James own scar had blended well, and while it would always be with him, it no longer made new acquaintances react.

"Any sign of Speir?"

"No sir," James responded. The lack of boats on board tells me that Speir must have taken a large part of the crew up river. Perhaps in search of slaves."

"You're probably right. In any case he won't bother shipping now and if they remain stranded in this jungle, we can only hope the natives will kill him. Would only be appropriate, don't you think?"

"Very much, sir," James said hoping that death would indeed be the end of the criminal. "If you will excuse me sir, I want to check on Private Collins. He was wounded on the brig."

"Ah, employment for the doctor, it's about time."

James turned on his heel and left the cabin. While he respected Robert Pelham, he had always felt distanced from him. A complete change from Captain Fletcher and not one he enjoyed.

"Hello, James," the doctor said straightening up from the flat board where Collins lay, resting on two large wooden chests.

One of the surgeon's assistant appeared at the doorway, a large bucket in one hand.

"Over here, Grant."

Jim Goodrum dipped a white rag into the water and gently dabbed the wounded man's chest.

"Damned lucky you are, Private Collins. Must be those big Irish ribs of yours. The blade slid right across, failing to do any fatal damage."

Collins turned his head, the sweat covering his face. "I'll be all right?"

Goodrum laughed, "Without question. Your ribs and that damned Cantu. I still don't know how he does it. It seems he can heal the wounds of the ages and make it look easy. Back in London I could make him a wealthy man if only he wasn't a blackie. Gentle persons don't accept ministrations from the colored races. Perhaps I could tell them he was a Mongolian? What do you say, James."

"You'll have to ask Mr. Granville about that, doctor."

"Mr. Granville, indeed," Goodrum chuckled, always amused by the use of Cantu's proper name.

"How is Will?" James asked, his concern evident for his friend.

Goodrum's expression changed.

"The fever still hasn't broken."

James heard the concern in the doctor's voice.

"Sometimes I think a cannon ball is the best way to go," James said quietly. "Not wasting away in a sweaty nightmare as you slowly slip away."

"I think you're right, my young friend. But there is still hope we can restore the balance of his fluids. I examined his urine earlier and I'm convinced of that."

Later in the wardroom the doctor and James sat at the table, a glass of wine in front of both.

"Will Collins live?"

"I should think so, as long as we can avoid putrification. With our new orders to sail for Boston, we'll finally escape this infernal tropical heat. With your Mr. Granville in attendance to deal with any fever using his herbal magic, the young man should heal good as new. In fact I asked Cantu to look at Mr. Thorpe. I know the first lieutenant would be horrified to have a blackie touching him, but he is well out of knowing at this point."

"He has a very special talent," James said. "I hope he can help Will."

"I've done everything I can for him, now it's up to God or the heathen."

The two men sat in companionable silence. Years together had established a bond that didn't need constant conversation.

James thought back to the arrival of the small sloop from Gibraltar with orders before he had left with the cutting out expedition. The Admiralty was sending a number of ships across the Atlantic in response to the recent trouble in Massachusetts. With the capture of *Serpentine, Challenger* would have to return to Gibraltar to replenish stores and regain the men from her prize crew, who were already enroute.

"What must the desk bound admirals be thinking? Warships to the colonies? To do what? These rebels have no navy. So what would they have us do, blockade our own people?"

Goodrum sighed and took a drink of wine.

"James, my expertise lies in the correction of human maladies. I'm afraid they do not extend to the lunacies of the senior officers in the Admiralty. Perhaps London intends a show of overwhelming force that will bring these fools to their senses."

Thinking of his last visit to New York two years prior, James knew there was a faction among the colonials that were vocally demanding more control of their affairs from Parliament. Surely these differences could be settled without violence? It was hard to imagine ships of the Royal Navy firing on New York or Boston. Madness, he thought, sheer madness.

"I hope the change will allow the cat to be returned to its bag."

Goodrum said nothing, but poured another glass for each of them.

"It was never like this in the old *Andromeda*," James added.

"And the captain is no Stephen Fletcher," the doctor said quietly.

When *Andromeda* had paid off in Portsmouth, both James and the doctor were fortunate that Captain Fletcher used his influence to have them both transferred to *Challenger*. Doctor Goodrum had no desire to go ashore and James's career as a new lieutenant would go no where if he did not get an assignment.

The time had gone quickly, with *Challenger* ordered initially to the America's and now with the Mediterranean Fleet. The almost constant time at sea had allowed James to gain invaluable experience and now he was returning to the land of his birth.

Chapter Twelve

Times Have Changed

A brisk wind cut across the deck and James pulled the collar of his boat cloak tight around his neck. As the end of the morning watch approached, he watched the routine unfold on deck as it did every morning at sea. From holystoning the decks to inspecting lines and tackle, the ship was now fully awake and ready for a new day.

"Deck there, land off the larboard bow."

Favorable winds and a lack of storms had allowed *Challenger* a swift passage from Gibraltar. Now, twenty six days out, they were in sight of the American coast. When they had arrived in Gibraltar the Admiral had told Captain Pelham that two regiments of regulars had landed in Boston in response to the recent unrest. *Challenger's* orders were to sail for Massachusetts and report to Vice Admiral Samuel Graves for duties in support. It appeared the unrest which began with the attempt by Parliament to tax the colonies was now coming to a head. James felt uneasy, but couldn't tell himself exactly why.

"My compliments to the Captain, Mr. Merriweather," James said to the young midshipman next to him. "And tell him we have land fall off the larboard bow.'

"America, so we return," Doctor Goodrum said as he stepped on the quarterdeck and crossed to where James stood.

"You have a good friend in Boston as I recall."

Goodrum grinned, "Indeed I do. Richard Warren, friends for over twenty years. A marvelous physician, he left London after falling in love with a young girl from Boston. He's practiced in America ever since."

"So you've been here before?" James asked.

"On the *Gorgon,* must have been in '67. A wonderful visit, I'll tell you. They make the most delectable fish cakes. The local cod, you know. Fried up in duck fat, it's a wonder to behold."

Friends for five years, James knew that the good doctor took his vittles quite seriously, always searching out the local specialties when in port.

"Captain's on deck," the helmsman called.

James touched his hat to Robert Pelham. "Good morning, sir."

"Mr. Addington, doctor," the Captain acknowledged them as he took a long glass and tried to glimpse the shore which still was not visible from the deck. "The wind's favorable for entering harbor, but I'm not sure we'll like what we find."

"Good morning, gentlemen."

They turned to see Will Thorpe, on deck for only the third time since he fell ill. His face was still drawn, but he moved with a steady step and smiled at them.

"Mr. Thorpe, good morning to you," Captain Pelham said. "The coast of Massachusetts is on our larboard bow."

"William, how do you feel today?" Doctor Goodrum asked.

"Appreciably better, doctor. I'm continuing with the mixture of herbs that Cantu prescribed. The effect on my constitution is remarkable."

"He's a talented healer. We are indeed fortunate to have his assistance," Goodrum added.

James thought back to that day when he first met the big man who had now become more of a friend than anything else. How many times had they shared danger and adventure, with Cantu always watching over him. Seeing Will back on his feet gave him no end of pleasure. He'd seen too many seaman die at sea and he wasn't ready to lose another close friend.

After weeks at sea, James's legs still felt a bit shaky as he and the doctor made their way from Market wharf up High Street. Locked away in the artificial world of the *Challenger*, the people hurrying down the streets seemed an alien world to James. Perhaps he was mistaken, but they seemed quite unsettled and several of the locals cast looks that James could only interpret as hostile.

In a short time they found Doctor Warren's home, an imposing two story gray house with fancy woodwork adorning the windows.

"Here we are, I remember it well," the doctor said, climbing the steps to the front door.

Shown into the sitting room by an elderly negro, the two officers remained standing awaiting Richard Warren.

"I received a letter two years ago after the death of Abigail. He was devastated, but immersing himself in his practice."

"Jim Goodrum, as I live and breathe."

Doctor Warren stepped across the room and embraced Goodrum.

"You look well, my friend," Goodrum said as they stepped apart.

"And you lie extraordinarily well."

To James, Doctor Warren did not look well, deep bags under his eyes, his skin appearing almost translucent against the pronounce cheekbones.

"Let me name Leftenant James Addington, my shipmate from *Andromeda* and now with me on *Challenger.*"

"Welcome to my home, leftenant."

The two shook hands.

"Please, sit. We will take some wine and throw caution to the winds catching up on the time we've lost." Warren seemed truly happy to have guests and called for his servant to bring them wine.

Seated around a low wooden table the men toasted to each other's health.

"I am so very pleased to see you, old friend. But I fear that these are not pleasant times in the colony."

Goodrum loosened his neck cloth and sat back in his chair. "Richard, we've heard the reports. It seems there's no controlling this group of hot heads."

Warren shook his head.

"Like every group, there are men with good hearts and bad. Some of the grievances are valid, I think. God knows I don't need to pay more tax to Parliament.

Unfortunately there's a faction that has decided breaking away from England is the only course to follow."

"Surely they can't mean that?" James asked. "These are English colonies. Founded by Englishmen under the mandate of an English monarch."

Doctor Warren shook his head. "Mr. Addington, most colonists have never travelled more than a day or two from where they were born. London means nothing to them. Many of our people are second and third generation Americans with few ties to the mother country. It is a common feeling that the English will always look down on us, the poor provincials, uneducated, far from the heart of civilization and in dire need of governance from their betters."

James realized he had never thought of these things as a young boy in Albany. Did New Yorkers feel the same way as the men of Massachusetts? Each colony was truly a world apart from the others. Separated by miles of forest and woodlands, there were few roads in the colonies, let alone between the colonies.

"But certainly that's not the way our government sees it," Goodrum retorted.

"Then why do we have regiments of British regulars occupying our city? Why are there warships anchored in our harbor?"

Suddenly the import of what might be happening hit James. *Challenger* was a ship of war. The twelve pound cannons which now sat quietly lashed down on the main deck could kill and maim at a word from the captain.

A pounding was heard on the front door.

"Lawrence, see who that is!" Warren called impatiently.

Barely a minute later, a tall, powerful man wearing the uniform of British infantry stepped into the room. His dark hair was disheveled and there were spots of mud on his white trousers.

"William," Doctor Warren exclaimed.

"Please excuse me, I didn't realize you had guests," the officer said as he glanced at the two naval officers. His tone was irritated which matched his expression.

"Nonsense, William, please let me introduce my good friend, Doctor Jim Goodrum. You have heard me speak of him."

"Of course, uncle, of course."

"And Leftenant James Addington. Gentlemen, my sister's son, Captain William Amherst of the 65th."

The three men shook hands, but it was clear to James that Captain Amherst's focus was not on his uncle's visitors.

"Let me pour you some wine," Warren said moving to the sideboard.

As Captain Amherst sat down, he asked his uncle, "Have you heard the news?"

"Apparently not, I've been in my study most of the day," Warren replied, handing his nephew a glass.

"It has finally happened! Open rebellion," Amherst said taking a large gulp from his glass.

The other three men looked at the soldier with surprise, awaiting an explanation.

Amherst continued, "A force sent out to confiscate illegal arms and powder was attacked at Lexington and again at Concord. Several thousand colonials were involved and a number of our men were killed."

"My God," Doctor Warren said quietly, "I never thought it would come to this."

Almost like eavesdroppers to a family dispute, Doctor Goodrum and James sat quietly, saying nothing.

"Of course it was going to come to this, Uncle! Those troublemakers have been preparing for it. Stockpiling weapons, organizing a militia, holding drills. General Gage has shown great restraint, but now there is no turning back. We shall have to crush this lawlessness with brute force. It's all this rabble will understand."

Surprised at the vehemence of the infantry officer, James began to think what this would mean as Englishmen turned against each other. My God, but it was hard to imagine, he thought.

"Then this is a sad day, gentlemen," Jim Goodrum said.

Warren nodded. "I'm afraid you're right, my friend. Once blood has been spilled, the anger and recriminations will only deepen. It's a dark path indeed I see for this colony."

This colony? Could this spread to the other royal colonies of North America, James asked himself.

"Has there been any word from the other colonies?" James asked.

"None," Amherst finishing his wine in one gulp.

"James grew up in New York, near Albany," Doctor Goodrum offered to his friend. "You still have family there, isn't that right?"

"You're a colonial?" Amherst asked, his hostility only thinly veiled.

"I am a king's officer as are you, sir," James replied, taking a dislike to the petulant attitude of this man.

"Gentlemen, please," Doctor Warren said quickly. "There have been enough hot emotions today. Let us deal with this crisis in a calm and measured manner."

"Tell that to the men of the light companies who are lying wounded in the infirmary on Charles Street."

"Perhaps we should return to the ship," Goodrum said to James. "There might be new orders."

"Do you hear that?" Doctor Warren asked.

The men turned in their seats toward the sitting room's windows.

A sharp rumble could be heard as the sun began to set over the harbor.

They looked at each other, knowing the sound but reluctant to acknowledge it.

"That is cannon fire," Amherst said at last.

"Naval cannon if I don't miss my mark," James added.

"What could be happening?" Doctor Warren asked. "Cannons firing within the city?"

"I must return to my regiment," Amherst said quickly and took his leave.

"We must get back to the ship," James said after Warren returned from seeing his nephew out.

"This is all so unsettling," the doctor said as he escorted the two officers to the door. "I can only hope this matter will resolve itself quickly and with no bloodshed."

But the doctor was not to have his wish fulfilled.

General William Gage sat at a large map table, his immediate staff standing around the large map of the Boston area.

"Is there any word from Percy?" Gage asked, but the question was rhetorical. Everyone in the room knew that any word from the general assigned to rescue the ill-fated Concord raid would be immediately sent to the British commander-in-chief.

"I'll check, sir," Captain Billingsworth said, and walked from the room.

Province House had served as the headquarters for the British occupation force since its arrival in 1766. The secret mission to seize the munitions at Concord had been drafted by the General's staff in the main dining room. The violent clash between the colonial militia and Gage's redcoats now had the headquarters alive with reports of what was beginning to look like a defeat for the British.

Initial reports had been sketchy, but contained enough information for Gage to understand that his force of 700 men, lightly equipped for fast marching, had encountered a large number of armed colonialists and was in danger of being cut off from Boston. Gage had dispatched General Percy to contact his men and protect their return to British lines.

The door opened and Colonel Bradbury entered carrying a single sheet of paper.

"I have word from Vice Admiral Graves, sir"

"Read it," Gage said impatiently.

"I have the pleasure to report that our contingent, under the protection of General Percy has occupied the high ground of Charlestown. H.M.S. *Somerset* is now providing artillery support for our troops. It appears the enemy has occupied Winter Hill and is taking up defensive positions. For now the situation appears stabilized. I have directed *Somerset* and *Exeter* to provide boats and their surgeons to help deal with the wounded."

Gage stood and walked to the window.

"The enemy, that is what the Admiral called them. It has finally come to that. Englishmen fighting Englishmen, my God."

"General, we're getting reports of armed men on the neck. We have to consider there may be a general uprising," Colonel Bradbury said.

"Very well, Colonel. Draft an order to all regimental commanders. Assume an active defense from this time forward. Positions as indicated during our last meeting will be occupied at your earliest convenience. Full provisions of ammunition and powder for all troops. Report your disposition at first light and any indication of hostile forces in your areas." Get that out as quickly as you can."

Major Highcombe, the provost martial, said, "I would recommend you declare martial law in the city. We know there are large numbers of rebels in the city and they are armed."

"I would still like to find some way to defuse this situation if possible, major. There is no doubt we have sufficient strength to hold the city, I'm not concerned to that end. I am more concerned what Parliament will say when they find out of today's events."

James Addington saw the neat sign hanging above the boardwalk on Albermarle Street. "Here we are, gentlemen," he said to Doctor Goodrum and Mr. Bennett, the carpenter.

"Walker and Sons, Ltd, Boston and New York," the doctor noted. "A reputable firm?"

"According to the Captain Symonds, they can be trusted to provide a good product for a fair price."

Assigned to the in-shore squadron, Captain Pelham had decided to replace a dozen of *Challenger's* oldest water casks which were leaking badly.

Several older men sat at a small table in one corner of the store. An assortment of nautical supplies lay on tables on both sides of a low counter. A young woman working intently on a large ledger book looked up as they approached.

James was struck by her beauty. Deep green eyes and her smooth complexion were framed by long dark brown hair.

She started to smile at them then seemed to catch herself. "May I help you," she said, her voice quietly rude.

"Yes," James replied, feeling a bit taken aback. His years at sea had not allowed him a great deal of time to socialize with the fairer sex. Now he realized he felt uncomfortable under her gaze. "We were told that Walker and Sons would be able to provide water casks suitable for our needs."

"We do sell water casks," she said, her tone now hostile. "But I don't know if we have any to sell to the English."

James suddenly realized this young lady's loyalties lay with the rebel cause. Several times in the last week, following the shootings outside the city, he'd encountered colonists who made no secret of their feelings.

"Perhaps I should talk with Mr. Walker," James said, his anger rising.

"I'm his daughter and I speak for him," she said, her anger obvious.

A man stood up at the table and walked to the counter.

"Samantha, I'll talk with the gentlemen."

"I told them we don't do business with the English."

Sporting a large bushy beard, the heavy-set man leaned on the counter and looked at James.

"And you might be?"

Removing his hat, James answered, "James Addington of His Majesty's Ship *Challenger*. This is Doctor Goodrum and Mr. Bennett our carpenter."

"My name's Silas Walker. I might have some casks for sale. But they won't come cheap, everyone is wantin' 'em now. But these are good New England oak, best in the world. The price is four pounds each."

"Four pounds!" Bennett exclaimed.

"That's my price. If you don't pay it, some other ship captain will."

"Then I want to see them," the carpenter answered.

"A splendid idea," the doctor said, a wide smile on his face.

"Very well. Lead on, Mr. Walker," James said, seeing the hostility on Samantha's face.

"But, father," she said.

"Samantha, it's business, now hush."

"I hate to admit it, but those were some of the best made casks I've ever seen."

"And I suspect you've seen many a cask, Mr. Bennett," Doctor Goodrum said as they walked back to the wharf.

But James thoughts were not on water casks.

Chapter Thirteen

Time for action

"Gentlemen, it appears the rebels have taken action to thwart our planned move out of the city."

Thomas Gage looked at the men sitting around the table. A distinguished group, the three generals had arrived from England two weeks prior as part of Parliament's plan to prosecute the war. William Howe, John Burgoyne and Henry Clinton were all experienced and capable commanders. While each man had his own motives for being in Boston, the common sentiment between them was that they could make short work of the rebel forces and return home.

"Damned inconsiderate of them to make us change our plans," General Howe offered. "Perhaps it won't cause unreasonable disruption. A damned lot of good staff work has gone into this."

"These fortifications above Charlestown must be taken before we can think of action," John Burgoyne added. Known as Gentleman Johnny, he had been a member of Parliament and was well-connected in the government."

"As I understand it, the rebels have occupied fortifications atop Breed's Hill overlooking Charlestown." Clinton pointed to a scale map of the harbor area.

"And we've had them under fire since first light," Gage interrupted.

Continuing, Clinton drew an imaginary line across Charlestown Neck. "Then we land a force here, cut them off and let them starve. Quite poor planning on their part, if I do say so."

The discussion flowed back and forth as the need to destroy the rebels took precedence for all but Clinton.

"Then it's decided," Gage finally said. "We shall move into action as quickly as we can distribute orders. General Howe, you are senior here, I feel the privilege of command on the field is yours."

"Thank you, General," Howe replied. "We shall make short work of it as long as the navy can accommodate our need for transport."

James Addington had never seen so many British soldiers in once place. In charge of one of *Challenger's* cutters, he watched as a line of ship's boats from the fleet converged on Common's Wharf. Will Thorpe had detailed him to lead the ship's boats from *Challenger* to support the army's attack.

Amidst the yelling of sergeants and boatswains, James saw troops moving down the wharf toward embarkation.

"There will be a battle today?"

"That is what we've been told," James replied to Cantu.

"Up oars," Cantu ordered and the sailors raised the dripping blades vertically as the cutter approached the stairs formed by carved logs.

"Hook on."

"Let's go you buggers," a beefy sergeant yelled as he motioned a line of grenadiers down the steps.

"Watch where you step if you don't want to go for a swim," James called as the men stepped gingerly into the cutter.

"Move to the rear and sit down, to the rear and sit down."

Three minutes later Cantu called, "Out oars. Starboard side, push off. Fend off up forward, Kelly."

James counted eighteen redcoats seated in the bow as the cutter moved into the stream, its place already taken by a large jolly boat.

"Give way together."

As the cutter turned north, James could see the line of boats moving past the anchored warships toward Charlestown.

Suddenly two frigates opened fire on the town, the crash of shot followed by billows of brownish smoke rolling across the water.

Amidst continued cannon fire the small boats continued toward the landing beach. With grenadiers aboard his cutter, James had been directed to land them on the left side of the town. There the light infantry and grenadiers would attack the rebel's flank while another force attacked the redoubt on Breed's Hill.

Approaching the beach James could see troops making their way toward formations that grew like a living thing. He could hear the curses of non-commissioned officers directing the soldiers toward their assembly area. Checking his watch he saw the time was approaching three o'clock. Still plenty of daylight left, he thought.

"Off you go, lads," the sergeant in the bow called when the cutter ground to a stop on the rocky beach.

Watching the men run toward the other troops, James watched a single red-coated officer approach the cutter.

"We need you here," the lieutenant called across the water. "The attack will begin shortly and you will ferry any wounded back to the city."

"Understood," James replied.

The officer moved down the beach and shortly there were ten boats being held on the beach.

"Well, my friend, it seems we will see the battle after all," James said to Cantu.

Situated on the left flank, the light infantry and grenadiers formed up four deep and several hundred across. Responding to shouted orders, the troops began moving toward a long fence that James decided must be a rebel position protecting the redoubt's right flank. Drums beat out a steady cadence as the red line moved forward, bayonets fixed.

Shots rang out from the rebels and soon a constant roar of musket fire almost drowned out the steady staccato of the drums. An acrid white smoke began to obscure the British ranks, the scene becoming something James had never imagined. Through the drifting clouds he watched as the redcoats took their firing positions, perhaps fifty yards from the fence. Rebel gunfire began to find its mark and before the British units could present and fire, their ranks were torn apart by massed fire from behind the fence.

It seemed to James that many of the companies were cut down by half in the first two minutes. My God, he thought, they just stand there and take it. He was close enough to see the men flung back when hit by the heavy rebel musket balls. Cries of pain echoed over the drums which continued to beat. Small groups returned fire, but their efforts were beginning to falter.

Just as in a sea battle, the horror of men killing each other brings out a wild madness that takes hold of everyone involved. For some, it drives them to acts of incredible courage, for others they crumble into the self made hell of cowardice and preservation.

The few red-coated officers still alive began to withdraw their men from rebel musket range. Here and there surviving sergeants tried to maintain control of their men who now saw a chance to escape the killing fire from the fence. As the mass of men moved back toward the beach, they left many wounded on the field like so many red blankets.

On the far side of the beach James saw a group of horsemen watching the retreat. That must be Howe, he thought. Occasionally a rider from the staff would gallop off with some order while the small knot of mounted men would adjust their location, several holding telescopes steady from their saddles.

Men began to straggle back from the larger formation which was now back near the beach, but broken into many small groups. Most of the soldiers approaching the boats no longer carried their muskets and they struggled with wounds. It struck James that none of the men were bandaged, some were bent over, others held an arm or a head, but these men were certainly coming to his boat.

"Out you go and help those men into the boat," James yelled.

Several of the wounded soldiers stumbled as they approached the water, falling on their knees in the shallow water.

No stranger to battle, James had always been in the action and focused on victory, his mind taken over by the fury of the fight. Now he was an onlooker and able to see the horror in a very different way.

"Stay here," James said quickly to Cantu and jumped into the knee-deep water at the stern of the cutter. Wading toward the beach he saw a young soldier walking tentatively toward the cutter, his bloody hands holding desperately to his left side, his white trousers now crimson.

"Easy there, soldier," James said as he grabbed the young private's shoulders. The boy's face was ashen. "Here, let's get you into the boat."

"It hurts," the soldier said through clenched teeth. "Christ, it hurts."

"Cantu, here."

The big coxswain easily bent down and picked up the soldier, setting him gently on the wide thwart.

Blood ran down on the weathered wood and the boy's breath came in short gasps.

James looked up and more men were being helped into the cutter by the sailors. Some of the men couldn't sit up and were laid gently on the bottom boards. The soldiers appeared dazed, whether from their wounds or the violence of the battle, James couldn't tell. But he knew their best chance to survive was to get them back to *Challenger* and Jim Goodrum.

Two more trips from the rocky beach of Charlestown left the cutter stained with the blood of over sixty wounded infantrymen. Those trips had ferried some of the most seriously wounded men. James knew that many of them were going to leave the *Challenger's* sick bay without an arm or leg if they survived the shock of amputation.

He had seen it too many times, the smashed flesh and bone, damaged so badly that there was nothing Jim Goodrum could do but remove the limb and hope the man survived. But what kind of a survival would it be? Begging on the streets of England? Turning to petty crime to feed themselves, the back of the nation turned on them after taking away their health. It was something that had always bothered James, but it was the way of things.

Ordered to return to the southern tip of the Charlestown peninsula as the day was waning, James found he was dreading what he would find. From a distance it appeared to him that the redcoats now were in place on the top of Breed's Hill, the redoubt now under British control. But at what cost?

A shout came from two sailors standing at the foot of a dilapidated wooden pier.

"Over here."

Groups of men stood waiting as the cutter bumped against the slimy wood posts.

"Sir, this officer needs transport to *Somerset*, he has dispatches for Vice Admiral Graves."

"Very well, help him down," James replied, relieved not to be carrying more wounded.

William Amherst looked very different from the first time James had met him. His uniform was filthy, stained by the mud and blood of Breed's Hill. Stepping into the stern of the cutter, the man was paying little attention to the boat or its crew.

"Captain Amherst," James called.

The infantry officer's eyes focused on James, his inattention broken for a moment.

""Yes........yes, do I know you?" A strong smell of cordite came off his muddy tunic, further testimony to the intensity of the assault on the redoubt.

Without offering his hand, James said quietly, "We met at your uncle's house perhaps six weeks past. My name is Addington, I was with Doctor Goodrum.

For a moment Amherst looked confused, then the light of recognition shone in his eyes.

"Quite right, yes. I remember."

The man was clearly dazed by the events of the day. James hoped he would regain some amount of composure prior to seeing the admiral.

"We'll have you aboard the flagship in less than a quarter hour. Will that be sufficient?"

Amherst nodded. "I'm in no hurry to describe the battle to Admiral Graves," he said, seeming to regain his sense of place and purpose.

"We've taken the redoubt. Wasn't that the objective?"

"But what will be the butcher's bill?"

James remembered the men cut down on the left flank.

"I saw a great number of wounded on this side. Did the main attack suffer similarly?"

"My God," Amherst said as he wiped his eyes. "The bastards held the high ground and waited until our men were at a perfectly lethal range. The first two attacks failed after most of the officers and sergeants were killed or wounded."

Discussion in the *Challenger* wardroom after Lexington and Concord had arrived at the conclusion that the colonials were very effective if fighting from the forest, much like the natives. But surely when they tried to fight a conventional battle against the experienced and disciplined British regiments, they would never be able to stand up. Perhaps these provincials had more spine than first thought.

"But you carried the day in the end."

The captain shook his head.

"From the few men we captured, it appears they ran out of powder and shot. If they had been fully provisioned, who knows?"

The tall side of the *Somerset* now loomed over the cutter as the crew made fast to the main chains.

As he rose and stepped to the boarding ladder, Amherst turned to James as if to speak. He stopped himself, shook his head and grabbed the rope handles on the tumblehome.

"Cantu, shove off and make for *Challenger.*"

Will met James as he climbed through the entry port.

"Is that it for today?"

"Let us hope so, my friend."

The two officers walked aft to the ladder way on the starboard side.

"I've been down with the doctor. He actually seemed happy not having to deal with wood splinters and the like."

"We picked up those men who could get to the beach, Will. I saw too many bodies on the slope of that hill. There were hundreds of dead, hundreds. These rebels are supposed to be undisciplined rabble, but they stood off some of the best troops the army has."

"You need a glass of wine, let's go below."

James turned to look across the harbor at the town of Charlestown, still burning in the sunset. What was happening here, he asked himself?

Chapter Fourteen

The Journey Home

"England?"

"That's the rumor, my friend."

Standing at the lee gangway, James watched the activity in the harbor as the end of his watch approached.

Doctor Goodrum leaned against a twelve pound cannon, his arms crossed on his chest.

It never ceased to amaze James that there were no secrets aboard a ship. No matter the subject, before the crew could be told officially, the word seemed to already be on the mess decks.

"Almost three years since we last saw home," Goodrum said.

James looked at his friend, knowing that England actually held nothing for him, his only living relative an aunt in Exeter.

"Why would they send a frigate home as the war here is becoming more involved?"

"Because we're fast and there's a general that requires passage," Goodrum answered.

"And who would that be, my nosy doctor?'

Goodrum's rosy face beamed and he grinned at his friend.

"None other than Gentleman Johnny Burgoync."

"Burgoyne? I would have thought he would be fully employed fighting the colonials," James offered.

"Apparently Billy Howe is in charge and there's only room enough for one commander-in-chief. So we sail on the morning tide tomorrow for Plymouth."

James shook his head, more rumors, the stuff of a sailor's life. "Any more word on the captain's brother?"

Goodrum frowned. "I checked with his clerk. The news was received by the captain the morning after the battle. His younger brother. William, was killed in the final assault on the redoubt."

"My God, he spoke very fondly of William the last time we dined in his cabin. Apparently he was always the rebellious of the two and rather than follow the family tradition of naval service, he purchased a commission in the 65th Foot."

"It appears the captain will be able to deliver the bad news to the family in person. Not a job I'd want, I'll tell you that, my friend."

"Nor I, my good doctor."

Major General John Burgoyne arrived aboard *Challenger* later that afternoon with several trunks and his aide-de-camp.

A member of Parliament, playwright and dashing soldier, Burgoyne easily captivated the ship's officers at dinner the second night after sailing.

Still stocked with fresh stores from Boston, the evening's fare consisted of baked pork, fruit compote, a passable wine and local cheese from Massachusetts. While Captain Pelham served as the host, the general dominated the conversation and soon the officer's were asking questions about the war.

"We divide the colonies," Burgoyne stated as he popped a piece of cheese into his mouth.

"Divide and conquer?" the captain asked.

"Exactly, sir. A fundamental military principle today just as it was in Julius Caesar's day."

"How does that translate to this war, sir?" James asked.

Burgoyne looked at James. "Mr. Addington, correct?"

"Yes, sir."

"The colonies are really divided into two regions. You have New York north to Canada, which is commonly called New England. And New Jersey south into the fertile farmlands of Maryland, Virginia and the Carolinas. The north relies on fishing and commerce while the south lives by farming. If we can split the colonies, we will have isolated Mr. Washington's army. He won't be able to protect the larger cities and they'll be hard pressed to supply him."

Doctor Goodrum sipped his wine then said, "Is that why you are returning to England, sir?"

Burgoyne smiled. "I'm afraid I'm not at liberty to say, doctor. Besides we wouldn't want the colonials to find out what we're up to."

"But, sir, Mr. Addington was born and raised in Albany, New York. So your cat appears to be out of the bag," Will Thorpe said dryly.

James felt his face redden slightly. He didn't notice the hard look from the captain.

"Albany?" the general asked, his interest genuine.

"Yes, sir. I lived there until joining *Andromeda* in '70."

"Quite interesting," Burgoyne said, his eyes showing an intensity that James thought strangely out of place. But generals were just like admirals, they were all a bit strange.

Favorable weather for the time of year provided a swift and relatively comfortable passage from Boston. General Burgoyne spent time with the ship's officers and enjoyed a number of meals with them over the six week voyage. His engaging personality quickly won over the officers and men, making it clear to see how he had been able to win a seat in Parliament while advancing to the army's senior ranks.

The crew remained busy with the many tasks needed to keep the ship in good repair, but as England drew closer, there was a sense of anticipation among the men. After years in the Mediterranean and off the coast of North America, they were coming home.

Following his morning watch, James walked forward to check the progress of re-reaving one of the large blocks on the foremast braces. The weather was cool, but not threatening and *Challenger* should make good progress toward Plymouth.

"Mr. Addington, might I have a word with you?"

James turned to see General Burgoyne.

"Good morning, sir."

Falling in step with the older man, the two made their way toward the bow.

"Have you ever been on the Hudson River?"

An odd question, James thought, but easy enough to answer.

"Many times, sir. My father would take me sailing in a small ketch he maintained on the river."

"Did you ever sail north to the headwaters?"

As they made a circular path around the main deck, James answered many questions from the general about the area surrounding Albany.

"You have been quite helpful, Mr. Addington. I find local knowledge always critical in war."

Burgoyne turned and walked aft, his stride moving with the rolling deck.

James watched him go and wondered about his last comment.

The future of *Challenger* became the main subject of conversation as the ship entered the English Channel. Some of the hands hoped that the ship would pay off, allowing them to return to their families ashore. The war in America led most to believe the ship would re-supply and put to sea in short order, probably back across the Atlantic.

While all ships at sea suffer over time from the ravages of the ocean, *Challenger's* condition was as good if not better than most of her peers. Captain Pelham had taken great care to maintain the miles of rigging, sails and timbers of the frigate. The only area that certainly needed attention was the marine growth on her copper sheathing.

Designed to protect the hull from boring worms and marine growth, over time the ocean's relentless attack would begin to win the battle. Many ships would enter shipyard docks with their hulls covered by marine grasses and barnacles. For a frigate, the decrease in the ship's speed due to this drag could possibly make the difference between victory and defeat.

"England."

James lowered the long glass and turned to the doctor.

"It's been a long time since we last saw the Isle of Wight."

"It's comforting in some strange way to see familiar territory."

"At least this is friendly territory," James added.

"Don't be too sure of that, my friend. While the colonies are split in their loyalty to the king, there is almost as much controversy across Britain over this war."

"It does seem tragic that we're fighting each other. Particularly when we know the French would attack in a moment if they thought they could win." James wondered if any of his boyhood friends were taking up the rebel cause. That time in his life seemed so long ago. He'd heard nothing from his brother and had only one letter from his father in the last six months.

"And I suspect the Dons would be right behind them," Goodrum added.

James thoughts returned to the present. "Well for now let's see if we can find some good food and drink to celebrate a successful passage."

The pleasures of Portsmouth were forgotten as *Challenger* entered harbor on the flood tide, passing the narrows and coming in view of over fifty ships anchored off Whale Island.

General Burgoyne had come on deck earlier and now stood next to James as frigate moved slowly ahead on topsails only.

"Quite an armada I daresay."

"Yes, sir," James acknowledged. Both transports and warships swung slowly at their anchors as the tide moved into the Solent.

Out of contact for over six weeks during the transit, *Challenger* entered the largest port of the Royal Navy totally unaware of the vast expedition being prepared for sailing.

"Signal from the *Orion,* sir. Captain repair onboard."

Challenger had barely taken full reach on her anchor as the flutter of signal flags danced from the *Orion,* a ship of the line flying the flag of a rear admiral of the red.

"Call away the gig, Mr. Addington, and tell Mr. Thorpe to arrange to replenish water and stores as quickly as possible, I want to be ready to sail at the earliest."

The initial flurry of activity on *Challenger* had served to distract the crew from their orders to sail as part of the large convoy enroute to New York City. Returning to America so soon after arrival in England told everyone the urgency of the crisis in the colonies.

Barely three days after dropping anchor at Portsmouth, *Challenger* weighed anchor and made sail as part of the largest overseas expedition ever launched by the British Empire.

Chapter Fifteen

A Foreign Shore

Extra lookouts manned both the maintop and also on the weather deck forward and aft. Sailing in company with many ships is a challenge in itself. When the sun sets, the difficulty of staying together and in any semblance of formation is sorely tested. With sufficient night lighting and vigilant lookouts, it is possible, weather permitting, to pass the night and emerge at sunrise with most ships still capable of signaling and rejoining the formation. While the weather had been accommodating, the nightly test of trying to keep the disparate merchantmen under control had made the passage a test for officers and crew of the navy escorts. Arrival at Sandy Hook would release the frigates and men-of-war from a truly onerous task of escorting the civilian mariners. But sailing alone, the transports could become easy prey for American privateers lurking off the coast of New England.

"A voyage home?"

James turned to see Will Thorpe watching the final shreds of daylight as the sun dipped below the horizon. Touching his hat out of friendly respect, he said, "I'm not sure anymore."

"These are trying times to be sure." The first lieutenant surveyed the horizon, the big merchantmen starting to fade into the twilight. "All in order with our charges?"

"For now. But by morning I trust we'll have to gather them up again. For the life of me I don't understand how they can get so far from the group in such a short time."

"Most of them are asleep. I expect they might have a master's mate and helmsman on watch, but that's it. Everyone else, including the captain is sleeping like babes."

124

"They won't be happy if a rebel privateer stumbles across them, I'll tell you that."

Thorpe chuckled, the rivalry between the navy and the merchant sailors still well in place.

A warm sun and clear skies greeted *Challenger's* arrival off Sandy Hook on the twenty first of August 1776. The twenty merchantmen, carrying both troops and supplies added to the impressive array of ships now gathered in preparation for Lord Howe's attack on Washington's army. The British had initially landed over 9,000 men on Staten Island and supporting forces had continued to arrive from Halifax, Portsmouth and the Carolinas. Now with a force of over 30,000 troops including Hessian mercenaries, Howe was ready to attack Washington's army.

James could see the results of the hasty retreat by the colonials from the city after their defeat on Long Island. While Washington had been able to rescue most of his army from the disaster on Long Island, it had become very clear he would not be able to hold Manhattan and in short order Howe's army had occupied the city.

Articles of clothing, broken wagons and smashed storefronts told the story of an army in panicked flight. He tried to remember where the Hunter Inn had been located, but the surroundings didn't match the memory of that young boy.

Will Thorpe and James had come ashore to investigate the availability of salted beef and pork to replenish *Challenger's* storerooms. Doctor Goodrum had also asked they try to locate any fresh fruit, particularly lemons or limes for the crew.

James and Will Thorpe were a good team on the ship as first and second lieutenant, but off the ship, their friendship made them just two young men on a run ashore. James felt himself lucky to have a friend and comrade like Will to face this new trouble in the colonies. The two of them would see it through.

"Quite a mess," Will offered as they stepped over a broken door that had been torn off its hinges and now lay on the wooden sidewalk.

The people on the street seemed oblivious of the damage and appeared to be going about their business as if nothing momentous was happening.

Turning a corner, Will glanced down the street and said, "Hold up there, James my boy. I do believe I see a public house." A large wooden tankard hung out from the front of the building.

"Would only be proper to check out the local flavor, don't you think?" Will said, the sarcasm plainly evident.

"Quite so," James agreed, grinning conspiratorially. "Lead on, Leftenant Thorpe."

Lit only by candles, the room seemed cool after the heat of the summer day. A tall man stood behind a counter, while several customers were eating at the small tables scattered in front of a fireplace. All conversation stopped when they saw the two naval officers.

"What would you recommend to quench our thirst?" Will asked.

The man didn't reply right away, but instead seemed to be considering the question.

"If it's cool you're after, I have wine and ale, both we store down below to keep away from this heat." His manner was not hostile, but he also wasn't as solicitous as most public house keepers.

"The two ales, if you please."

Will and James took seats at a table set against the far wall.

Sitting down, James had time to survey the customers and came to the conclusion they were mostly working men taking a noon break. The finery associated with businessmen was missing from this group.

When the man brought their ales, Will asked, "We're looking for a chandler who can help us procure salted beef or pork. Is there anywhere you might recommend?"

The man thought for a moment then said, "At the end of Market Street, down near the water, you'll find Walkers. They deal in those things."

James thought of the water casks they had procured from Walker and Sons in Boston. And he remembered the girl Samantha.

126

After two ales, the officers decided to resume their search. Fortified with spirits and a recommendation, they went to find Walkers.

Working their way down Market Street, the masts of the British ships seemed to cover the water south of the island. How could a piecemeal army hope to stand up to the might of England? James wondered. What could possibly make them believe they could ever be victorious? Not only did they have to face British regulars, but Hessian mercenaries who were renowned across Europe for their prowess on the battlefield.

At the end of Market Street a sign which James had seen before hung over the door, "Walker and Sons, Ltd, Boston and New York." As they approached the door he saw a woman come around the corner toward them. It was Samantha Walker.

Waiting at the door, he watched her approach and was struck again by her beauty. Dark brown curls were highlighted by a white bonnet which matched her dress. She hadn't noticed him, her attention directed at trying to avoid the debris in the street.

"Good afternoon, Miss Walker," James said as she approached and took off his hat.

At first there was no recognition, only her formal nod. Then her expression changed as she realized who he was.

"You're the officer who wanted water casks."

"James Addington, Miss Walker."

"You're with the occupation army?" she asked, her tone sharp.

"Actually the navy, but I can see you would prefer we were somewhere else."

"Would you be happy to see the French army setting up camp in London? I think not." She pushed past him opening the door.

"But we are all Englishmen and subjects of King George."

She turned to face him.

"Not any more, we have declared our independence, sir. You're not welcome in New York."

Turning, she entered the shop.

He called after her, "I was born in New York. I'm not welcome in my home colony?"

She reappeared in the doorway. "New York is a state, Mr. Addington, not a colony. And as long as you wear that uniform, you are not welcome, sir." Anger shone in her eyes and defiance across her face. Waiting for a reply, she saw the surprised look on James's face and her expression softened just slightly.

"I'm sorry you feel that way, Miss Walker. And the purpose of my visit was to purchase provisions. Are you telling me you won't sell us food?"

She paused, looking at him, her eyes searching for something.

"Then come in. I will sell what I have, but supplies of everything are already getting short. It seems that war has a way of eating through the larders of the people."

Will looked at James and grinned, "My, you do know how to charm the locals."

Later, when the purser inspected the first cask of salt pork, he found it was of the highest quality. All subsequent casks were in the same condition, something highly unusual if the pork had been procured in Portsmouth.

James went ashore again later that week in company with Cantu to meet a Mr. Guiliboys, a supplier of charts and maps. While *Challenger* carried sufficient charts of the northern colonies, Captain Pelham wanted chart coverage of the Carolinas in the event they received orders to proceed south. Working his way north along the battery, they found the address just as the sun was setting.

Mr. Guiliboys proved to be not only knowledgeable about the waters off the Carolinas, but was also well equipped with charts for sale. In short order James procured a dozen charts and maps which would be sufficient for a journey south.

"So what do you think of New York?" he asked Cantu as they began to walk toward the Market Street landing.

"Too many people."

"There are a great number of people. But there are more in London."

"Too many people in London, also."

James laughed. "You are probably right, my friend."

Suddenly there were shouts of "Fire" coming from down the street.

In the darkness, a glow rose from the other side of the rooftops. The two men ran down a side street, taking a shortcut to Market Street.

The scene that greeted them was chaotic and terrifying. Flames sprang from a number of buildings on both sides of the street. A scream came from within one of the houses and men ran about in confusion trying to organize a bucket brigade.

Fires don't start on both sides of a wide street at once, James thought as the smoke and flames were now fanned by the breeze coming off the harbor. More people poured into the streets and some men tried unsuccessfully to toss buckets of water onto what were already a fully developed fire.

He thought of Walker and Sons. It had come out when they purchased the salt pork that Mr. Walker had sent Samantha to New York when his agent had suddenly died. She was responsible for the store and its contents.

"Come with me," James told Cantu and ran south on Market.

A musket shot rang out from somewhere as they reached the store but neither man paid attention. Flames leaped from the storefront windows and reached upward toward the second story. Across the street a window burst, the glass spraying into the roadway.

"Stay out here with the charts," James yelled over the noise of the flames and kicked at the store's front door. A second kick flung the wooden door wide open and a blast of hot air rushed out. Ducking inside, James saw that the fires were spreading from what looked like torches that must have been thrown through the window. Those flames were now climbing to the ceiling and he knew the building was doomed. But was she here?

Flames had already spread to the stairway at the back of the room. Taking a chance, James ran to the stairs and looked up through the smoke that was now filling the room.

"Samantha, Samantha, are you up there?" he yelled at the top of his lungs, the smoke immediately sending him into convulsive coughing. He couldn't stay here much longer.

"Help me," came a cry from above. "I can't get the windows open."

Flames continued to consume the stairway, which was now impassable.

Looking around, James saw a wooden ladder lying against the far wall and he staggered toward it.

In a moment he pushed the ladder out the door and was caught by Cantu as he crumpled to the ground, his body racked by coughs.

"Get an axe or a bar, anything, we have to get into the second story window," he cried.

Cantu immediately understood and picked up the ladder, placing it under the largest window on the second floor. He turned, searching the area around them for anything to use as a tool.

"Never mind," James called, remembering his sword. Pulling it from the scabbard he climbed the ladder and saw a thick layer of paint covered the window joint. Using the tip of his sword he ran the blade around the window, using the leverage to break the frame free. Just as he finished, the blade snapped off six inches from the hilt.

Using the remaining blade as a lever, he pried the window up until he could get his hands under the frame. Pulling with all his strength, he ripped the window out of the surrounding frame and dropped it into the street.

"Samantha, here, the window is open," he yelled.

Smoke poured out the opening and he waited for her response.

"Samantha, can you hear me?"

Without waiting, he stepped through frame and into the room, smoke engulfing him.

Coughing hard, he moved slowly toward the far side of the room, his hand stretched out trying to find his way. Stumbling, he knew he'd found her. Coughing as the acrid smoke burned his lungs, he knew they had only one chance. He lifted her body between fits of coughing and staggered toward the window but realized he'd lost his direction.

130

"Here, here," Cantu yelled through the billowing smoke.

That was all James needed and in a moment he'd handed the girl through the window to Cantu and followed them down the ladder.

"Over there," James called, directing Cantu over to a patch of grass on the far side of the next lot.

Samantha coughed violently as he laid her on the grass. Desperately trying to clear her lungs, she continued to cough in spasms.

James knelt down, unbuttoning the tight neck collar of her dress.

"Miss Walker, Miss Walker," he said shaking her shoulder.

Slowly her eyes opened, a hint of recognition and then her head rolled to one side as her body went limp.

He had to help her, but what could he do?

"The smoke is taking her," Cantu said quietly.

"Can you do anything?"

"I will try."

He knelt down next to James and lifted her head slightly. Bending down he put his mouth over hers and blew.

The shock of the fire was nothing compared to what James felt when he saw Cantu's mouth on hers. What was he doing? This was an abomination, he reached to grab Cantu's shoulder then stayed himself. He'd known the big man for five years and in that time Cantu had never done anything but right. By James or other men, Cantu always did right. Now he must trust him.

Several minutes passed as James watched Samantha's chest rise and fall with Cantu's breath. Shouts continued throughout the street and men ran by in confusion. But on that small patch of grass, something was happening. Samantha's left arm, lifeless and limp, twitched. Then her legs began to move, slowly then with more force.

Cantu rose up from over Samantha and she coughed hard twice.

James leaned down and saw her eyes were open although there was no recognition.

"We have to get you out of the street," he said.

She didn't respond, but coughed again.

131

"I know a house where we can take you," James said remembering his trip ashore with Will the day prior. They had visited Will's only living relatives, the Whitfields. He turned to Cantu. "Get back to the ship and bring the doctor. Thrusting a handful of coins into Cantu's hand, he said, "Help me pick her up."

In a moment, they went their separate ways.

"She's resting now." Jim Goodrum sat down at the small table.

"Will she live?"

"I should think so," the doctor replied to James, wiping his face. "But she's still a very sick young woman. How did you find this place," he said, looking around the room.

"Will Thorpe brought me here yesterday. The Whitfield's are Will's only living relatives. Mrs. Whitfield was Will's mother's sister. You remember both his parents died last year of the pox? I couldn't think of anything else at the time." James paused then continued, "Jim, after we pulled her out of the building I asked Cantu to help her." How would he say this? But the doctor had to understand. "He blew his breath into her for three or four minutes, then she revived. Have you ever heard of this?"

Doctor Goodrum smiled. "There are some in my profession who think aeration of the lungs is critical in some maladies. Rejuvenation of the critical bodily gases, if you will. While I have no opinion one way or the other, it apparently did no harm. Perhaps it made the difference, who knows? As advanced as the medical profession is, there are still many things unknown. But if a man's breath can recapture a victim's wind, so much the better."

James never ceased to be amazed at the wonders of medicine.

Chapter Sixteen

A Blurring of Loyalties

White spray burst over the beakhead as *Challenger* sliced into a heavy swell. A clear but windy day found the frigate off the coast of New Jersey in pursuit of colonial merchants trying to run supplies to the rebel army.

For most of the morning watch the British warship had been slowly overtaking a ship moving south, paralleling the coast. Weeks patrolling off the coast from New York to Virginia reminded the crew of the size of the colonies and the length of the coastline. It seemed there were innumerable coves and small rivers that could shelter the sloops and brigs that the rebels preferred to use in their contraband runs. It reminded James of chasing slavers off the African coast.

Only one successful prize capture in the three weeks since leaving New York had put the captain and crew in a foul mood. Prize money for any ship and cargo captured would handsomely increase the meager pay of the men and make any captain independently wealthy over time. But the prizes must be found and then taken. So far that task had been painfully illusive to Captain Pelham.

"Mr. Addington, if you would be so good as to take a glass aloft and tell me what we have as our prey."

"Aye, aye, sir."

James removed his coat, pulled a long glass from the rack, placing the cord over his shoulder and proceeded to the weather rail. Pulling himself up he climbed into the ratlines, briefly remembering his first climb aboard *Andromeda*. Seaman Stevens had watched over him like a mother hen, even though James hadn't known it at the time. Now, many years later, he was able to quickly climb the swaying rigging to the maintop, barely losing his wind.

"Morning, Mr. Addington," Monroe, the maintop lookout said.

James moved carefully and sat next to the young seaman who had returned to looking at the sail with his own glass.

"What can you see, Monroe?"

"Looks to be a sloop, but the haze is something fearful. And at this distance a man just can't be sure."

The lookout was certainly right about the haze, James thought as he focused on the small white shape that appeared to be five or six miles on the larboard bow.

For several minutes he let the glass follow the strange vessel as both the *Challenger* and the stranger worked with the wind. It wasn't one particular sight for James, but more an opinion after many small variations of viewing that brought him to the conclusion that Monroe was indeed correct.

"I believe you are quite right," he said lowering the glass. "Well done. I'll make sure Mr. Thorpe knows of it." James gripped the futtock shrouds and called down to the deck. "A sloop, captain. Running before the wind, estimate five miles."

"She may be running for Great Bay," the master said slowly. "The bar at the mouth is treacherous and shallow. We'd be hard pressed to follow her."

Pelham looked up at the straining sails, rigid against blue sky. Turning to the sailing master he said, "Set the t'gallants, Mr. Mudge. Let's show these rebels what a real ship can do."

Two hours under every sail she could carry brought *Challenger* within a half mile of what now was clearly a fully rigged sloop making desperately for the mouth of the bay. While she flew no ensign, her flight clearly indicated a contraband cargo or purpose.

Captain Pelham had stayed on deck during the pursuit as the master adjusted the sails and rigging to capture every possible bit of speed from the ship. Now their efforts were bearing out and the frigate surged toward the smaller vessel.

"Beat to quarters and clear for action, Mr. Thorpe," Pelham finally called and the entire ship reacted as if they had all been holding their breath.

Feet pounding on the deck mixed with the steady beat of the Marine drummer as men moved in all directions at once. Gun crews crowded around their guns, making sure the rammers, spikes and other tools were ready. The young boys, aptly named powder monkeys ran to the guns carrying the charges from the magazine.

At each main hatchway Marine sentries took their posts to prevent any weak-hearted sailors from going below when the cannon began to fire.

"Load and run out the larboard battery, if you please."

"Aye, aye sir," the first lieutenant answered.

James, in charge of all the guns on the main deck, echoed the order to load and run out.

In a moment gun ports slammed open and the squeal of gun trucks could be heard as the twelve pounders rolled out to a firing position.

"Mr. Hitchcock," the captain called to the warrant gunner, standing on the main deck.

"Aye, sir," the big gunner replied.

"Sight the port bow chaser and put a chain shot into her rigging."

Pelham turned to Will Thorpe and said, "I'll be damned if this one will slip away from us."

On the up roll Mr. Hitchcock touched the quick match to the priming vent and the big cannon recoiled back against the rope tackles. Making a different sound, the chain shot whistled across the half mile of water and ripped into the rigging of the sloop. Slowly, then with more speed, the foresail and rigging collapsed on the sloops forecastle.

"Damned fine shooting, damned fine, I say. She's ours now."

As *Challenger* closed the sloop, James could see there were smaller cannons on the ship's main deck. He guessed they might be six pounders, certainly deadly in some situations, but against a frigate they were ineffective save a lucky shot.

From the mainmast of the sloop a flag broke, prompting Mr. Furlong, the signals midshipmen, to raise his big glass.

"It's one of those rebel flags, sir," he called across the quarterdeck. "Red and white horizontal stripes."

Just then the sloop fired two of her deck guns, the ship having paid off enough to bring the guns to bear.

Above the *Challenger* a hole appeared in the main course, followed immediately by a block falling to the deck.

"By God, they intend to fight," Will Thorpe exclaimed.

"Then a fight they will get, Mr. Thorpe, starboard two points." Pelham said coldly and the frigate began to turn, the main deck guns turning toward the smaller vessel.

"Fire as your guns bear, Mr. Addington," Pelham called.

As the ship came abeam the sloop each cannon on the larboard side roared, sending its twelve pound iron ball across a distance that had now closed to only a quarter mile. Slamming into the small hull the iron ripped swaths of death across the deck, hurling men, cannons and boats across what was now a killing ground.

"Sponge out and reload," James called automatically, the hours of gun drill making his actions secondary.

"Grape if you please, Mr. Addington."

For an instant James thought he must have misunderstood the captain. The sloop was already a shambles, no guns were firing and with the mainsail now at half mast, the ship was no longer under command. Surely they would strike and the captain would confiscate the sloop as a prize.

"Grape, sir?"

"You heard me, now quick about it," Pelham called, his voice hard over the wind.

The packed grapeshot would murder anyone still alive on the sloop, now identified as *Julie Ann.* But to what purpose, James asked himself. This made no sense.

As Pelham brought the ship around, the crews made the guns ready.

As the horror unfolded, James felt as if he was part of a terrible dream.

On the *Julie Ann* the red and white striped ensign still flew defiantly. Was there anyone alive to strike?

Suddenly James saw the flag disappear from the staff. Thank God, he thought.

"They've struck," a voice called

Pelham turned to Thorpe. "Shot away by my estimate. They're continuing to run from a king's ship. Fire as the guns bear, Mr. Thorpe."

Will Thorpe looked at the captain, his face showing the conflict.

"Is there a problem, sir?"

Will realized the order of his captain must be obeyed. He walked to the quarterdeck rail and looked down at James. "Fire as your guns bear," he said dully.

James started to protest, then knew it would do no good.

Behind him Mr. Hitchcock called, "Fire as your guns bear."

The sloop slipped beneath the waves only minutes later. Amidst the broken spars and debris floating on the surface there were several bodies, or what was left of them, mostly torsos without arms or heads. There were no survivors.

Later that night, James sat in the wardroom with the doctor and first lieutenant, his mind still reeling from the day's events. A bottle of wine sat on the table, the third one of the night.

"We've been over this before, James. There's simply nothing you or I or the doctor can do about what happened today." Will Thorpe topped off his glass and sat back in his chair.

"The authority of the captain is and will always be supreme," Jim Goodrum offered.

"That's rubbish, Jim. You of all people have always taken the side of honor in these things," James said.

The doctor shook his head.

"This is open rebellion against the king. Even the most brutal means are acceptable for good order."

James snapped back, "You sound like that fellow Amherst. Damn it, these people are Englishmen. Perhaps they have legitimate grievances, I don't know. But does that allow us to ignore the rules of warfare and chivalry? I think not."

"Careful, James. You are among friends here, but those words could be seen as dangerous by others," Will said, "Particularly from someone born in the colonies."

What his friend had said came like a slap to James. Were lines being drawn, even aboard this ship?

"Here, Mr. Cantu, tea for Miss Samantha."

Abigail Whitfield was a large woman who never seemed to rest as she went about the many duties involved in taking care of her husband and house. The unexpected arrival of an injured woman might have thrown her routine into terrible disarray if it had not been for the presence of Cantu since the *Challenger* had departed New York. Through the collusion of Will Thorpe and James, they had been able to list Cantu as "sick, transferred ashore" in the ship's log, duly approved by the ship's surgeon.

While the change from the deck of a frigate to the parlor of a gentlewoman's house would have been difficult for most sailors, Cantu found the change welcome and Mrs. Whitfield most agreeable. While the lady had been childless, she looked at Will as hers now that her sister had died and any connection with the navy was welcome.

"Yes, ma'am," he said, taking the small tray and climbing the stairs to Samantha Walker's room.

Her recovery had been slow to be sure. For almost a week, she had drifted in and out of sleep, occasionally touched by a slight fever. But with rest and several of Cantu's potions, she had recently been able to sit up and take nourishment. He knew she would soon be well.

Walking up the stairs he remembered the morning when she had first awakened after the terrible ordeal. He'd been sitting in her room, watching and waiting for any movement.

Her eyes had opened as if they were reluctant to face the world. Cantu watched as she slowly looked around the room, her head not moving from the pillow. He rose carefully, not wanting to startle her.

"How do you feel?" he asked softly.

Samantha looked up at him, showing no surprise that a huge black man stood over her bed.

"Where am I?" she asked, her eyes firmly fixed on Cantu.

"Borden Street. The Whitfield house."

Opening her mouth to speak, Samantha stopped and appeared to be thinking.

"The store……the fire."

"Yes, miss. There was a fire."

She wiped her hand across her forehead.

"Here, take some water," he said holding a cup to her lips as he raised her head.

After swallowing the liquid, she laid her head back and looked at Cantu.

"Who are you?"

He smiled. "My name is Armand Cantal Granville. But I go by Cantu. Leftenant Addington asked me to watch over you."

She looked hard at him.

"Now I remember," she said, her eyes closing as she drifted back into sleep."

He knocked twice and opened the door.

"I have tea for you," Cantu said, putting the small tray on the night stand.

Samantha sat upright in the big bed, a small book at her side. She smiled at the big man who moved so lightly.

"Thank you."

"You look very well this morning, Miss Samantha."

"I do feel so much better. It's time I leave my sickbed and get on with sorting out the fire."

Cantu sat in the chair by the door. "I hired two men to pick through the remains. It doesn't appear there will be much to save, perhaps some of the metal tools, that's all."

"Did the letter get off for Boston?"

He nodded. "Mrs. Whitfield wrote it and I took it to the post house. But with the trouble, who knows when it might get to the city."

"What would I have done without you," she asked.

"It was Mr. Addington, most surely."

She remembered her encounters with Lieutenant Addington. Could this be the same man she perceived as an overbearing officer of the Royal Navy?

"Why do you serve him? Surely every officer in the Royal Navy doesn't have a servant."

"I am not his servant," Cantu said quietly, "I am his friend."

Samantha looked skeptical. "I know enough of the sea to know that common sailors do not have lieutenants as friends. You must think me a fool."

"When he was young midshipmen, he saved my life. Since then we have taken care of each other and I will take care of him for as long as I live. He is a good man and I am his friend."

Samantha sipped her tea, her mind taking in what Cantu had said about Lieutenant James Addington.

Chapter Seventeen

The Winds of Change

The first day of October dawned clear, the last vestiges of summer remaining in New York as a jolly boat approached the Market Street landing. In the harbor, *Challenger* swung at anchor preparing to re-supply after almost a month on patrol. The continued presence of the Royal Navy filled the inner harbor anchorage with warships and transports.

James saw Cantu standing on the jetty, his arms folded across his chest. The big man smiled and he moved to the stone steps as James stepped from the boat and climbed up to shake hands. Will Thorpe followed his friend

"All is well?" James asked quickly.

"It is indeed. The young lady is healthy again."

He knows me too well, James thought. Was I that obvious?

"And my aunt? How is she holding up?" Will asked.

Cantu grinned.

"Mrs. Whitfield is quite a woman, sir. I think she has enjoyed having a young person in the house and has taken to using some of my medicine on her husband."

Will laughed, "That's my Aunt Abigail."

They walked north, Cantu describing the last month and Samantha Walker's progress.

"So she's left the Whitfield's?"

Cantu nodded.

"She took a small house in the next street while she waits for word from Boston. For now she is running her business from there."

"And you see her every day?"

Cantu chuckled. "I do."

"Well, what can you tell me?"

"That lady does not like King George or Parliament, I can tell you that."

"Damn, man, I knew that. What else?"

"Very stubborn.   Yes, I would say she is very stubborn."

James remembered her prickly temperament.

"I think I knew that too. Can you think of anything more?"

Cantu stopped. "Why not find out yourself, we're here."

"James, I'm off to see my aunt. Come by later and we can have dinner ashore." Will said and patted his friend on the back. "Plus, I'm not sure I'd want to see this."

The small house was very different from the former establishment of Walker and Sons, but the makeshift sign told the world the shop was open for business.

Opening the door, James stepped inside, not sure what to expect.

"May I help..."   Samantha had just stepped from behind a curtain on hearing the door and stopped when she saw James.

"Miss Walker.....good morning."

She broke the awkward silence first.

"Do come in, Mr. Addington.   Cantu would you please get a chair from the back?"

He watched her straighten her green dress, pulling herself up to her full height. Her green eyes brought back memories of their first meeting in Boston, and he was again struck by her beauty.

"May I offer you some tea?" she asked as James took the offered chair.

"I would like that," he said, feeling extraordinarily awkward.

"Let me get the tea, Miss Samantha," Cantu said. "While you two talk."

She sat down gracefully, her back straight, hands in her lap.

James said, "I'm so very glad you seem to have recovered from the fire."

"I am in your debt, sir. If not for your actions, I might well not be here." Her voice was soft, but she had turned to look directly into his eyes.

"Thankfully Cantu and I were there for you."

Samantha smiled. "Mr. Granville has been an angel from God, to be sure. I don't know what I would have done without his help."

"You're not the first person who has felt that way, I assure you."

She watched him as he smiled at her. This is the same man, but he seems so very different to me now.

"And I have found a true friend in Abigail Whitfield. She is a dear and we have seen each other every day since I left."

"Will is very fond of her, she's all the family he has left."

Cantu brought in a teapot and two cups, quietly pouring for James and Samantha.

"I understand you're awaiting correspondence from Boston?"

"It has been several weeks since a letter was posted. But with the war...." Her voice trailed off.

"Ah, yes. It has been disruptive throughout the colonies."

"And certainly not helped by your patrols."

He noted the sharpness in her voice and understood. In the past he might have taken exception to her words. Now he remembered the little sloop torn apart by *Challenger's* guns.

"War is difficult for everyone, miss. I assure you most in my crew would much rather be in England."

"Then why don't you all go and leave us in peace?"

James thought for a moment then answered quietly. "If it were up to me I would do exactly that."

"I'm sorry, lieutenant. I didn't mean you. It's just that this war has turned our world upside down. You've been nothing but kind to me and I must seem ungrateful."

Looking into her eyes he felt that she wanted to say more, but couldn't. He also wished he possessed the words to try and tell her what she meant to him. But for now, a barrier lay between them, a barrier neither knew how to surmount.

The return trip to *Challenger* in the cutter across the choppy harbor could not have been described by James, who was surprised as the boat bumped against the big ship's side. Sitting in the stern with Will after their dinner, he'd tried to make some sense of how he felt. Never before had a woman attracted him like this Boston beauty. One way or another he would find out if Miss Samantha Walker was going to be part of his future. But how?

As he climbed up the ladder to the entry port and raised his hat to the quarterdeck, Andy Thorton moved across the main deck toward him. He could see by the look on his friend's face that something was amiss.

"It's not good, James," Andy said, taking him by the arm and directing him toward the quarterdeck. Will followed, listening to the exchange.

"What do you mean?"

"A man from your division was overheard by the master-at-arms telling two other men that our attack on the rebel sloop was a massacre and we should have never used grape!"

James heart sank, he knew this would end very badly. "Who was it?"

"Able seaman Kelly. The captain had him put in irons immediately. He's talking about hanging him for seditious talk."

The power of a captain of a king's ship was absolute. He certainly had the power at sea to hang anyone who violated the Articles of War.

"Will he do it?"

Thorton shook his head. "I don't know. He was as angry as I've ever seen him. But hanging a sailor in port with an admiral as the senior officer, I think not. He'd have to explain the attack on the sloop and Howe might not like the full story."

He thought of Kelly, a good sailor who never complained and could always be counted on in a fight. So I wasn't the only one who felt the attack crossed the boundary of decency, he thought.

"I'll go see Kelly. Then try to intercede with the captain."

"Tread carefully, James," Will said quietly, "He hasn't been right since his brother died."

The small confinement cell on the orlop deck was not designed to do more than hold a man awaiting execution. Stepping onto the lower deck, James saw the sentry standing outside the big wooden door, a large bolt holding the cell secure.

"Open this, I have to see the prisoner," James said with an edge on his voice.

Reacting as expected, the man acknowledged James's order and slid the bolt out.

As the man swung the door open, an odor of urine and sweat met them. A single lantern carried by the sentry cast a pale yellow light into the small fetid space.

Kelly, sitting with his back against the wooden timbers squinted at the light, his eyes adjusting from the pitch black. Seeing James he pushed himself up the wall and stood with his head just barely under the overhead planking.

"I came as soon as the first leftenant told me what happened," James said briskly, trying to sound irritated for the sentry's benefit. He knew the story of this visit would be all over the ship in thirty minutes. It wouldn't due to be seen as sympathetic to a seditious sailor, even if he might be.

"I'm sorry, sir. I should've kept my mouth shut."

James turned to the sentry. "Leave us."

"Now, tell me what happened," he said quietly after the Marine closed the door.

Kelly took a deep breath. "I was talking to Donahue on deck. We was forward by the bow chasers. I told him I thought what we did to that sloop weren't right. Then I turns to see the master-at-arms listening. 'For I knew it, I was in the big cabin with the captain screaming at me and then down here."

"Christ," James said. Kelly had probably signed his own death warrant. "But whatever made you say that? You've been in battle before, you know what it's like.'

"But, sir. I'm from Boston, pressed about three years ago. I found this life is just fine with me. But my brothers are all sailors sailing this coast. They could have been on the sloop, or someone just like 'em."

James could see the pain in the man's face. This was the tragedy of a civil war and this was now a civil war, the rebels against the loyalists. The horror of war rises to new levels when a people declares war on its own.

"What will happen, Mr. Addington?"

"I don't know. I'll go to the captain, but what good that will do I don't know."

"The boatswain said what I did's a hanging offense."

"I'll not lie. The Articles of War say any man who utters words of sedition shall be punished by death or as a court martial may decide. But you have a good record and I'll speak up for you as will others. That will count for something, I know it will."

Captain Robert Pelham looked up from a letter he was writing. His eyes were cold, his lips set in a firm line.

"What do you want, Mr. Addington?"

"Sir, about Kelly, I…"

"Be very careful what you say, sir. I am now writing a letter to the admiral recommending flogging around the fleet for the traitor."

While James had heard of the gruesome form of execution, he had never witnessed the spectacle. Taken to each ship at anchor, the man was given a dozen or two lashes by that ship's boatswain while the entire crew officers and men watched. Then cut down from the grating, he was rowed to the next ship and the punishment repeated. Most men could last through four maybe five ships until the cumulative effect of the slashing cat 'o nine tails would kill him from shock and loss of blood. By comparison, hanging was infinitely more humane. But by asking for this punishment, Pelham would tell the admiral he felt any seditious actions must be dealt with in the most brutal manner.

"Sir, what the master at arms heard was not the whole story."

Pelham stood and slowly walked to the big windows at the stern of the cabin. Without turning to look at James, he asked quietly, "And just how would you know that, pray tell?"

"I went down to the orlop and talked with him, sir."

146

Slowly the captain turned, the anger clearly in his eyes and voice. "You tread very dangerously, sir. Anyone might think that you are sympathetic to a fellow colonist."

Never since his first ship had anyone indicted him for his land of birth. Suddenly James felt angry himself. The captain had no right to assume that James's birthplace would override his loyalty as a king's officer. Trying to control himself, James said as steadily as he could, "Do you think that is the case, sir?"

"How dare you," Pelham screamed. "Get out, get out, now! SENTRY..."

The cabin door opened and James saw Private Gorris standing with his musket. "SIR!"

"Escort Mr. Addington to the wardroom. Sir, you can consider yourself under close arrest."

Sitting on his cot, James's mind kept going over the events in the captain's cabin. What had happened? Certainly going to see one of your own men didn't cross any lines of discipline, did it? What could have given the man any idea that James's loyalties were to anyone other than the king and the navy? This made no sense.

A knock on the flimsy door was followed by Will's voice from the other side.

"James?"

"Come ahead," he answered, not wanting to see his friend, but hoping the first lieutenant might shed some light on the situation.

The look on Will Thorpe's face told James that this was serious trouble.

"What in God's name did you say to the man?"

Shaking his head, James honestly answered, "I told him that there was more to what happened than what the master at arms reported."

"Oh, Christ. I know where this is going."

"Will, he questioned my loyalty to the navy because I was born in New York." James voice quivered from the emotion as he described the captain's actions.

"James, you've been around enough to know he can do anything aboard his ship that he damn well pleases."

"Including impugning the honor of his officers?"

"Yes, if that is what he wants," Will almost shouted. "Damnation, man, this is bad, very bad."

James had never known Will Thorpe to exaggerate or spin excesses. If Will felt this was bad, the truth could not be far from it.

"What will happen," James asked, imagining himself being taken to the flagship, under arrest, to stand trial by court-martial.

"For now, you're ordered to remain aboard the ship until specifically directed otherwise by the captain."

"What?"

"I think the captain may be realizing that he let his temper take charge. If you're restricted to the ship for a reasonable period of time it will give him a way out of this situation without losing face."

"The devil he will."

"Shut up, you fool. There's nothing you can do for Kelly. Throwing your career and perhaps your freedom away to prove a point is senseless. Surely you must understand that?"

James found his fists clenched so tight that they began to hurt. "The bastard."

Will said nothing.

Lord Howe, commanding the naval forces in the colonies had considered Captain Pelham's request and disapproved it. His reasons were not conveyed to Pelham, only a short note telling the captain to "handle as you see fit, within the confines of *Challenger*."

The following morning the cry was heard at two bells on the forenoon watch, "All hands lay aft to witness punishment."

Kelly, escorted from below stepped into the harsh sunlight and had to shade his eyes. Pushed from behind by the burly boatswain's mate he stumbled his way to the after part of the main deck where a deck grating had been rigged against the quarterdeck rail.

Quickly the punishment party pulled Kelly's shirt off his back and tied his wrists and ankles to the grating with leather thongs.

Standing with the officers on the main deck across from the grating, James felt as if he was living a nightmare. Standing with his feet slightly apart, he felt the steady motion from the waves against the hull. It was very quiet despite the presence of over two hundred men in ranks facing aft waiting for the captain.

What were these men thinking, James asked himself? Did they feel anything at all? Anger, pity or perhaps relief it was Kelly and not them on the grating? Most of this crew knew Kelly as a good sailor and shipmate, a man who they could count on in bad weather or a fight. But now they would watch him whipped for words, not actions.

"Attention to orders," the master at arms called.

Captain Pelham stood at the quarterdeck rail, a book open in front of him.

"If any person in or belonging to the fleet shall utter any words of sedition or mutiny, he shall suffer death, or such other punishment as a court martial shall deem him to preserve." The captain closed the book and looked out across the assembled crew. "Master at arms, six dozen lashes."

On the main deck, Silas Lloyd, one of the boatswain mates pulled the cat from a red leather bag. Its long knotted cords uncurled from the bag almost as if they had a life of their own. At the end of each thong the cord spread into three strands which would lacerate as it hit the bare back of the prisoner.

Lloyd looked up at the captain who simply nodded.

Remembering the first flogging he had witnessed aboard the *Andromeda*, James had never learned to accept the brutality of the cat. It seemed to him that a man was reduced to lower than an animal as his back turned bloody red from the lashes.

"Crack" brought him back to reality as Lloyd made the first swing with brutal force. For just a moment Kelly's back appeared unblemished, but then the red welts appeared as he shuddered from the pain. In the background the steady roll of a drum came from the Marine squad giving the spectacle its own macabre symphony.

By the first dozen lashes, Kelly's back was now a bloody mass of torn skin and blood oozing down and mixing with the sweat on his back. His jerks and shudders had ceased, and James knew he must have passed into semi-consciousness.

Standing behind the boatswain, Doctor Goodrum watched, his face impassive.

"That's enough for now," the doctor said at the end of four dozen lashes. He walked forward to examine Kelly. Stepping to one side he put his hand under Kelly's jaw and slowly moved the sailor's head. Goodrum put his other hand on Kelly's neck for a moment. Stepping back he turned toward the quarterdeck.

"He's unconscious, sir."

"But alive?"

"Yes, sir," Goodrum answered with little emotion.

"Can he take two dozen more?" Pelham asked.

"I should think so, sir."

"Very well then, boatswain, complete the punishment."

Jim Goodrum moved behind the boatswain.

"Crack."

James looked at the doctor sensing that something had changed. Will Thorpe stood behind the captain, his face impassive. The world was turning upside down.

Chapter Eighteen

A Question of Loyalty

Samantha Walker looked up as a tall, well-dressed man entered Walker and Son's shop on Albermarle Street in Boston.

"Miss Walker?"

She stood up and nodded. "May I help you?"

"My name is David Addington. I believe you know my son, James."

For a moment Samantha examined the man's face. Could this be the man James described as "the admiral?"

"Yes, sir, I do. Although it has been two months since I've seen him." Her voiced sounded bitter.

He smiled slightly. "I think I can explain that."

Her heart sank, while she had been confused and upset when she learned *Challenger* had left New York without a word from James, she decided he simply hadn't time to come ashore. When her father had sent a new manager for the New York office, she had left the city to return to Boston thinking she would never see James Addington again. Secretly she'd worried that he might have been injured or killed. Now the truth would be known and she wasn't sure she was ready to face it.

"Please sit down," she said, indicating a straight-backed chair at the end of the counter. Watching him move across the room, Samantha saw more traces of resemblance, how he walked and the set of his head.

Pulling another chair around to face her visitor, she remembered her manners. "A cup of tea, perhaps?" Trying to sound calm, she knew her voice was anxious.

David Addington shook his head. "Thank you, no." He paused for just a moment then continued, "Miss Walker, I'm here at the bidding of my son." He saw the surprised and happy look on her face and countered, "Let me explain. I received a letter from James a month ago. It was the first communication we had shared for nearly half a year."

"Were you in Albany?"

"I was preparing to leave for Boston when the post arrived. James has been restricted the ship for the last two months."

"Restricted, is he in trouble?" she asked quickly.

"Apparently his captain felt that James had been too sympathetic to the rebel cause. It resulted in a confrontation and when a lieutenant takes on a captain he will always lose."

Sympathetic to the rebel cause. The words seemed so powerful and not whatever she would have expected from him. Surely his father must be angry with his son and now me.

"That must bring you great distress," Samantha said quietly.

"Miss Walker you are quite correct, but not for the reason you suspect. I am very angry with my son for having a confrontation with his captain. Right or wrong the captain of a king's ship deserves the loyalty of his officers."

"And to think he feels sympathetic to the rebels must surely raise your wrath."

David Addington smiled. "That is where you are mistaken, Miss Walker. I'm in Boston at the invitation of the Naval Committee."

The surprise in her eyes was matched by the tone of Samantha's voice. "But, sir, you're an English admiral."

"Young lady, I am a New Yorker. While I'm proud of my service to the king, I have no use or respect for the sniveling politicians in Parliament or the Admiralty. These colonies have passed their time of servitude. I aim to do everything in my power to assist them."

Samantha found herself at a loss for words.

Two months of patrolling, interspersed with infrequent port visits for re-supply, had resulted in two minor engagements with colonial traders. *Challenger* had captured one large sloop while a small barquentine had escaped during darkness. The back-breaking routine of working the sails and rigging in frigid weather began to take its toll on the ship and crew.

"Sweet Christ, it's brutal up there," Will Thorpe said as he pulled off his oilskin cloak.

"And a happy Christmas to you as well," Archie Tatnall added as he lifted a glass of port, holding it level as the deck canted to the force of another heavy roller.

James picked up a hard ship's biscuit and dipped it in his glass of wine to soften, then took a tentative bite. His mood was as dark as the sky that scudded over the frigate as December drew to a close. The captain had been quite proper in his deportment toward James and on the last port visit to Halifax had informed him that the restriction to remain aboard was lifted. That did little to lift James's spirits, the damage having been already done to his reputation. His future in the Royal Navy seemed bleak at best.

"Bugger off, Archie, and pass the bottle. I'm wet and frozen," Thorpe wiped his face, the spray still evident on his face. He quickly drank from an offered glass then turned to the table. "But I do have a Christmas present for you poor unfortunate sots."

They looked at him with curiosity.

"We head for Halifax at first light. Re-supply and refit. We'll be able to clean the copper and replace the damaged spars and rigging from the last storm."

Everyone in the room knew the ship needed a great deal of work to say nothing of the crew's need to rest from the fury of the North Atlantic during winter.

Since the flogging of Seaman Kelly, there had been tenseness in the wardroom. While the doctor and James were certainly civil, the warmth of the friendship had faded, adding to the dreariness of constant patrolling and bad weather.

"What made up the captain's mind?" James asked.

"We can thank the good doctor. He stood his ground that the men needed fresh supplies and water or he wouldn't answer for their health."

James knew the doctor was concerned for the crew. Several men had died of consumption in the last two weeks. Another topman fell to his death one morning trying to reef a frozen topsail. The crew was as tired as the ship and it was beginning to show.

"Remind me to buy the old boy a toddy," Archie said, grinning as he finished his port.

"I'll buy you all a round, but we need to get this ship safely to Halifax." Thorpe grinned.

"A toast to Halifax," James said.

The chorus of replies was drowned by the sound of a wave crashing against the side of the ship.

Challenger found Halifax busy for the middle of winter. A full anchorage told the story of a build up of forces for the coming summer campaign against the rebels. Captain Pelham's anger over the loss of his brother had seemed to abate and the ship settled into as pleasant a routine the cold winds and frigid temperatures would allow.

Supervising the repair and re-rigging of the ship kept both officers and men busy during daylight hours. But at night the discipline was relaxed and the crew took advantage of the reduced watch requirements in port. Several young ladies of the docks were permitted a discrete opportunity to practice their trade. In a move that surprised the experienced hands, all mates were allowed to go ashore in small groups to explore the hospitality of Nova Scotia.

Two weeks after entering port, James watched the sun setting on what had turned out to be a crisp clear day. The thick green forests visible from the anchorage reminded him of the area around Albany. He had always thought it strange that England seemed to be so devoid of trees compared to the Americas. But then the demands of the navy for centuries had stripped the once lush English forests of much timber. Perhaps the same would happen here one day.

"A good day, if too cold as always."

James turned and nodded to Cantu.

"Not like your home I daresay."

"I think everyone believes their home is the best place. But I know that my island truly is a paradise."

Trying to remember Albany he wondered if he felt the same way? Most of his strong memories were of ships and the sea. Perhaps he was a man without a home now.

"You have received no letters?" Cantu asked.

Shaking his head, James said, "No."

Cantu had taken the letter for David Addington ashore to post during *Challenger's* last visit to New York.

But the reliability of the post combined with the hostilities made James wonder if the letter would ever reach his father. He could try to send a letter directly to Samantha, but he had less faith that mail would make it into rebel held territory. His restriction had seemed less important once Cantu informed him that Samantha had left New York for Boston. But he also knew he very much wanted to see her.

"Would you like me to post another?"

James turned to look at the man who had become his friend. Cantu seemed to sense how the young officer felt at any given time. Now he must decide if there was any chance he would ever see Samantha Walker again. It certainly seemed like a remote possibility.

"I received a dispatch from the Admiralty on the last packet."

James watched the captain with a wariness born from the last two months. He said nothing as Pelham glanced down at the single piece of parchment lying open on the desk.

"Most unusual, but as I consider all aspects of your situation, it is probably for the best. You are hereby directed to leave *Challenger* and report to Major General John Burgoyne who will be arriving in the near future."

Trying to absorb what the captain had just said, James was at a loss for a response.

"You have done a fair job in *Challenger,* Mr. Addington. Let us leave it at that and part companies with civility. I will also send the man Cantu with you as the army expects officers to have a servant."

"Yes, sir.....thank you, sir."

"I trust you will continue to do your duty. A replacement for you will be sent from Plymouth and for the immediate future you will be attached to the staff of Sir Guy Carleton, the governor-general. Here is a letter for you."

Thoughts raced through James mind, what did this mean? Why was he being singled out? It must be connected with Burgoyne's journey in *Challenger,* but how?

Pelham looked down at his paperwork as he said, "You are dismissed, Mr. Addington."

And you are still a bastard, Captain Pelham, James thought.

"Leaving to serve with the army?" Will asked after James told him of the arraignment. "For how long?"

"It appears I won't be returning to *Challenger*," James said.

"Christ almighty," his friend said, shaking his head.

"The captain is allowing me to take Cantu with me, so that's something."

Will said, "Hell, he knew that if he didn't let him go with you, your large friend would get busy with that damned machete' of his."

James smiled, he would miss Will's wry sense of humor.

"Have you seen the doctor?" he asked Will.

"In the wardroom I suspect."

"Jim, I will say good bye to you, it seems I'm being seconded to the army."

The doctor looked surprised.

"To do what?"

James shook his head, "No idea, but I am supposed to be on General Burgoyne's staff."

Jim Goodrum rubbed his chin. "Must be something afoot if I don't miss my guess. Perhaps another landing by the army and they need naval expertise."

Hesitating, James said, "Jim, we've been good friends. I know what happened created a problem, but I'm still your friend, don't ever forget that."

The doctor smiled and extended his hand.

"I never will, my young friend."

PART THREE

1777-1778

Chapter Nineteen

A Fish Out of Water

The letter which Captain Pelham had delivered to James only served to further mystify the young lieutenant. Arriving ashore he was directed to the Provost's Office in Halifax where, to his continued curiosity, another letter waited for him.

Now, attired in a hastily purchased pair of civilian trousers and heavy coat, James saw the small house on the southern end of the waterfront which was his destination. He stepped quickly through the slushy water that lay in wide puddles on the dirt road. The gray sky showed no hint of warmth and despite his curiosity James hoped there would be heat inside. A thin trail of smoke rising from the chimney kept him hopeful. He stepped onto the bare porch and knocked hard on the door.

In a moment the door swung open to reveal a tall, hard looking man wearing the heavy clothes of a dock worker.

"You are?"

"Addington."

"Come in, leftenant," the man said moving from the doorway.

A bright fire did indeed burn in the fireplace and the interior was remarkably comfortable.

The man had taken a seat at the wooden table and gestured to a chair on the opposite side.

"My name's Porritt. Major Richard Porritt."

"Sir," James said, trying to establish some familiarity to what seemed a very unusual situation.

"I understand you've served in the navy for the past six years?"

"Yes, sir."

"Well this is not the navy, sir, not by a long mile. The army has a different way of conducting business and you've been pulled into that world."

"I'm not sure I understand, major," James said, unsettled by the man's gruff manner.

"You, my fine young sailor boy, crossed paths with Gentleman Johnny Burgoyne. The general has a long memory, even for a politician, and he remembered the young man from Albany."

The situation was becoming even more bizarre, James thought. What could that possibly have to do with this?

"And he intends on using your knowledge to help defeat the rebels."

"But, sir," James protested, "I find myself at a loss to understand what this is all about. It's quite unusual indeed."

"My word, but you are very perceptive for a sailor." Porritt laughed and stood up, picking a piece of wood from the pile next to the fireplace. He tossed it on top of two burning logs, throwing sparks up the chimney.

"Do you drink, Addington?"

"Why, yes," James answered as Porritt poured measures of a dark liquid into two battered pewter mugs.

"Then to your health, sir," the major said, raising the mug to James then taking a long drink.

Cautiously James took a sip, the raw liquor burning his throat.

"My God, what is this?"

"They call it rum, but I think that is a very loose description."

James sniffed the mug then set it down on the table. "Major, why I am here?"

"Because you've been assigned to me until Burgoyne arrives from England."

"He's coming here?"

The major poured another measure into his glass and offered the jug to James.

"Uh, no thank you."

"As you wish. But it might be easier to hear what I have to say."

James picked up the jug and splashed some of the dark liquor into his mug.

"Much better, you certainly learn quickly." The major laughed but his eyes didn't show any humor. "You are going to be a spy, Mr. Addington." He paused. "It takes many things to win a war and information is one of the most critical."

The word spy seemed to hang in the air. James had always thought of spying as something done with no honor by brigands for money. Now, as he looked at Porritt, the word brigand seemed quite appropriate.

"I seem to have put you at a loss for words."

James stuttered, "Sorry, sir. I never considered I would become a spy, certainly not for the army."

"For England, leftenant, for England. And you won't be alone either. I'm sending you in company with a young cavalryman down into the colonies in search of information."

The fantasy that James was hearing prevented him from even considering the many questions he knew he should be asking. But better to hear this man out first, he thought.

"In both Rhode Island and Massachusetts, the rebels are trying to put ships of war to sea. While we don't much fear a challenge to our Atlantic Squadron, they might indeed allow more contraband to get past our blockade. We also need to know more about the civilian ships that are trading in illegal goods. Who owns them? Where do they put their cargoes ashore? And how do we get a warning on their sailings?"

The major poured himself another full cup of the horrible liquor and continued, "You know ships and what questions to ask. But you haven't been recently ashore in the area and don't understand the many changes since the rebels declared they were independent. For that reason we are sending a captain from the Queen's Rangers with you."

James had heard of the Rangers. A loyalist cavalry regiment, they had gained a reputation as brutal fighters who gave no quarter nor asked for any.

A knock came from the door.

"I believe that would be your counterpart."

A tall dark haired man about James age entered the small room. He wore leather britches and a heavy woolen coat. Dark hair protruded from under his leather tricorn hat framing an honest face.

"Leftenant James Addington, meet Captain Justin Thompson."

The tall man showed no emotion, but offered his hand.

"My pleasure," James said, trying to be pleasant.

"Mine as well, Mr. Addington," the stranger replied.

"Now sit down and we'll go over the plan," Porritt said, returning to his seat by the fire.

Using a map of the northern colonies, the major laid out a route of travel for his two newest agents. Acting on messages from loyalists in Providence, Rhode Island, Porritt was sending the men to survey the Providence River for signs of ship-building.

One of the continental navy's new frigates was reported to be outfitting near the shipyard at which she had been built. The ship was named the *Warren* for General Joseph Warren, killed on Breed's Hill. A new design, the frigate was rumored to carry 34 guns, including a dozen 18 pounders, heavier than any carried by frigates of the Royal Navy. It was up to James and Justin Thompson to verify the ship's exact status and future plans.

The major also ordered them south to Boston to find out more information on the cargo vessels that continued to elude the navy, carrying stores and munitions from Europe to the rebels. While most of the contraband came from France, the trade was expanding to Spain and Holland also.

The two young officers were directed to return to Halifax within sixty days to await the arrival of Burgoyne and the forces he was due to bring from England.

"As the weather improves, the general will begin to make plans for the spring campaign against the rebels."

"Where will he attack?" Justin asked.

"He's not confided that to me," Porritt replied, a touch of sarcasm in his voice. "But I trust you will know at the proper time."

"And we will travel by ship?"

"Correct, Mr. Addington. Travel by land is too hazardous this time of year and would take too much time. I have a small coaster that will take you from here to just south of Portland, Maine."

"My contact will be waiting for us with horses," Thompson added. "From there we go overland to Providence then to Boston."

James realized he didn't know if Cantu could ride a horse or not. The subject had never come up and he hadn't thought to ask.

The sun had not yet shone itself as the three men walked through the cold wind toward the waterfront. Bundled against the winter weather, each man carried a canvas bag with his belongings. Armed with both a blade and a pistol provided by Major Porritt, they were traveling light.

James and Cantu had met Captain Thompson at the stable on Front Street as agreed upon the night before. Now they walked in silence, their breath visible in the frigid air, the frozen ground crunching under their feet.

"I don't like ships," Thompson offered, breaking the silence.

James had already seen their destination the evening before and laughed. "Well, captain, I think you will find this is not a ship, it's what we in the navy call a boat."

"A boat?"

"Not large enough to be considered a ship," James replied, smiling in the darkness.

Thompson stopped and looked at James. "Not large enough?"

Cantu chuckled.

"Should make for a spirited ride in this wind," James said, continuing to walk, grinning to himself.

The cavalryman watched the other two as they walked on toward the water. "Not large enough?" he asked himself and followed.

The three men went aboard the small lugger *Amelia* which tugged at her ropes against the wind and tide. Though smelling faintly of spoiled fish, the sixty foot ship appeared to be well-maintained to James, who surveyed the deck in the growing light.

A tall man stepped from behind the deckhouse.

"Welcome aboard, gentlemen."

"Captain Adams?" James asked.

The big man nodded. "I'm Adams."

"I am…"

"Best I don't know, better that way," the man said turning. "Follow me. Crew's eating. We sail on the morning tide, that's about thirty minutes."

The three passengers stepped carefully around coiled ropes as they followed Adams toward the main cabin hatch.

"I'll take you below," the captain said. "Stay there until we get out of the harbor. Better that way."

The three found a small area to stow their bags and tried to get comfortable as they began to hear commands coming from on deck.

"Here," James said to Cantu, offering a hard piece of bread he had just torn off a loaf given him by the captain.

The deck canted slightly and the mast groaned in its mount behind them.

"It seems we're underway. Here," James said poking Justin Thompson with another piece of bread.

"Not just now, thank you."

"Go on," James insisted. "No one does well at sea without a little something in their stomach."

"He tells the truth," Cantu added and bit into the bread.

Thompson took a small bit and began to slowly chew.

"I don't like boats, either," Thompson said, looking around at the cramped and crowded area.

"We should only take two days to make Portland, if we don't hit a storm," James commented. "Who will meet us?"

Thompson looked at James, wondering what the question meant. Were these two sailors questioning him?

"Surely you can tell us that, captain."

Thompson took another bite and caught himself as the lugger heeled over.

"Perhaps it would be wiser not to use rank in our conversations."

James thought for a moment and nodded.

"I agree. I prefer James. And this is Cantu."

"Most people call me 'JT.' It's common enough where I come from to use initials."

The groan from the mast told them the lugger was now making good time in the stiff morning wind.

"And where's that?"

"North Carolina, Raleigh."

James had never set foot in the colony, but knew it was very important to the rebel cause.

"What do you mean two days if we don't hit a storm?" Thompson asked.

James smiled. "To get to Portland, we must cross the Gulf of Maine after rounding the Hawk at the southern end of Nova Scotia. If a storm moves into the gulf, we would have to turn east and ride it out. That could take days and send us hundreds of miles out to sea. Then we have to claw our way back west to Portland."

The look of concern was evident on JT's face.

"I didn't understand."

"Don't worry, I'm sure we'll be fine. Now who's meeting us?

The shock of facing an Atlantic storm had taken the immediate brusqueness out of the cavalryman's demeanor.

"Caitlin. Caitlin McKenna."

"A woman?" Cantu interjected.

Now it was Thompson's turn to smile. "Oh yes, and quite a woman."

The name raised a vague question in James's mind, but he quickly disregarded it. There were more important things to occupy his thoughts.

The vagaries of winter weather were kind to the little lugger and the passage was made with a minimum of discomfort. James was thankful they had enjoyed relatively good conditions as even the modest rolling of *Amelia* had resulted in great personal discomfort for Captain Thompson. Only the efforts of Cantu, using several herbs, had allowed the poor landsman to barely tolerate the voyage.

The captain and crew had kept mostly to themselves, although Adams had been good sharing navigational information with James as they crossed the gulf. Surprisingly to James, the captain possessed a creditable sextant and the weather had allowed several position fixes as they approached the mainland.

Many years of sailing the coast had allowed Captain Adams to make landfall only ten miles north of the small bay where he was to land his passengers. A decreasing off shore wind allowed a swift passage south along the coast and by mid-morning on the second day after leaving Halifax, the *Amelia's* anchor splashed down into Saco Bay.

"That beach yonder is Pine Point."

The captain handed JT a long glass.

"If you're satisfied, I'll drop the jolly boat and my men will row you ashore."

JT handed the glass to James. "They should be waiting for us beyond those dunes."

"Then let's be on our way," James said. "Better that way," he added, cutting his eyes at Adams.

The salt spray stung like needles as they were pulled toward the low spit of land. While the wind was not strong, the swell coming off the ocean would make for a challenging run into the beach. James only hoped these oarsmen knew what they were doing. A dunking in this frigid water could kill a man.

He looked over to Justin who huddled next to him in the stern. The poor man's face looked gray in the morning light.

"You'll be on dry land shortly," James said, noting that JT kept staring straight ahead.

In the bow, Cantu seemed oblivious to the pitching of the jolly boat. He had their bags with him, his responsibility was to get them safely ashore.

The coxswain knew his business, James thought, as he watched the bow remain dead straight to the surf as they accelerated toward the sand.

"Up, oars!" the man bellowed, taking the control of the boat entirely on himself with the rudder.

In what seemed like an instant the boat ground to a stop on the sloping sand, water sloshing past the sides and then flowing back out with the next wave.

"Thorne, Baker, over you go. The rest of you hold fast."

Two men jumped from the bow into the foaming water. Each grabbed a line which ran down each gunwale.

"Here you go, gents," the coxswain called.

James had already starting moving forward.

"JT, follow me."

Cantu jumped to the beach, all three of their duffel bags under his arm.

Following James, JT jumped the short distance to the wet sand, stumbled and found himself in the vise-like grip of Cantu.

"Easy, sir, easy."

JT was already surveying the bleak landscape as if orienting himself.

"We'll move toward those sand dunes," he said after a moment of composing himself. Without another word he strode up the beach.

James looked slightly surprised, then turned to Cantu. "He must know where he's going."

"One would hope, sir."

The two stragglers followed Justin Thompson across the deserted beach.

Chapter Twenty

A Different Kind of Woman

As the three men approached the dunes, a man appeared from one of the many ravines that ran through the sandy mounds.

"Do you know him?" James asked.

"Most assuredly," JT replied and waved his hand.

The man did not move to meet them, but stood with his legs apart and hands on his hips. Clad in buckskin, the man seemed to be a statue. Barrel-chested, it was as if he was guarding the entrance to the dunes.

"Robert," Justin said, using the French pronunciation.

"Hello," the man said, his eyes moving to James and Cantu.

"They're with me," he immediately said as if they were in danger of being attacked.

"I see."

James decided that Robert looked like someone you did not want as your enemy.

"Is she here?" JT asked.

Robert nodded toward the dunes.

Without a word, Justin walked off leaving James and Cantu with Robert.

"Follow me," the big man said and turned to follow Justin.

James fell in trail, noting the largest knife he had ever seen on the man's hip. No, this is not the man you want opposing you, he thought, wondering what they would find on the other side of the dunes.

When he later thought of his first impression of Caitlin McKenna, it was that she could not be the woman that Justin had told them about aboard the *Amelia*. Justin's description had prepared him to meet a renegade. He had told them of a woman who had spurned polite society for the dark world of smuggling. On her own from an early age, she'd learned to fight for what she wanted and in fact several men now lay dead who had tried to cheat her.

Justin had described a firebrand, who was competent with pistol or blade and willing to use both to get what she wanted. What James saw did not support that description.

A slight figure, she wore a leather coat and pants. The shock of seeing a woman in pants was only matched by the short sword she wore at her waist and the large pistol jammed in her belt.

Standing in front of Justin, her head only came up to his chest. She can't weigh more than eight stone soaking wet, James thought. This woman couldn't be the firebrand that Justin had described.

The two turned as James approached. Her expression was that of someone completely in control.

"Leftenant Addington, this is Caitlin McKenna."

James removed his cap.

"Miss."

The woman looked again quickly at JT then back to James.

"Did he say your name was Addington?"

"Yes," James stammered, "James Addington."

Her eyes betrayed surprise.

"Never mind," she said quickly. "I knew an Addington family once, but that was in New York."

"I see," James said, deciding that perhaps he should be on guard until he found out what the woman really meant. It couldn't be my family, he thought. But McKenna was his mother's maiden name.

"It's time we get off this beach," she said. "There are several houses on the point and I'd rather not meet anyone coming out of the dunes."

Cantu dropped the bags near the small fire and crouched down to warm himself.

"Your slave?" she asked.

James noticed the bite in her words. "My friend," he replied. "His name is Armand Granville."

Caitlin appeared not to have heard James, but said, "Robert, fetch the horses. Take Mr. Granville with you."

"Come on," Robert said.

"Call me Cantu."

The burly Robert turned and a hint of a smile showed from his mouth. "Much better than Armand, I'd say, by a damn sight," He continued toward the tethered mounts.

"Who's the big man," James asked.

Justin looked at Caitlin, who nodded.

"His name is Robert Schlatter. He's French Canadian. Drunken British soldiers killed his wife and family about ten years ago. He came south and has worked with Caitlin ever since. Hates the British with a fury."

"Good man with a blade and strong as the day is long," Caitlin added.

"I don't think I'd like to find out," James said and they all smiled.

Traveling across Maine in the winter was difficult at best, dangerous at times. The first leg south to Manchester proved difficult. Strong winds and cold temperatures made each hour a trial and the need to find shelter at night critical. Caitlin McKenna's knowledge of the country had resulted in the small group finding suitable shelter each evening of the five days it took to make the passage south to Lake Massabesic where they found a small cabin on the edge of the water.

A light snow had left them wet and cold, their normal state over the last several days. But the cabin proved to be their best overnight stop since leaving Pine Point. Caitlin had used the cabin many times and kept it supplied for situations like this. An adjoining enclosed lean-to provided a place for their horses out of the cruel wind. A common opening allowed the heat from the fireplace to warm the animals also.

Settling in to the cabin, the small group talked very little. Robert, who turned out to be a Canadian trapper by birth, lit a fire from his tinder box. The wood shavings quickly ignited and he carefully fed small pieces of dry wood into the rock fireplace.

"I'll get water," JT said. Picking up a metal jug and a small hatchet he left to chop through the shore ice to get water.

"How far to Providence," James asked Caitlin who was unpacking a saddlebag.

Without glancing at him, she replied, "Eighty miles." She put a slab of bacon on the wooden table, the grease staining the muslin carrying bag. "But the weather is changing. I can smell it in the air. If I don't miss my guess we'll have a storm by morning."

Years at sea had led James to believe he understood the signs of an impending weather change. But nothing he had seen today indicated anything serious in the offing.

"Most interesting," he replied nonchalantly.

"You doubt me?" she shot back.

He looked at the anger in her eyes. What was this about, he wondered?

James had been watching Caitlin and Robert closely, trying to get a sense of who they really were and would they help him complete Major Porritt's mission. The two of them had quietly gone about their business and the trip so far had been hard but uneventful. It was also clear that JT and Caitlin were more than just comrades in arms, but they kept it to themselves.

Robert had proven to be as dependable and physically powerful as Cantu. The two of them struck up a comfortable relationship, the Canadian trapper and a sailor of the Caribbean. James felt the mission was on good footing, but something still bothered him.

It had taken two full days for the storm to pass. While Caitlin never said it, her observations on the weather every few hours had a particularly biting tone to them. Finally they were able to start south toward Providence. The storm thankfully did not drop much snow and they were able to make good progress.

The small group met few travelers on the road south to Providence. James had yet to see any evidence of rebel troops or colonial authorities.

Caitlin had proven to be very accurate with her directions and they first sighted the upper reaches of the Providence River on the second day.

"We'll follow the river as we go south," she said as they moved down the crude road. "There are outposts along the river from here south we can use each night."

During the storm, Caitlin had related a report that one of the new frigates was in fact fitting out in the river.

"How far to the shipyard?" JT asked.

"Two days," she answered. "But the ship's not in the shipyard. At least that's what my contact told me."

"And he said no army troops in the area," James added.

"There weren't then, but that was almost a month ago," Caitlin answered.

"Most of the army is still in New Jersey," JT added. "But there is the constabulary and you never know where their loyalty lies."

The curse of any civil war, James thought, the lines of battle were never clearly drawn and apparently in this area it was no different.

Caitlin went on to explain that despite the main British bases of operation such as New York, clearly under control of the crown, the countryside and small towns were by and large open territory where the local authorities might support the king or the Continental Congress.

James still felt there must be some military or naval presence nearby if the frigate was preparing for service. But that shouldn't prevent an observer from determining the actual status of the ship. At least that was his hope.

A small roadhouse sat on the bend of the river that was now almost half a mile wide. The early dusk made it a good location for their last night before Providence.

Two horses were already in the small shed when the four unsaddled their mounts.

"Room?" JT asked when they stepped inside.

From behind the counter a man nodded. "One room for the four of you."

"All right."

"Food?"

"Cost ya extra," the man said with little enthusiasm. "Ready in 'bout an hour. Rabbit stew."

They laid their bags against the wall and sat down at one of the two tables in front of a small fireplace. Two men sat at the other table, a jug in front of them.

"That's your room there, but you pay in advance."

James took out several coins and paid the man.

"What have you got to drink?"

"Hard cider, rum and a fair ale," the fat innkeeper said, examining the coins in the poor light.

Caitlin returned to the inn later that evening to find James and JT still awake.

"The ship is eight miles south on this side of the river," she said. "A man told me there's a small wharf at the yard they're using for the fitting out."

James knew there was only one key question.

"How close can I get?"

She shrugged. "I guess that's up to you."

"We can be on the road at first light," JT said.

James nodded. Their first objective was close.

A swift start in the pre-dawn light put the small party approaching the area where the *Warren* should be moored as the sun came up. Three masts catching the early light confirmed the new warship was around the next bend in the river.

Fifteen minutes later they came around a turn in the road and saw their objective. Smoke rising from a storage shed was the only sign of activity around the ship. Two lanterns still burned near the entry port and James could see several men standing on deck.

"We need to keep riding," Caitlin said as she looked at the deserted wharf.

James knew she was right. If they stopped now it would look suspicious to the men on the frigate's deck.

In the distance the road wound past a stand of elm trees as it moved south.

"Stop past those trees and make a fire. I'll be back when I can," James said and turned his horse toward the wharf.

"You sure?" JT asked.

"That's what we're here for. I'll simply ask for directions."

Caitlin said, "Tell them you're looking for the Arrington farm."

"Arrington?"

"It's about five miles south, but hard to find. They should know of it, it's one of the biggest farms around."

As he approached the ship, James tried to take in everything possible to determine when the *Warren* might be ready for sea. The ship was definitely riding high in the water. Perhaps she didn't have all of her cannons aboard yet. Closed gun ports added to the mystery. Her rigging appeared completed, only the mizzen topsail was missing, the remaining canvas reefed tight against the yards.

James dismounted when he reached the wharf and tied the reins around a small railing. Noting the thin wisp of smoke coming from the galley smokestack, he decided some of the crew must be living aboard.

"Hello," James called as he reached the short gangway.

"Good morning," a short man holding a truncheon answered.

"Beautiful ship," he said brightly as he stepped on the gangway.

"What's your business, mister?"

"Looking for directions." James answered one of his questions as he walked toward the man who was now joined by his companion. Some of the main deck armament was indeed in place, squat cannons on their trucks behind some of the gun ports. But these were 12 pounders, the rumored heavier cannons nowhere to be seen.

The second man also carried a small club and was looking hard at James.

"Directions?"

"That's right, friend. I'm headed for Arrington's farm. Thought you might know the way."

Two of the main deck cargo hatches were open, making James think the on loading of supplies and final ballasting hadn't taken place. But there still should have been more men on deck at this time of day.

"And what be your business at Arrington's?" the larger man asked, his tone hostile.

Damn, James thought, I should have thought this through. "It's private. All I need is directions."

A man emerged from a small wooden shelter at the far end of the wharf. James could see he carried a musket and it was leveled at him.

"You'll be talking to our officer, so just stay right there." A pistol emerged from the man's belt as he gestured James onto the frigate's deck.

"Fergus, take this man down to the big cabin."

The second man was holding a short cutlass and motioning James aft.

Moving past several crewmen, James noticed their curious stares and desperately thought of a plausible story. He was going to Arrington to investigate a stallion for stud. That would make sense, he hoped. Any large farm would have livestock for breeding.

He ducked his head as he stepped down the ladder moving toward what must be the captain's cabin.

"Wait in here," the man said, motioning to what must become the chart room when the ship went to sea.

"What's your name," the man asked as he made to close the door.

Hesitating as he searched for something to say, James answered, "Richard...Richard Porritt."

The door closed and James heard the hasp close. He was on an enemy ship, in civilian clothes with no good story and a false name. The image of a hangman's rope running up to the foretopsail yard made him shudder. He had seen it only once as a senior midshipmen. A gunner had killed a messmate in a fight and the captain had sentenced him to hang. James could still remember the drum roll, the man's pathetic cry for mercy and his feet jerking as the rope pulled him off the deck.

Twenty minutes later the door opened.

"Let's go."

Passing through a temporary screen, James entered the big cabin dimly lit by two lanterns.

"Here he is, Mr. Brown."

James stared with total shock.
Sitting at the small desk was Lucas Brown.

Chapter Twenty-One

A Test of Friendship

Smoke swirled into the bare branches of a small grove of trees. Two hours had passed waiting for James to return from the frigate. Robert had worked his way through the woods to survey the ship and wharf, but saw nothing unusual. It was as if James had simply disappeared.

"The rebels must have taken him," JT said, knowing their mission just became more dangerous and perhaps deadly.

"How many men did you see?" Caitlin asked Robert.

The burly trapper shook his head. "Maybe ten."

"What do you think?" Cantu asked JT.

"We watch the wharf until the sun goes down. Then move in and try to find him. I only hope the rebels haven't taken him somewhere else."

Caitlin turned to JT and said, "How do we find him?"

"We ask."

Her eyes flared at him.

"Justin!"

"If they have him, people will know about it on the wharf. We take someone aside and convince them to tell us where they're keeping him. Once we know that, we go get him."

Cantu nodded, his expression grim.

JT looked around the group. "Robert, you and Cantu go back to the edge of the woods and keep an eye on the ship. Let us know if you see anything. Otherwise we'll all head back to the ship when it's dark."

When the two men had disappeared into the underbrush Caitlin asked Justin, "Can we get him back?"

"I don't know. But if we can't, he's a dead man."

"Have a seat...Mister Porritt." Lucas motioned to a chair. "You can return to you duties, Fergus."

The two men looked at each other across the desk.

"A most unusual circumstance I think you'd agree," Lucas said.

James searched his friend's face, but saw no apparent emotion, anger or humor.

"I would."

"A king's officer, out of uniform, inspecting a colonial warship? The situation certainly seems to be damning if I am any judge."

"I lost track of you, Lucas, heard you were second leftenant in *Tiber.*"

A slight smile broke on Brown's face.

"*Tiber*, quite right. We were in Boston when the trouble began. I decided to stay."

"You deserted?"

"I chose to stand by my home colony," Brown said his tone sharp.

James saw the anger in Lucas's eyes and remembered the mauling of the little sloop off North Carolina. *Perhaps I do understand how he feels.*

"I was in Boston when the army attacked Breed's Hill. I'd never thought that Englishmen could savage each other like they did."

Somewhere on deck a man yelled, his voice muffled as work continued to get the ship ready for war.

Memories of his time with Lucas came back to James as he watched his friend rise and walk to the stern windows.

"Do you know the name Nathan Hale?" Lucas asked.

"Should I?"

Lucas turned, his face hidden in shadow. "I expect not. Captain Nathan Hale volunteered to go into New York City to spy on Howe's troops for General Washington. They caught him and without trial or appeal hung him."

The image of the gunner being jerked off his feet as his messmates ran with the bitter end of the hanging noose flashed back into his mind.

"He wasn't a good spy, but certainly a brave man. The last words he said, 'I regret I have but one life to give for my country.' That's right, James, his country. Those fools in Parliament and the king refuse to recognize that we have moved past being colonies. And if you believe our declaration of independence, it is our right as freemen to choose our own destiny."

This was not the glib young midshipmen who had befriended him years ago, James thought. But this was Lucas. I see everything I liked in him then and I understand what he means.

Lucas returned and sat at the desk.

"James, we were friends. You saved my life and that's something no man can ever forget. But if it means your death to preserve a chance for my country to survive, I will gladly sacrifice you."

He remembered Lucas careening toward the side of *Andromeda* during a terrible storm. Only James's desperate lunge kept him from being swept overboard into the crashing waves. "So what now?"

"I don't know," Lucas said, sitting back in the chair. "I'm senior on board until the captain returns from Boston. While no one else on board knows who you are, I do."

Since his first awareness of his military past, James had learned that honor was the one thing that no one can take away from you. In the horror of war or the fury of a sea fight, honor must be paramount. And honor meant doing the right thing.

"Lucas, you must do your duty. I would not hold it against you, know that. In this terrible war we must be honorable men if there is any hope for the future."

"You will likely hang."

Suddenly James felt old, as his friend was likely correct.

An early sunset brought the first sign of fog drifting south on the river. A damp cold this time of year was only made worse as the visibility on the river dropped to almost nil.

Caleb Hunter wondered why he had ever left his farm outside Newport to join the Continental Army. Now he stood a lonely guard in the frigid winter weather, his toes numb inside his worn boots. With his eight pound musket slung over his shoulder, the short Rhode Islander walked a slow circuit up and down the wharf. The occasional muffled conversation from the frigate made his post even more lonely.

Adjusting the scarf around his neck, Hunter made a cursory glance north on the river. The mist reflected from the single lantern near the frigate's beakhead. Only two more hours, he thought, turning south on the wet planks.

"Don't say a word or you'll die."

Suddenly two men had him by the arms, pulling him into the darkness. He felt a blade against his throat and knew he was about to die. Instead he was dragged behind the wooden guard shack and forced to his knees.

"Keep your head down if you knows what's good for you," one man whispered and pulled the musket sling off his shoulder.

A second voice came from behind him, "Answer my questions and you'll live. Understand?"

The Rhode Islander had always thought he was a brave man. But now Caleb knew he was afraid of what these men might do to him. He was outnumbered and only a fool would resist them. He nodded his response.

"Do you know of the man they are holding on the ship?"

"Yes.....yes, I heard about him."

"What did you hear?"

"That a man had been arrested. They said he might be a spy."

"Is he still aboard the ship?"

Another nod from Hunter, "Far's as I know."

Cantu asked quickly, "Where are they keeping him?"

"I heard the cable tier, but don't knows for sure."

JT whispered, "What's a cable tier?"

"The cables for the ship's anchors. Forward part of the ship, down to the keel."

"Can we get there?" Caitlin asked.

"I can get there," Cantu replied, the tone of his voice leaving no doubt he would reach and release James.

Sitting in the damp compartment, James huddled under a wool blanket and watched the dim flicker from the single lantern on the bulkhead. Where would this journey end, he wondered? He thought for a moment of Lucas. He didn't bear his friend any ill, knowing he would have done the same thing if positions were reversed. But what struck James was the passion he has seen when Lucas talked about this new country. It was a side of Lucas Brown he had never seen. Do I have that amount of passion about anything, he asked himself. He reflected on his life at sea. James knew he'd always felt a loyalty to the navy, but England was just a place to him. His true devotion had always been to his shipmates and ship. Then why had he felt such anger when Captain Pelham butchered the men on that sloop? Does one's birthplace determine your loyalty or should it be something greater?

The latch on the cable tier hatch squeaked as it was lifted out of place. James looked up in the dim light to see the access open slowly.

"Cantu!"

The big man smiled and held up his hand signaling the need for quiet. Without a word he motioned James forward.

Once past the hatch, Cantu said quietly, "Follow me."

Carefully the two men moved up the ladders on the larboard side, arriving on a darkened deck.

James saw the thick fog and knew how Cantu had gained access to the ship.

After surveying the deck for any activity, Cantu motioned James to the starboard side where they quietly slipped over the side and made the short jump to the wharf. Quickly, but with care not to attract attention, they crossed the darkened quay toward the guard shack.

Dawn found the group almost ten miles south of the *Warren*. Caitlin had guided them southeast away from the river road in case the rebels sent men after them.

"We can cross the river farther down, but splitting up makes sense in case they send riders to alert the constables in the area."

"Did you learn everything you needed back there," JT asked as they crested a small hill.

"No, I think we should go back," James said with a tone of friendly sarcasm. "Actually I did see enough to tell me they could put to sea within the next several months."

"What's keeping them?"

"They don't have all of their cannon. Also they still need to provision and come up with a full crew. Both of those are harder than it might seem," James answered.

"Why's that?" JT came back, his interest seeming genuine.

"A ship that size needs a great deal of powder and shot. That'll be hard to provide quickly. And they need a crew that can operate an extremely complex vessel. While there are lots of sailors in this area, the experienced hands for the sails and guns are not so plentiful. And then you have to mold the crew into a fighting unit. Any captain would require many days of gun and sail drills before he would want to engage a king's ship."

Later that night they sat around a small fire, deciding to avoid any local inns until they were farther south. A lack of wind or rain had made the night tolerable and Robert had been able to shoot several fat rabbits for an evening stew.

"So this rebel officer was once a friend?" Caitlin asked.

"I like to think we're still friends," James replied.

"But he was going to let you die," Robert said, his tone curious.

"And I would have killed him if our ships met at sea. But that doesn't mean I don't respect him."

"You people are crazy," Robert said and finished his stew.

"I knew Mr. Brown," Cantu added. "He's a good man. But now he's fighting for what he believes is right. Shouldn't every man do that?"

James was struck by the simple logic that his friend offered. Why shouldn't each man fight for what they believe in? Isn't that what JT and I are doing?

"JT, what are you fighting for?"

Justin turned to look at James. "For the king, I guess. And so North Carolina can continue the way it is. What about you?"

James didn't answer, but stared into the fire. *What am I fighting for?*

Caitlin, who'd been listening, now turned to James.

"What are you fighting for?"

"I guess I'd have to give that some thought."

Chapter Twenty-Two

A Question of Loyalty

Splitting into two groups the next morning, they cautiously made their way south and finally rendezvoused at Cambridge before continuing on to Boston. James's escape from the *Warren* apparently had not raised a widespread alarm and they blended into the populace going and coming from the big city. The large number of travelers and bustle of Boston should ensure they wouldn't receive any great notice from the authorities, at least that was their hope.

Approaching Boston, James knew he had to try and see Samantha. Had she received his letters? He hoped that talking with her would help him try and understand what his future might hold or if the two of them might have a future together. And in the back of his mind, the question that he continued to struggle with, what was he really fighting for? If he considered himself a professional sea officer, perhaps he was simply discharging his responsibility and duty. But then how did that make him any different from the German mercenary soldiers now fighting in the colonies. Perhaps it really didn't matter as long as he did his job. Why should he bother with trying to make sense of the politics of the time? He had his orders and that should be all that he needed. But he thought back to his meeting with Lucas Brown. Had he ever felt as passionate as his friend for any cause? And Samantha's own burning fire for her country had always struck him as a bit dramatic.

"You've been here before," JT said as they crossed the narrows from Roxbury. "Where do we go first?"

"The waterfront," James answered. "We find a lodging house where we can mix with the sailors. It shouldn't take us too long to find out what's happening. Most sailors love to brag and a little rum will only make them more talkative."

"Then why are you always the quiet one," Caitlin asked.

Cantu laughed, his deep voice accentuating his humor.

"All you people talk too much," Robert growled. "Spend a winter alone, trapping beaver and talking to yourself. You'll soon learn to keep your mouth shut."

"And I thought you were just naturally unfriendly," Cantu said and laughed again.

Robert looked at his friend and scowled.

One street back from the east wharf, they found lodgings in a reputable inn with the comfortable name of Toby's Tavern. Clean by the standards of where they had been over the last two weeks, the owner turned out to be an old sailor, paid off from a Royal Navy ship almost twenty years before.

Tobias Sims served as cook, barman and bouncer to a continually changing crowd of sailors from the ships in the harbor. From early in the morning until late into the night, a small crowd could be found in the inn's main room eating, drinking and gossiping. The big ex-sailor kept up a lively banter with the customers while drawing ale and tending to his cooking pots. An old black woman named Tinky helped in the kitchen, serving portions of the hearty stew that were always cooking in a big pot over the fire. Tobias also baked a crusty bread which his customers used gratefully to sop up the gravy from their bowls.

James had been able to procure three rooms, sharing his with JT while Cantu and Robert bunked together next door. Caitlin was given a small room at the opposite end of the upper floor.

"So tell me Tobias, how's business this year?"

Putting down two tankards of ale on the table, Sims shook his head. "I get by, people always comin' in for a drink or some stew. Course I gets my provisions from right around here locally and the damned blockade doesn't make it any easier."

"Surely our boys can give the navy the slip?" James asked.

"Sometimes, sure. But it's a dangerous business and if'n they gets caught, I've heard they hang 'em, no questions."

"But that goes against English law," JT said.

"Only law on the Atlantic is cannon and shot in my book."

Later that afternoon, James sought out Tobias, finding him cutting up meat in the back room.

"It strikes me that there's money to be made for anyone who can run the blockade."

"You're right on that, young fella."

"I've spent some time at sea, maybe I should see someone."

Tobias looked up from the bloody cutting board. "Make your fortune, heh?" He grinned.

"Why not?"

"Right you are. Long as you don't get caught and hung, you'll be a rich man."

James said calmly, "I'll willing to take that chance."

The cleaver slammed down, severing a bone joint.

"I believe you are. Tells you what. I'll talk to some of the boys and see if there's anyone taking on hands. Fair enough?"

Sitting in the main room James knew he'd be able to find out what was happening amongst Boston's blockade runners. In particular he hoped to find out if there was some method to evade the blockading ships or was it simply each captain taking his chances. But he also knew that he would be seeing men that would surely end up under the guns of a king's ship at some point. Would they encounter *Challenger* and the burning hatred of Robert Pelham?

Cantu came through the main door from the street and sat down.

"I've seen Miss Samantha."

James felt his stomach tense. What was wrong?

"And?"

A smile broke on Cantu's broad face as he chuckled.

"She's anxious to see you."

James felt his spirits soar.

"I told her you would be around to call within the hour."

"Thanks, my friend."

Cantu nodded.

"I'll show you the way when you're ready."

Walker and Sons was a thirty minute walk from Toby's. James saw little evidence of the war as he made his way through the mid day traffic in the streets. He knew it was potentially dangerous to see Samantha but he was willing to take that chance. Perhaps he was being a fool, but he thought not.

Reaching the chandlery he paused for only a moment before opening the door and stepping inside.

Samantha was standing at the far side of the room, holding a small book, which she slid into a shelf, turning to face him. Her expression was calm, almost serene but her eyes told him that the fire from their last meeting was still there.

"James."

"I've missed you Samantha Walker."

She walked to him, her eyes fixed on his.

"And I you," she said softly, raising her hand to his cheek.

Carefully James took her hand and lightly kissed her fingers.

"I think I love you, dear lady."

Samantha said nothing, but gently kissed James on the cheek.

He took her in his arms and they stood in the empty store for what seemed like an eternity.

"How can you be here?" she finally asked.

"That's not important," James said quietly.

She seemed to accept that answer and led him to a pair of chairs on the far wall.

"I'd heard you were restricted to the ship."

He nodded. "Not my happiest moment, but it was for something I felt strongly about."

"I know," she said quietly.

"You know? How could you know that?"

186

At that moment the door opened.

"He told me," she said as David Addington entered the shop.

James found himself on his feet and confused as his father walked up to him.

Taking his son by the shoulders, David Addington said with obvious pleasure, "It's good to see you, son."

"Father, how?"

"There's time for that later, more to the point, what are you doing here?"

Events were moving in a direction James could have never imagined. His father in Boston, what did that mean?

"Have you left the navy?" his father continued.

James shook his head.

"Then how have you come to be here?"

"I was ordered," James said quietly.

"What? That's absurd. Espionage?"

There was no reason to deny it. He'd never been able to lie to his father. "Checking on rebel shipping."

"My God, James, you shouldn't be here. You're a naval officer not a spy."

A look of alarm spread across Samantha's face.

"Who sent you here," David Addington asked his son, his anger very apparent.

"A major working for General Burgoyne."

"Gentleman Johnny's returning to America?"

James nodded. "Halifax actually."

While distant from active service, David Addington had not disregarded the strategic efforts of either side in the conflict. Now as a member of the Naval Committee he had gained important information. What was the army up to?

"You've placed both of us in grave danger, James."

"I know I'm in danger, but you?"

David Addington sighed. "I'm a member of the Continental Navy Committee. If it became known that I allowed a British spy to escape from Boston, I would be considered a traitor. But I will not allow you to sacrifice yourself for those fools in England."

Hearing his father's words, James felt as if he had been slapped in the face. Lucas Brown and now his own father in service with the rebels.

"I want you to leave the city instantly. You were raised to do your duty at sea, not skulking around back alleys with scum." He put his hand on James shoulder. "When this is over, we'll see each other in peace. But until that day, you must be leave Boston and quickly."

When he first left his father to join *Andromeda*, James had felt empty. Now his heart felt like ice. He looked at Samantha, her eyes moist with tears. They're both in danger if I remain, he thought. He walked to the door and looked back at them. "I will come back," he said and stepped into the street.

Walking north on the waterfront, James should have been surveying the shipping. But his mind kept going over what had just happened. His father, on the rebel's side. An Admiral of the Red, Knight Commander of the Bath, David Addington had thrown in his lot with this new upstart confederation. James had heard how the leaders would be taken to England and hung for their treason when the war was won. Washington, Adams, Jefferson and now Addington. My God, the world has gone insane? How can these men, how can these people, risk everything simply to govern themselves? It made no sense, he thought, but it bothered him greatly.

"Can I walk with you?"

James turned and looked into the concerned face of Tom Faircloth. Never far from the admiral, the coxswain must know the situation, James thought.

The two men shook hands.

"Have you talked with my father?"

Tom nodded. "Aye."

"I'm in a terrible predicament. But you know that."

"The admiral is rightly concerned. If you're found out, it's a hangman's rope."

"But my father has taken the enemy's side."

Faircloth chuckled.

"He could say the same about you."

James noticed two men in military uniforms coming toward them and directed Tom onto a cross street.

"What do you think?" he asked Faircloth.

"Doesn't matter what I think. What matters is your decision to remain loyal to the king. That's fine by my reckoning. A lot of good men are fighting for England just as there are good men on this side."

"That's what makes this war insane."

Faircloth stopped and looked back at the two men who had passed the intersection without paying them any attention.

"Not just this war, all wars make no sense. But you and I aren't going to change that, my boy. What you need now is to get back to the navy and to sea."

Somehow that sounded very inviting to James. The routine of shipboard life and leaving all of this behind. But that also meant leaving Samantha and his father.

"I don't know what to do," James finally said.

Faircloth put his hand on the young officer's shoulder.

"Don't worry, you'll figure it out."

Chapter Twenty-Three

A Change of Direction

Justin was not to be found when James returned to the inn. Just as well he thought, I need time to think. His world had been truly unsettled by his meeting with Lucas and now his father. Why was he wearing the king's uniform and fighting for the crown? He couldn't answer that question.

Cantu could sense that something was not right with his friend. They had shared a quiet dinner with Robert, but Caitlin was also no where to be found.

All that James had said to Cantu was that it had been good to see Samantha. That has seemed to satisfy him and they finished their meal quietly.

Returning to the inn late, JT found James in the room, lying down but not asleep.

"James, wake up."

"I'm not asleep. Where have you been?"

"Caitlin and I had to see someone."

James sat up, the tone of JT's voice told him something wasn't right.

"Is there a problem?"

The big soldier lit a second candle from the single nub almost out on the window sill.

"Things are not what they seem, James."

Now with his feet on the floor, James watched his friend pace the small room.

"What do you mean?"

JT hesitated.

"You and Cantu need to leave Boston right away. Tonight."

"Why would I want to do that?"

Sitting down opposite James, JT said, "Because if you don't, you'll be arrested."

"How do you know that?"

"Caitlin and I both work for the Continental Army."

The impact of those words could not have been greater if a blow had accompanied them.

"So this is a trap?"

'No," JT answered. "It was originally only a way to get me back from Canada with critical information. When Porritt added you I figured it would be a bonus."

"And what's changed?"

"You've gained only a little knowledge about one ship. But we can't have you uncovering any of the secrets of the blockade runners."

"And you're going to let us simply leave Boston? Why?"

"No one else knows about you and Cantu. Not yet at least."

"What makes you willing to let us go on our way."

Justin smiled slightly. "Because you're a good man, James. Call it respect for one's enemy. I think if all lobster backs were like you, we wouldn't have a war on our hands. I don't want to see you swinging from a gallows because of me."

"And Caitlin, I don't sense she is quite so magnanimous."

"She isn't, generally. But you're family."

"What!" James said.

"After talking with you and Cantu, she realized that your mother was her sister. Caitlin's your aunt."

Two hours later, James and Cantu were in the stable to saddle their horses. As always, Cantu seemed unperturbed by the turn of events. They went about saddling their horses without talking, the animals providing the only noise as they protested their rude awakening at this time of night.

"I have to tell you I'm sorely confused, my friend."

"What can I do to help?" Cantu asked.

"Tell me I should go back to Canada and to my duty."

"You should, if it's the right thing for you."

James finished checking the belly cinch.

"How do I know that?"

Cantu chucked.

"You have to answer the most important question."

"What's that?" James asked.

"What's in your heart?"

"I don't know, damn you," he replied, the frustration obvious.

"Only you can finally decide. Once you've done that, everything will be clear."

"You should be gone by now, you're taking a foolish risk," JT said, rolling over when James entered the room.

"Sometimes you have to do that."

"I don't understand," JT said, now fully awake.

"I remember you said you were fighting for the king to keep things the same."

Justin nodded, "I had to say something."

"And I couldn't really say why I was wearing the king's uniform."

"Right."

"I've been asking myself that question ever since we talked. And it took Cantu to make me realize that I was simply doing what I thought was expected of me by everyone else. When I went aboard my first ship as a boy, no one asked me what I wanted to do. So I became a king's officer because that's what my father decided I should become. But I never thought about why I fought for the king."

"You sound much as I did last year."

"When did you decide to change your loyalty?"

JT rose and lit another candle and sat back on the bed.

"We knew there were rebel soldiers near Louisberg who were ambushing army supply wagons. My colonel volunteered our services to Lord Howe to crush them. But we couldn't find them in the thick forests of the valley. But we found where many of their families lived. When we were done almost fifty people were dead and the town on fire."

James could see the pain still on his friend's face.

"So I decided to do what I could to stop these men who would make war on women and children. That's when I met Caitlin. I didn't know it at the time, but she was already working for Hamilton. It didn't take long before we were working together."

"I watched our captain massacre the crew of a sloop off North Carolina. He kept shooting even when the ship had surrendered. The memory has bothered me ever since. Hell, I'd seen battles at sea, but never anything like that. It made me ashamed to be a king's officer."

"So what now?"

James sat down.

"I found out that my father is not only in Boston, but has joined the rebel cause."

"We prefer to call ourselves continentals."

"Sorry."

"Then you need to meet Colonel Hamilton. He's normally with the army, but they're in winter quarters and he had business in Boston. I'll tell Caitlin to arrange it."

James knew that he was about to make a decision that was irreversible. He also knew that he would be casting his lot in with these strange people who were willing to die for the right to govern themselves.

"Will they take an English officer into their cause? They might still want to hang me."

JT got up and pulled on his over shirt. "I think not."

It was mid morning when Caitlin and Robert returned to the inn. James had not seen her earlier and now looked at her with curiosity. He had thought of his time with her over the last two weeks and now knew he could see his mother in Caitlin. That rebellious nature was very characteristic of Rowena Addington. And both were certainly forthright and not in the least retiring as so many women of the day seemed to be. There was a slight resemblance, but Caitlin's hard life had given her a much harder appearance than his mother.

Taking off her hat and shaking off the water, Caitlin sat down in front of the fire to warm up from her short journey.

She held her hands out toward the flames then rubbed them together briskly.

"So Justin has let you in on our little secret?"

"Would that be your work for the army or our relationship?" James asked, finding it still difficult to talk with her.

"My sister married David Addington several years after I'd left our farm to move to Boston. I was a good deal younger and decided to make my life in Massachusetts."

"But she never mentioned you," James said, relaxing as she began to describe her early life.

Caitlin had always been a wild spirit and when her father had forbidden her to leave home, a terrible fight resulted in a bitter estrangement. Rowena had sided with her father and the family had chosen to isolate Caitlin emotionally and financially. Finding herself in a demanding world that didn't provide much freedom for young women, particularly unmarried young women, she had fallen in with a group of smugglers that worked the northeastern seaboard. Over time she had proven her strength and had been accepted into their dark and shadowy world. She'd heard that Rowena had died, but by then Caitlin considered her family only a memory.

"Your mother was my older sister and we always were close friends. I guess that's why it hurt so much when she sided with father over my decision to leave. But that was a long time ago. Now it seems I do have a family and you're it. The truth be known, you remind me of her."

She looked up as JT handed her a steaming cup of tea.

"I spoke with Hamilton," she said. "He wants to see James before returning to Washington's headquarters."

"Who is Hamilton?" James asked.

"Originally an artillery officer, he's become an aide-de-camp to General Washington. He handles many things for the headquarters including intelligence gathering. A good man. You'll like him."

Alexander Hamilton was staying with a Mr. Thorton who had a neat brick house on the west side of the Commons. JT waited until just after sunset to escort James to see the young officer.

"Mr. Addington, do come in," Hamilton said when a servant showed them into the small parlor.

James was surprised to see a very slight figure in the uniform of the Continental Army. He'd been working on a letter, but now he stood up to offer his hand.

"James, this is Lieutenant Colonel Alexander Hamilton of General Washington's staff," JT offered.

"Please sit down, sir. Captain Thompson, would you please ask Howard to bring us some claret."

In short order, the servant had returned and Hamilton poured glasses for the three of them.

"Now Mr. Addington, exactly what is your status?"

James took a deep breath. "Leftenant, Royal Navy, on detached duty from *Challenger* to General Burgoyne."

"And that duty included gathering information on our shipping?"

"It did."

Hamilton's features remained impassive as he took a sip of wine, then continued, "Captain Thompson tells me that you were afforded an opportunity to return to your forces. While I might question his decision at first examination, it certainly demonstrates your change of loyalty is sincere. I have great respect for Justin. He's provided exceptional service to our country and has earned the discretion which he exercised."

Looking at his friend, James saw that JT looked uncomfortable on hearing Hamilton's compliment.

"It seems a curious assignment for an officer serving at sea to be seconded to a land command, wouldn't you say?"

James replied, "No one was more surprised than I was, I assure you, sir."

Hamilton, a lawyer by trade, responded instantly. "Then why were you singled out for this duty?"

Relating the story of General Burgoyne's voyage to England in *Challenger,* James offered that the interest shown by the general in New York must be at the heart of the matter.

"You grew up in Albany I understand."

Surprised that Hamilton knew his origin, James nodded, noting that he'd not lived there in over six years.

Hamilton turned to JT.

"Are you thinking what I am?"

"Invasion from Canada?"

"Yes, my Carolinian friend. We thought they would stage their forces in Canada for another sea invasion using the fleet to outflank our army. But it appears they want to split our forces. Leave Howe to confront Washington while Burgoyne invades and draws manpower away from New Jersey."

Immediately James understood what Hamilton was proposing. It made complete sense. Divide and conquer. If you have numerical superiority, which the English did, split the inferior force and crush each part separately.

"Damnation," JT said, his drawl accentuating the word.

"And you, Mr. Addington, have perhaps given us the key to beat them at their own game."

Hamilton's words had a strange effect on James. He was now part of this insane cause. Remembering the desperate battle on Breed's Hill, he'd always respected that those men had been willing to die for what they believed. Now he'd joined their ranks.

"But we must take action on this without delay," Hamilton added. "Justin, I want Mr. Addington to accompany us back to Morristown. General Washington will want to consider how this will affect the army. Can you leave tomorrow?"

"We'll be bringing Caitlin with us," JT replied.

Smiling for the first time, Hamilton said, "Then I suspect we won't worry about getting lost. That woman could find her way to Babylon if necessary."

Chapter Twenty-Four

Caught up in the struggle

A break in the winter weather allowed the small group to make good time to New Jersey. Caitlin McKenna saved them several days by guiding them via a route that was not generally used for east to west travelers. On the afternoon of the tenth day after leaving Boston they spotted the rising smoke from the township and encampment of the army. Morristown was a small town with no more than two thousand souls but located in a strategically advantageous position between New York and Philadelphia.

Small snowflakes were just beginning to fall as they dismounted from their horses behind Jacob Arnold's tavern. Hamilton had told them that General Washington was using the building for his headquarters while the army remained bivouacked just on the edge of town.

"Robert, have the stable boys take care of the horses and then join us inside," Hamilton said. "Follow me."

The small group trailed Hamilton around to the front of the two story building. Several guards stood on the porch, muskets at their sides. Recognizing Hamilton they nodded as he opened the front door. They all followed him into the tavern's great room, grateful for the warmth after the day's ride.

Perhaps twenty men were standing or sitting around the room, most within ten feet of the fire. James could see all of them wore some type of uniform or at least had a piece of uniform apparel as part of their dress. Hamilton, with the exception of his muddy boots, wore a complete uniform of the Continental Army, his blue coat and white breeches very proper for the headquarters.

"Hamilton, bless me you look frozen, come here by the fire before you catch your death."

"Wait here," he said to the group and approached the fire place. "Colonel Tilghman, it's good to see you. And I confess, my bones are starting to creak from the cold."

"Didn't think we'd see you for at least another month, did you complete your business?" Tilghman was a tall man of six feet, his frame solid like a blacksmith's.

"Events compelled my return earlier than I would've anticipated. But I'm sure the general will concur that the journey was justified."

Tilghman smiled. "Well you're in luck. He's just finishing a meeting with Mr. Lawlor and you'll be able to pay your respects momentarily."

Thirty minutes later James, Justin and Caitlin were ushered into the back dining room which George Washington used as his office. Sitting at a simple table, the general looked up as they entered.

"General Washington, this is James Addington. You've met Captain Thompson and Miss McKenna."

Washington motioned to chairs.

"Colonel Hamilton has relayed the substance of his conversation with you which prompted his return to this headquarters. If what he believes is in fact true, we might be able to gain great advantage for our cause."

James considered the general as he spoke. He was indeed as large as was rumored. But what struck him was the earnestness of the man. He wasn't the bombastic or domineering leader which James had so often encountered aboard ship. He knew the general had been active in the war with the French and then returned to his farm in Virginia. Now this man was risking everything for an idea.

"The British Army seems to be preoccupied with seizing territory almost to a fault," Washington continued. "But I remain convinced that the area of our new country is simply too large to hold with any permanence. King George has neither the soldiers nor the money to even attempt to seize and hold our main cities. But if Burgoyne has returned to Canada and he's inquiring about New York and the lakes region, then he must be contemplating a march south into New England."

The general traced a line across the large map on his table.

"Of course this could all be a clever plan to deceive us, wouldn't you agree Colonel Hamilton?"

The small man looked at James and smiled.

"Certainly a well conceived and reasonable plan I'd say, sir. But yes, I see how the enemy would see an expected invasion from Canada as a reason to split your forces and opening up an opportunity for them."

"What say you, Mr. Addington?"

James found himself momentarily flustered as the general's stare fixed on him like a musket barrel.

"Sir, you have me at a disadvantage. All I can offer is what I know to be true. If you want assurances of my intentions, I would certainly offer them. But that is all they'd be, words with no way to prove or disprove their veracity."

For the first time, the general seemed to brighten.

"Well said, sir." He paused then fixed his eyes on James. "I understand your father is a member of the Naval Committee?"

The change of direction surprised James.

"Yes, sir, he is."

"So there is at least some reason for your change of heart, wouldn't you say?"

James didn't hesitate. "General Washington, my father had no bearing on my decision other than providing a degree of reinforcement. No, sir, it was when asked what I fought for, I realized I couldn't answer with any strength of feeling. Only after reflecting on what I'd seen in this war so far did I decide that men do indeed have a right to determine their own future. What men have built in this land should not be controlled at the whim of men in Parliament who've never set foot on the continent."

The tall man leaned back in his chair.

"What is the penalty for desertion in the Royal Navy?"

James answered quietly, "Death, according to the Articles of War."

"And you freely take it upon yourself to desert your service?" Washington's tone was almost frigid.

Perhaps the general thought that any man who could betray his duty was not trustworthy.

"Sir, I consider myself resigned from the service. There is a difference." James had not intended his tone to be so sharp, but he felt that what he was doing did have honor. Certainly Washington could understand that?

Washington said nothing for a moment then said, "If our cause fails, I am certain I shall pay with my life. Perhaps I will fall in battle in any case. Are you willing to take active service for this country? If captured you would most certainly not be accorded prisoner of war status. I suspect you would find yourself at the end of a hangman's rope."

James found the general's sincerity in such a valiant cause heartening.

"General Washington, it is rumored throughout the fleet that if we lose, you will be taken to London to hang.........I will be in good company."

Washington smiled, the lines around his mouth showing the deep creases of exhaustion. He stood up slowly, his frame extending to a full six feet, three inches. "Let us endeavor to ensure that doesn't occur." The general extended his hand to James. "Colonel Hamilton, please find our visitors something to eat and drink. I must attend to a pressing matter."

It was later that day when James and Justin were summoned back to the general's office. When they arrived, Alexander Hamilton stood behind Washington who remained sitting at his desk.

"Do sit down, gentlemen," Hamilton said.

"The survival of this army will determine the success or failure of our cause. If a force is to attack from the north, I must be able to take action to defeat that force. Finding out English intentions is imperative. I need you to return to Canada and discover their plans."

Washington's word hit James like a full broadside. He was being asked to continue as a spy, now for the colonials. He remembered the name Nathan Hale.

"There are some on my staff who feel I'm foolish for offering you the opportunity to return north. If you are indeed an agent for the British, you'll return with information which would aid them to defeat us. But I trust my judgment and that of Captain Thompson. In point of fact, he has volunteered to go with you."

James swallowed to clear his throat and said, "When I left Halifax, sir, I understood I would be returning to

General Burgoyne's staff upon completion of this mission. I believe it would be quite possible to discover their intentions."

Washington's eyes met James. Both men knew what had been offered and accepted. The risks and potential reward were pointedly obvious. These were events upon which battles and wars were decided. A venture worth risking one's life for.

"Let us drink to your success, sir. Also, you will be commissioned as a captain in this army. I fear that status will offer no great protection, but will give legitimacy to your actions for history's sake. Your rank and status will remain a secret between the four of us until you return from Canada. The fewer who know of your conversion, the better for everyone, wouldn't you agree?"

Hamilton poured glasses of claret and handed them around.

James thought of Samantha and his father, both under the impression that he had returned to service with their enemy but also committed to a reunion when the war ended. Caitlin and Cantu would have to know they returned north on a mission of deceit, but she was family which would stand him in good stead and faithful Cantu would stand by him even if enlisted by Satan against the Lord.

"Agreed, general. Until we return." He raised his glass and glanced at JT. The tall cavalryman nodded slightly but the message was clear...we will return.

"What do you propose for the journey north?" James asked JT as they walked down the busy street toward a boarding house that Hamilton had recommended.

"It will take two weeks to make Portland. From there another two weeks to Halifax," JT answered. "Caitlin, will the weather hold?"

"It should," she replied, her manner abrupt since learning of the turn of events.

"We could go by ship from Portland, that would save time," James offered.

"Too dangerous, if you ask me," JT said. "Passage from Portland to a British port would raise too many questions, to say nothing of finding a captain willing to do it."

"You wouldn't be trying to avoid a pleasant ocean passage, pray tell?"

JT glared at James, then grinned.

"Man was not intended to sail out of sight of land. I am simply trying to use common sense."

James laughed. His apprehension over spying on the army was muted somewhat by the knowledge that JT would be with him.

Chapter Twenty-Five

A dirty business

A journey of six weeks was required to reach Major Porritt who had traveled to Quebec to meet General Burgoyne. Robert rejoined the group after traveling to the cabin at Lake Massabesic to meet with a man who was willing to sell information to the army.

They'd been fortunate to encounter a British column as they crossed over the border and had learned of the growing forces in the west. A Colonel McGowan knew Major Porritt and had told James that Porritt had left Halifax three weeks prior.

As they traveled west, Robert's knowledge of the country replaced Caitlin's expertise farther south. Several storms had blown through the region which gave the former trapper an opportunity to demonstrate how to survive in the Canadian winter. While Cantu had never expressed any love for the cold and frigid climate, he appeared to be comfortable going about his daily tasks.

The potential power which might be unleashed on the continentals became very clear when they reached Quebec. Passing through the regimental bivouac areas, James realized that Burgoyne was building a powerful force which included artillery and cavalry. He remembered the ill-fed and poorly equipped soldiers he'd seen in Morristown and didn't feel confident in any potential outcome of battle.

"The major will see you now."

Nodding to the skinny corporal who manned a small desk outside Porritt's office, James entered, followed by JT.

The change from their first encounter with the major was startling. Gone were his rough civilian clothes, replaced by an impeccable uniform of a king's officer. His red wool coat with its white facings lay across a chair, but the rest of his uniform had every indication of being freshly laundered and perfectly adjusted.

"Ah, our wandering souls return." Porritt stood and offered his hand to James and Justin. "Please have a seat."

"Thank you, sir."

The major poured three glasses of wine, setting one in front of each of his visitors.

"You look none the worse for your winter journey," he said with a friendly tone.

"On the whole I prefer to travel by ship, sir." James tried to sound relaxed but knew he was nervous.

Porritt laughed. "Quite right, I'm sure. Never took to the ocean myself, too damned unstable."

"At least we were spared the trip to Halifax," JT offered.

"Ah yes, I knew there was no way to communicate our move. I'm very glad it worked out well. Now to more pressing matters, what did you discover?"

For the next thirty minutes, the two men, primarily James, passed on their observations and information on the frigate *Warren* and the colonial shipping system. A great deal of the information was accurate, but entirely useless for achieving any advantage of arms. Porritt took notes, asked questions and seemed satisfied.

"We were also able to get to Morristown," JT said. "We saw what the rebels call an army."

JT now lead the conversation, describing the army's condition with a degree of embellishment from the real situation.

"So you saw both artillery and cavalry?" Porritt asked with a hint of surprise in his voice.

"Yes, sir. The horses looked healthy for the time of year and weather, perhaps they're new mounts from the south.

"Possibly," Porritt responded almost absentmindedly.

"We saw at least a dozen cannon, mostly three and six pounders."

The major seemed lost in thought, then quickly stood up.

"I had a new assignment for you both," he said. "Now it is even more critical. I need to know where those forces are headed."

This was not what James wanted to hear, but he fought the urge to protest.

"Also, General Burgoyne is aware of your return to the army and wants to see you straight away. Is there anything preventing you from leaving immediately?"

"I can think of nothing, sir," JT answered.

James wondered how they could get answers for General Washington in this current situation?

The next morning the two officers waited for over two hours before an aide-de-camp showed them into the general's large office in State House. The headquarters seemed to be alive with soldiers going about their business with certain purpose. The level of activity might be their first indication that something was in the offing.

James felt oddly calm as he waited to see Burgoyne. He remembered the pleasant and casual conversation that last day before reaching England. The man certainly was friendly enough, for a general. But then he was also a politician and didn't all politicians seduce people with their words?

He was not disappointed. John Burgoyne greeted him like a long lost comrade. His warm reception for JT made them both feel as though they were part of his personal staff.

"What was the attitude of the rebels?"

James asked, "How so, general?"

"Did they seem in the fight, as it were? Ready to smash on regardless of the price?"

Caution rose in James's mind. Be careful how you answer. "I heard no great enthusiasm, but then there was little complaining either."

"We found some shortages," JT added. "But nothing that seemed to affect the population in any great way."

"That is the key, gentlemen. We can make assaults on the periphery, in fact occupy key locations. But as long as the rebels can move unfettered within their borders, we can't bring enough pressure to bear. That is what I intend to remedy."

Burgoyne opened a map case and pulled out a large rolled parchment chart.

"Here," he said, unrolling the map.

James and JT rose and approached his desk.

"The key is the Hudson valley. If we can move down Lake Champlain, take Ticonderoga and then push south past Albany, the colonials will be split open like a suckling pig."

"Is your objective Albany?"

Burgoyne shook his head.

"Not in the main. I'm more concerned with removing the rebels from Ticonderoga and the valley. Putting a British force in that area will prevent flow of men and supplies which now are allowing Washington to survive. And if the navy can squeeze the flow in the south, he will soon lose his ability to field an army."

The men looked down at the chart, each considering the possibilities and hazards.

"That is where you come in," Burgoyne went on. "I must know the disposition of the rebels. While their occupation of Ticonderoga is certain, what other forces are in the area? Our native scouts are not always reliable and simply do not understand the subtle indications of a modern army."

"If I might ask, sir, from what tribe do your scouts belong?"

Burgoyne looked surprised then pleased.

"Very astute question, Mr. Thompson. They are Oneida. We've established a strong relationship with Shelitta the strongest chieftain in the valley. Are you familiar with these tribes?"

Justin nodded. "A number of our scouts were Oneida. I found them to be reliable, but I'm not convinced of their ultimate loyalty to the crown."

The general chuckled.

"Your opinion is in direct opposition to Governor General Carlton. But I'm sure you're quite aware of that?"

"No, sir. I can only tell you what I've seen."

James had always found the native tribes interesting, but he also never felt quite safe around them. The history of the last war with the French had been rife with stories of treachery. But that was years ago, perhaps they had changed.

"I expect to commence my move south within two months. By that time I need you to find out all you possibly can of the rebel strength and disposition south of the Lake

Champlain. Major Porritt tells me you have a local travelling with you that is well capable of guiding you in that area."

"Quite correct, general. She has always proved very reliable."

"She?"

Justin continued, "Yes, sir. She grew up in the valley and has spent years in the area," he paused trying to think of an appropriate word to describe smuggling, "uh, trading."

Burgoyne grinned.

"These colonial women, my God but they're a different breed."

Later that afternoon, James and JT met with Major Porritt, who outlined the move south by the general. It had been decided that there would be two groups. Burgoyne would lead the main group while Colonel St. Leger would take a smaller force and proceed down the Mohawk River from Oswego. The first march south would occur in two weeks time.

Burgoyne's journey, while tedious, should present no significant obstacles until they came upon Fort Ticonderoga. The general hoped that the arrival of such an overwhelming force would result in a quick capitulation by the fort's garrison. With that fortress in British hands, they would then strike out for the Hudson River valley. The location of any rebel forces and loyalty of the Indians were two unknowns that could threaten the success of that move.

It was up to James and JT to travel south and determine the disposition of any opposing force. They were then to travel north and meet Burgoyne in the vicinity of Ticonderoga. Porritt did not say if there were other scouts with the same assignment.

"Well that summarizes your task, gentlemen. Any questions?"

The two officers continued to examine the chart, but raised no issues.

"Very good. I want you on your way today. Be back to Ticonderoga no later than the middle of July. Clear?"

"Quite clear, sir," JT answered.

Major Richard Porritt seldom ventured into the area of the city known as the "belly." But tonight he knew he would endure vile smells and a parade of the unwashed of Quebec. Tonight he was buying insurance.

The lack of street lighting made his journey more difficult, but several shillings bought him directions to Andre's and he found the building in little more than twenty minutes. Two lanterns burned on each side of the single door. Down the street the figure of a man lay on his side on the raised walkway, probably the result of heavy drinking in one of the many public rooms in this part of the old city.

Inside, the light of a small fire was augmented by candles on each of the four tables that stood against the wall. Looking around quickly, Porritt saw there were only two other men in the room in addition to the proprietor. But he relaxed when he saw the familiar figure of the man farthest from the door. He walked over to the table and sat down.

"Right on time," Robert said as he took a drink from the wooden mug in front of him. The single candle flickered and threw a pale light on the man's rugged face.

"I don't know how you can stay in these places," Porritt said, his voice harsher than he intended. The unpleasant journey coupled with his knowledge of the danger at night in this part of Quebec made him testy.

"Because you don't pay me enough money to do your dirty work," Robert said. "Besides, the ale is cheap and so are the women." He chuckled to himself and took another drink.

"To our business. What can you tell me?"

"Nothing yet. All the woman said was be ready to leave tomorrow."

A skinny man with dirty shoulder length hair and a pock-marked face walked up to the table. "You want anything?"

His tone told the major that the man didn't care either way. Porritt realized he could smell the man's odor, a mixture of sweat and smoke.

"No."

Robert spoke up, "Another for me."

The man turned wordlessly and returned to the counter.

"She didn't say where you were going?"

Shaking his head, Robert said, "Down the Hudson Valley, that's all."

She could be lying, the major thought. But they had to take a chance.

"All right, then. You know what I require. Watch them closely. I trust them, but I can't take any chances. If you see anything wrong, get the information back to me and you'll be rewarded handsomely."

Robert looked up from his drink, the anger clear in his eyes.

"I'll take your money, major. But don't ever think I'm doing this for the money."

Porritt remembered that terrible night almost ten years before. His voice softened. "That's why I trust you."

"And what makes you think those two could be a problem?" Robert asked as he drained his cup.

"That's not anything for you to be concerned about, just do your job."

Caitlin led them out of Quebec the next morning. The busy preparations by the army were evident as the small band made its way toward the post road. There was little talk among them despite the clear skies and arrival of spring in Canada.

James rode behind Caitlin, but his mind was totally focused on the conversation from early that morning. He knew he must think out all the aspects of what was now becoming a very clouded situation.

He would never forget the simple statement by Robert when he returned to the lodging house in the early hours.

"They suspect you."

The looks of surprise were replaced by concern as Robert related his conversation with Porritt.

"Must have something to do with Morristown. I'm to stay close and report back to him if I see anything suspicious."

They were stunned. How had anyone identified who they were unless that person was privy to the business of Washington's staff? They must get word back to Hamilton and carry news of Burgoyne's plan. But if they arrived back at the headquarters without knowing who was the spy, the British would know their plans had been compromised. And what other British spies were working among the senior officers of the Continental Army?

That evening they made camp near the post road, hidden in a thick stand of birch trees. After a short dinner of bread and cheese, they sat around the small fire talking.

"It appears that Carlton has decided to support Burgoyne's march," Justin said.

"What makes you think that," Caitlin asked.

"Did you see all of the new carts and wagons that lined the streets today?"

She nodded.

"Newly made. The army brought a large number of horses, but no wagons or carts. Word around the streets is that Carlton ordered two hundred built for the army."

"Why so many?" Cantu asked.

"They must be planning to carry a lot of supplies south."

Robert shook his head. "But the area south of Ticonderoga is dense forest. They'll never get wagons through there."

"We have to get word to Washington," JT said. "Without letting Burgoyne or Porritt know their plan has been compromised."

"How do you intend to do that?" Caitlin asked.

"Why not go directly to Schuyler?"

They all looked at James.

Caitlin nodded. "Why not, indeed."

Chapter Twenty-Six

The tide begins to turn

Captain Mordecai Stone led the small party past two sentries who stood to each side of the large canvas tent. Commander of a company in the New York militia, he felt it was his responsibility to take these strangers to see the general. Not trusting the men who claimed to be from General Washington, he detailed a dozen of his men to accompany them. The militia troops were armed with an odd assortment of weapons, including the British Brown Bess musket. But there was no mistaking their seriousness as they carried their rifles at the ready.

"These men are looking for the general," Stone told the young officer who stood just inside the tent flap.

"The general is quite busy," the man said, his tone slightly imperious. "What's your business?" he asked JT.

"A message from General Washington," the tall man replied, not much liking this officious little pip.

"I'll take it," the officer said dismissively.

"It's extremely critical we see General Schuyler as soon as possible," James interjected.

"What is the blazes is going on out there, Miller?"

The voice from within the tent was deep and clearly belonged to a man that was agitated.

"These men claim they have word from General Washington, sir."

"General Schuyler, it is imperative we talk with you," JT said with an authoritative tone.

General Phillip Schuyler appeared at the tent's entrance, his appearance that of a man who has been disturbed from an afternoon nap.

"Very well, come in," Schuyler said, returning to the dark interior of the tent.

The general had a long patrician face, but his language gave no such indication.

"God's teeth, Miller, where's the bloody wine?" he hollered as he sat heavily in the single camp stool.

Only JT and James had entered the tent and they now stood to each side of the entrance watching the now frantic lieutenant enter with a dark green bottle, which he set down next to Schuyler.

"You can stand or sit down, your choice," the general said, his attention focused on pouring wine into a single worn cup.

James looked at JT then spoke, "General, we're on duty with General Washington."

Schuyler took a drink and looked up.

"So I have deduced, young man. Now tell me who you are and what you have to tell me."

"Left…Captain James Addington and Captain Justin Thompson, sir."

The general narrowed his eyes, "Not sure of your rank, sir?"

"Recently promoted, sir," JT said quickly.

"If you say so. Well, get on with it."

James felt his anger rise and decided he didn't care what this popinjay thought about him. "Three weeks ago we were in Quebec City."

Schuyler looked up, his look of surprise quite evident along with a degree of confusion.

"And according to General Burgoyne, he was preparing to move his army south toward Ticonderoga and then down the Hudson Valley."

Enjoying the general's quandary, James preempted JT and continued. "We thought you might like our assistance."

"You say those are Burgoyne's intensions. What proof have you?" The general's tone had changed from one of bored skepticism to intense interest.

"He told us as much," JT added. "And we saw an army preparing to march with perhaps six thousand men and two hundred wagons."

"Good Christ! And I'm to meet them with what?" Schuyler paused for a moment, his mind digesting the news of invasion. "You say you work for General Washington?"

"Yes, sir, we do."

"And he knows of this?" the general asked, now mildly agitated.

James shook his head.

"Sir, time is critical and we felt that coming directly to you was prudent in view of the imminent move south by Burgoyne."

"Let me gather my regimental commanders and you'll relay your information to them. Perhaps we'll have a surprise for Gentleman Johnny."

Caitlin had argued when JT told her to find General Washington and tell him what was happening. Having broken camp at Morristown, the main army was moving north in preparation for renewing its campaign against Howe. She understood how important their information was, but didn't want to leave JT.

"I can't have Porritt questioning Robert," he told her. "The man is smart and we can't continue this ruse for long. We have our orders from Schuyler and that's what we must do."

Caitlin knew he was right, but still rebelled at leaving his side.

"You have to find Burgoyne in that mass of wilderness. Robert knows that area well. Without him you might waste weeks trying to find the British."

"We know they intended to move down Lake Champlain and then south toward Ticonderoga."

She remained silent, knowing he would not be deterred from his plan.

As Schuyler's army began to prepare for battle, two small groups left the headquarters, one moving north, the other west.

"I will get this news to the general right away."

"JT and James have headed north to find Burgoyne to lure him toward a trap that Schuyler intends to set south of Ticonderoga."

Alexander Hamilton sighed.

Meeting in a small grove of trees over a mile from the headquarters, Robert had been able to get Hamilton away from the crowd around Washington to prevent any possible compromise of her message.

"Then you'll have to go after them. Our agent confirmed that the British are onto them and will arrest the two on sight."

She knew how futile it would be to try and reach them before they might walk into a trap set by Major Porritt. But she had to try.

Fort Ticonderoga commanded the key passage at the southern end of Lake Champlain which entered into the Hudson Valley. Captured in a surprise attack by Benedict Arnold in May 1775, the garrison had been expected to be able to withstand even the most spirited attack by British forces. What they had not expected was a very determined John Burgoyne who was able to emplace an artillery battery above the fort which rendered the bastion indefensible. On July 5th, the defenders abandoned the fort and escaped south. When word of the loss of Ticonderoga reached Congress, furious law makers replaced General Schuyler with Horatio Gates, who left immediately for New York.

James leaned his head back against the rough wheel of the wagon, the beads of sweat rolling down the small of his back. The heat only added to his sense of failure and futility. Mud covered his boots and breeches, the result of days of struggling through the morass of forest the army was fighting its way through. Insect bites covered his face and hands, the mud he smeared on them barely deterring the attack of the ravenous mosquitoes.

He kept remembering the look of contempt on Porritt's face as he had related the story which General Schuyler had crafted to draw Burgoyne's army into a trap. Barely finished, James had looked with astonishment at the pistol the major had leveled at his chest.

"You disgust me, sir. If not for General Burgoyne's desire to make an example of you, I'd shoot you now."

Immediately pinioned by two red-coated soldiers, he had been manacled and shackled since. Chained to a wagon during the day, he'd walked along as the army slowly made its way south from Ticonderoga.

On the second day after his capture, he had been taken before Burgoyne at the end of the day's march. The general's anger was obvious and his desire to see James Addington hung from the mast of a king's ship in New York harbor absolute.

"You are a spy and traitor, Addington. A son of an admiral, no less. I know a little of the navy and you certainly warrant a flogging around the fleet. The jack tars would love to see a leftenant on the gratings, trust me of that."

The only solace to James was that JT had taken ill and Cantu had remained behind to take care of him while James rode ahead. But that had been two weeks prior. Where were his friends now? He could only hope they had learned of his arrest and returned to Schuyler's camp with news of the British march south. It's strange, James thought, I began my naval career with a journey to New York City. Now this march south will truly be the end of my journey. He thought of Samantha and of what would never be. But he couldn't have any regrets, he'd done what he knew was right. Now he would have to face the consequences. He remembered Lucas Brown's tale of Nathan Hale and wondered if he would be as brave when the time came?

Justin Thompson lay on the bed of ferns that Cantu had built when they had first stopped in the clearing. The two blankets over him were just enough to hold off the early morning chill, despite the crackling fire only five feet away from his lean-to. Only now did he truly believe he would survive to leave this wilderness. While he could remember the long and terrible day prior to stopping here, the time before that was a blur of images and recollections by Cantu. Never had he felt as sick and helpless. He wouldn't have ever believed a man in his prime could be so weak and incapable of helping himself.

"You look better today," Cantu said as he knelt down with some warmed water for JT.

Taking a sip, he lay back on bed. "I think I do feel like I'm better."

"Fevers like yours take much time to overcome. It can't be rushed."

"But it's been ten days, you tell me, since I fell sick and James left to find the army." JT frowned, his head still aching. "Why hasn't he come back?"

Cantu was silent, he didn't like to think that something had gone very wrong.

"You should go find him," JT continued. "I can take care of myself now."

The big negro smiled at him. "Maybe tomorrow, if you can stand."

"Then today I will eat and drink and rest. Tomorrow you must be on your way and find out what happened."

Again the big man smiled but inside he was very concerned for his friend James. He would have returned as soon as possible having seen how ill JT had been. Something must be wrong.

And so they passed the day which warmed to a pleasant temperature in the shaded woods.

"On your feet," Sergeant John Rial ordered James as he kicked him hard in the side, spit flying from his mouth as the bellowed out his order.

Struggling to his feet, for a moment James felt dizzy but was able to hold himself upright by bracing on the wagon.

Rial was a beefy man and sweat was already showed through his heavy redcoat. In need of a shave, he put his florid face three inches from James.

"Another day closer to the hangman, ain't that right?" He turned to the skinny private leaning on his musket next to the wagon. "Foreman, keep him moving or I'll have you up on charges," Rial barked as he hit the private with a polished maple stick.

"I know, sergeant."

Rial turned and strode off toward the head of the column, his maple walking stick resembling a commissioned officer's swagger stick.

James took a deep breath as the private propped his weapon against the wagon and reached over the rearboard to grab a small chain with a slip link.

In a drill that had been repeated each day for the last week and a half, the private fastened the chain to James's manacles.

216

Quietly the young soldier said, "I'll get you some water once we start moving."

"Thank you."

Walking off, the private muttered, "Filthy bastard sergeant, he didn't have 'ta bleedin' hit me."

Cantu knelt down at the small stream and began filling the water bags. They'd been lucky to be so close to fresh water when JT had fallen ill. He had just topped off the first bag when he thought he heard something moving in the thick underbrush on the far side of the stream. Reaching down, he felt the reassuring shape of his pistol which he had freshly loaded and primed only this morning. Probably an animal, he thought and went back to filling the second bag while still paying attention across the stream.

"You'd be a long way from home," a voice said.

Standing up abruptly, Cantu pulled out his pistol, then checked himself realizing the voice belonged to Robert. He watched his friend push through the foliage.

"You're a tough man to find," Robert said as he waded across the stream, stepping on the bank and taking Cantu's offered hand.

"I'm glad you found us, I need your help."

Robert looked at his friend.

"What's wrong?"

"James has gone missing and Justin is just recovering from the fever."

Knowing what Caitlin had said about the British knowing about James and JT he realized the worst must have occurred.

"Where's Miss Caitlin?"

"Should be three miles northwest. We spread out trying to catch some sign of you. She and I will meet just before sundown.

Progress by Burgoyne's army had been painfully slow. Several small battles between the advance companies and the continental troops fleeing Ticonderoga had been inconsequential. However the farther they tried to move south, it became clear the rebels were intent on slowing their progress. The few bridges in the area had been destroyed and in many areas the trail was blocked by fallen trees.

James had been put to work chopping and clearing these trees and under the watchful eye of Sergeant Rial, he labored in the oppressive heat of late summer.

"Not used to doing a real days work, are we, Addington?" Rial sat on a fallen tree watching James chop another tree to facilitate removal from the road. The ever present Private Foreman stood guard, his musket and bayonet ready if needed.

James's hands were bloody with broken blisters and calluses mixed with filth from the pine tar and sap. Bringing the axe down one last time, the tree broke into two pieces.

"Come on, now. Get a line on those and pull them off to the side," Rial growled as he cracked his walking stick across James's back raising a bloody welt.

James glared at Rial, his anger rising as his thirst raged.

"You'll get more than that if you don't get this tree moving," the sergeant yelled.

Wondering if he could reach the sergeant to deliver a fatal axe blow before the private shot or bayoneted him, James suddenly he knew what he would do. Burgoyne's reference to flogging around the fleet had made its point. Rowed from ship to ship, flogged at each, most men died on the grating after a hundred lashes. For anyone who survived, the hangman's noose would await. While James had only seen it once, he now decided he would not take the chance that Admiral Howe would break with tradition and allow an officer to suffer the cruel and humiliating punishment. And he would kill Rial in the process. Suddenly he felt better and pulled one half of the small tree to the side of the road. Yes, very much better.

"At first light we find the army. Then we follow until we can find James." Justin sat with his back against a tree, the flames of the small fire illuminating his determined face.

Caitlin knelt next to him, having smoothed a patch of ground next to the fire.

"Robert knows this area well. The British must travel through two valleys if their destination is Albany. But where they are now? He thinks we should move northeast to the Shining River, which they will pass through last. It's about one day's ride from here."

"Because they have wagons, they have no choice but to pass there," Robert added.

"But how do we find out if James is with them?" Cantu asked.

JT knew of British drumhead justice, they might very well have already executed James.

"We'll find a way," he said, not sure he believed it himself.

If he is there, Cantu thought, I will find him.

Chapter Twenty-Seven

The Bond of Friendship

Hoping that Sergeant Rial would remain occupied, James held a piece of hardtack in the small cup of water that Private Foreman had given him. Sitting in the dirt next to his wagon, he waited a full minute for the biscuit to soften enough to make it chewable. James knew he must eat something if he was to have the energy to attack Rial the next day. His mind made up, he would wait for the sergeant to close within the range of an ax blow. He knew that surprise would allow him two maybe three blows before anyone could shoot or bayonet him. Would the young Private Foreman be able to kill him after becoming friendly? Perhaps it would be possible to disarm the private and seize his musket.

"Don't let me disturb your evening repast."

James looked up to see Major Porritt, looking quite presentable for having spent two weeks on a wilderness march.

While he would have expected Sergeant Rial to kick his food away, James knew that a gentleman like Porritt would never think of doing something so uncouth.

"I thought I would inquire how you are enjoying your journey."

The smirk on the major's face infuriated James but for now he knew he must keep eating for strength.

"Quite marvelous," James said after swallowing. "Exercise and fresh air, couldn't be any better I daresay."

His expression hardening to James sarcasm, Porritt stood over James and crossed his arms.

"You will hang in New York, of that be sure. But if you would consider providing me with some information, the general is willing to intercede on your behalf to prevent a flogging around the fleet."

James looked up at Porritt, wondering how he could wear his coat in this heat. "Everything has a price, doesn't it?"

"Don't be a fool, Addington. Tell me what I want to know and you can die like a gentleman, not some common sailor."

"I happen to respect the common sailor, something your type wouldn't understand."

"Ah, the romantic if ever I heard one. Please spare me the theatrics. I'm offering you a chance to at least die with dignity, not that you deserve it."

I will not give him the satisfaction, James told himself, more to strengthen his own resolve.

"What you ask is quite impossible, major," James said, trying his best to sound dismissive.

Porritt looked at him with a malevolent stare, turning to leave but then stopping long enough to say, "I hope my schedule allows me to witness your trip around the harbor, it should be quite entertaining."

James's hunger seemed to disappear and he sat back against the wagon wheel.

Once the army had been located, the small group worked its way to the northeast on the northern slope of the Shining River Valley. The trapper's experience around the British regiments made the final argument for who would try to locate James.

JT knew he was still weak and wanted to save his strength for whatever was needed to rescue his friend.

"I must go with you," Cantu said, his voice insistent.

Turning to the big man he put his hand on Cantu's arm.

"If he's there, I'll find him. Trust me, my friend."

To Cantu, James Addington had become more than a friend. The young man was his partner and companion, his only true friend on the entire continent, although he did feel a strong bond with Robert.

"He's right," Caitlin added. "He can blend in and move throughout the camp. You might be recognized."

Cantu knew she was referring to the color of his skin. While there were negros throughout the colonies, in Canada or with the army it was rare.

"What can I do?"

Robert grinned. "If I'm not back by morning, come find me."

Of course, Cantu thought. Of course I will.

The trapper laughed.

"Until later."

It had been a fitful night around the small fire, each person taking a one hour watch to tend the fire and watch for danger. But the night had passed quietly.

Only an hour before the sunrise, Robert walked quietly into the camp and saw Cantu standing at the fire.

"Did you find him?"

Robert nodded.

"Is there anything hot to drink?"

Cantu poured a cup of hot tea into one of the communal cups and called to JT and Caitlin.

Pausing to drink half of the warming tea, Robert immediately launched into his report.

"He's alive and under guard. A shackle binds him to a wagon that's in the middle of a column of maybe a hundred wagons. There are redcoats everywhere."

By now several pieces of wood had been tossed on the fire and the four of them stood in a circle, the light reflecting off their concerned faces.

"Can we get close?" JT asked.

Robert nodded while finishing his tea.

"The forest is thick and it will be dark."

"Guards?" Caitlin asked.

"There were soldiers all around."

They knew that whoever was in their way must die and quietly.

"Then tomorrow night it is," JT said, his tone deadly. "Cantu, you stay here with Caitlin. The fewer of us, the less chance of being seen."

"No, I will go after him."

"Christ, man," JT said, the anger apparent. "I understand how the army works and Robert has been there. We'll get him back."

Cantu said nothing as he poked the fire with a stick.

It had been strange, James thought as he swung the axe almost automatically. When he awoke this morning, his first thought had been that he would never wake up again in this life. Lying quietly looking up at the lightening sky the thought had increased his resolve. He would not go quietly to the gallows nor become a spectacle.

The column had stopped only an hour after the march commenced, a burned bridge over a steep creek delaying the advance indefinitely. James had been put to work cutting down trees for the engineers to patch together into a temporary bridge. Late summer heat and insects made the work unpleasant but James was oblivious. He was waiting for Sergeant Rial.

A drummer boy came through the undergrowth, several wooden canteens slung over his shoulder. The skinny youth wore a thin jerkin stained by dirt and tree sap.

Private Foreman, who had been watching the larger group while guarding James, called to the boy.

"It's about bleedin' time, get over here."

"The sergeant just let me go, honest," the boy protested.

"A likely story," Foreman said, pulling the cork from one of the canteens and drinking deeply. "That's right good, doesn't taste like mud for a change."

"I took it from the bank where the horses can't get to," the young man said grinning, "All water and no horse piss."

"All right, pass 'em out and be quick about it."

The men laid their axes down and eagerly took the offered water.

"Ten minutes, no more," Foreman called and sat down on a recently downed tree.

While he took a drink, James looked through the trees trying to catch a glimpse of Rial. Just my luck, he thought, the son of a bitch was sent off somewhere.

Later in the afternoon, after the engineers directed where the felled trees should be dragged, James's group worked four teams of horses to drag the limbed timber to the edge of the stream. A steep bank made the work hard and it was almost sunset when the major overseeing the construction was satisfied. While the other men returned to their units, James was escorted back to his wagon where Private Foreman reattached the manacles.

"I haven't seen Sergeant Rial today," he said as the private locked his manacles.

"Then that makes you a lucky man, now don't it?"

Then it'll be tomorrow, James decided. I guess I'll wake up one more time on this earth. Then that bastard will die.

Justin Thompson realized what the fever had taken out of him after creeping through the thick woods toward the British column. His head still ached and the humidity seemed to be sapping his strength by the minute. Luckily he only had to follow Robert and make as little noise as possible.

The trapper stopped and waited while JT joined him behind a rotting tree trunk.

"See those four wagons?" Robert pointed toward the camp where the dim light of several camp fires illuminated the canvas wagon covers.

"Yes," he whispered.

"James was chained to the second one, on this side by the fire."

"Let's move closer."

James ignored the insects that dodged the fire smoke while looking for victims among the sleeping soldiers. His thoughts kept returning to ships, the sea and Samantha. Streams of what had been and might have been kept him from sleep. This forest was a festering shit-hole and here he would die, he finally reflected as he gave up on sleep. But he also knew he could have just as easily died on St. Lucia or a dozen other times at sea. What difference did it really make?

A commotion in the darkness, followed by several shouts roused James from his focus.

"Over here, sarge," a voice called out and two men with small torches moved toward the darkness.

James could see a group emerging from the trees, the torches lighting the way. Two men in civilian clothes were walking with their hands on their heads, followed by several soldiers carrying muskets. Another group of men from Ticonderoga was James's first thought.   The Americans had split into many small bands as they made their way south. This must be some of the unlucky ones.

"Take 'em over to the traitor's wagon," Sergeant Rial barked, his voice especially loud against the dark trees.

As the men walked into the light from the small fire, James's heart sank.

Major Richard Porritt walked into the light and inspected the two men standing with their hands tied behind their backs.

"Why it's none other than Captain Thompson, late of the Queen's Rangers," he said sarcastically. "And pray what brings you into our camp, sir? Perhaps you were looking for the other traitor?"

JT stared back at the imperious Porritt who had now clasped his hands behind his back and turned toward James.

"Mr. Addington, now you will have company on your march to the gallows."

Porritt turned to Sergeant Rial. "Release that man, he works for me," he said nodding toward Robert.

As the large man untied the trapper's hands, Porritt turned to JT.

"Quite right, I'm afraid. Your trusted man was in fact my agent. Never underestimate your betters, Thompson."

JT stared at the tall officer, his eyes flashing hatred but he said nothing.

"Mr. Schlatter, please follow me," Porritt said over his shoulder, walking toward the head of the column.

"Over there," Rial ordered harshly, shoving JT toward the wagon and James.

"Where is the woman," Porritt asked Robert, who sat across from him at a small camp table.

"They sent her south to find General Schuyler."

"When did she leave?"

"This afternoon. She was going to Albany first then south if she had to."

Porritt thought for a moment. Although Schuyler must assume the British would continue south trying to force an engagement, there was no benefit in confirming Burgoyne's location during the march.

"Can you catch her?"

Robert nodded. "She'll stay on the main trail. I know a shorter way."

"Then leave now. If you can bring her back, I'll question her. But don't hesitate to kill her if you have to, I don't need her helping the rebels."

Private Foreman walked into the darkness after locking JT to the same chain which held James to the wagon.

"Looks like I've made a mess of this." JT said after a moment.

James nodded.

"No matter, where's Caitlin and Cantu?"

"They were to wait for us at the camp."

Both men sat thinking, wondering what their companions would do.

The sun was just breaking the horizon when a small group of soldiers approached the wagon. Major Porritt was accompanied by Sergeant Rial and two tall grenadier guards.

"Get them on their feet," Porritt said, his voice quiet.

The two grenadier guards pulled James and JT to their feet.

Private Foreman stepped up as if he'd been briefed and unlocked their manacles from the long steel chain.

"This way," Rial ordered and the two prisoners were pushed toward the dark forest.

With the way lit by two torches carried by Rial and Foreman, the small party moved toward the rising terrain north of the river.

"Where are you taking us," JT asked.

"Shut up," Sergeant Rial said without looking back, his normal brashness strangely subdued.

James realized what was about to happen and suddenly felt his heart pounding. So this is it, he thought, stumbling on the underbrush.

"You bastards," JT said, also realizing they had only a short amount of time to live.

"Let us behave as civilized enemies if you please," Porritt said from the rear of the column.

They stopped in a small clearing, the grenadiers stepping to the side, their muskets at the ready.

Major Porritt stepped in front of the two prisoners.

"The arrival of Captain Thompson prompted the general to bring this affair to an end and focus on the battle at hand. He has decided that you two will simply be executed and left behind. He has offered you the honor of death by firing squad, a consideration seldom shown to traitors. Mr. Addington, it appears you will escape the hangman's noose after all."

A strange calm came over James. He had done his duty and that could never be taken away from him. It did provide solace. Thinking back to his walks with Burgoyne on the deck of *Andromeda*, he found that he held no animosity toward the man.

"Please thank the general for me," James said. "And Major, may I ask a favor of you?"

Porritt's face remained impassive. "Perhaps."

"Would you get word to my father? I shouldn't want him to wonder as to my fate."

The major stared back at him, his eyes hard. "I think not. Thompson?"

JT shook his head, the resignation now evident by his stance.

"I will have my men reload to make sure there will be no problems with the damp. You have ten minutes."

James and JT stood side by side, their hands manacled behind their backs.

"Damn."

"Are you a church-going man?" JT asked.

James smiled. "I guess so."

"Never much cared for preachers."

They watched the soldiers discharge their muskets then begin the ritual of reloading.

Major Porritt stood ramrod stiff to one side, his sword still in its scabbard, arms folded on his chest.

A musket blast came from the far side of the clearing throwing one of the grenadiers backwards, a dark spot instantly visible in the center of his chest.

"What..." A second shot struck the second guardsman in the head as he turned toward his fallen comrade sending a large piece of bone and flesh into the air.

Private Foreman reached down to prime the pan of his musket and was hit in his back by a musket ball, knocking him to his knees, his weapon clattering on the ground.

James dropped to one knee searching the woods for the shooters.

Sergeant Rial grabbed one of the grenadier's muskets, the long bayonet now pointed toward JT. The big man moved quickly, his intent now clear as the bayonet was now leveled at Thompson.

James saw that his friend was the target of Rial's charge and knelt, ready to lunge and knock the sergeant off his mark.

Facing the charging Rial, JT stood ready to dodge the blade, his hands useless behind his back.

From the brush at the edge of the clearing, a figure in dark clothes rushed Rial, a long machete' raised high over his head.

Turning in response to the assault from his side, Rial hesitated in his charge and started to bring the musket around to fend off his attacker.

A viciously hard swing of the blade hit the British sergeant at the base of his neck almost severing his head, blood spurting from the massive wound. Cantu turned toward the major who had drawn his sword and was advancing at the ready.

From the right, Robert and Caitlin pushed through the bushes, a large knife in her hand, a hatchet at the ready for the trapper.

Porritt lunged with his sword, but stumbled on a large tree root. Off balance he was able to parry the slashing attack by Cantu, but was driven to the ground.

Robert rushed forward, the small axe raised for the killing blow.

"Stop," James yelled.

As if on order, the violence of the past minute was frozen into suspense.

"Quick, that man has the keys to these," James said nodding toward the prone figure of Foreman.

Caitlin had checked the two grenadiers and said simply, "They will die."

Private Foreman coughed, a red froth appearing at his mouth.

"Him too," she said.

Robert released James manacles and moved to JT.

James walked to Cantu who stood with his machete' in the major's back.

"Let him up," James said as he held out his hand for the machete'.

Porritt scrambled to his feet, brushing the dirt and brush off his uniform.

"Pick up your sword, sir."

The major looked at James in the early morning light.

"A sporting chance?" Porritt said as he carefully picked up the sword and circled to his left.

James said nothing holding himself opposite of the major as they both circled.

Porritt lunged quickly, making a feint as if testing his opponent. He knew that James was weak from lack of food and the march.

A second lunge was parried by James who staggered slightly, only then realizing how tired he was and pulling back to a defensive position.

"Shall I kill the man," Cantu asked of JT without taking his eyes off the fight.

"I shouldn't think that will be needed," he answered.

Two more slashing blows by Porritt were followed by a vicious lunge at James's midsection which he was able to parry.

Both men were now breathing hard, sweat now evident in the morning light.

James felt a surge of confidence, he was alive and he would kill this man. He feinted to his left then brought the blade over hard right and caught Porritt's shoulder, opening a gash in his red coat, the major crying out in pain.

Grunting to fight the pain, Porritt stepped back, his face pinched. He desperately raised his sword as James attacked again.

Bringing the big blade down hard, James knocked the major's sword aside, the machete's blade cleaving into Porritt's chest.

James stepped back, his breathing labored as Porritt fell to his knees his arms clutching his chest as if to hide his wound. He stared at the dying man who said nothing as he pitched forward into the dirt.

For a moment, everyone stared as if in a trance, then Robert spoke up.

"We must hide the bodies and leave, now."

The moment broken, each of them began dragging the wounded and dead into the underbrush. Within several minutes the clearing looked as if men had never been there.

JT walked over to James who sat on a fallen tree trunk. The fury of his fight had drained and now utter exhaustion consumed his body.

"How are you?"

"Well enough," James said standing up and stretching his back. "We've got to find Schuyler, let's move."

Chapter Twenty-Eight

An Unlikely Victory

James Addington felt a bone deep weariness that reminded him of the effect of a week-long storm at sea. Their journey south in search of General Schuyler had ended with the surprise that Horatio Gates had taken command of the northern district. The new commander had sent them back north to scout the enemy advance. James and JT had been able to provide critical information which helped set the stage for a series of battles that had resulted in the surrender of John Burgoyne to Gates at Saratoga.

While the army had always talked of defeating the British head to head in a large battle, the true feeling by many was that the continentals simply could not prevail against the training and experience of the British army. Now as their small group approached Washington's headquarters, the reality of the victory was hard to comprehend.

Across the Atlantic, the French had taken notice of the remarkable battle and now the rebellion began to affect the always tenuous relationship between England and France. The small amount of support in both arms and men which had trickled into the colonies now accelerated as an agreement between the former British colonies and the government of France put real teeth into the battle being fought in the hills of New Jersey.

"We're looking for General Washington," JT called to several men who appeared to be sentries standing guard at a fork in the trail.

A tall, hard looking man with several days growth of beard walked up to them as they pulled their horses to a halt.

"And who might you be?" he asked, his musket now held at the ready. His clothing gave no hint of a military uniform, except for the piece of red cloth that was attached to his cap. The same marking adorned the caps of the other men standing back from the road.

"Captain Thompson, attached to Colonel Hamilton. This is Captain Addington. The two men and the woman are with us."

The man eyed them with less concern, but certainly with no deference.

"'Bout half mile in that direction," the man said, nodding toward the trail that ran to the west."

"Obliged," JT answered, spurring his horse into motion.

James let his horse follow the other animal's lead. His mind was replaying the last month and he felt as if he was simply a pawn in a huge chess game. Never schooled in land battle, he'd felt like a novice as they scouted Burgoyne's forces and carried the information to Gates. It had been JT who invariably knew what to look for and what things a general would need to know before a battle. James knew he was not of great assistance to his friend, although JT had never said anything. Caitlin had sensed his discomfort and on two occasions had approached him, asking him what was wrong. He hadn't told her that he felt like an imposter.

"Captain Thompson, it is indeed a pleasure to know you are safe."

"We got back here as soon as General Gates released us," JT replied to Alexander Hamilton.

Washington's aide shook their hand and asked them to take a seat on a large log which ran parallel to a fire burning inside a circle of large stones.

Over the next hour, they related the entire story of their journey north, capture, subsequent escape and finally the lead up to the recent battle.

"Your service was exemplary, sir. Please accept my thanks. I know the general will want to talk with you later. For now, get yourselves settled in camp and we can talk about your next assignment."

"If you have another minute, colonel, might I talk with you?" James asked.

JT looked surprised, but said, "I'll take care of the horses," and strode off.

Hamilton smiled. "What's on your mind, captain?"

"I belong at sea, sir. While I'll do whatever you or the general requires, I feel very much like a fish out of water. I trained as a naval officer. I know how to fight at sea but here on land I feel the fool."

"But you seemed to accomplish a great deal in the last two months."

James shook his head. "If it hadn't been for Captain Thompson I'm not sure what the results might have been."

"I see. Well let me think about it. For now get some rest, you do look a sight."

When the two young officers had met with General Washington later that day, the subject of James's future came up again.

"I've been informed that you desire a return to naval service?"

"Yes, sir. I honestly feel I would be more effective on the deck of a ship, any ship, than here with the army."

Washington smiled briefly. "I never enjoyed the sea, I must confess. But to each man his own calling I suppose. You know our navy is very small and you might not be needed."

James had indeed thought of that.

"Sir, my father is with the Naval Committee. If there are no billets available at sea, I will outfit a privateer and add my weight to the fight."

"You would certainly hang if ever captured. There's not a letter of marque in the world that would protect a former officer who had defected to the enemy."

"Sir, I'm quite aware of that and willing to take that chance."

"God knows we need to control as much of our coast as we can if this war is to move forward in our favor."

"Captain Thompson, were you aware of your comrade's desire?"

JT answered, "Yes, general."

"And what do you say?"

"Sir, I travelled south from Halifax on a ship with Mr. Addington. I was truly out of my element while he was completely comfortable. If Mr. Addington can contribute more to our victory as a naval officer I think it worthy of your consideration."

James looked at his friend and realized how much they had come to respect each other.

"Well said, captain. Now leave me to consider this question. I will let you know in short order."

To Captain James Addington:

You will consider yourself detached from duty with the army and are requested and required to proceed to Boston and present yourself to the Naval Committee for duties as they see commensurate with your rank and experience.

/S/ Alexander Hamilton, Lt Colonel

A week later the ship's masts in Boston harbor were visible to the two men riding down the Cambridge Road toward the city.

James had been grateful for the time on the trail to think about his future and how he would approach his father. He meant what he had told the general that if he couldn't sail with the navy, he would become a privateer. In his mind the financial support for this venture would come from his father or perhaps Samantha's family. He hoped it would not come to that, he wanted to wear the blue coat again but for this new country.

His parting from JT and Caitlin had been bittersweet. He'd come to care very much for both of them and knew that somehow they would meet again. For the first time James saw something in Caitlin's eyes that betrayed a warmth beneath her normal hard exterior. He knew the tall cavalryman and this slip of a woman would find some way to stay together and that pleased him. It seemed he was acquiring the family he had never had.

A chill in the air gave emphasis to the activity on the streets leading into Boston from the surrounding towns.

The final preparations for winter were evident as fodder and carts loaded with wood made their way into the city. But despite the press of people and animals, in less than an hour after crossing the neck, the two men arrived at Toby's Tavern.

"Well, well. Back from the sea, Mr. Addington?" Tobias Sims grinned across the counter as they entered the main room.

"No, just a trip up north. We hoped you'd have room for us?"

The big man nodded. "Room and some hot soup if you're needin' it."

An hour later James had to admit, the warmth of the tavern and a hot beef stew made the world look like a much better place. He was now ready to clean up and find Samantha. The Naval Committee could wait.

Walking north to the Walker and Sons store, James's thoughts were torn. He longed to see and hold Samantha, but he would also have to tell her he intended to return to sea. Would she understand? Would she still feel the same way about him as she did before? Of course he told himself, he felt even more committed to her now and she must feel the same way.

Opening the door to the store, he felt his heart beating and getting his wind seemed a test. Quickly looking around he saw she wasn't there. A young man stood behind the counter, reading a pamphlet.

"May I help you?" he asked, putting down his reading.

Stammering, James said, "Miss Walker, Samantha, is she here?"

The man looked at James curiously then shook his head. "She went to Providence on business. Should be back later in the week.... if the weather holds."

Not sure if he was more angry or frustrated, James walked south toward the Commons. He had simply never expected to find her gone.

At Government House, he discovered the Naval Committee did not meet every day. A friendly clerk told him that he would likely find Admiral Addington at either his lodgings near the waterfront or at a local tavern known as The Dutch Maiden on Gloucester Street.

"May I join you, sir?"

David Addington looked up from his plate with surprise followed by concern.

"James," he said standing up and embracing his son.

"It's good to see you, father."

"Here sit down, sit down."

The two men looked at each other, seemingly at a loss for words.

"What in heaven's name are you doing here?" David Addington finally asked.

"Looking for you, sir. I have orders to report to the Naval Committee and you're still a member, are you not?"

"Well, yes. Of course I am." The older man paused, taking in what his son had just said. "James, you have me at a disadvantage. What do you mean orders to report? What orders?"

James smiled and reached into his inner pocket producing an envelope which he handed to his father.

The admiral examined the packet, squinting slightly in the fading light. Without a word he broke the seal, withdrew the inner letter and began to read.

Through the window, James watched a small chaise made its way toward the waterfront, the two matched horses indicating the occupants were likely well off. Against the shabby men and women in the street, the gleaming panels of the chaise seemed to highlight the difference between the rich and poor of the city.

"Damned remarkable, James. I'm at a loss to respond to what I've just read. Do you know what's in here?"

"Colonel Hamilton gave it to me sealed."

Sitting back in his chair the admiral looked hard at his son. "This describes your activities over the last several months while in the service of... General Washington?"

"Yes, sir."

"My God, James. Why didn't you tell me of this?"

"Sir, General Washington felt the fewer who were aware of our real identities the safer we all would be."

"Quite right, I'm sure. Quite right. Damned unusual though, I'll tell you."

The admiral now sat back in his chair looking at his son with both admiration and curiosity.

"You remind me of your mother, quite the independent soul."

"It must run in the family. I met Caitlin Mckenna, mother's sister. She's quite a woman."

David Addington's eyes reflected a piece of the past and he said, "Caitlin, I'd almost forgotten her."

"Twice she helped save my life."

"Then I owe her a debt of gratitude," the admiral added softly. "And I expect to hear all about it. Now, what's this about you holding a commission in the army?"

"General Washington thought it might provide some protection if I were captured. I was skeptical, but went along with his orders."

"And now?"

"Father, I realized my ability help our cause would be best served at sea. For that reason the general released me to petition the committee for a position with our navy."

"Now I understand."

"If nothing is available on a man of war, I'll ship out on a privateer. I know they're active off the coast."

"Indeed they are, however my experience has been that they are closed to outsiders."

The serving woman approached the table, wiping her hands on her apron.

"Would you be requiring anything further, sir?"

"Yes indeed," the admiral answered. "Ask Mr. Partridge if he has any good brandy. I believe this is an occasion to celebrate. Yes, indeed, providence has smiled on us."

Chapter Twenty-Nine

A New Commission

Two days later James was summoned to Government House. The note said only that the secretary of the Naval Committee, a Mr. Hobbs, requested his presence on a matter of great urgency.

Always at James's side, Cantu remained in the street when they arrived at the appointed hour. While still not accustomed to the bitter cold of Massachusetts, Cantu had learned to dress warmly and now did not dread going out. His heavy coat always concealed two small pistols and his machete' hung from a scabbard at his side.

The offices of the Naval Committee were sparse, the few desks taken by several clerks who seemed to be fully engaged in copying from letters into large ledger books. James was shown into see Mr. Hobbs after only a minute or two.

"Ah, Addington, good to meet you. My name is Hobbs, Horatio Hobbs."

The short round man reminded James of a large pumpkin, his flushed face adding to the glow from several candles burning on his desk.

"The pleasure is mine, sir. James Addington."

"I will have a number of pieces of business with you after you meet with the committee. Let me see if they are ready for you, please wait just a moment."

David Addington sat on the left of rest of the committee who all were seated at a long table. Piles of papers covered most of the table and from their appearance the men had been busy for hours.

"Please do come in," the man in the center said as James entered the room. "My name is Moore and this is Mr. John Adams."

There were no chairs on his side of the table and Mr. Moore made no offer for James to sit down.

"Mr. Addington. Your father has been so good as to share his letter from Colonel Hamilton. We congratulate you on your contribution to the magnificent victory over Burgoyne. The admiral has also given us a summary of your service with the Royal Navy. He told us that you desire to go to sea and relinquish your commission in the army."

"Yes, sir."

"We are prepared to offer you a commission as lieutenant in the Continental Navy and a mission which could result in a posting to one of our ships already in European waters."

"Yes, sir."

Adams now spoke, "Make no mistake, Mr. Addington, this is an assignment that is not without risk. We'll be asking you to serve as a messenger for both information and valuables. We have no doubt that the British will try everything in their power to intercept and detain you. While you will travel in uniform, your former position would likely make your capture a death sentence."

"As it would be for any of you, sir."

"Quite true. But we will have to lose this war for them to get their hands on us and we don't intend to lose," Moore said with little emotion.

"If you agree," Adams continued, "You would embark within the week for France."

James knew his answer without having to think about it.

"I place myself at your service, sir."

Two days later, Cantu entered James's room with a sly smile. They both had been busy with arraignments for their impending voyage. They were to sail three days hence onboard *Invictus,* a barquentine bound for Le Havre, France. From there they would take the overland coach to Paris with dispatches and bank drafts for Benjamin Franklin, United States representative to the court of Louis the 16th.

"Is it the opportunity to visit France that creates that glow on your face, my friend?"

"Miss Samantha is back in Boston."

Samantha Walker thought it curious that the frigid weather in Boston seemed easier on the spirit than the cold in Providence. Enjoying her morning walk to the shop, she felt comfortable despite the chill in the wind. Her trip to Providence had proved partially successful. She had met with a man who was willing to provide a number of items they needed for inventory but had been unable to procure now that trade with England had ceased. In particular the merchant was able to obtain nautical chronometers and charts previously only available from London. But because of the uncertainty of the war, Walker and Sons must send someone with gold to pay for and take delivery of the merchandise. She knew there would be a battle from Silas Walker, but her father was too ill to make the voyage and she had to.

"Good morning."

The greeting broke Samantha's deep train of thought and she looked over at the tall man. Her momentary confusion was replaced by a smile that conveyed the true happiness she felt at seeing James.

"James!"

They grasped each other's hands and he squeezed hers as he looked into her eyes.

"You are truly lovely, Samantha Walker."

"What are you doing here?" she said, looking around as if they might be under observation.

"I'll tell you everything. But for now let me just look at you."

The young man looked up as Cantu shut the door to Walker and Sons.

"I have a message for Mr. Adkins."

"I'm Mr. Adkins.

"Miss Samantha told me to tell you she has returned home, but will be here within the next several hours."

"She told you that?"

Cantu nodded.

"That is rather odd. Why would she send you?"

"I am a friend of Leftenant Addington. She is talking with him."

Now Mr. Adkins understood.

As James related the events of the last several months, Samantha said nothing. Their tea grew cold as he described his capture, escape and the victory at Saratoga.

"I've been commissioned a lieutenant in the navy and will leave in two days for France."

Samantha rose and came to his chair. Kneeling at James's side she took his hand and brought it to her lips.

He gently turned her head and kissed her lips for the first time, his heart pounding in his chest.

They stood together and embraced with hesitation then pulled each other close.

James could feel every curve of her body pressed hard against his as she kissed him again passionately on the lips.

James's excitement on going to sea was tempered with the happiness of the last two days with Samantha. It seems as if the two of them had known each other forever. The intimate moments seemed so natural and he felt that now he understood how powerful love could be. Yes, he did love the young lady and it made him smile.

When he had taken his leave of her, late the evening prior, she had told him she would be on the dock before sailing. While the parting would be bitter, he knew that nothing would prevent their future together now.

His thoughts were interrupted by the sound of a carriage coming down the street toward the wharf.

Mr. Tredegar, the Walker's long serving coach driver brought the carriage to a stop and set the brake. Samantha sat in the seat, a heavy coat, scarf and bonnet protecting her from the cold.

Opening the door, James helped her down, taking the opportunity to hold her for a brief moment.

"Sailing within the hour, get all gear aboard," a tall mate onboard the *Invictus* yelled down to the pier.

James looked around, not seeing anything in the way of cargo.

"Could I get a hand with these," Mr. Tredegar called up to the deck.

"What?" James asked.

"My bags," Samantha said.

"Your bags? Why?"

"I'm sailing on this ship for France."

James found himself ready to argue then thought better of it.

"Cantu, help with the bags."

The big man grinned as they all walked up the gangway.

"What in heaven's name do you think you're doing?" James asked Samantha once they were on deck.

A rebellious look in her eyes told James that he was in love with a remarkable young woman, but what she was doing made no sense, no sense at all.

"Walker and Sons have business in France. My father isn't well enough to travel and so the journey is left to me."

"Isn't there anyone else that could go?"

"James, we're a family business. While we do have several men who might go, we prefer it remain in the family when the task is so critical to the survival of the firm. You can see that can't you?"

"I'm not sure. Sailing the Atlantic in the winter is dangerous in itself. But we're at war and as a privateer, *Invictus* is likely to be involved in some type of fight. Are you willing to risk that?"

"I have no choice. Besides, I've never taken passage in any kind of ship. It's time I learned the ways of the sea."

"Let go forward.....let go aft," came the call from the quarterdeck.

The captain's voice boomed across the deck as hands struggled to pull the mooring ropes aboard.

"Hoist the jib, if you please, Mr. Langdon," Captain McMahon called to the chief mate.

Standing on the deck, the captain surveyed his ship with an experienced eye. His face, weathered and tanned by years at sea, was accentuated by a firm jaw. A moustache flecked with grey gave him a distinguished look that added to his look of authority.

A light off shore breeze began to slide the ship away from the wharf, helped by the triangular jib now raised fully to the foremast.

"Lively there, Mr. Langdon, get those lines stowed and ready for open water."

The mate raised his hand to his head in the manner of a military salute and went forward.

"Now, if you will excuse me, leftenant," Samantha said, smiling, "I must, as you say, go below and stow my gear."

As she walked aft toward the main hatch, the young officer remained confused but oddly happy.

Chapter Thirty

An Unexpected Prize

Commanded and owned by John McMahon, *Invictus* was a true hybrid. Originally built as a fast packet, the barquentine had been modified when the war started. She now mounted a respectable battery of eight 6 pound cannons and two swivels. In addition McMahon had procured two 32 pound carronades which were mounted on each bow. These weapons were especially lethal at short ranges, particularly when loaded with grapeshot.

Armed with a letter of marque from the Naval Committee, he had made several successful voyages as a privateer. A profitable enterprise to be sure, the ship was well known by the Royal Navy's Atlantic Squadron and would be feather in the cap of any captain that could capture the Yankee privateer.

Transporting passengers was not a normal activity for either John McMahon or *Invictus.* But maintaining his letter of marque could possibly make him a very rich man and if the Naval Committee needed a vessel to sail for France, he couldn't easily refuse them. And never a man to pass up a profit, when Walker and Sons offered hard gold to transport Miss Samantha across the Atlantic, he readily acquiesced to that also. A voyage of many purposes.

The well-maintained ship was used to having a woman aboard as McMahon's rather fiery wife Caroline had sailed on almost all of the ship's voyages. The daughter of a ship captain, she was more at home on a ship's deck than ashore and had become something of a legend in and around Boston. Often wearing man's pants, she had taken to wearing two pistols in her belt and the lady knew how to use them.

"You must be Addington," a voice called from behind James as the ship cleared the harbor and headed into the open ocean.

He turned to see Caroline McMahon, her arms folded in front of her, surveying the deck as the crew went about their duties after leaving port. She was just a slip of a woman, but her strong chin and piercing blue eyes told him she was not someone you wanted to anger. She indeed was wearing leather buckskin trousers, but the pistols were nowhere to be seen.

"At your service, ma'am."

She walked up to him, her gaze clearly sizing him up against her measure of a sea officer.

"My husband tells me you were a lieutenant on the British frigate *Challenger.*"

"That is so, ma'am. Why do you ask?"

Her eyes went cold, her features grim.

"That bastard Pelham attacked a sloop off the Jersey coast. I was told that the bloody swine kept firing even when the sloop had struck."

The horror of that day flooded back into James's memory.

"My brother commanded that ship, Mr. Addington. And I will hate you British until the day I die."

Taking a deep breath, James said slowly, "Ma'am I don't blame you. And I'm not British, I'm a New Yorker."

For a moment her eyes showed confusion, then curiosity.

"A New Yorker?"

"Born in Albany. But I did serve in the Royal Navy for six years. And what you were told was correct. I saw the sloop strike and Captain Pelham ordered us to continue firing."

"But why?" she asked the pain evident in her voice.

"Pelham's only brother was killed at Breed's Hill. Never an easy man, after learning of his brother's death, he was even worse."

Caroline McMahon turned to look at the horizon. "A brother for a brother," she said quietly, then walked aft toward where her husband stood watching the sails as *Invictus* moved steadily into the Atlantic.

Despite the cold, James and Samantha had gone on deck to stretch their legs on the first morning at sea. The ship had enjoyed a comfortable first night out, the winds remaining steady and the sea calm for the most part.

"Oh my," she said as they walked carefully to the windward rail. Before them stretched an endless panorama of water which appeared more blue than green and flecks of white capped the procession of rollers moving from the north east.

James caught her as the ship hit a deep wave trough and she lurched toward the rail. The feel of her body in his arms brought him immediate surprise and pleasure.

"You must be careful," he said holding her longer than necessary.

Samantha seemed quite happy to be where she was and simply turned her head to say, "But I have you to take care of me."

He helped her to the rail and continued to hold her steady.

"I never imagined it could be like this," she said, staring out across the sea.

He had never thought he would be standing on the deck of a ship holding a beautiful woman either, but here he was.

"The ship seems so small now," she said. "Not like yesterday in port."

James smiled, the smell of her perfume seeming so out of place at sea.

"The ocean is always to be respected. You must never let her lull you into thinking she is your friend or she will turn on you."

He felt her shiver.

"Are you cold?"

Shaking her head, she continued to look across the large expanse of the North Atlantic but said nothing as the brisk wind blew her long brown hair into James's face.

The passage fell into a comfortable routine after several days. Meals in the large aft cabin with McMahon and his wife were pleasant enough and the food better than James had expected. Caroline McMahon always went to sea with her husband now that their children were married and gone from their home in Marblehead. Her sometimes acerbic wit spared no one and she always spoke her mind. There was also no doubt she was going to do what she thought was right for the *Invictus* and her husband. After their first exchange, Caroline had warmed to James and made him feel welcome aboard the ship.

John McMahon spent most of his time on deck and James found himself doing the same. Naval officers, as a rule, looked down at merchant sailors, thinking them unprofessional. But aboard *Invictus* there was no question the ship was run smartly and the crew very capable. He liked the quiet sometime taciturn captain of the barquentine and James decided that in a fight, the ship would acquit herself well.

Caroline McMahon and Samantha had taken to each other from the first day. The two women seemed to be of similar demeanor which made James curious how his Samantha would change as she grew older. Would she someday wear pants and carry pistols? The thought was unsettling to James.

While invited to take his meals with James and Samantha, Cantu chose to mess with the ship's doctor, an odd character named Roger Hanson. While most ships like *Invictus* would rely on the master to care for sick and wounded men, John McMahon felt a medical man was an appropriate precaution for a vessel that carried a letter of marque and would likely fire weapons in anger. He had found Roger Hanson in one of the many waterfront pubs that dotted Boston's waterfront. Rather worse for drink, the middle aged healer apparently had few means of support and the potential for prize money was all he needed to be lured away from the bottles of rum that were his usual companions. Strangely, Cantu seemed drawn to the doctor and in short order they became comfortable companions.

The weather remained calm for this time of year, allowing the men to continue with routine maintenance of the ships rigging between standing watches. One rather encouraging practice by McMahon was to exercise the gun crews several times a day. Carrying a larger crew than in peacetime, *Invictus* was able to man four guns on one side while still working her sails. James could tell from watching the men service the guns that some of them must have spent time in a king's ship. A quiet Rhode Islander, Hiram Perkins, served as the ship's gunner and appeared quite well versed in the mysteries of naval ordnance. But how would they stand up to a well-trained king's ship?

Ten days out of Boston, *Invictus* spotted the first strange sail of the voyage. James knew that McMahon wanted to run south east for a week to clear the area where the British squadron actively patrolled. Now clear, they were not as concerned to see another vessel.

"What do you think, leftenant?" John McMahon asked as he handed a long glass to James.

Stepping to the shrouds, James supported the glass on the rat lines while focusing the eyepiece. Always a challenge to identify a ship across several miles of pitching sea, this time it was easy for the young officer.

"A sloop would be my thought. Running easy, she might be making for the West Indies. I saw a lot of rigs like that around Antigua over the years."

"Guns?" McMahon asked, raising the glass back to his eye.

"Sometimes. The navy will often press larger sloops into service. If she's a sloop of war, you can expect a dozen guns."

"I feel inclined to close for a look. We have the weather gauge and if we need to run, I'd put this ship up against any."

James knew from the first mate that the bottom had recently been cleaned and some of the copper replaced. She should be able to fly before the wind, particularly in the hands of an experienced mariner like McMahon.

Thirty minutes later the guns were manned as *Invictus* rode down on the stranger. Now less than two miles away, it was clear the ship was indeed a sloop, but the stranger flew no flag.

Samantha appeared in the main hatchway with Caroline McMahon.

"Perhaps I should escort the women below," James offered to the captain.

The tall man laughed.

"Good luck, my young friend. I gave up trying to tell my wife what to do many years ago."

The two women made their way aft past the guns and climbed up to the quarterdeck.

"Well?" Caroline asked her husband.

"We don't know anything yet."

"Captain, she's British!" John Langdon, the first mate, called as he saw the white jack of the sloop break from the gaff.

"Run up our colors," McMahon ordered, "Bring her one point into the wind,"

The two helmsmen strained on the big wheel, the bow responding quickly.

"Mr. Perkins, prepare to fire"

Standing behind his gun crews, Perkins answered, "Aye, sir."

The two ships were now less than a mile apart. All preparations were completed and now James knew the last few minutes before the action would seem like an eternity. Why is it always this way, he asked himself?

James examined the ship closer using a long glass. Not just a sloop, she was a British sloop of war. Over 100 feet in length, she likely mounted a dozen cannon, probably four to six pounders. A deadly package, manned by over one hundred sailors, this battle could go very wrong for *Invictus.* But with her lee rail under water, the enemy ship would be hard pressed to fire her cannons.

James could see two men on the quarterdeck of the sloop, their dark blue coats indicating officers of the Royal Navy. Do I know these men, James wondered?

"Caroline, would you be so good as to escort Miss Walker below?"

Saying nothing, the captain's wife took Samantha by the hand and quickly walked her by the guns and down the hatch.

"Stand by to fire on the up roll," McMahon bellowed over the roar of the wind, Invictus now committed to battle.

It seemed to James that the British captain had misjudged his approach and waited too long to pay off so that his guns could bear. James watched the two ships closing and knew the sloop would take the worst of it.

"FIRE!" Perkins yelled and one by one the six pounders jerked back on their carriages as the two ship passed. Wood flew from the sloop's sides as cannon balls slammed into her at short range, her gun ports finally opening above the tossing water.

The late turn by the sloop allowed her to only get two rounds off from her aft most cannon, but at such close range both slammed into *Invictus,* violently tearing large pieces from the starboard bulwark, sending splinters across the deck.

"Standby to come about," McMahon yelled as they watched the sloop pay off.

"Sponge out, reload and run out," Perkins yelled over the squeal of lines running through blocks on deck.

James knew the next time they wouldn't be so lucky.

From behind him came a guttural cry, a sound James had heard before from grievously wounded men. He turn to see one of the helmsmen named Jacobs laying on his back, blood covering the deck from a leg that was torn almost off.

"Mr. Langdon, a hand here," McMahon called and three men ran aft to tend to Jacobs. Perhaps Hanson could save him, James thought, if he can get the leg off and stop the bleeding the man has a chance. Returning to the fight, he felt the deck steady under him.

Invictus gained speed as the wind filled her sails, her bow again pointing at the enemy. Spray flew back as the ship plunged into the blue gray waves, closing again on the enemy sloop.

James watched with professional curiosity, wondering why the sloop seemed so sluggish as she came around. A sloop should always gain a turning advantage over a ship like *Invictus*

"Captain, she's struck," the first mate called, his glass held to his eye.

"Perhaps the shot carried her flag away," McMahon said.

"No, sir. I watched two men lower the colors."

McMahon looked at the ship as they closed, his concern evident over this bizarre twist of events.

"Standby to fire, but only on my order, Mr. Perkins."

"Aye, sir."

Steadily riding down on the sloop which now lay to, her sails luffing, the men on *Invictus* were strangely quiet and subdued. Was this a trick? Would they close only to suffer a full broadside at close range? But they had struck their colors, the time honored mark of submission which obligated the victor to show quarter. But what of this time?

Unwilling to give up his speed advantage, McMahon passed the sloop, calling across with a speaking trumpet, "DO YOU STRIKE, SIR."

"We do," came the reply across the water.

James could now clearly see the quarterdeck and the complete devastation.

"The officers are dead," he said quietly to himself.

"Standby by to wear ship and lower a boat, Mr. Langford," McMahon called over the squeaking of line and tackle. "Mr. Addington, perhaps you would lead the boarding party?"

As the jolly boat was being swung out, James ducked below to find Samantha. He hoped she had been taken into the hold by Caroline, but realized he didn't really know. I should have said something, he told himself then knew that Caroline McMahon would have watched over Samantha like a mother.

He found her, not in her small space or the big cabin, but forward where Roger Hanson had set up his surgery and was being assisted by Caroline McMahon. In the muted light from two lanterns, the unfortunate Jacobs lay on his back, his arms held fast by two sailors. The man's pitiful moans had subsided as rum had been rapidly administered by the captain's wife.

"Come on, my boy," she coaxed. "I know you love your drink, so down the hatch."

Approaching the sloop's side, James realized he knew this ship. She was the *Eagle* from Gibraltar. He remembered she'd been commanded by Commander Percy Shilling, who had a reputation as a strict captain. But James could remember nothing else to set her apart.

Climbing through the entry port, he saw that Perkins's shots had indeed taken a bloodytoll. Two upended guns and at least six bodies lay on the deck. A tall man dressed like a petty officer approached him.

"Who are you," James asked.

"Rush, ship's boatswain....sir." The man's face was bronzed by the sun, his long hair streaked with gray and bound in a ponytail above his collar.

James glanced around.

"Where's your captain?"

"Dead, sir. Along with Mr. Paine, the gunner and the master."

"You have no officers?"

The man shook his head.

"Only Midshipman Rogers, but he took a bad splinter in the gut."

James walked toward the quarterdeck, seeing the bloody remains of the ship's two officers.

"Mr. Addington?"

Turning toward the familiar voice he saw an old shipmate grinning at him.

"Dick Stevens?."

"Aye, sir. I never expected to see you on an American ship."

James remembered that first time aloft in *Andromeda* and how the wiry sailor had watched out for him.

"I changed sides, Dick, decided this new country might just be the right place for me."

"I see you still have Cantu with you."

James laughed, as always the big man was at his back.

"But why are you on *Eagle*?"

By now a group of men had gathered to watch one of their own talking with the strange officer.

"*Challenger* put into Gibraltar and this here sloop needed crewmen. So I decided to get off while I could. The ship just weren't the same after we sank that sloop. Damned if it wasn't just as bad here."

Thoughts ran through James head. Why did these men seem eager to be around him? They didn't look like a crew that had just surrendered.

"But why did you strike?" James asked Stevens, but looking around at his shipmates.

No one said anything for a long moment then Stevens spoke out.

"Begging your pardon, sir, but Commander Schilling was a right proper bastard. Leftenant Paine weren't no better. Half of these men have been flogged and everyone was treated like dogs."

Several of the men nodded.

Taking in everything, the realization hit James. "Do you mean John Paine who sailed with us in *Andromeda*?"

"That's him all right."

"We hear if you join up with the Yankees you get land when the war's over," a man asked from the crowd. "Is that right, leftenant?"

James looked toward the two blue clad bodies on the quarterdeck as memories flooded back to him. He saw the taller of the two lying on the deck, half of his chest gone, the blood pooled under his body. John Paine. Refocusing, he answered the question.

"It is, anywhere from 40 to 160 acres depending on what state you're in."

James looked across the faces. He could see that look of the British tar he'd always admired. These men had put up with a bastard for a captain and now saw the promise of a new life.

"Cantu, return to *Invictus* and tell Captain McMahon that we'll get *Eagle* underway and match his course. I need the doctor over here right away." He turned to the boatswain, "Rush, is it? You're the senior boatswain's mate."

"Aye, sir."

"We'll get underway as soon as the doctor is aboard. Let's get the men fed so we can start on repairs. Have someone show me the sick berth."

His look of surprise did not keep the newly appointed sailing master of the *Eagle* from calling, "Lacy, take the...uh....captain down below."

James saw the wiry little gun captain grinning at him.

"That's *Mr.* Lacy, Mr. Rush, our new ship's gunner."

His confusion now complete, Rush watched the odd pair move aft, talking like old shipmates.

"Tell me about Boatswain Rush," James asked as they entered the big cabin.

"Right fine sailor, sir. Been at sea his whole life and knows his job. A good shipmate if you ask me."

"Would he make a good ship's master?"

"Aye, sir, that he would." Lacy grinned.

"Well then, Mr. Lacy, as gunner of this ship, ask Mr. Rush to come see me."

Rush entered the cabin tentatively, his cap in his hand.

"Sir?"

"Come in," James said.

"What's your given name, Mr. Rush?"

"William," he blurted out, the confusion evident on his face.

"Tell me, William Rush, what did you think about Captain Shilling?"

Hesitant, he answered, "What the men said was true, but he was the captain."

"Some captains forget that it is the men that make the ship. Treating them like criminals is without honor."

"No, sir, I mean, yes, sir."

"Mr. Rush, you were highly recommended for the job of sailing master by our new gunner. Do you feel ready to be master?"

"Aye, sir, I do."

The young midshipmen's face appeared waxy and white in the late afternoon light coming through aft windows. Leather straps tight across his thighs, several crewmembers also held the boy's arms and feet as Roger Hanson prepared to remove the large splinter.

Cantu watched as the older man gently examined the torn skin, now swollen around the wood projectile.

"Ah, much better than I originally had thought, my friend."

Cantu leaned closer and saw what Hanson meant. The wooden splinter, perhaps the thickness of a man's thumb had hit Midshipman Rogers from the front, but at the right extremity of his mid-section. While there had been a great deal of blood, it appeared to Cantu that a fatal puncture of the viscera had been avoided.

Hanson wiped his forehead, sweaty despite the cool temperature. His hand shook slightly as he turned to Cantu.

"Before we start, I believe a tot of rum would be beneficial."

"He's had a full cup, doctor," Cantu answered. "And the area around the wound has been soaked as you ordered." Now he could see that both of Hanson's hands were trembling.

"For me, my friend. It helps me concentrate on the job at hand."

Cantu found the decanter and poured a large measure into a pewter cup which he handed to Hanson.

The doctor took one sip of the liquid then drained the rest in one quick motion. Pausing a full fifteen seconds, he handed the empty glass to Cantu and said, "Now I'm ready."

The doctor's hands no longer trembled.

Two days were required to complete repairs and take care of the wounded. James used the time to talk with the crew and examine the ships records. The men had not exaggerated the severity of punishment under Schilling. The captain had used the cat as almost a daily weapon in response to many trivial offenses. He's lucky they didn't mutiny before this, James thought.

"Beg your pardon, captain."

James turned from his thoughts to see the master.

"Mr. Rush, what can I do for you?"

"We're set on the larboard tack, *Invictus* to leeward at two miles. I'd recommend we shorten sail with this wind picking up."

He saw the look in Rush's eyes and realized he didn't feel confident of the trust that James thought he had given him.

"Mr. Rush, you're the sailing master. I trust your ability and judgment. If you feel it would be prudent to shorten sail it's not necessary to ask my permission. Notification by the messenger of the watch is all the courtesy I require."

"Yes, sir. Thank you, sir."

He's a good sailor, James thought. And he knows it. But he doesn't know he's a good sailing master. Not yet anyway.

"Cantu pick a boat crew, I need to talk to Captain McMahon. Mr. Rush, signal *Invictus* we would like to hove to."

As the small boat moved quickly across the waves, James knew what he must do. And he thought he knew John McMahon well enough that the older man would support him.

Walking aft to the main cabin behind McMahon, he saw Samantha standing in the doorway to the chartroom.

"John, if you would excuse me for a moment or two?"

McMahon turned and saw Samantha. He smiled and nodded as he opened the door to his cabin.

James took her hand in his and they stepped into small space.

"I don't have much time, but I knew I had to talk to you."

She looked apprehensive, her eyes questioning.

"I intend to take command of that sloop and press her into service for the United States."

Her eyes widened and she started, "Oh, my."

"Sam, I could travel the length and breadth of Europe looking for a berth and not find one. Here's an answer to my problem and a way to help the cause. I just hope that Doctor Franklin will feel the same way."

"What do you mean?"

"My father told me that Franklin is our naval contact in France. Not officially his mission, he will, in any case, try to help raise money and ships for the navy. I'll deliver a manned ship of war at his feet. He must provide his support."

Her expression was positive, but she said, "What if he gives command to someone else. Perhaps someone with more influence or money than you."

The idea shocked James. He was bringing the prize in to Le Havre and would be offering her to Franklin. The only other man who could lay claim to the sloop would be John McMahon and he intended to address that shortly.

"I'll have to deal with whatever happens, of course. For now I intend to sail *Eagle* for Le Havre in company with *Invictus.*" But there were now doubts in his mind.

John McMahon had poured two glasses of wine and waited at the wide stern window.

"What's the mood on the ship?" he asked. "Harding passed to me that the officers had all been killed. Do you think I have to keep the guns on her for the entire trip?"

Depending on the situation, a prize crew would often lock the captured crew below decks if it was thought they might attempt to retake the ship. If the prize was to remain in company with the ship that captured her, loaded cannons would provide an additional deterrent to a wayward crew.

"They struck because they had no intention of fighting once the officers were killed. The captain was a cruel bastard and I sense they're happy to be free of him and the Royal Navy."

"Not unheard of, certainly," McMahon said.

"In fact, I want to press her into service for our navy."

The master looked at James with surprise.

"You want to do what?"

"There are men I've have sailed with on that ship. I think with a promise of prize money, freedom from the press and free land after the war, many of the men will gladly join. By my guess almost half of the crew aren't British anyway. I saw blacks, and northmen to say nothing of the dons."

"That ship would bring a pretty price as a prize."

James nodded. "I know that and I'll ask Doctor Franklin to issue vouchers to completely pay you off as the prize captain."

McMahon sat down and rubbed his face, now in need of a shave.

"If we sailed together, we could make quite a powerful little force. There might be a lot more prize money to be had."

James extended his hand and they shook on the deal.

By sunset on the second day, James decided it was time to call the crew together. The navy discipline was still in evidence as the men lined up quietly at quarters. Their faces did not show fear or anger, more a tired acceptance that they did not nor never would control their own destiny.

"Men, when you struck to the American captain, you put your future in his hands. I'm going to take that responsibility away from him. As you know my name is Addington. I was a leftenant in both *Andromeda* and *Challenger.* Some of you sailed with me. I'm also from New York and have decided to support the American's fight for independence. Right or wrong, that is my choice. I am now a leftenant in the new Continental Navy. As such, I'm taking this ship for service in that navy. It appears to me that many of you would like to follow the same path I've chosen. The difference in this new country is that a decision like that is your choice. We don't press men and your free will determines what course you take. If you choose to sail with me, we'll make war on British trade. For those who choose to leave, I'll put you ashore in a French port and you're free to go. I would like to set you ashore in England, but I'm sure you understand that would be a foolish thing to do. You can ship out from France and go home or back to sea, your choice."

A man called from the back. "Do they have prize money in your new navy?"

James laughed. "Indeed we do. I'm not promising to make anyone a rich man. But if we take prizes, whoever is with me will share in those prizes."

"If we go home, the navy can press us back to sea."

"That's right," James answered. "You might think about choosing a new name if you return to England."

The men laughed.

"How's Mr. Rogers, captain?" a man asked from the front row.

"Doctor Hanson removed the splinter. He's doing as well as we could have hoped. The rest of the wounded are progressing and I think they wouldn't mind a visit from their mates."

A chorus of murmurs told James the wounded would soon have company.

"Now set the evening watch, Mr. Rush, we sail for Le Havre."

James returned to the captain's cabin where Doctor Hanson sat beside the wounded midshipman. On entering, the smell of rum and sweat greeted him. Young Rogers was asleep, his breathing steady, a slight sheen on his brow. The doctor appeared to be dozing and James closed the door quietly. This man is certainly an odd one, he thought. While the doctor appeared to be partaking of spirits any time he was awake, he never appeared to be drunk. Cantu had relayed that the doctor also had some very unique ideas on medicine that the island healer felt might have merit. Hanson had also eagerly embraced Cantu's island medicine and several of the wounded had poultices made from the ingredients in his travelling bag.

Cantu had also assisted Hanson when he removed the wood splinter from young Rogers's side. A liberal application of rum before and after to the wound were a departure from normal protocols. The doctor had told Cantu he felt that the cleansing properties of spirits were important in promoting a quick return to a balance within the body. Interesting to Cantu, Hanson had also told him he felt that bleeding was an inefficient way to rebalance. He felt that proper ratios of warm and hot spirits coupled with a special diet would repair the balance more quickly. In any case, the wounded seemed to be getting better in the sick berth, while the ship's cook complained that the doctor made unreasonable demands of special meals for his patients.

Now looking at Hanson he saw the doctor open his eyes, momentarily disoriented.

"Doctor, may I pour you a glass of wine?"

"Indeed you may, sir. I feel mightily rested and a little wine is all I need to complete my bodily restoration."

James poured two glasses and handed one to Hanson.

Holding the glass up to one of the lanterns hanging from the overhead he examined it carefully.

"I understand the former captain was a cruel and vicious man, but I do like his choice in wines," the doctor opined.

Laughing, James sat down at the table next to the doctor. "And well supplied. I checked the hold, there's enough wine and rum to last two years, if a day."

"Well prepared, that's what I always say, you must be well prepared if you're going to sea."

James tone turned serious. "Doctor, I intend to place this vessel in service as sloop of war. My understanding is that the Continental Navy does not currently have such a vessel. Once I talk with Mr. Franklin and send several dispatches to America I plan to put to sea in search of prizes. Would you consider staying aboard as the ship's doctor? I'm not sure I can pay you what Captain McMahon does, but I would be willing to give you a ten percent share of any prizes."

Hanson's eyes widened. Ten percent was well above the range normally received by ship's doctors or surgeons in the Royal Navy. McMahon had promised him three percent of any prizes captured by *Invictus*.

"And what makes you think you'll capture any prizes?"

"Because that's what I do, doctor. Just like you heal the body, it's what you do."

Hanson looked at his wine then took a large drink.

"A ten percent share you say?"

James nodded.

"Free access to the spirit locker?"

"As long as you do your job," James replied.

The doctor slowly smiled then said, "Agreed."

Chapter Thirty-One

Seek Out and Destroy

A fellow traveler on the Paris coach told James that Benjamin Franklin was the talk of the city. The famous scientist had been warmly received by the wealthy and powerful of France and was making quite the case for the French to support the new United States against the British. How would the wily diplomat react to James's proposal?

"The doctor will see you now," the young secretary said to James who had been waiting in the drawing room of the suite of rooms Franklin had occupied since his arrival.

"Please do come in, sir," came the friendly greeting as James entered the small study. A large desk sat in front of the only window and Franklin rose and came around to shake James's hand.

"James Addington, at your service, sir."

"Do sit down, Mr. Addington. I understand you have a packet for me."

Opening up the leather valise, James handed the bundled papers, wrapped securely in oil paper.

"I shall read them later, but thank you for your efforts to bring them to me. I hope your trip was uneventful."

Now was the time, James thought and took a deep breath.

"Sir, that is what I would most urgently wish to discuss with you."

Franklin looked up from the packet, his expression one of curiosity.

"That certainly sounds ominous."

"No, sir. I mean it's very important, but the news is good, surely."

"Then let us have some tea and we can discuss whatever you would like."

Over the next thirty minutes, James recounted the events that now placed the young lieutenant in Benjamin

Franklin's study with the offer of a warship for the new Continental Navy.

"My goodness, sir, that is a most remarkable account. Now what exactly are you proposing?

"Sir, if you commissioned *Eagle* a Continental sloop of war, I would sail in company with John McMahon in *Invictus* and we would do our best to disrupt local British commerce while awaiting formal orders from the Naval Committee."

The older man stood and folded his arms as he looked out the window. Without looking back at James, he said, "I do believe my authority would allow me to do what you ask. But there would be the matter of money to purchase supplies and pay the crew."

"Doctor Franklin, for now the ship is relatively well victualed. A more important issue would be the ability of the crew to be compensated for any prizes that are taken. Besides the cargoes we might confiscate, sale of the vessels would be strong incentive for the crew."

"Quite so, quite so. I don't see a problem there. I've actually discussed the possibility with several senior officers of the French Navy. Let me give this some thought. While inclined to do what you ask, I must consider other factors not directly related to the navy, we are still very much on thin ice with the French."

The young lieutenant stood to take his leave, hopeful, but also trying to remain cautious.

James found Samantha at the small inn in Le Havre where she had secured rooms on her arrival. While near the waterfront, Samantha had been told it was a clean and safe lodging house, close to the businesses she needed to deal with. Good weather had allowed a trip back to the coast in only two days and now he was in a hurry to tell her the good news.

"He agreed?" she asked, her eyes widening in surprise.

James smiled. "I have a copy of the commission with me which I'll read to the crew tomorrow."

"And then you'll be like the *Invictus*?"

He shook his head. "John McMahon is the master and owner of *Invictus*. He carries a letter of marque and by law is allowed to attack enemy ships. *Eagle* belongs to the United States. The crew will be sworn into the navy and we'll take our orders from the Naval Committee or any officer in the navy senior to me."

"But you can sail together?"

"We can and will. Both of us want the same thing, victory over the British."

She took his hand. "Then that makes three of us."

The time at sea as the *Eagle* sailed to Le Havre had been exceedingly valuable to James, allowing him to get a better sense of the crew and the ability of the key men.

William Rush, the senior boatswain, elevated to master, had proved to be a very good seaman and a steady leader. Having gone to sea as a ship's boy at eight, over twenty years ago, he knew the ocean and sailors. James's selection of him as master gave the man a great deal of pride and he clearly was not going to let his new captain down.

With Rush's promotion, James had appointed Dick Stevens as the ship's boatswain. He was very comfortable with the wiry topman's ability and felt he would also provide stability on the lower deck.

The doctor had proved to be an even more enigmatic character. In addition to a prodigious knowledge of medicine, complete with his own unique theories of treatment, he was also pleasant companion with definite opinions on the world around him.

Jebidiah Lacy remained the ship's gunner. He was indeed one of the senior gunners aboard and commanded the respect of the gun crews. His life manning the guns of many ships would be a strength for *Eagle*.

Only eight crewmen had chosen to leave the ship. Most had wives in England or families and their departure actually tightened the bond of the remaining sailors who all knew they were there by choice.

There was one last promotion that James knew would be a key to the success of the ship in the future.

"We are almost ready for sea, my friend."

James sat at the small table in the captain's cabin going over the list of provisions which had arrived on board that day. Samantha had been their agent with a local purveyor to arrange for flour, hardtack, and several pigs. With the stores already aboard, they would be able to stay at sea for at least six weeks. The fresh water casks had been cleaned and filled. A small amount of powder had been purchased to replace a cask found contaminated by sea water.

"Aye, I think so."

"What do you think of the crew?" James asked.

"They know their jobs."

"We're only lacking one thing."

Cantu frowned, he'd gone over all of the preparations for getting underway and saw nothing missing.

"What would that be?"

"I need a first lieutenant."

"Where can we get an officer in such a short time?"

"He's already here," James replied, knowing his decision was the right one.

"Who?"

"You, my nautical friend."

Cantu frowned even harder.

"Hear me out," James said quickly.

"I've watched you at sea for years. You know the wind and how to sail a ship. You've always been a leader, even that first day. You're a better man than most lieutenants in the Royal Navy and this new navy needs you. I need you."

"I don't know."

"I have a commission signed by Doctor Franklin appointing you a lieutenant in the Continental Navy."

"But you're a lieutenant."

"Actually I'm now a commander. Franklin felt it was appropriate based on the size of *Eagle.* Now go ashore and find Miss Samantha, she's been busy on your behalf."

The next day with John and Caroline McMahon standing on the quarterdeck alongside Samantha, James read the commission to the ship and swore in the crew.

When the formalities were completed, James removed his hat and looked across the ninety or so men who had chosen to sail with him.

"Tomorrow we sail in company with *Invictus*. Our mission will be to make war on British shipping. I don't know what the future will hold, but I do know that we can and must do our best. We're a long way from America. That means we can't count on anyone but the men standing on the deck of this ship. But remember, we're fighting for ourselves and this new country of ours. It makes a difference. I saw that at the Battle of Saratoga. General Burgoyne never imagined that a militia could defeat a trained professional army. But they did. This is no different. We're not the Royal Navy, but the navy of the new United States. Remember that as we sail."

Standing behind James was the first lieutenant of *Eagle* in a blue coat with white trousers looking very much the part.

"Lieutenant Granville, you may dismiss the crew."

Chapter Thirty-Two

They acquitted themselves well...

"Standby by to come about, Mr. Granville!"

"Aye, sir," Cantu called back, holding himself steady against the cant of the deck.

"Put her on the port tack, and conform with *Invictus,* Mr. Rush."

"Aye, captain."

Three weeks had passed since sailing from Le Havre and the Americans had taken six prizes in and around the approaches to the English Channel. John McMahon had shown James that his ability to handle a ship was second to none and most encounters were over almost as soon as they started. The extra hands carried by *Invictus* allowed the captured vessels to make for Le Havre for sale on the prize blocks.

Now, tacking north toward the Irish Sea, James wondered how long before they would have to return to Le Havre. Their provisions were sufficient for perhaps a month, but it was always better to plan cautiously and be ready for any turn of events.

Pleased with the crew's performance, any questions James might have had about their loyalty had been put to rest. In fact he had begun to hear laughter on the lower deck and each night the men would play music after dinner.

He'd made the decision that he would eat with the officers and he had come to enjoy the different personalities.

Cantu, or Lieutenant Granville as James now normally referred to him, had blossomed given the chance to exercise authority coupled with his common sense. The men took his position as nothing abnormal while Stevens and Lacy knew the quality of the man and gave him their full support.

Roger Hanson had become the life of the mess and soon had even both Mr. Rush and Mr. Lacy discussing everything from astronomy to zoology.

Despite the harshness of the weather on deck, the main cabin was warm and ready for the evening meal.

"Ah, roast pork. Would that our last pig taste as good as the other two," the doctor said when Horton, the mess servant, brought in the main course.

"We have to enjoy this, gentlemen, back to salt pork until we make port," James said.

Mr. Rush picked up the sliced pork and offered the plate to James. "Ever since Higgins came aboard as cook, *Eagle* has been a good feeder."

"What say you, Mr. Lacy?"

Looking slightly uncomfortable in his clean shirt and coat, the wizened little gunner grinned at them. "I remembers the old *Canopus*, even the cockroaches and rats wouldn't touch the food coming out of the galley."

They all laughed and settled down to slicing the fragrant meat, and dishing up the boiled peas.

"Do you think *Invictus* will close the Irish coast, captain?"

James nodded as he took a bite. "Unless that last fisherman we stopped was lying, we should find good hunting, particularly off Holyhead."

The messenger of the watch stepped into the mess and came to attention. "Sir, Mr. Granville's respects and Invictus's course is west northwest. We're making six knots and the wind is steady from the north."

"Thank you, Phillips. I'll be up directly."

"Glass is steady, sir. Normally that north wind would have me worried, bad blows this time of year." The master mopped up his gravy with a piece of ship's biscuit.

"At least we have open water south of us, let's me sleep a little better at night," Lacy added.

The doctor poured more wine in his glass. "And why's that, Mr. Lacy."

"The doctor knows the human physic, Mr. Lacy, but not the ways of the sea. If a strong storm comes in from the north, doctor, we would normally run before the wind with minimum sail. If a ship is caught with a lee shore blocking her way, it can spell disaster if the storm continues unabated. A wind from the north would allow us to run south toward France and shelter."

"And more fresh pork, I daresay," the doctor laughed.

"Indeed."

Shifting the tone, Jack poured wine in his glass and passed the decanter to Rush.

"Gentlemen, so far we've had good luck and done well taking prizes. But I have to think that before long the navy will learn of our activities and send out a warship to find us. Are we ready to take on a man of war?"

The *Eagle's* officers didn't respond immediately. Roger Hanson sat with an expectant look while the master and gunner looked at each other.

"Don't be bashful, gentlemen. Are we ready?"

"Sir," Lacy said, putting down his glass. "I would match these gun crews against any in the bloody fleet. It would only depend on who they send out. I think we can best any sloop or brig. I think a frigate we need to avoid if only for the weight a frigate can throw at us."

The combined weight of the cannon balls discharged during one broadside was a common method of comparing the capabilities of adversaries.

"Mr. Rush?"

"The rigging and sails are in good order and should hold up well in a fight, all things being equal. I think we can jury rig with the best if damaged. And the new copper on her bottom makes her as fast as any in the fleet."

"And the crew? Will they fight a Royal Navy ship?"

Rush answered quickly "Sir, they're in a new navy now and they know the Admiralty would look at every man jack as a mutineer. These men know what's at stake and you can count on them."

"Thank you, Mr. Rush, I feel the same."

"Sail in sight to the nor-east, sir"

James put his feet on the cold deck, rubbing sleep from his eyes.

Two days closer to the Irish Sea, James expected they would have encountered more shipping, but the sea had been empty. Perhaps now they would get some action.

The sailing master and first lieutenant were already on deck when James arrived, their long glasses trained over the port bow. About two miles to the east, *Invictus* rode easily under moderate sail.

"Hard to make out in this light," Mr. Rush offered, lowering his glass to greet James.

"Any signal from McMahon?" James asked as he tried to locate the far sail through the lens of the glass.

"Nothing yet," Cantu said, "But surely they see the sail."

James rubbed his eyes, but he knew from the deck he wouldn't be able to discern anything at this range. Slinging the glass over his shoulder he walked to the mainmast shrouds and began to climb. Wishing immediately that he had pulled on his heavy sea jacket, the cold pierced into him like a knife.

By the time he arrived at the mainmast cross trees he felt numb and wind whipped.

"Morning, sir," the lookout said as he slid over to make room for James.

His breathing labored, James said, "Atkins, looks like we have a stranger come to see us."

"Aye, sir, bearing down on us from the noreast."

Steadying the glass against a stay, James blinked his eyes to clear them and stared hard at the sail. The stranger was carrying more sail than might be prudent in this weather, main and forecourses plus t'gallants. She was certainly in a hurry wherever she was bound. There was something about the outline that seemed familiar to James, but with the ship still hull down, he couldn't put his finger on it.

"Keep a close eye on her, could be prize money in it for all of us," James said as he reached for the back stay and descended to the deck.

"Signal from Invictus, sir. 'Intend to close.' Any response?" Rush asked.

James shivered. "Acknowledge, Mr. Rush. All hands to quarters, clear for action."

"Aye, sir."

The word began to be passed throughout the ship as James ducked down to the cabin to get his heavy sea coat.

It would be an action before breakfast he thought as his stomach grumbled.

No different than in a ship of the line, the gun crews ran to their guns, making them ready by laying out spikes, swabs, rammers and powder bags. Behind the gun captains, a slow match burned in the tin, ready to ignite each individual match. The depleted gun crews manned the entire starboard side, after preparing the larboard battery in case those guns were needed.

Mr. Lacy raised his hand to James as the last gun captain raised his hand. "Guns manned, sir. Ready to load on your command."

Suddenly James remembered where he had seen that profile, it was *Challenger* bearing down on them. A cold chill ran through him, it had to be Pelham, carrying a broadside that would crush *Eagle* in a blinding instant. He turned to see *Invictus* with her bow as close to the wind as she could hold, closing on the stranger, McMahon unaware that disaster waited for the two smaller ships. Damn, he thought, telling McMahon to veer would make no difference at this point, the big frigate bearing down on them held the wind gauge and would certainly overhaul them in short order.

"Run up a signal, Mr. Rush. 'Enemy frigate in sight,'" if you please."

The master turned sharply to James.

"That's right, Mr. Rush. I recognized her as my former ship, *Challenger*, 28 guns."

A look of despair told James that Rush knew what the outcome would likely be, but the man said nothing other than acknowledging James's order.

Pelham must still be there, James decided. Unless he'd died of illness or been killed in a battle, both of which were unlikely, the man with the scarred face would be standing on the quarterdeck, his guns manned and ready. For a long moment, James felt himself slipping into a terrible acceptance of what was about to happen in a very short time. Death by fire or death by hanging, one or the other was now very much in his future. His thoughts went quickly to Samantha, thank God she was safe in France. But she would find out of this soon, Le Havre only a four day sail south.

"This will not be good," Cantu said quietly from behind James.

Turning to his friend, James smiled. "No, I think not, Lieutenant Granville."

The big man put his hand on James's shoulder. "You will find a way to win."

Heroic words, James thought. A true friend always and he knew that Cantu would be standing on the quarterdeck beside him when they took the *Challenger's* broadside. James didn't fear what was coming, but he wished that Robert Pelham was not going to be the engine of their deaths. The pompous overconfident man would revel in their destruction and there was nothing they could do about it.

"*Invictus* closing fast," Cantu said, breaking into James's thoughts.

With the frigate carrying a massive amount of sail and John McMahon close on the wind, the distance was rapidly closing. How do we approach, James asked himself? Some of Pelham's guns would likely be loaded with chain shot to dismast the two smaller ships. Then it would be a simple matter to pound the rebels to pieces using the superior weight of his broadside.

The hull pounded into the waves, white water flying high over the deck. On the guns, the crews waited knowing the fear of those last minutes before the fight is joined.

James pictured Robert Pelham, imperious on his quarterdeck, the first lieutenant by his side. My God, could Will Thorpe still be aboard? One man he hated, the other a close friend and now he would try to kill them both. But he also saw the gun crews crouching by the cannon, the men counting on him to do the right thing.

"Look at her move, my God that's a thing of beauty," the master called as *Invictus* pulled ahead of them past the starboard beam as if she was racing to beat her consort to battle.

"Mr. Rush, we won't let anyone show up *Eagle,* bring her one point into the wind and try to close McMahon."

"Aye, sir," Rush answered, stepping back to the helmsman and looking up at the mainmast pendant. "She'll do just fine."

Across the rapidly narrowing distance to Challenger, the two rebel ships closed their own distance abeam. James steadied himself and trained a glass on the barquentine's quarterdeck. He could see McMahon standing at the lee rail staring toward him. The old fox knows what I'm thinking, he knows!

"Mr. Lacy, load with grape and shot on the starboard guns and be ready to run out at my command," James called to the gunner.

"Grape and shot it is, captain."

"Mr. Rush, I want you to slowly fall back, putting us on Invictus's port quarter as close as you dare."

Both Cantu and the master looked at James as if he had lost his mind.

"Captain, the sloop is closing our port quarter," Mr. Langdon called to John McMahon.

Moving to the lee rail, McMahon could see the sharper angle as the *Eagle* drew closer to *Invictus.* They do train them well in the Royal Navy, he thought to himself. Dear God that he makes it in time. The tall master turned back, his gaze returning to the British frigate now only two miles across the tossing gray water.

McMahon looked forward to the starboard carronade, the crew standing behind the short ugly weapon. Loaded with over 500 musket balls in a tight packed wad, the effect on another ship's deck could be devastating if fired close enough. He also knew that most British frigates were not equipped with the new innovation in gunnery, his carronades only aboard due to his relationship with a rather unsavory smuggler named O'Hara. His gunner stood with the gun captain to ensure their one chance to deal *Challenger* a crippling blow would not be missed. Now if only Addington will do as I hope.

"I intend to wear ship, crossing McMahon's stern to rake the frigate," James said, his eyes not straying from the ship bearing down on them.

"Aye....sir," the master answered, his voice questioning.

"McMahon will shield us until we turn. By the time *Challenger* knows what's happening it should be too late to change course enough to avoid our guns. Mr. Lacy!"

The old gunner made his way to James's side. Out of habit he knuckled his forehead.

"Be ready to have the guns fire on your order as we cross the frigate's stern. We'll have one chance to cripple them by putting shot and grape down her gun deck. If we can make each shot count, we can win this fight. Are you with me?"

Aye, captain. The boys won't miss," Lacy shot back, a grin covering his weathered face.

"I then intend to come about and lay us alongside on their starboard side. If McMahon can strike them hard, they may not be able to re-load and run out in time to fire on us."

The men around him said nothing, now understanding the plan. There was nothing else to say, it would either work or they would die.

"Boatswain Stevens, be ready to wear ship. When I give the order, smartly as you can, we're all depending on you, sir."

The looks from Dick Stevens's weathered face told James that if it could be done, it would be.

James pulled his sword from its scabbard as the other two ships converged. On the *Eagle's* deck, only the boatswain was moving, making last minute adjustments on the lines and instructing the line handlers. The only sound was now the rush of water on the hull and wind through the rigging. Across the waves he thought he could hear the sound of drums from the frigate's deck, probably the Royal Marine drummer boys. It was time.

With a sickening lurch, *Invictus's* bow came right as McMahon made one last effort to close the distance to the frigate. The sound of the carronade crashed across the water as tongues of flame began to belch from *Challenger's* side. *Invictus's* guns answered as they passed abeam.

"HARD A'STARBOARD," James called, the two helmsmen and Mr. Rush immediately hauling on the wheel with all their strength. At first James thought he'd ordered the turn too early, the *Eagle's* bowsprit seeming about to ram the stern of *Invictus,* but with a lunge, the sloop cleared the barquentine's stern and pointed her bow at *Challenger.*

His hand griping the weather rail hard to steady himself, James watched as Eagle's bowsprit swung to the frigate's starboard quarter, the distance now closing rapidly. On the British quarterdeck he could clearly see Pelham who was gesturing to his gun deck. With a sickening realization he saw that a stern chaser had been mounted on *Challenger*, and now was the only British gun that would bear at the sloop.

A horrific blast at the close range ripped across *Eagle's* deck, tearing her jolly boat apart in one blinding explosion of wood and ripping out a ten foot piece of the railing. Two men standing by the mainmast were thrown viciously across the deck like rag dolls, blood spraying from multiple wounds. As the ship heaved, their bodies rolled back across the bloody planks.

James staggered from the impact and caught himself as *Eagle* surged toward the frigate. It had to be now, his mind screamed, NOW.

The forward gun fired, its vivid flame reflecting against the glass windows on *Challenger's* stern. In quick succession the starboard guns crashed back on their tackles as *Eagle* passed behind the frigate. James watched the shots crashing into the unprotected stern, shattering planking and windows. He knew the shot and grape would tear down the length of the gun deck ripping the gun crews to ribbons. How many do I still know, he asked himself?

"Stand by to come about," the master yelled as *Eagle* cleared the frigate's stern.

Shaken from his thoughts, James looked for *Invictus* and saw her off his bow, bearing down on them, only two hundred yards away.

"Belay that," James called, "Follow McMahon."

"Aye, sir."

Invictus had shortened sail and was running with the wind, the distance closing rapidly. The close exchange with *Challenger* had spared her rigging, but James knew there had to be damage to the sleek barquentine's hull. Be that as it may, the wily old McMahon must know the damage *Eagle's* raking would have caused and now was the time to strike.

"Follow her 'round, Mr. Rush. Be ready to make for *Challenger's* larboard side."

Cantu joined him from the gun deck.

"They did well," he said looking back at the gun crews sponging out the barrels.

"Tell them to load, but not run out, my friend," James said. "I intend to go alongside her larboard side, but we may still need those guns."

The big man nodded, he knew what a boarding would mean. More men would die, but they could take the frigate if enough of her crew had been killed when *Eagle* raked her.

"Stevens, be ready with grapnels," Cantu called down to the boatswain. "And open the arms chests."

The wiry boatswain ordered two of his mates to retrieve the grappling hooks, and another man to open the ready arms chest near the mainmast.

"And Mr. Stevens, get those bodies over the side."

The two men cut down in the first exchange were dragged to the entry port and unceremoniously rolled into the ocean.

James knew there would be more dead before this day was done.

Challenger surged ahead, the steady wind driving her southwest with the two smaller ships in full pursuit.

"Match their course, Mr. Rush," James called as *Eagle* settled on the larboard tack.

"Aye, sir, southwest full and by."

Trailing *Invictus* by only half a mile, *Eagle* sliced into the rolling waves, her sails straining as she tried to close the distance. Ahead, the barquentine neared the frigate, much like hounds catching the fox.

From *Invictus*, the port carronade boomed across the narrow gap of less than 50 yards. Across the frigate's deck the hundreds of balls tore men, lines and sails to shreds. Parting lines could be heard across the water and on the starboard side the mizzen mast stays parted like a shot. Immediately the mast bowed forward, throwing *Challenger's* bow to larboard. A splintering sound echoed across the deck as the mizzen mast split in half, the sails and rigging crashing down like an avalanche.

"By God, he's hurt her bad," Rush called watching the sails and lines cascade across the quarterdeck, sliding over the side into the grey water.

"Larboard two points, Mr. Rush," James ordered as *Challenger* wallowed across their course, and get the main and fore course off her."

Eagle's speed began to diminish as the big driver sails were hauled up to the yards, the topmen securing the flapping canvas as the masts swayed in the rolling sea.

A long splinter flew off the deck near his foot as, a musket ball thudding into the thick planking. In the maintop of *Challenger*, James could see the red coats of the Marine sharpshooters and knew where the ball had come from. He knew those Marines, many he had led on cutting out parties, were now aiming for the blue coats on *Eagle's* quarterdeck. His heart pounded knowing that any moment he might take a ball and he fought the urge to take cover or at least take off the coat that identified him as an officer. Then he thought of Cantu.

"Cantu," he called, forgetting Lieutenant Granville in the heat of the moment, "Get that coat off, the lobster backs are shooting at us."

To emphasize the point, two more musket balls whipped by them, the ugly sound he had heard too many times before.

His friend looked at him as if to ask if James would do likewise.

"That is an order, Lieutenant Granville."

Cantu turned back to look at *Challenger.*

"Captain, if you intend a boarding party I will ensure we are ready."

James nodded, knowing it was futile to challenge his friend's courage.

"Sir, *Invictus's* laying off to use her guns, she's not boarding," Rush said, his voice now hoarse from yelling over the din of the guns.

James remembered Robert Pelham, the man who showed no compassion for the enemy or his own men. He would never strike.

"Aye, but we are, Mr. Rush, so lay her alongside!" James felt a wild fury as he moved to the rail.

"As you say, sir."

The reality of what he was about to do struck James as he gripped the rail. Sloops of war simply did not grapple with frigates. But he was only minutes from doing just that. Was he leading these men to their deaths? Was he being a fool, only driven by his hatred of Robert Pelham?

"We're ready," Cantu said, returning James's focus to the immediate.

He looked at his friend of these many years, now wearing the uniform of a ship's lieutenant, holding a machete' in his right hand. His expression told James that only death would stop him from doing his duty.

"Victory will go to the ship that attacks, my friend, so let us not hesitate." James pulled his sword from the scabbard and took one last look at the sails.

Between the hulls, now separated by only thirty feet, grey green water collided with itself sending spray across both decks. James could see the destruction wrought by the carronades of *Invictus* and his own raking of *Challenger's* stern. A musket ball whizzed past him, the ball grazing the cloth of his coat but doing no harm.

Cantu had moved amidships and stood amongst the crewmen waiting to board. Boatswain Stevens crouched next to one of his mates who held a long coiled line with the grapnel on one end. Forward, another boatswain's mate awaited Stevens's order. In almost a last act of defiance, one of the aft guns on *Challenger's* deck fired as the hulls closed for impact. Normally the sloop's lower deck height would have made a hit impossible, the shot traveling harmlessly above the smaller ship's deck. But the ocean's swell heaved *Eagle* up and the ball crashed into the bulwark, throwing debris across the deck, knocking several men down, hit by wood splinters. The ball ricocheted off one of the six pounders almost cutting Seaman Andrews in half, his torn body slamming against another man and falling to the deck spewing blood across planks.

The impact came hard and James struggled to stand upright. "Over all lines, boatswain," he called.

Dick Stevens knelt on the deck, a massive piece of wood protruding from his right leg. Looking left and right he yelled with a voice now overcome by pain, "Grapnels away, grapnels away."

"Kelly, their swivel," James yelled desperately at one of the younger gunners who had been detailed to man the quarterdeck swivel gun. Across on *Challenger* James saw Archie Tatnall turning the frigate's swivel toward the men on *Eagle* ready to go over the railing. James could see bloody stains on his friend's left leg, his white uniform trousers torn by shot.

"Aye, sir," Kelly called back, slamming the barrel around to point directly at the wounded Royal Marine who seemed to be waiting with patience for *Eagle's* boarders.

The horror of the moment did not stop James from screaming "FIRE."

Archie Tatnall was spun around viciously as the grape from *Eagle's* swivel hit the left side of his body and tore the swivel gun from its mountings.

"AT 'EM," came the cry from amidships as Cantu led a dozen men over the rail. Screaming like banshees they clawed their way across the frigate's bulwark and threw themselves toward the enemy seaman now fleeing aft from the charge.

More men swarmed up to the gangway as James ran forward and called, "Let's go, lads." Jumping for the frigate's rail he pulled himself over on to the deck.

The crew of the frigate had been literally shredded by the carronades and swivels. Mangled bodies and pieces of bodies lay strewn across the main deck amidst the overturned guns. The remaining British sailors were turning in rough lines, their weapons ready for the final clash.

Through the smoke, James could see Robert Pelham by the wheel, several Marines on each side, their muskets at the ready. Knowing that the frenzy of a boarding crew would rapidly wane, he screamed, "Forward you sons of whores," just as *Eagle's* swivel fired again tearing into the packed crew of *Challenger*. Four men were torn apart, their blood and flesh flying across the rest of their shipmates mates who jerked away from the horror.

As the Eagle's crew surged forward, a guttural cry that only can come from men ready to die echoed across the deck.

His feet slipping on the bloody deck, Cantu ran forward, leading the men on the left of the charge, his machete' held high. An enemy seaman stepped forward, thrusting a boarding pike toward the big man, but Cantu struck first. As chaos erupted across the deck, the lone sailor dropped, blood streaming from a massive wound in his chest.

James met the front rank of the enemy, bringing his sword down hard on a man's shoulder. Pushed from behind, he used the hilt of his sword to slam into the next face he saw, the man's mouth exploding in a rush of blood.

Around him the battle became a series of individual battles, men living and dying within a space of feet.

James checked to each side, fighting for space to move forward. Next to him a pistol fired, the white smoke surging into the bloody fight and blocking his vision. From the corner of his eye, James saw a cutlass slicing at him just in time to step back and parry the thrust. He turned to see Seaman Rowland, a man who had been in his division. The look on the man's face was a mixture of anger and surprise, but it turned into horror as a blow from behind the sailor drove a boarding ax into his back. Rowland fell to the deck without a word, the ax still buried in his spine.

"I want him alive!" Captain Pelham yelled at his Marines, pointing his sword at James Addington.

"Alive, I want the bloody traitor alive, do you hear me?" he screamed, but his Marines were already pushing into the crowd.

"Behind you," Cantu bellowed as he slashed his way toward James.

Sensing more than seeing the danger, James knelt and turned sharply, his blade swinging in a protective arc.

Redcoats were converging on him and only the crush of the crowd prevented the bullocks from using their bayonets.

James recognized Private Collins, now wearing corporal stripes, smash his musket into a seaman's face as he fought his way into the throng of bodies.

The sounds of men struggling and dying, the clash of weapons and angered shouts seemed to cover the deck of *Challenger* as the battle surged back and forth.

Trying to fend off a sailor's clumsy swing with a cutlass, James was pushed hard from behind. As he desperately struggled to maintain his footing, he slipped in a pool of blood and fell sideways onto the deck. Scrambling upright, James found himself past the mass of fighting and at the ladder to the quarterdeck. Without hesitating, he took the steps two at a time, stepping onto a quarterdeck to find two helmsmen, Mudge, the sailing master and Captain Robert Pelham.

With *Challenger's* sails flapping, the two helmsmen weren't needed to steer the ship and James saw a man he remembered as Adams move forward, a cutlass in his right hand. Most sailors understood only that a cutlass was for slashing and used it like an axe. Faircloth had taught James from his first lesson to use a blade in the proper manner. Through the years he had honed his skills and now approached the man with his sword at his side. Keeping his eyes on the sailor, James called, "Hiding behind your men, captain? Adams, stand back, my fight's not with you."

The sailor lunged forward, the cutlass coming down like a truncheon in a street fight. James pivoted around, delivering a swift but not lethal strike on the man's right shoulder, sending him sprawling to the deck.

"Strike, I'm telling you!"

"Not to the likes of you, you bloody bastard," Pelham yelled and withdrew his own sword.

James realized in all his years serving the man, he had never seen him use his blade. Could Pelham use a sword?

Two quick moves by the British captain answered James's question. Lunging forward and side stepping, he flicked his blade at James's exposed arm, barely missing a crippling strike.

Pulling back, off-balance, James parried a second quick stroke, the blades clashing.

Both men circled, looking for an opportunity to strike, their eyes fixed on the others.

A primal urge began to take control of James, he would kill this man and nothing would stop him. Blocking out everything but Pelham and his blade, he felt a surge of confidence and lunged as Pelham raised his foot to move to the left. Slightly off-balance, Pelham parried the thrust but not enough to escape a severe slash to his left forearm as James pulled back.

Seeing no reaction to his blow, James lowered his blade as if inviting an attack.

"Stand where you are, Mr. Mudge," Cantu called from the group of men that had climbed to the quarterdeck. On the main deck, the Challenger's crew had thrown down their weapons and were now trying to help their wounded shipmates.

The old master stepped back to the lee rail without saying a word.

"Captain Pelham, your crew has surrendered. Thrown down your blade," Cantu called at the two men who remained face to face.

Blood flowing freely from his arm, Pelham moved to his right, the deck showing a trail of red.

James knew it had to be finished, there would be no surrender.

Their eyes met and both men knew it was time.

Pelham feinted with his bloody arm and brought his blade up from his side trying to drive it into James's midsection.

Stepping left, anticipating Pelham's attack, James brought his sword down hard, slicing the man's sword arm to the bone.

The English captain fell forward to his knees, the sword clattering to the deck. He remained upright, blood flowing from both arms.

"Finish it," he said through the pain.

James raised his blade, ready to drive it home, and then he hesitated. Looking around the quarterdeck he saw Cantu.

"Call the surgeon, Mr. Granville."

Chapter Thirty-Three

Hands that heal...

The aftermath of a battle at sea lingers for many days. Torn and ripped sails can be mended in short order, while repairing damage to the hull might take the carpenter several weeks. For the men wounded, the road back to health may take much longer if they survive at all. The horrendous wounds almost certainly would result in death, perhaps following an amputation which was the only true remedy for most wounds. Injury to the head or torso most often was a lingering sentence of death, only the length of suffering at question.

James Addington and John McMahon did what they could for wounded on both sides while they made all three vessels as seaworthy as possible. Fortunately none of the ships suffered any damage below the waterline and only the frigate's loss of her mizzen mast materially affected her sailing qualities. But lingering so close off the coast of England was not something either captain wanted, and two hours later the three ships set a course south for Le Havre.

Standing on *Challenger's* quarterdeck, James tried to make some sense of the recent battle. Had they been lucky or had their tactic been the key to their success. The two captains had talked briefly of the battle but were intent on making sail.

John McMahon had offered to send his first mate, John Langdon over to *Eagle,* freeing up Cantu to help James on *Challenger.* But James knew that it was only correct that a commissioned lieutenant should assume temporary command of *Eagle.* Instead, Langdon would transfer to *Challenger* as James's second while Cantu took over the sloop. One additional transfer sent Roger Hanson to *Challenger* in view of the extensive casualties on the frigate.

"Quite the butcher's bill, I'm afraid."

James turned to see the doctor, his white apron almost red from the blood stains.

"What's the count?"

"Hard to say for sure. Well over half the company is dead or wounded. Those carronades...."

"Nothing to be done about it. If we hadn't had them, the result would have likely been far different," James said, knowing that many of the wounded would surely die in the next few days.

"The surgeon is quite a fellow, working non-stop although I can't say I agree with all his methods. I think he said his name was Goodwin....Goodrum, something like that."

James turned. "Goodrum did you say? Jim Goodrum?"

Hanson nodded. "Yes, I believe that was it."

"Hold him, Grubb, damn you."

James recognized his friend's voice over the moans of wounded men. The orlop deck stunk of sweat, urine and rum. Dimly lit by several lanterns, the macabre theater would be the last stop for many of these men. Sewn into a canvas hammock, weighted down with shot, many of them would never see the light of day again. Watching his friend begin to saw, he knew the man on the table was about to lose an arm.

Doctor Goodrum turned, wiping the sweat from his forehead, leaving a red streak below his hairline.

"Doctor, is there anything you need?"

"God's intervention would be welcomed," he said as he continued to saw on the man's arm, the rasping of the saw filling the space. Suddenly he stopped and turned to see James.

The grim look from the doctor was something that would always be burned into his memory.

"So it really was you. I didn't believe them at first, but it seems I was wrong. Well Mr. Addington, here's a piece of your work, damn you! Now get out." Goodrum turned back to his patient and began to saw again.

On the bloody wooden table, strapped and held down by two loblolly boys, lay Will Thorpe.

"Thank God the main and foremast weren't damaged too badly," James observed to John Langdon as they both watched the sails, taut from a following wind.

"A wind out of the north is just what the doctor ordered, sir."

What the doctor ordered, James thought. The anger of his old friend stung badly, but James understood.

A darkening sky found the wind still from the north, but it had slacked a bit and James was confident the current main course and topsail rig would ride comfortably through the night. It had been strangely quiet aboard the ship during the day. The heavy casualties among the crew had made an attempt to retake the ship unlikely, particularly with *Invictus* and *Eagle* maintaining close station. The barquentine's carronades provided all the security the prize crew needed. But James had also asked Andy Thorton, who had assumed the position of second lieutenant on James's departure, for the parole of the ships remaining officers. Thorton had maintained a formal demeanor but assured James that he would not take any action to retake the ship. The truce allowed both crews to work on repairing damage and minister to the less severely wounded.

James walked back to check the compass, remarkably untouched during the battle. South by southwest and at this speed they should sight France by late tomorrow afternoon. Returning to the lee rail, he looked forward to see Jim Goodrum leaning on the starboard bulwark.

"Doctor, may I ask how Mr. Thorpe is?"

Goodrum turned, his face weary in the fading light. He looked back at the sea before he spoke.

"He should live."

"I'm glad. And the captain?"

"Without his arm, but he should also survive."

The two men stood at the rail, the only sound coming from water and wind.

James wanted to say something, to explain to his friend what had happened, but he knew this was not the time. Perhaps there never would be a good time.

"Might I see Will?"

"It's your ship, I'm certain you can do what you will."

"God damn it, Jim. I did what I had to do, whether you believe it or not, this is a civil war and I've chosen my side." James turned and strode aft.

The doctor turned, the look on his face softened.

"As have I my friend, and that's the damned shame of it all."

A day after the battle, enough of the stern had been temporarily covered to allow Doctor Hanson to transfer some of the wounded from the hell of the orlop to the relative spaciousness of the great cabin. Fueled by a constant supply of wine, Hanson had worked through the night tending the wounded alongside Jim Goodrum.

Initially keeping to himself, Goodrum realized as he watched Hanson that the Yankee knew his medicine and was working hard to save as many Englishmen as possible.

"Do you hold a warrant in the rebel navy?" Goodrum finally asked when they had moved a dozen men up from below.

"Me? Heavens no. I only joined this little expedition for money and wine, two things I never seem to have adequate amounts of."

Goodrum laughed then his tone changed.

"You strike me as a man who has seen battle before, doctor."

"That was a long time ago and I don't speak of it much."

The older man nodded, understanding that each man had his own demons. "Thank you for what you've done for these men,"

Hanson shrugged, "You would have done the same thing."

"I don't know, doctor. James Addington and I go a long way back, to when he was a midshipman. I can't countenance what he's done."

Hanson turned. "Then you've been at sea too long, sir. I've watched Addington. He believes in this new country and he cares deeply about his men. This is not some silly European war like you people have been fighting for centuries. It's about a new way for men to control their own destiny."

"I'm loyal to our king," Goodrum replied, his voice steady.

"And that's fine for you, but not for everyone, doctor. Just as in medicine, with new methods being discovered every day, perhaps this is the discovery of a new way for men to govern themselves. All I know is that men like Addington are willing to die for this new country and if you're willing to die for an idea, that's a powerful force."

Jim Goodrum didn't reply, but walked over to where Will Thorpe lay in his cot.

An hour into the noon watch, James scanned the horizon, grey under low clouds. Damaged rigging creaked as the wind drove their makeshift array of sail, but he knew *Challenger* would survive. They should reach Le Havre by mid-day tomorrow and secure the damaged frigate in the French dockyard. Surveying the wrecked main deck, only perhaps half of the guns appeared to be undamaged. The remnants of the four ship's boats had been thrown over the side, each hull torn to pieces by grape and shot. But the true damage was to the crew. At last count, eighty six dead, twenty three gravely wounded and another forty were injured enough to be off duty. At sunset, Andy Thorton would read the burial at sea as the dead made their plunge to the sea bed, sewn in canvas shrouds. When asked to perform the last ceremony for his fallen sailors, Andy had shown a brief recognition of their previous friendship. It was something.

"James, may I have a word with you?"

Turning he saw Jim Goodrum at the quarterdeck ladder.

He walked over to greet the doctor, "Of course, please come up."

Goodrum stepped onto the quarterdeck and his eyes went to the jackstaff where the British ensign flew under the horizontal red stripes of the new United States.

"These are difficult times," he finally said with a tone of sadness in his voice, "And I've thought about what has happened here and what you've done."

Watching the doctor search for words, James understood that this was not easy for him.

"Once I saw past my anger, I realized that you indeed did do what you had to. Your decision to follow the flag of your birthplace is no different than mine. But because of what I know of you, your history and our friendship, I felt betrayed. And I hate what you've done, the killing, my God, James, you knew these men. And I thought I knew you."

Goodrum turned away to lean on the rail as if his admission had taken every ounce of his energy.

James looked at his old friend and said quietly, "I'm sorry. I wish there were a different way, but there isn't." Turning, he walked aft, the ship suddenly a small place.

The doctor watched James and thought how the young boy had changed. It made Jim Goodrum sad in a way, the goodness of youth now dirtied by the demands of a bloody war.

In the fading light, the great cabin seemed smaller than James remembered it. The cots were lined up athwart ship where the captain's desk had always stood. After the din of battle and chaos of the fight, the silence seemed like a bandage applied to a terrible wound. Here men lay quietly, some knowing they would not survive, others hoping they would be able to return to some type of life. James saw Will on the far cot, his eyes open, staring at the overhead beams.

James said nothing as he walked over and stood next to the cot.

His eyes moved to the left and Will saw his visitor. With some effort, he turned his head on the sweaty pillow.

"Ah, the victor," Will said quietly.

"How are you?" James asked, knowing how hollow his words sounded.

"Without a hand, James. But compared to many, I guess I'm fortunate," bitterness evident in his tone.

"Will, I'm sorry for that. But you're alive and the doctor feels you'll recover in time."

"James, whatever made you betray your king? I thought you of all people would understand loyalty." Will's outburst drained him and he lay back on his pillow, his eyes returning to the overhead.

Not wanting to discuss his own decision, James asked, "Is there anything I can do for you?"

"Yes, James. Tell me what's to become of me. No family, no money and now I'll be invalided out of the service, not even on half pay."

He knew Will was right. The navy had no use for crippled officers and there were no provisions for those who were unable to serve. Reliance on friend or family was the normal plight of those unfortunate few. In some ways, death was easier that becoming crippled. Perhaps Will would find employment in the shipping business as a clerk or some such duty?

"Something will turn up, I'm sure of it. Put that out of your mind right now. Get some rest, tomorrow we'll be in France and I'll find a way to get you back to England."

Will stared at the closed door for some minutes after James left. He looked down at the bandaged stump, the pain aching but bearable and wondered what would become of him?

Chapter Thirty-Four

Find a way or make one...

The arrival of a prize of war, signified by the victor's flag flying over that of the defeated ship was not unfamiliar in the French harbor. But the American flag hoisted over the red British ensign brought a focus of attention. Coming after the defeat of Burgoyne, here was more evidence that this upstart nation was making itself felt.

James stood on the quarterdeck as the skeleton crew manned only the jib and topsail to nurse *Challenger* quayside. Several port officials and French naval officers were present along with a company of infantry led by several lieutenants on horseback.

He remembered his conversation with Will last night and knew he must try to help his friend.

"Be ready to get those lines over, Mr. Langdon," James called to his temporary first officer as the ship angled in to the quay. Always a tricky maneuver, James felt confident that with the light winds parallel to the pier, he could put the frigate alongside with little problem.

A last minute flurry of orders to the sail handlers and helm put the damaged frigate gently alongside the pier, made fast with both bow, stern and spring lines in short order.

The first man up the gangway was a short officious man in a drab brown suit.

"Commander Addington?" he asked on seeing James uniform coat.

"I'm Addington. And you are?"

"Humphries, Elijah Humphries. I have a message from Doctor Franklin." The man reached in his coat and withdrew a small envelope which he handed to James.

Checking the address and seal, James opened the envelope and pulled out a single piece of paper. Looking up after reading it, he asked, "Do you know what is in here?"

Humphries nodded, "I have a carriage waiting, are you ready?"

"Tell the good doctor that I must attend to my duties here until tomorrow morning, at which time I will make all haste to Paris."

The man didn't look surprised at James's response, but said. "I will be ready when you are, shall we say first light right here?"

His mind distracted by Franklin's message, James didn't see the remaining visitors crossing the wooden gangway. What would the good doctor have to say about the newest prize? Would there be money to complete the extensive repairs she would need to return to sea? Who would be given command?

"James?"

Drawn back to the present he found himself turning to see Samantha standing on the battle damaged deck, her face hopeful and at the same time apprehensive.

"Heavens, Sam, you're here," he blurted out without thinking.

She stepped to him and he reached out to hold her.

PART FOUR

1781

Chapter Thirty-Five

The World Turned Upside Down

Gray clouds scudded across the dark water as *Eagle* drove into a quartering sea. Three days out of Boston, the sloop was under orders to sail south in search of the French Fleet and Admiral Comte de Grasse. James watched the men move about their duties, his confidence in them and this sturdy ship supreme. Three years of war had seen many miles of water pass under her keel in search of British merchant traffic and carrying messages for the Naval Committee. But this time the message came from none other than the commander in chief of the Continental Army.

He remembered seeing General Washington at his headquarters in White Plains, New York. Almost four years has passed since he had last seen the general and when ushered into his office, the change had been shocking. The strength of youth that had been so evident at their last meeting had left George Washington. While his confident manner and courtesy had remained unchanged, physically the war had taken a toll. Still commanding in bearing, the strain of four more years of checkmating a stronger British army had aged him. But it was the way of things, James told himself. The last meeting with his father had also surprised him. The admiral had walked with more of a stoop and seemed to be tired after what previously would have not taxed him in the least.

Washington had remembered James, although his aides most surely had prompted that memory. Colonel Hamilton greeted James with great enthusiasm having kept track of the young commander's exploits through JT who still worked ad hoc for army headquarters. Hamilton told James that JT was currently in Virginia keeping track of Lord Cornwallis and British forces in the south. The true difference from earlier years was the strong presence of French troops under General Rochambeau.

The two commanders had been planning their assault on the British forces currently occupying New York

City. With almost 8,000 troops including a strong contingent of artillery, both felt that if they could get support from the French fleet, a decisive battle could be fought, eliminating a large part of the enemy forces at one stroke. However after exchanging communications with Admiral de Grasse, it became clear that the best opportunity to deal a crushing blow would be an attack on Cornwallis who was far from his supplies and could be isolated with the help of the French fleet. The two generals had decided to march south while continuing the deception that they would attack New York. This gamble could prove to be a turning point.

Washington had stood when James entered and extended his hand.

"Commander Addington, it is indeed good to see you again."

While he looked tired, Washington's handshake was firm and strong, reinforcing the strength that James always felt from the general.

"Thank you, sir."

"I have a critical task for you that could contribute to resolution of this terrible war in our favor."

James could sense the gravity of Washington's words as he continued.

"With the French at our side, we can finally attack and not just joust with the enemy. We have received word from Admiral de Grasse that he will sail to the Chesapeake to support us in an attack on Cornwallis. Our intention is to continue as if we will attack New York while moving the army south. It is imperative that de Grasse knows we have accepted his offer of support and are moving to Virginia. We have received word from Lafayette that the British have moved to Yorktown and are fortifying the town. Until we arrive I am counting on his forces to hold Cornwallis behind those fortifications while de Grasse prevents the British fleet from evacuating the army. If we can do that, Cornwallis is ours and half of their forces are out of the war."

The realization of what could be hit James like a hammer. After years of cat and mouse, Washington was going to possibly strike the killing blow and end the war.

"What would you have me do, general?"

Washington looked up from the chart.

"Find de Grasse and tell him we are indeed marching south to force the issue. If the admiral can prevent the British fleet from intervening, I believe we will prevail. I need you to take that message to him as quickly as possible. While we expect him to stay in the area of the Virginia Capes, we cannot count on it unless he knows the importance."

Now as he looked across the blue green water James knew he must find the French fleet. If not, the future of the army could be at stake.

"Could we have passed them in the night?"

James turned to see Cantu lifting a glass from the rack and scanning the horizon.

"It's possible."

Cantu said nothing as he continued to sweep the empty sea.

Sailing to the mouth of the Chesapeake had been his plan. If the French weren't there, *Eagle* would retrace a course back to the island of Hispaniola where de Grasse had said he would sail from. But that course might have been altered by storms or even battle with the British. He could only hope they would have luck on their side.

"Might I offer you a glass?"

Roger Hanson filled his wine glass and reached behind to the shelf for another.

James sat down and loosened his collar, rubbing his face after several hours on deck.

"Any sign of the French?" the doctor asked, sliding the glass over the James.

"None."

Taking a long drink he thought again about his plan. Was he making the wrong assumptions? General Washington had left finding de Grasse to him. His knowledge and experience was enough for the general, why was he doubting himself now?

"We'll reach the mouth of the Chesapeake at first light. I can only hope the French are there. If not, we have a long journey in front of us."

Justin Thompson crawled forward through the thick underbrush as the sunlight began to fade. He knew that

British pickets or patrols could be around as he worked his way toward Yorktown from the northwest. All he had seen since earlier in the afternoon was signs that the British had passed through on their way toward the river. Estimates of British strength put their total numbers over 6,000 troops. But JT knew that wounded from Guilford Courthouse and sickness would make for a much lower number of effectives. Always the unknown, it seemed to JT that he had spent the entire war trying to determine the actual truth over rumors. He'd learned to disregard the opinions of others. The civilians almost always estimated enemy strength too high, while the militia's reports were wildly inaccurate. He had to see for himself and count tents and horses, whatever was in real evidence, to determine truth about the enemy's strength. But determining the enemy's intentions was different. Loose lipped soldiers, whether drunk or amorous were often the best way to determine what the army was about. For that reason, Caitlin was now making her way into Yorktown to find out what she could from careless soldiers.

Attached to Lafayette's staff during the recent fighting in Virginia, JT had watched the British movements since their Pyrrhic victory at Guilford Courthouse. Tracking the enemy column north, he'd helped direct Lafayette to Richmond in time to prevent an attack by the forces of General Phillips, who had set up headquarters in Petersburg. Now it appeared that all of the British forces had arrived at Yorktown, the harbor town at the mouth of the York River. His job now was to try and discover the British intentions. He knew that Lafayette felt they were trying to rescue the army and transport it north to join forces with General Clinton. If that happened, the on-going stalemate would continue and perhaps the French would withdraw their support. Between Caitlin and JT, they must find the truth.

Shadows were finally fading as twilight began to slide into darkness. The underbrush ended in front of JT as he reached the edge of a small field. Low grass covered the ground ahead of him and he stopped to survey the scene. The only noise was a slight rustling of the branches over his head as a summer wind blew toward the river.

There were no signs of troops, wagons or horses. Where had the British gone?

"You'll do well to stay out of the streets, missy," the British soldier called across the road as it turned into Yorktown. His compatriot laughed and they watched the young woman as she made her way into town as the sun continued to set.

The small harbor on the York River had been transformed from a quiet village into a bustling military depot. Wagons and horses lined the dark and narrow streets now lit by cooking fires. There weren't as many soldiers on the streets as she had seen in the defensive positions, but she could tell this was a large force of many thousands of redcoats.

Caitlin McKenna had seen a large number of troops building revetments as she walked northwest through the countryside toward Yorktown. The soldiers were digging emplacements which encircled the town. She'd seen two rings of defensive positions, many already displaying the sharpened tree trunks that were designed to thwart frontal assaults. A number of artillery pieces were being dug in by their crews, showing that the British were determined to transform the town into an impregnable fortress.

"You, what's your business here?"

Caitlin turned to see two soldiers walking across the road toward her. They looked lean and hard, veterans of the recent battles in the south. One man had a dirty bandage wrapped around his left hand.

"That's right, I'm asking you," a large man wearing sergeant's stripes said as they stopped in front of Caitlin.

"What have we here, a lady selling her wares?"

The two men sniggered, then pressed closer to her.

"I'm bringing medicine to my uncle," Caitlin said, hoping to sound convincing. Barring that, in her coat pocket was a mixture of dried herbs and ground bark that should pass as a local remedy for the fever.

"Maybe her uncle has the pox, Harry, whaddaya say?"

The large sergeant grinned at Caitlin. "But I'm thinking this one don't, do you, love?"

"Let me pass," she said with a sharp tone in her voice.

"I think we need to search you, little lady. You might be a spy carrying messages to the damn rebels."

She could see the looks in their eyes and knew she was in trouble.

"Please let me go, I'm telling you the truth," she pleaded, trying to sound frail and weak.

The big sergeant looked around in the growing darkness and quickly pulled his bayonet from its scabbard.

"Not a word, love," he said maliciously and leveled the long blade at Caitlin's stomach. "Move over that way."

With one man on each side, Caitlin was pushed toward a small building that looked like a tool shed.

"Please don't, please don't," she pleaded as the men opened a ramshackle door and shoved her inside.

Caitlin moved to the far wall and faced the two men who had leaned their muskets against the wall. The sergeant slipped his bayonet back into the scabbard and dropped the belt.

Light from a hole where a window had been, cast a pale light across the room, lighting the men as they moved toward Caitlin.

"Keep your mouth shut and we'll be easy with you," the smaller man said, removing his leather belt and dropping it into the dirt.

"You ever had a real man, love? 'Cause I'll show you what it's all about, right?"

The sergeant pulled off his coat and slipped his suspenders off his shoulders.

"Come to Harry, my little lovely."

Caitlin moved like a snake striking as she came out of the shadow, her hunting knife slashing toward the sergeant, catching him full across the throat. The man staggered, clutching at this throat, stumbling backwards and falling against the wall.

"What's this," the other man said in confusion, turning his attention to the sergeant as Caitlin stepped toward him from the side and rammed the knife into his throat up to the hilt.

"Ahhhhhhhhh....." the man gurgled as his hands clutched at the knife, now covered with his blood. Tripping over his feet, he fell to the ground and collapsed on his side.

Caitlin stepped back, her heart pounding and breath coming in short gasps. A pitiful moan came from her first attacker who lay on his side against the far wall. Taking two steps, she grabbed one of the muskets, raised it above her head and slammed it down hard on the sergeant's head.

Taking a deep breath, she stepped over to the second man, ready to do the same, but then she held herself, the frenzy subsiding as she slowed her breathing. She rolled the man over, his body like so much dead meat. Grasping the bloody handle, she yanked hard pulling the knife out of the wound. The man was dead, a large pool of blood spreading in the dirt, filling the little shed with the sickly sweet smell mixed with voided bowels.

Moving to the opening in the wall, she looked outside and listened for anyone close by. Satisfied she was undetected, Caitlin opened the shed door and disappeared into the dark.

Private John Scrapper squatted down in the bushes, his soiled britches down around his ankles. Sweat beaded up on the man's face as his body convulsed from another spasm of diarrhea. The attacks had started three days prior, his body now at the mercy of the attacks which drained him of energy and stamina.

The young man was a good soldier and because of that, his sergeant had been easy with him as the company dug into and constructed a large redoubt northwest of the town. Light duty and permission to head for the bushes when necessary had made life at least bearable. While nothing had stopped the attacks so far, Private Higgins had made him a potion of charcoal water which he swore would stop the constant shitting. All Scrapper could do was hope, as another spasm squirted fluid between his legs. As the urgency slowly receded, the private realized there was a man creeping across the field in front of him.

Damned odd, Scrapper thought as he grabbed a hunk of grass to wipe his bottom.

"Shit," he said quietly realizing that some of his excrement had landed on his boot.

But this was something to take his mind off his pain. He quickly pulled up his britches and slipped his coat on. Picking up his musket, he slowly withdrew the long bayonet and fastened it with a quiet click on his musket. Moving slowly, using a bush for cover, the soldier moved behind the strange man who kept moving toward the far brush.

Closing the distance from behind, Scrapper saw the man wore civilian clothes, and appeared to be wearing a sword.

JT heard the click behind him and knew the sound was a musket being cocked. He froze and slowly turned to see a British soldier with a musket leveled at his chest.

"Deck there, masts visible beyond the point," came the cry from the masthead lookout.

James grabbed a glass, moving to the side and raising the long brass cylinder. It had to be the French, he thought. There must be thirty ships of the line, their masts clear of sails now as they lay at anchor.

Cantu climbed up from the aft hatch, his face set in a grin.

"Did I hear masts ahead?"

"Indeed you did, Mr. Granville," James answered.

"French frigate clearing from behind the bluff."

James shifted his glass to this new sighting, knowing that the French admiral would have pickets protecting his anchored ships.

"Bend on the recognition flags," James ordered. The signal had been given to James by Hamilton who received the code from Rochambeau's staff. While the ensign of the United States should be enough to prevent a hostile reaction from the frigate, he wanted to take no chances. But his mission had been accomplished, now to convey Washington's message to the French Admiral.

Attired in their finest coats and britches, James and Cantu sat in the stern of the quarter boat as it approached *Ville de Paris,* the flagship of Admiral Francois Joseph Paul de Grasse. The massive first rate towered over them and they closed on her entry port, which appeared to be twenty feet above the waterline. Along her side, gun ports closed, James could see the evidence of her one hundred and ten guns. He knew that the lower deck would be carrying the massive 32 pounders that could crush the sides of most ships.

Following the formality on the quarterdeck, the two American officers were escorted aft by the Captain, a tall lean man who had introduced himself as Saint-Cezaire. Cantu had provided the necessary translation although James's French allowed him to understand most of what the French Captain had said. The fleet had arrived five days prior and had completed unloading troops to assist in the attack on Cornwallis. Now they were considering putting to sea as a barrier to any British attempts to relieve their troops on the peninsula.

An aide took them into the large, well-appointed cabin where they found the admiral examining a large chart which lay across his desk. The count was a large man, his full face framed by a small powdered wig. He wore only a white shirt, with the neck open, clearly the arrival of two junior officers did not merit donning his gold covered coat which hung on a peg beside the desk. The aide introduced James as the commander of "the American sloop, *Eagle*."

The admiral smiled and gestured to the two officers to sit.

"Addington?" de Grasse asked.

James felt confident enough to answer in French.

"I knew of a British admiral named Addington."

"My father, sir."

"And now his son fights against England."

Now it was time for James to smile.

"My father is a member of the Continental Navy Committee. He's fighting for his adopted country."

"I am pleased to hear that, your father always had the respect of the French, now even more so. Now tell me what message you bring?"

James recounted his conversation with Washington and the voyage south.

"That is marvelous news, marvelous!" He turned to the flag captain. "This will make our decision much easier, eh?"

"Indeed, sir."

A knock at the door was followed by the aide who entered and   said quickly,

"*Intrepide* passes from *Infante* 'many sail approaching from the east.' It must be the British fleet."

De Grasse stood and told Saint Cezaire, "Pass the signal, prepare to get underway. Gentlemen, you must return to your ship immediately. You are welcome to attach yourself to our fleet for protection or retire up the bay until the British depart."

James and Cantu stood and moved for the door.

"Good luck, sir," James said quickly.

The admiral looked surprised at James's comment for a moment then grinned broadly. "And to you also, Commander Addington."

On returning to *Eagle,* James surveyed the anchorage and was dismayed to see ships boats not only in the water, but many were ashore. How would the French be able to get underway before the afternoon tide? Looking at his pocket watch he saw it was ten minutes after ten. The tide now was incoming, making the challenge of getting a large formation underway even more challenging. The British ships were now in view from the anchorage, but the patrol frigates couldn't be more than ten or fifteen miles at sea or their signals wouldn't have been picked up. Would the British try to close the anchored French ships and attack with the wind and current at their backs?

"Stations for getting underway, Mr. Granville. We will stay out of the way of the battle line, but I think we need to watch and report what happens to Lafayette."

An hour later, James watched as the French began to cut their anchor cables.

"By God, he's going to do it."

"He's still fighting the tide," Cantu added.

"And it looks like most of their boats are still ashore, how many of his crews are absent?"

"This could turn out very bad, I'm thinking."

"Be that as it may, my friend, we'll be there to watch. Break the anchor free and be ready to make sail."

Sitting under a large oak tree, JT shifted his weight trying to ease the ache in his shoulders. The British soldiers had tied a rope to one hand, then run the rope around the tree trunk, securing JT's other hand. He'd spent the night sitting in the damp grass cursing himself for letting a single soldier catch him off-guard. The British soldier had marched him at bayonet point to a redoubt where a company of redcoats manned the hastily constructed position. Fortunately the sergeant who appeared to be the senior man hadn't wanted to question him. He could only hope they believed his story why he'd been walking around the British positions after dark, armed with a pistol and sword.

Chapter Thirty-Six

The Tide Turns

By noon all of the French line of battle ships had gotten underway and were clawing for the open sea while trying to organize their formation. James had cleared the headland then waited under minimum sail for the rest of the ships to make their way out of the Chesapeake. In the distance the British fleet was in sight, although it was hard to make out details.

The center of the French line established itself, but a large gap had opened between the center ships and the four ships in the van, leading the formation.

The British fleet was closing fast, both fleets now establishing on easterly courses. A northwest wind had given the English the wind gauge, but also was keeping their lower gun ports masked. As in all battles, the hours of planning and preparing seldom prepare anyone for the chaos of real time crises. This engagement was going to be no exception.

James watched the scene unfold as he drove *Eagle* into the gap between the French center and van. Watching the English warships bear down toward the French, he made a decision that his task must be to observe the action, being careful not to be drawn in or blunder into a fight. He couldn't see any small ships among the British squadron, although he knew there must be frigates on the perimeter of the fleet. An inadvertent encounter with a more powerful frigate would most likely be the end of *Eagle*. He also knew that while he might be able to out run many frigates, there were some fresh out of refit that would best the little sloop.

"Bring her a point closer to the wind, Mr. Granville, I want to close the van."

"Aye, captain. Helm a point closer, if you please."

The first British ships were closing for action against the French. Signals were flying from all the ships as commanders and captains tried to anticipate the other side's tactics. James could see gun ports open on the leading English ship with guns run out.

Suddenly an exchange of gunfire echoed across the water, ugly clouds of brown and white smoke masking the ships the British ships as they drove closer. James pictured the gun captains barking orders to sponge out, load and run out in preparation for the next salvo.

"The French are aiming for their rigging," James called. Shot from the French van sliced into the British sails as the two lines of ships converged. The British were also at a disadvantage, their rearmost guns unable to be trained on the French.

British salvos were hitting the French, but it didn't seem the amount of fire would pose a deadly threat. Looking west, James saw the center of the French line continuing to close and wondered why the British commander didn't break the line to rake the sterns of the French. It had now turned into a battle of trading salvo for salvo. James knew that the advantage would go to the British ships who had always been able to best the French in rate of fire. Now it might very well come down to the luck of well-placed shots.

After two hours of running up and down the lines of battle which did include eluding a British frigate who finally broke away back to his larger consorts, James watched the battle slowly wind down, the two forces separating as evening approached. To his way of seeing things, the battle had been inconclusive for the day. But what would happen tomorrow? Closing on the French flagship, James decided that *Eagle* would wait and see.

It was mid-day when the man JT recognized as his captor, approached and began to untie the ropes binding his wrists. Two other soldiers stood behind watching, but took no action to help the man.

"Come on, now," Private Scrapper said as he pulled JT to his feet.

Rubbing his hands and exercising his shoulders, Justin followed the man. The other two soldiers fell in behind him.

A tent had been erected under a large tree behind the redoubt where JT could see a man sitting inside.

"Here he is, sir," the private called at the tent entrance.

"Very well, bring him in."

Entering the tent, James saw a tall officer sitting at the table reading from a small notebook.

"Your name?" the officer asked almost dismissively.

"Justin Taylor."

"From where?"

"Just outside Williamsburg, sir." JT lowered his head after answering.

"And pray tell, Justin Taylor, whatever could possibly possess you to skulk around his majesty's fortifications at night, armed to the teeth?" The man's voice now had a hard edge to it.

"My wife, sir. I was trying to find my wife, I promise you."

The officer, who had been examining his fingernails, looked up, surprised.

"And you thought she might be entertaining my troops?"

"No, sir.......... no, that's not what I meant. I.... I saw all the army men in Williamsburg and knew you were around Yorktown and my wife's uncle's sick with the fever and she was taking her special medicine to him but I thought she might be in danger, so I followed her..."

"Enough! Good Christ, man, slow down and let's go over this absurd story one step at a time."

Marching toward Yorktown with his hand tied behind his back, Justin wondered if any story would have convinced the English bastard who now walked several yards in front of him. The officer, who finally did identify himself as Major Ian Parker, announced that if JT's story was indeed the truth, then there should be a wife and uncle in Yorktown. If not, Major Parker felt that Lord Cornwallis would be obliged to hang Justin Taylor as a spy.

It had taken Caitlin until midnight to locate the small house on the northwest edge of Yorktown proper. While she had never been there, the description was accurate and even in the pale moonlight there was no question she had arrived at the Thompson house. While Justin was from

North Carolina, his family had originally settled in the Tidewater region of Virginia. His cousin Andrew lived in Yorktown and made his living ferrying cargo up the York River to the settlements and plantations further inland. This was his house.

Two small lanterns were burning in the window as she arrived and unobtrusively stepped to the porch.

Despite the late hour, the door opened almost instantly and she immediately felt relieved. Standing in the door, like a huge bear, was Robert.

"Come in here, woman," he said ushering her inside and closing the door behind them.

"Lord, I'm glad to see you," she said, grabbing him by the shoulders.

Robert sensed that something was wrong and led her into the small parlor.

"Were you followed?"

She shook her head.

"Two soldiers attacked me on the far edge of town. They took me in a shed." Caitlin paused, her memory still so vivid. "I killed them."

Robert looked at her. Despite her tough exterior, he knew that she was upset.

"No alarm?"

"Nothing yet," she said. "The town was jammed with troops, perhaps they won't be missed."

"You better stay here until we leave," Robert told her, pouring a measure of rum into a small metal cup and handing it to her.

She took a deep drink and nodded.

"As soon as JT can finish," she offered. "He should be here soon."

While the next day after the battle dawned with good visibility, the night had allowed the fleets to separate and proved inconclusive. James kept on the outside of the French formation waiting for what he felt must be the decisive battle.

Both admirals still sought the advantage and the next several days became a succession of sightings and maneuvering by each, culminating with both fleets retiring, the British north to New York and De Grasse back to the

Chesapeake. But the die had finally been cast, Cornwallis was cut off.

"By the mark five," the leadsman called aft as *Eagle* moved under reduced canvas up the James River toward an anchorage near Jamestown. The ship had cleared Old Point Comfort at first light and now moved steadily up river. On the shoreline the crew saw no evidence of the impending battle, the troops and emplacements far from the southern shore of the peninsula.

"My friend, I have a feeling that we are finally ready to prevail. My God, the French fleet fighting for our new country, it really is possible?"

The first lieutenant of *Eagle* leaned on the starboard bulwark. It was always the same, he thought, returning to the land brought out reflections on what had happened at sea. But he too knew that there was a new feeling from the crew. They had watched the battle fleets of England and France clash head to head and the English had been driven back to port. An English army now stood with its back to the sea with a force twice its size ready to strike a killing blow. These were times that would change the world around them.

"I've never thought much of these things. But something very important is happening." Cantu paused then turned to James. "It has been quite a journey."

James looked across the deck at his friend. So very different when they met, the two of them had seen and done so much together that they now seemed like brothers. Perhaps it was like this new country, a wild mix of so many different people who all shared the same view of their future. Where would it go?

Entering Oldham Bay, the anchorage on the north side of Jamestown came into view. The only other vessel within sight, a small lugger, appeared to be moving down river and would pass wide abeam of *Eagle*.

James called to Boatswain Stevens, "Have the cutter ready to put in the water as soon as we have the anchor down."

Still limping slightly from his wound suffered in the battle with *Challenger*, the now grey-haired sailor nodded. "Aye, sir."

Proud of his crew, James had watched as they became more than a group of men assigned to a ship. The men who had made the decision to cut their ties with the old country were of the same mind and because of that had developed a camaraderie that was seldom found in ships of the Royal Navy. Most of the original crew was still onboard and, thanks to smart tactics and the ministrations of Roger Hanson, still in good health.

"Mister Alexander, go below and see if the good doctor is available to join me on deck."

"Aye, sir," the skinny midshipman answered and disappeared through the aft hatchway. Aboard for almost a year, the sixteen year old had proved to be an able young officer.

Ten minutes later, Roger Hanson, dressed in a clean white linen shirt and blue britches, appeared from the hatch. He squinted from the early morning light, shielding his eyes before walking across the deck to James. Other than needing a shave, he appeared to be quite aware of the world around him.

"My God, why is it that everything done at sea seems to be at the crack of dawn. It ain't civilized. But you know my feelings on the subject, what can I do for you this bright morning?"

"Doctor, it's what I can do for you that prompted my request."

Hanson looked askance at his friend.

"Why does that frighten me?"

James laughed. "Truly it is for your good and the good of the ship. I will be going ashore as soon as we anchor. I have to find Lafayette and tell him of the battle. Likely he is in Williamsburg. I thought it would be a good chance for you to replenish your medical supplies or perhaps your wine stock."

"Well that is a truly capital idea, I do say. But how are we traveling?"

"We'll hire some mode of transportation in the village, could be horses or a wagon, whatever will get us there the fastest. Cantu will remain with the ship to replenish our water casks."

"A cross country jaunt, I shall look forward to it," the doctor said, walking back toward the main hatch. He turned back to James. "But I do have a request if we are to travel on strange soil."

James looked back at his friend, never truly surprised at anything he might say.

"And that would be?"

"Might I borrow a sword for the journey?"

"Well, of course. But doctor, I wasn't aware you knew how to use a sword."

Hanson smiled.

"You never asked. Let's just say I spent my younger years in other pursuits. Many of which were of less than an honorable nature and over time I found a need to learn to defend myself."

He never fails to surprise me, James thought, chuckling at the picture of the doctor leaping from a window in the night chased by a cuckolded husband.

In stark contrast to the last time James had seen the rag-tag soldiers of General Washington, the troops in and around Williamsburg appeared to be healthy and well equipped. The presence of so many French infantry made this combined forces a formidable opponent for Lord Cornwallis. With the British fleet held at bay by de Grasse, the scales had tipped away from the red coats.

The sound of cheers greeted James and the doctor as they approached the center of Williamsburg on two rented horses. A local farmer had happily accepted two barrels of flour in payment for the use of the two mares for the day. Thankfully the two horses were docile enough as the experience of the doctor on horseback was minimal.

Riding through the late summer morning, the two had for a short time been able to forget that a momentous battle was in the offing. The morning turned out to be warm but not uncomfortably so and the humidity that the region was famous for had not made itself felt by mid-day.

"What's happening?" James asked a soldier who sat with his back against a large oak tree, his musket on the ground next to him.

"It's General Washington, down from the north," the man replied without making any effort to stand. "Looks like there's gonna be a big battle."

Washington had arrived, as he said he would, James thought. But was he going to attack an experienced British force behind emplacements? The advantage was always to the defender in cases like this. Would the general attack or lay siege? I must get my news to him.

As they rode on, the streets became more crowded, the day's heat and increasing humidity descending on the marching men like a blanket. But these men were marching like an army, their faces showed a grim determination that James had not seen before.

"Where is headquarters?" James asked a sergeant who stood watching the arriving ranks of troops.

The tall man looked up and asked, "American or French?"

"American."

"About a quarter mile down," the man said pointing along a parallel road.

The jangling of trace chains preceded the arrival of four towed cannon, their brass barrels dull in the noon day sun. Immediately behind the cannon, a company of cavalry cantered by, their hoofs clattering on the stones in the roadway.

"I'm afraid that man was right," Roger said, thinking of the men that must still die before this war was ended.

"Come along, my friend, we might find some wine at the headquarters."

Hanson spurred behind James.

"I most certainly hope so."

The only way to describe the scene when they arrived at the large house which served as the American headquarters was chaotic. Soldiers were taking reins from the officers as they dismounted and advanced to the porch where greetings were being exchanged. The two sailors worked their way around to the right of the house where a young private approached them.

"Take your horse, sir?" he asked, while examining James dark blue coat. Not what he was used to seeing around the army. "You an officer?"

"Navy," James said, chuckling.

"You say?" the boy replied, a degree of wonder in his voice.

310

"Have you see General Washington?"

"Yes, sir, your lordship, he's inside. Been here almost an hour. Had some Frenchies with him."

"Roger, why don't you see if you can find some refreshment, I want to find Hamilton."

"Where can we retrieve our horses, young man?"

"Next block, Loughlin's stable."

"Hamilton? He's now in command of a New York battalion," a youthful captain told James in the main hallway of the headquarters.

"Colonel Tilghman? Is he still with the general?"

"Down the hall on the right last time I saw him," the man answered and turned away to address another.

James recognized the beefy aide-de-camp from his previous visits.

"Colonel?"

Tilghman looked up from a letter he was reading.

"My name is Addington."

"Of course, Commander Addington," the colonel said standing and offering his hand. Then the realization hit Tilghman. "Did you find de Grasse?"

"I did sir and he was victorious over the British. I'm here to tell the general."

Coming around the table, Tilghman grabbed James by the shoulders.

"A victory?"

James nodded, "The French fleet commands the approaches to the Chesapeake. Likely the British have returned to New York."

"Then Cornwallis is cut off?"

"Yes, sir, I believe so."

"Come with me," he said and rushed out the door.

George Washington looked tired to James, but peaceful and determined. After a polite greeting he had remained silent as James recounted his meeting with the French admiral and the ensuing battle.

"By heaven's," Washington said when James had finished. "We shall prevail."

James saw that the general was not addressing him, but seemed to be lost in thought. He wondered what

311

Washington must be thinking at a time like this? After five long years of war, always on the edge of defeat, the tide had turned.

Rising, not wanting to intrude on the great man's thoughts, James said quietly, "I will await outside, sir."

Washington looked up, returning to the present.

"Sir, you have done us a great service. Might you remain close if there is a need for your ship during the final battle?"

"Of course, general. I will remain at anchor off Jamestown awaiting your orders."

Collecting Roger at a small tavern where he had spent the afternoon enjoying the wine and the company of a young woman tending tables, the two walked back toward the headquarters to find their horses.

"I quite forgot the pleasure that can be obtained from enjoying the solicitations of a lovely tavern wench. It quite restores my vigor."

"Then I will make it one of my constant endeavors to conduct you to taverns at every port we might enjoy."

Hanson grinned, "You, sir, are a true friend and companion."

The heat of early afternoon had reduced the activity in and around the Wythe house where Washington was staying. James decided to return to the ship rather than remain in Williamsburg, but would send Midshipman Alexander back to Williamsburg to await any orders from the commander in chief.

As they turned the corner toward Laughlin's stable, the two men saw a temporary stockade set up on the opposite side of the street. Perhaps forty men sat on the ground behind a hastily erected rail fence. Several trees provided a little shade from the fierce afternoon sun and the men sat or lay in the heat, brushing bugs away from sweaty faces.

"Makes a little sea breeze seem welcome, I'd say,"

Roger, who was beginning to sweat profusely after his afternoon of wine, agreed.

Surveying the prisoners, it appeared to James that there were Royal Marines among them. Strange he thought, they would be off ships, how did they get here? Then he saw something that seemed very familiar. One of the prisoners was older and next to him a blue coat hung on the fence.

Approaching the British, James was confronted by a corporal carrying a musket.

"Prisoners, move along."

Looking past the man, he now felt he was sure.

"Where's your officer?" James asked, his voice hard.

The corporal immediately re-evaluated the man he'd stopped and brought the musket down, butt on the ground.

"He's over there......sir."

A youthful lieutenant sat on a wooden box, concentrating on a small leather-bound book. He stood when James and Roger approached.

"I am Commander Addington of the *Eagle*, who am I addressing?"

The young man came to a degree of attention and replied, "Lieutenant Thomas, sir, Virginia Militia."

"I need to see one of your prisoners?"

"Sir?"

"I've just come from General Washington and I need to see one of your prisoners."

The invocation of the commander in chief's name coupled with the strange uniform and title won the day and Lieutenant Thomas told one of his men to bring the older man over to them.

Despite the heat, the prisoner moved purposely toward James, the look on his face changing from curiosity to incredulity.

"My God," James Goodrum exclaimed, stopping in his tracks when he realized it was James.

"Doctor, I have been instructed to take you to *Eagle*. Lieutenant Thomas, this man is a naval surgeon. My ship is in desperate need of his services and headquarters has released him to my custody."

Roger Hanson stared at James, trying not to smile.

"Sir, this is very unusual."

"That might well be lieutenant, but it is what it is. Now where would you like me to sign for the prisoner, and do you have manacles we can use during transport."

Thomas was now completely befuddled.

"Manacles, no sir, we don't have any, and I don't have anything to sign."

"Very well, a good length of rope will do, we will tie his hands and he will walk to Jamestown."

Fifteen minutes later, a tightly bound prisoner walked down the busy street between two mounted men.

On turning the corner off the main road, both men dismounted, Roger holding the horse's reins.

James quickly untied Jim's hands and grabbed his friend by the shoulders.

"It is good to see you."

Jim, his face sweating after walking three blocks, wiped his brow.

"I never would have believed it."

Roger handed a canteen of water to Jim.

"Now, tell me what the hell brings you to Virginia?" James asked.

Taking a long drink, Jim smiled. "I was going to ask you the very same thing."

That night, as the sun slowly sank in the western sky, the two men stood on the deck of *Eagle* and watched the preparations for setting the night watch.

"How many sunsets have we watched together?" James asked..

"I would ask in how many different places around the world," Goodrum countered.

"We've seen a lot, my friend."

Goodrum turned to James. "My loyalties haven't changed, James. I'm grateful for your help, but I consider myself your prisoner."

James smiled. "You can consider yourself anything you would like, Doctor Goodrum. But you are a guest on this ship and under my protection until we can get you safely home."

The doctor laughed. "Home, hell's teeth, I never got around to having one. Just expected to stay at sea until I died."

"On that sentiment, I think a drink is in order."

Chapter Thirty-Seven

The Terrible Truth

It had been a long and sleepless night for Caitlin. Thinking that JT would arrive, she had dozed in the front room, listening to the noises of the night. Her mind kept returning to the two men in the shed. She had killed before, but never like that, always with a pistol or a sword in the light of day. But there was no remorse, the men were animals and they got what they deserved, although her knife stuck in the second man's throat still bothered her. But where was JT?

At sunrise, Robert had decided to walk into Yorktown to see if he could find JT. While he tried to reassure Caitlin that she had nothing to worry about, he knew that an army with their backs to the sea can be more than dangerous. He was sure that the British provosts would be patrolling the streets and knew he must be careful as well.

Cornwallis's men were waking up and beginning the day's routine when Robert arrived on the outskirts of town. Smoke from cooking fires rose in the still air and men went about their business quietly. While it was cool from the night, he could already feel a touch of the heat that was only hours away. God I want to go back to the north country, he thought, skirting the largest groups of soldiers as he worked his way to the harbor.

Arriving at the small wharf, he saw that there were three ships anchored close in shore, all looked like single deckers, none of the bigger warships were anywhere to be seen. A boat was approaching the dock, likely coming in from the ships, but it didn't appear to be anything of great import. Looking up the shoreline, Robert could see several white tents with men milling around, campfire smoke rising straight up in the nearly clear morning sky.

Drums sounded from the small group of tents and he heard shouts as men began to fall into formation. Two men, wearing officer's uniforms, walked down from the encampment toward the boat, which was now tying up at the pier. A blue-coated officer climbed onto the wooden planks and strode to meet the army officers.

Robert sat down with his back against a large oak tree and pulled out a small knife. Finding a small branch at his feet, he began to whittle and think of where to look for JT. Perhaps he'd taken refuge in one of the small houses that fronted the harbor. Strangers would often prevail on the hospitality of locals if there was no inn nearby. Maybe JT had still not found his way into town with the British continuing to expand their defensive positions around Yorktown.

A small party left the British camp and began to move toward the pier. Five or six soldiers were escorting a man in civilian clothes. There was something familiar about the man's walk and with a sickening feeling in his stomach Robert recognized JT as the man who was clearly now a prisoner, his hands bound in front of him.

Forty minutes later Robert watched the boat go alongside the larger of the three ships. He could see men scrambling up the side and the boat being secured. He didn't know much about ships, but this one had two tall masts. The other ships anchored in the roads each had a single mast and were at least thirty or forty feet shorter than the large ship. He could also see gun ports on the main deck of the larger ship. He had to find out the name of the ship.

"Call the captain," Cantu ordered the messenger of the watch, "Boats approaching."

James appeared on deck several minutes later and walked to join his second in command and Mr. Rush.

"Perhaps some word from Williamsburg," Cantu offered.

"Anything would be greatly appreciated. It seems we're destined to remain here while the world goes on around us."

"I'll be ready to get back to sea, captain," the master said. "Never did much like swinging on the anchor."

The last two days had indeed gone slowly. Settling Jim Goodrum in and catching up had been a welcome distraction, but James knew that events were unfolding ashore and his frustration grew as nothing was heard from Washington or his staff.

The small boat's passenger was hidden by the backs of the men rowing and James couldn't make out a uniform, even with his long glass. But this boat certainly did not present the impression of a naval craft, if only from the patchwork clothes he could see on the crew.

"I'm sure this is nothing of any import, my friend. Call me if the need arises," James said and went below.

Fifteen minutes later, James had returned to the book which he had been reading over the last two weeks. It was remarkable he thought, at sea there is almost never time to read, although there should be. But between constant attention to the weather, navigation and the ship's rigging, there seemed to barely be time to sleep and eat. Perhaps on a larger ship with more officers to handle the critical tasks, the captain might actually be allowed some time to himself.

A knock sounded on the door and Cantu put his head into the small cabin.

"There is someone here to see you," he said and opened the door wide to reveal Caitlin McKenna.

James rose with surprise and pleasure, almost cracking his head on the low overhead.

"Caitlin, my heavens, it really is you. Come in, come in."

He took her hands, guiding her into the cabin.

In the light from the rear windows, her face revealed the strain of the days since she had escaped Yorktown and rushed to Williamsburg.

"You look tired," James began.

"I need your help," she blurted out, reaching for his hand. "Justin's been captured."

The words hit James like a blow.

"Tell me what happened."

"We were in Yorktown, trying to get information on troops and fortifications. Something went wrong and Robert saw him under guard, taken aboard a British warship."

James knew what the British did to anyone suspected of spying and he had to ask one crucial question.

"Caitlin, was he wearing a uniform?"

Slowly she shook her head, knowing the consequences only too well.

"Damn. What else can you tell me?"

She continued in a more measured manner.

"Robert told me it was the only warship in the harbor, but it was a smaller ship, not a big ship of the line. He came with me, you may ask him."

My God, James thought, the British must have two or three dozen frigates and sloops in the Americas.

"Was the ship still there when you left Yorktown?"

She nodded yes.

He pulled a chart from a lower draw. Yorktown lay only eight miles across the peninsula, but it would be closer to fifty sailing miles for *Eagle*. But what could he do? A cutting out expedition made the most sense at first consideration. Steal aboard at dark, overwhelm the crew and set sail before anyone on shore could put the ship under shore fire. But what was his target? If another sloop or brig, he felt confident his crew would prevail. However a frigate was another matter with over two hundred crewmen, it would be a long chance to expect victory. But how could he not try?

"Cantu, send word to Mr. Alexander. Inform the general's staff that we are sailing. I will draft a short letter to Tilghman to explain."

"Can you save him?"

James put his hand on her slim shoulder. "Of course we can. I've got you to help me, now don't I?"

She tried to smile, but her eyes betrayed her fear.

"Now go find that trapper friend of yours and send him down to me, I have some questions for him."

The gentle motion of the ship kept JT slightly sick to his stomach adding to the misery of the sweltering temperature on the lower deck. His Majesty's Sloop *Pigeon* had lain at anchor since he had come aboard and been manacled forward under the main deck. He hadn't been mistreated, but more ignored by the ship's crew that seemed to always be busy completing ship's chores. No one had chosen to tell him why he was aboard the small warship or where he might be bound. But the ship's failure to sail told him that his presence aboard was to get him away from Yorktown, not necessarily to anywhere else. Perhaps Cornwallis would address his situation when events ashore had played themselves out.

"Up you go," a big burly man in a short blue coat ordered him, grabbing the manacles that held JT's wrists securely to chains anchored deep in the wooden bulkhead.

Normally taken to the privy at sunrise and sunset, this might be his first chance to find out what was in store for him.

"Let's go, you're going aft to see the captain," the man said, pushing JT aft toward a small ladder.

Emerging into the light, he raised his hand to shade against the glare. A fierce sun beat down from a clear blue sky, the only clouds visible far at sea on the horizon. He glanced shoreward, wondering if he could swim that far. It was a foolish thought, the only time he was unchained, he was under guard. But if he could overpower the guard and avoid discovery, could he make it to the shore? He looked down at the greenish water sluicing alongside. The current might help him, but it could also carry him further out into the river.

The small cabin seemed spacious after where he had been held forward. His guard pushed him in front of a desk where the man he assumed was the captain stared up at him.

"My name is Culley, Mr. Taylor, commander of this vessel. I've been instructed to tell you that the authorities ashore did indeed find the house you claimed your wife was taking medicine to, however was no one there. Rather strange, I'd say. You claimed she was going to minister to a sick relative?"

"Her uncle, sir."

"It's odd that there was no one to be found, wouldn't you say?"

"They must have traveled elsewhere, sir. Maybe your soldiers didn't go to the right house. All I know is that my wife was going into Yorktown to find her uncle and give him medicine."

"Yes," the captain said, his interest seeming to wane. "For now you will remain under arrest, awaiting resolution to this affair. That is all."

JT's mind raced as he was escorted forward. If Caitlin and Robert we not at the house, where had they gone? Had something happened to them? A feeling of helpless frustration gripped the tall officer. Where was Caitlin? What had happened?

A strong off shore breeze had provided *Eagle* a swift passage down river to the roadstead where they would turn north toward the entrance to the York River. Despite the afternoon heat, the cooing effect of the water and wind made the ship almost comfortable during the two hour journey downriver.

James leaned against the starboard bulwark going over options in his mind. The presence of more than one ship off Yorktown could mean more enemy ships might be found near the mouth of the York. It was strange he thought, the French had retired to their Chesapeake anchorage, allowing English ships continued access to the stranded army at Yorktown. Of course the few ships that were in the area would not be able to effect a withdrawal, but it did allow Cornwallis the ability to communicate with New York. In any case, a night raid made the most sense. His crew knew their business and could prevail over any ship of *Eagle's* size, but what if their target was a frigate?

"You look deep in thought," Caitlin said from across the deck.

James, broken from his thoughts, smiled.

"Many ways to skin this cat, I'm thinking."

She walked to his side.

"Let me help," Caitlin said, the tone of her voice betraying her fear for JT.

Holding his immediate negative response, James considered her request. Perhaps there was something here.

An hour later, the captain called Cantu, the master and Stevens, the boatswain, to his cabin.

Chapter Thirty-Eight

Beware of Strangers

A light wind played over the darkened deck of H.M.S. *Pigeon.* Two bells of the mid-watch had just been struck and Midshipman Drager wondered if he could ever stay awake until eight bells when he was due to be relieved. Aboard the sloop for over a year, Timothy Drager had decided that a life on the ocean was not what he wanted. But at this point he had little choice, with the small ship thousands of miles from England and his home in Essex.

"Boat approaching, Mr. Drager."

Torn from his thoughts of the Essex countryside, the young man walked to the entry port and confirmed that there was indeed a small boat rowed by one man approaching the ship. Not a great threat he thought, the small lantern in the stern of the boat illuminated what looked like a woman sitting on the stern thwart.

"I'll be damned if I'll wake the captain for this," Drager said under his breath and turned to Wood, the boatswain's mate of the watch. "Tell them to secure to the main chains, let's see what this is about."

Several minutes later a woman wearing a hooded cloak appeared at the entry port. She stepped tentatively on deck and looked around expectantly.

"My name is Tarleton, Miss Lucy Tarleton of Williamsburg."

Not unpleasant to look at, Drager thought, his seventeen years making the female form something he was constantly considering.

"Allow me to introduce myself, miss, Midshipman Drager, of His Majesty's Sloop *Pigeon.* How may I be of service?"

"Lord Abernathy directed me to your ship, sir. I was delayed making my way from our plantation and missed the ships going to New York."

Drager had watched earlier when two transports crowded with loyalists had sailed for New York to escape the wrath of the rebel army.

"Uh……I see," he answered, knowing that he would be hard pressed not to call the captain over this matter, the woman was asking for passage. While Captain Culley had been known to bring women aboard during port calls, he had never taken one to sea on *Pigeon.* His attention was drawn to the entry port where a huge negro, dressed as a common sailor climbed on deck after securing the small boat.

"Sir, I have nowhere else to turn," she insisted. Would you have a loyal daughter of England ravaged by that pack of animals that Washington calls an army?"

"No, of course not, miss. But we don't know where we're bound, it could be New York, but it could just as easily be Plymouth or Bermuda."

She stepped close to him.

"Anywhere is preferable to Virginia at this time, sir, anywhere. Lord Abernathy and my family have very close ties and he assured me that that Royal Navy would stand by me."

While trying to frame some type of diplomatic response Midshipman Drager felt a sharp stab in his side.

"What!" he exclaimed stepping back.

"Cry out and I'll kill you," Caitlin said in a quiet and vicious tone, a short knife in her hand.

The confused young officer looked with incredulity as she now produced a pistol from under her cloak which she aimed directly at his stomach.

The big negro moved fast toward the two sailors standing watch with Drager, a pistol appearing from behind his back.

"What are you about, woman," Drager finally managed to blurt out.

"You'll find out soon enough, Mister Drager. Now tell me where you're holding the prisoner?"

Forward in the darkness, Seaman Smithers checked the anchor line in preparation to reporting to the officer of the watch. He never could understand why the anchor line had to be checked every hour of the day while anchored, even if the ship had been in the same place for two weeks.

Made no sense, but then most of what the navy did made no sense. As he walked aft, an odd scene greeted him. Two strangers, one a woman, seemed to be holding the watch at gunpoint. Suddenly he realized the danger and ducked down behind the four pound cannon. Christ, he thought, what am I supposed to do? Get below and wake the boatswain, he thought, he'd know what to do.

The cutter gently bumped against the starboard side of the sloop, hands reaching up to secure and brace the boat against the wave action. *Eagle's* largest boat carried eight oarsmen and twelve more crewmembers to board the sloop. Armed with cutlasses and pistols, the boarding crew scrambled up the side and over the starboard bulwark.

James quickly surveyed the deck, which seemed almost deserted except for the small group aft, where he saw Caitlin and Cantu.

"Spread out, quickly now," he said quietly and moved aft with his sword now at the ready.

The crewmen moved down each side of the main deck, stationing themselves at the forward and aft main hatches, ready to deal with any crewmembers coming on deck.

"You have a prisoner aboard, I want to know where he is," James demanded of the midshipman who stood next to Caitlin.

"He's up forward, below deck." Drager said, realizing this man was ready to do him harm.

"Let's go," James said, shoving the midshipman toward the forward hatch.

"To arms, to arms," a cry came from the bow as a group of British sailors burst on deck, immediately clashing with the *Eagle* men guarding the hatch. The sharp sound of steel meeting steel mixed with grunts and yells as the forward deck turned into a brawl.

James grabbed the midshipmen and shoved him hard to the deck, cracking him on the back the head, then lunging toward the men fighting in the bow.

"Alarm, all hand to quarters," a shout came from aft as several men attacked the Americans at the aft hatch.

Cantu knew any ship's officers would be aft at this time of night and ran to the hatch, his pistol aimed at the first man clearing the deck. The sharp crack of the pistol echoed across the deck, the man flying back from the hatchway to sprawl on the aft planking.

"Watch out, Cantu," Caitlin yelled on seeing a man climbing over the starboard bulwark. She could see the man wore white britches and an open white shirt. In his right hand a sword blade flashed in the lantern light.

Cantu ran toward the man in white who now was on deck, his sword at the ready.

Paul Culley fought hard to take in the scene on deck. It had only been five minutes since the Boatswain had burst into his cabin to alert him of the rebel boarding party. Sending the man back forward to rally the crew, Culley had climbed out the cabin's side gallery and up to the deck. Now forward he could see a group of men fighting hand to hand while at the aft hatch, the boarders appeared to be in control. Then from his left he saw a man charging him.

Cantu knew the man was an officer by his dress and lunged forward his machete' swinging down with a force that would kill or stun almost any man.

Fear clutched at Paul Culley as he saw his attacker carried a huge blade which was descending for the killing stroke. Desperately he ducked to his left and jammed his sword toward the man's stomach, knowing that it was a futile gesture.

Watching from across the deck, Caitlin watched in horror as Cantu's foot slipped as he lost his balance, throwing off the attack. Before he could recover, the Englishman's sword ripped into his side, the point exiting Cantu's back.

Cantu's forward momentum threw him into Culley, ripping the sword out of the Englishman's hand and sending both men to the deck.

The fight in the bow was beginning to turn against the Americans. Desperately chopping and hacking at the British sailors trying to fight their way on deck, the sheer numbers were starting to turn the tide. Wounded and dead from both sides littered the forward main deck around the hatch as a huge sailor emerged from below deck, slashing left and right with a cutlass.

Pulling back, James reached for the pistol in his belt, kneeling down as he cocked it, dropping his sword to the deck.

The sailor swung hard to his left, catching Seaman Abbott above the elbow, the blade cutting flesh before it hit bone. Abbott's terrible cry echoed over the deck, the young man staggering back, his arm hanging from only a thread of skin and tendon.

As the man turned to face him, James aimed directly at his chest and pulled the trigger. The force of the large pistol ball at close range threw the sailor backwards and he collapsed back through the hatch. Turning toward a group of three British sailors, James now knew they were outnumbered but there was nothing to do but continue fighting. He lunged forward, catching one man on the neck, then rolled to the right, his back against the bulwark, sword ready to take on the other two. As he parried a clumsy cutlass blow, James was aware of cries from the aft part of the ship. The second man came at him with a billy club, swinging it hard toward James's head. Instinctively he ducked and slashed his sword horizontally catching the sailor across his stomach. Then shoving hard, he pushed the fatally wounded man backwards and turned to face his companion who was swinging a cutlass down toward James's head.

A pistol cracked from over James's shoulder and the sailor was thrown backwards, his cutlass falling from his hand as the pistol ball ripped into his chest.

In a fury, James turned, ready to attack, only to see Roger Hanson lower the pistol.

"Doctor!"

Hanson said nothing, but ran up the deck toward several enemy sailors, his sword already slashing toward the closest one.

James looked aft and realized that the doctor had brought the second boat and now there were almost twenty *Eagle* crewmen on deck, throwing the tide of battle to the Americans.

Paul Cully pushed the big man over, trying to scramble to his feet. He could make out more men on deck but the sounds of fighting were fading.

"Wait, Robert, no," Caitlin yelled. "Don't kill him."

Culley turned to see a man dressed in buckskins charging down the deck, a cutlass poised for the killing stroke.

Robert slammed the sword hilt into Culley's jaw, dropping the captain to the deck stunned and bleeding.

Caitlin rushed to Cantu who lay on his side, the sword imbedded in his chest.

"My God," she said, reaching over to touch the big man's sweaty face.

"Is he all right?" Cantu asked, his voice strained.

"What?"

"James, is he all right?"

She looked up at the deck to see the few remaining British sailors throwing down their weapons.

"James," she called up the deck.

"Mr. Lacy, take five men and go below and find Captain Thompson, he's been held there. Big tall bugger, you'll know him. I'll be aft."

A minute later James knelt down next to her and saw his friend's terrible wound.

"My God, Cantu...."

"It had to happen," Cantu said and he smiled through the pain, his jaw tightening.

"Rest easy, we'll get you back to the ship."

"Can you do anything for him?" James asked Roger after Cantu had been taken below to the big cabin.

"If we get him to Goodrum, he may have a chance," the doctor said. "He has a great deal more experience in these types of wounds."

"Here he is, captain," the gunner said.

James turned to see Justin Thompson standing next to Lacy.

The men shook hands.

"You're a welcome sight, James. What now?"

"We have to get this ship underway and find the *Eagle*. Cantu's been gravely wounded and I must get him back to the ship."

"Is there anything I can do?" Justin asked, understanding the friendship between James and Cantu.

"Make sure the ship's crew is disarmed, locked forward and keep them under guard while I get the ship underway."

"It would be my great pleasure.....and thank you for what you've done."

James knew he would do it again, but to lose Cantu was something he could not let happen.

"We're short about ten men to get her underway, sir."

James trusted Lacy's judgment and knew where he would get the extra men.

"Bring their captain here. What was his name?"

"He's a shipmate of ours, sir. Mr. Culley, off the old *Andromeda*."

His eye almost swollen shut with the side of his face terribly bruised, Paul Culley tried to carry himself with the dignity required of a ship's captain in the Royal Navy.

"So it appears that John Paine was correct about your loyalty, Addington."

James looked at his former messmate from so long ago. That remark should have enraged him, but James thoughts were focused on saving Cantu.

"Yes, I suppose he was. By the way, we cut John Paine down with a broadside when we took his ship three years ago. Damn pity, wouldn't you say?"

Culley glared back but said nothing.

"I will make this brief. We have taken your ship and intend to get underway before sunrise. I need ten men from your crew."

"Go to hell," Culley spat out.

"I need ten able seamen who can work yards and lines. You can select them or I will run you up the foremast with a halter around your neck."

"You wouldn't dare. My navy would hunt you down until your dying day."

"I'm willing to take that chance, are you?"

James stood up and walked over to Cully.

"It's your sword that is still inside my friend. And if you don't help me get him to a doctor, first I'll turn you over to that trapper and then I'll hang whatever's left over. If you don't believe me, consider this. I already have a death sentence hanging over my head, hanging you wouldn't change a thing. And I'm ready to do it, now damn you, provide me with those names!"

Culley's eyes betrayed his understanding that Addington did indeed have nothing to fear. With the tide turning in this war, perhaps discretion was the better part of valor.

A light wind stirred a slight chop on the water as the pair of warships made their way south around the end of the Yorktown peninsula. Pigeon sailed about one quarter mile astern Eagle, the American colors flying above the British ensign on her gaff. There was little evidence of the fight earlier that night and both ships appeared on routine passage.

Below decks in Pigeon's main cabin, Cantu lay quietly as Jim Goodrum carefully probed where the sword blade entered the big man's lower chest just under the rib cage. Dried blood coated the blade and the skin had swollen around the torn flesh. Protected from the ship's roll by several pillows, the tip of Culley's sword extended from below his shoulder blade for almost an inch. There was little blood evident on the blade and minimal swelling around that wound, but the horror of a weapon driven deep within a man's body could not be hidden. The doctor finished his examination and sat down on a small stool, the look on his face betraying his fears.

Roger Hanson sat on a small stool, his eyes watching Goodrum's examination. He had been surprised that the older doctor had not seemed particularly upset on seeing the sword still lodged in Cantu's chest. Instead he had immediately ordered that several men be brought into the cabin to make sure the big man didn't move and aggravate the already serious wound. To the great surprise of both physicians, Cantu had remained not only conscious, but conversant throughout the ordeal.

Now, on the low cot that served as the cabin's bed, he lay quietly as Goodrum continued his examination.

"In some ways it's almost like a huge wood splinter and I'm seen plenty of those wounds. Wood presents its

329

own set of problems, with smaller splinters or clothing being drawn into the body." He paused in thought.

"Can we simply pull it out?" Hanson asked.

"What many don't realize is that the flesh grabs the blade once it penetrates the body. That's the reason for grooves or canals on the side of swords or bayonets that are designed to thrust, so they can be withdrawn. While this sword clearly has those, it's been in the flesh now for a long time. But I feel that attempting a slow withdrawal does make the most sense." Goodrum looked down at Cantu.

"Cantu? I've watched you heal a number of wounds, what would you have us do?"

Turning his head slowly, the sweat glistening on his brow, Cantu said, "If the sword has not proved fatal by now, perhaps it can be pulled out."

"Sometimes the simple cure is the best," Hanson added. "I would be ready with bandages to bind the wounds quickly."

"Curcuma, " Cantu said slowly. "Doctor Goodrum, you have seen it on the *Andromeda*."

"By God, I do remember. You used it on James when he was wounded as a young midshipman. I do indeed."

Hanson jumped in, "Your bag, we need your bag." He turned toward the door, "I'll send a boat for it immediately."

James quickly scrambled up *Pigeon's* side with Cantu's healing bag to be met by Roger.

"Will this work?" James asked as he handed the heavy leather pouch to the doctor.

Roger turned aft.

"It's our only hope."

The unique smell of the poultice filled the cabin. Mixed in a small metal cup over a large spirit lamp, the glutinous mixture looked like thick, black mud. Roger had followed Cantu's directions, adding seven different ingredients before putting it on the heat. Fifteen minutes later Cantu had pronounced it ready by the odor and watching Roger stir the mixture.

Four men stood ready to hold Cantu steady against the movement of the ship and his own possible reflexes. Refusing to take the leather bite piece he watched the overhead beams as Goodrum and Hanson prepared to withdraw the sword.

James, who had been at the cabin door, walked over and knelt next to Cantu.

Their hands met and the two friends said nothing for a moment then they both nodded to each other.

"It is time," Cantu said, the four men taking their places beside the bed.

Looking down at the man who had been at his side for ten years, James found he was afraid. The big quiet man had become a part of him and the thought of losing him was more disturbing than going alongside an enemy ship in battle. He moved back against the bulkhead, his mind torn by what might be.

"We have our bandages laid out, the poultice is ready." He turned to Cantu.

"I want you to take more tincture of laudanum. Doctor Hanson, do you agree?"

Roger answered by locating a spirit bottle and pouring a dose of the medicine for Cantu.

Swallowing the mixture, Cantu lay his head back on the pillow.

"Don't forget rum for the doctor," he said, closing his eyes momentarily.

"Not this time," Hanson said and moved to Cantu's left side.

Jim Goodrum wiped his hands on his apron and moved to the patient's right side where the steel hilt and blade entered Cantu's lower chest cavity.

"Is everyone ready?" he asked as he carefully moved his hand to the sword's handle. Water slapped against the Pigeon's side rolling her slightly to starboard.

"Very well, I will begin."

Goodrum was a strong man and he set his body against the edge of the cot and began to pull on the hilt.

Cantu groaned, his breath coming faster as Goodrum continued to exert pressure on the blade, rivulets of sweat running off his body.

The doctor knew that he had to twist the sword ever so slightly in an attempt to break the hold of the flesh. But how could he twist the blade knowing that he might be causing more damage.

He used his fingers to push down the skin which was adherent to the blade, gently working his way around the margin of the wound, and instructed Hanson to do the same on his back, freeing up the skin's hold on the blade, and had Hanson apply a layer of whale oil from the lamp to lubricate the tip so it would slide less traumatically thru the body.

"Doctor, a small pressure on the tip, please."

As they had previously discussed, Roger Hanson used a leather sail maker's hand palm to gently push the sword tip.

Goodrum began to feel the sword move ever so slowly and he kept a smooth steady pressure, trying to reverse the course directly as it had followed into Cantu's body.

Cantu's body shuddered slightly and the blade began to emerge.

"Hold him, damn you," Goodrum hissed at the men holding Cantu.

"The tip has been withdrawn," Hanson offered, but Goodrum seemed not to notice, his focus totally on the effort to smoothly withdraw the blade. Slowly, inch by inch, the wicked steel blade slid out of the wound, fresh blood mixing with the crusted blood, turning the blade crimson.

Rising on his toes to accommodate the curve of the blade as it emerged from the wound, Goodrum breathed a sigh of relief.

"Out!"

Cantu opened his eyes and his body appeared to relax, the invasion of steel finally over.

"By God, it worked," Hanson said as he motioned the assistants to relax their hold. "Cantu?"

"I feel whole."

James moved to his friend's side, gently placing his hand on Cantu's shoulder.

"Thank God," he said.

"It was certainly the Almighty, not me," Goodrum said as he sat down heavily on a stool, the sword still gripped in his hand, the bloody tip resting on the deck planks.

As Hanson moved to Cantu's side with the folded bandages, the patient seemed to have trouble breathing, his face swelling, and his neck veins distended. Goodrum, jerked his head up and reached for Cantu's arm, which flayed the air as his body shook from convulsions.

"Sweet Jesus, what's happening," James yelled.

Hanson held Cantu's head in his hands to try to help stabilize his airway while Goodrum stood examining Cantu, both doctors knowing that their patient was not moving air into his lungs, in spite of massive respiratory efforts. Years of experience allowed Dr Goodrum to notice that Cantu's right chest was over distended. He used his fingers to percuss the chest on each side, noting the hyper resonance on the right as he drummed his fingers.

"He has an air leak in his chest!" Goodrum shouted to Hanson.

Every time Cantu attempted to take a breath, more air collected in the right chest cavity, outside of the right lung, building up pressure to the point where it forced the lung itself to collapse, and gradually started pushing on the heart and left lung also.

Goodrum confirmed his suspicions by placing his hand over the left chest. He could feel the heart beat becoming more and more displaced to the left, and increasingly weak as the right chest pressure started to even displace the flow of blood to and from the heart.

Cantu was dying.

Acting almost on instinct, and to every ones horror, Doctor Goodrum forced his finger into the anterior chest sword wound, and immediately a loud hiss of air resulted as the pressure was released. Almost immediately color returned to Cantu's face, his neck veins deflated, and he seemed to stabilize for a moment. His breathing became less labored and yet at the same time there was a ghastly sucking sound at the wound site. With each breath Cantu was moving air in and out of his mouth, he was also moving it in and out of the wound held open with Goodrum's finger. The doctor knew he couldn't take his finger out or the pressure would accumulate.

"By the Saints, I'm damned" Goodrum said.

Hanson thought for a minute and ran from the cabin. He reemerged with a clay tobacco pipe. "Thank god the smoking lamp is out" he exclaimed, "or I wouldn't have been able to borrow this".

Goodrum looked quizzically then his eyes brightened, "It's perfect!"

Breaking the long stem off of the pipe, and tapping the residual ash from the bowl, Hanson then handed it to Doctor Goodrum who removed his finger from Cantu's chest wound and replaced it the pipe. The horrible sucking sound was replaced by a quiet whistle. It was just enough to keep pressure from building in the chest. Both men looked at the curious sight of the clay pipe bowl sticking out of the chest, rhythmically whistling along with Cantu's now more easy respirations, then both started to laugh uncontrollably, their tension gone. "I hope he likes to smoke" Hanson quipped.

Looking around for the bowl of poultice, Jim grabbed a handful and a bandage, smearing Cantu's back wound with the sticky goo and putting a triple wrapped bandage on top of it, laying Cantu down on the cot. With another handful, he placed the tar-like mess around the clay pipe. "That lung should heal in a day or two and we will declare success."

They looked in wonder as Cantu took one easy breath after another, then opened his eyes and smiled up at them.

British surprise at seeing an empty anchorage when the sun rose was echoed by the Americans at Jamestown as two warships dropped their anchors just before noon off Jamestown.

"Anchor's holding, sir," William Rush called back to the quarterdeck as *Eagle* swung with the wind.

Above the decks, sailors were securing the sails and rigging on both ships as the late morning sun rose toward noon.

James stood by himself looking over the taffrail at the nearby shore. He felt tired and after the events of the last day, he should be collapsed in his cot. But perhaps the emotion had yet to let him go. Returning to *Eagle* just before dropping anchor, he had spent the last two hours of the journey sitting with Cantu, who continued to rest comfortably. Hanson and Goodrum were pleased but perplexed on the turn of events. All they could surmise was the application of the poultice had immediately provided a return of Cantu's bodily balance. James didn't much care as long as his friend continued to recover. He would get him back to Boston and under the care of Samantha as soon as the doctors felt it safe to sail. All that was needed now was to collect Mr. Alexander and obtain General Washington's permission to sail. And perhaps find another tavern for Hanson.

JT and Caitlin emerged from the main aft hatch and walked aft to James.

"We must go ashore, James," JT said.

"You'll avoid any more trouble I trust?"

"He will," Caitlin said taking Justin's arm in hers.

"What will you do?" JT asked.

"Take Cantu and Doctor Goodrum to Boston. Then, who knows?"

"When will we see you again?" Caitlin asked.

"At your wedding," James grinned.

They both seemed taken aback.

"You will certainly marry, I only ask to be present. So send that rascal Robert to find me when it's time."

They all laughed as the gulls wheeled overhead the anchored ships.

Epilogue

Despite the imminent arrival of May, the weather in New York City remained brisk as a steady stream of travelers converged on Manhattan. Eight years after Cornwallis's defeat at Yorktown, the unthinkable was about to take place in the former colony of New York. George Washington would take the oath of office as President of the United States at Federal Hall the following afternoon. That the country remained whole and Washington alive, would have been unthinkable at one time during the struggle for independence. Now amidst an atmosphere of jubilation and excitement, a great experiment would take its next step.

On Church Street, the large Walker store, which replaced the building burned in the fire, was busy for a Wednesday afternoon. The coming of spring had prompted many ship owners and masters to make long delayed repairs in preparation for the coming summer.

Despite the British occupation during the war, the business had survived and with the support of the main Boston warehouse it had blossomed when hostilities ended. Samantha always regretted that her father didn't live to see the rebirth of the business he had worked so hard to build, but she had continued in his spirit, building a strong reputation for honesty and fair prices. Now Samantha had two more establishments, one in Philadelphia, the other in Charleston.

Two ship's officers stood at the counter, samples of hemp rope on display. The store manager, Mr. Richard Stevens, was explaining the availability and prices as the men examined their options. Still lean as he was as a young topman, only the grey running through his hair betrayed his age. Behind the counter he leaned on a cane, the wound to his leg suffered on *Eagle*, still with him.

"You can provide five, 200 foot lengths of this half-inch?" The taller man asked.

"Aye, that we can, they're in our warehouse near the battery."

"I've done business with Walker twice in the last few years," the man said to his companion, "And it's always been good quality."

"I'm glad to hear that, captain," Dick Stevens responded.

"By the way, is Mr. Thorpe in today?"

"I'm sorry, but he's down at the waterfront. One of our ships is arriving from Boston today."

The second man spoke up, "Big doin's with the swearin' in I suppose?"

"Quite true, the whole city seems alive with it."

"Tell, Mr. Thorpe I paid my respects."

"I will, captain, good day."

Will Thorpe, the managing director of Walker and Sons stood at the head of the wharf, watching the busy traffic off the southern tip of Manhattan. His posture was erect and from a distance, the empty sleeve of his coat was hardly noticeable. That coat was cut from the best broadcloth and his clothes told the story of a prosperous business man out on the town. But Will was oblivious of activity around him, instead focusing on a ship coming up the harbor.

"Never did like the water," Robert Schlatter commented. "Can't understand how JT and Caitlin took to it so easy."

Thorpe smiled to himself and turned to his burly companion.

"Mr. Schlatter, they had a very good teacher."

"I'll give you that much, but I still don't like the water," he grumbled. And I don't like these damned big cities, either."

"And soon you will see your friends," Will continued. "When did you last see them?"

"Must have been three years ago. They were in Boston and sent word north. We met in Portland. It was good to see them again."

Will reflected on what Robert had said. Yes, he thought, it will be good to see all of them, particularly James.

Samantha Addington walked aft on the starboard gangway to where James stood with Caitlin.

She wore a bright green dress, a black shawl over her shoulders against the chill of a spring morning in New York. But as always, her long dark brown hair blew freely in the wind and it caught James's attention.

"Your wife seems very pleased this morning," Caitlin observed.

"This trip has gone very well and truth be known, she was anxious to reach New York," James said.

"But she almost died here during the war."

James thought back to the night of the fire and shuddered to think how close he had come to losing her.

"She's been wanting to sit down with Will to discuss expanding the business."

"They've become quite a team, haven't they?"

"Indeed they have."

"Good morning, Caitlin," Samantha said smiling at the older woman.

"A brisk one to be sure," Caitlin replied, although her oilskin cloak provided a warm refuge from the morning breeze.

"How long?" Samantha asked, turning to James and pulling the shawl tight on her shoulders.

James paused then said, "With this wind, we should be pierside within the hour."

"Are you excited?" she asked him.

Truthfully he said, "Yes, I am. It's been a long time. Too long."

When word of the inauguration reached Boston, James had just returned from a voyage through the islands of the Caribbean. While busy with business and at sea much of the time, James had followed the birth of this new nation with great interest. Now he would see a momentous step for the new United States of America.

The two old friends smiled then embraced, oblivious of the activity on the pier.

"You're looking well, my friend."

"It is good to see you, James. A safe voyage?"

"A profitable one," Samantha interjected as she walked up to the two men and embraced Will.

"I'm glad you're finally here, I thought you might miss all the festivities."

The three of them began to walk up the pier to where Caitlin and JT were talking to Robert with great animation.

"The last time we were all together was at their wedding," Samantha said.

"You're right," Will said. "That was quite a party, but I'm sure tomorrow will be memorable as well."

"What have you heard?" James asked.

"That Washington would have preferred to stay in Virginia and out of the public's eye."

"Too much honor and sense of duty." James remembered the intensity of focus that Washington had always radiated. "He couldn't refuse the country that lives because of his efforts."

"It will be quite a day," Samantha said as they drew up to Caitlin and JT who were watching Robert stride up the pier.

James asked, "He's heading back for the woods already?"

They all laughed.

It took Robert only fifteen minutes to walk to Lampe's Inn on Broadway. The streets were crowded and by the time he arrived at the two story building he was ready leave that instant for the northern woods.

The reception area had several small tables and they were all occupied, the town's boarding houses full for the big event. Robert saw his friends at the far table and was happy he didn't have to search for them.

The gentlemen were attired as would befit three of the most successful Bostonian physicians who had travelled by private coach to attend the inauguration.

Roger Hanson saw the trapper first.

"Are they in?" he asked.

"Within the last hour," Robert replied. "They were all on their way to Fraunces Tavern." He looked at the tea cups with a wry expression. "And it looks like you need to do the same thing."

Jim Goodrum laughed.

"It is certainly late enough in the day to splice the mainbrace as we used to say.."

"I know......in the navy," Hanson finished the phrase for him.

"If anyone knows about drinking aboard ship, sir, it would be yourself and you would be well to remember that." Goodrum's tone was full of good natured sarcasm.

"Did you see James and Samantha?" Doctor Armand Granville asked.

"I did and they are well," Robert said.

Cantu smiled and thought to himself that is what I wanted to hear.

"Well, gentlemen, in keeping with my rather sordid reputation, let us be off for the tavern, where I will happily buy you all a celebratory libation."

"What in the hell did you just say?" Robert asked.

"First round of drinks is on me."

"Then what are we waiting for?"

The early afternoon crowd at the Fraunces Tavern was noisy and many had clearly been there since before the noon meal. The spirit of expectation which gripped the city was reflected in the level of animated conversations and number of empty bottles on tables.

Arriving within minutes of each other, the reunion of old friends blended well into the festivities. Since the end of the war, these kindred spirits had formed unique bonds of friendship, which carried over into both a thriving medical practice and a shipping enterprise that only kept expanding. There were now six ships that traded in the Atlantic under the flag of Eagle Shipping Ltd. Until the tragic loss of *Invictus* off the Virginia Capes with all hands the previous year, there had been seven ships working for the company, which had allied itself with Walker and Sons ever since the end of hostilities. That alliance included Will Thorpe also serving as the President of Eagle Shipping while James and his father remained as owners.

David Addington had returned to his farm in Albany, but twice each year he would make the trip to Boston to visit his two grandchildren, John and Rowena. Tom Faircloth made those journeys each spring and fall at the admiral's side until he came down with small pox and died in 1787.

Using the influence of everyone from Alexander Hamilton to Benjamin Franklin, James had been able to have Cantu attend the medical school in Cambridge. After two years of study, the man who had started his medical career as a natural healer, joined the clinical practice started by Roger Hanson and Jim Goodrum after the war. Despite rumors that Doctor Granville used unusual potions and techniques, his success had been rewarded with an expanding list of patients who enjoyed being cured regardless of what method was employed. Apparently some of his clients quietly referred to him as "the Witch Doctor."

"It is good to see you, my friend," James told Cantu. The conversation had moved away from them as a spirited argument between JT and Roger sprung up over the merits of Irish whiskey.

"Why is it that we both live in Boston and it seems that we seldom see each other?"

James laughed. "I'm at sea and you're busy healing the sick."

Cantu sipped his wine.

"You're right and I wish it wasn't so."

"We both know that so much of our lives are out of our control," James replied.

The big man nodded as he considered what James had said.

After a long pause and laughter coming from the far end of the table, Cantu said evenly, "I want to go back to sea."

For a moment James thought he'd misunderstood his friend.

"To sea?"

Cantu nodded.

"By God man, you make no sense. You've found success as a doctor in Boston. Respect, wealth, friendships, what more do you want?"

"I learned healing early in life from my father. Now I have learned English medicine as well. The sum of the two makes a stronger whole, like braiding two strands of rope together."

"I'm not sure I follow."

Setting down his glass, Cantu began to speak, his tone earnest.

"English medicine is very good. For surgeries or wounds there is none better. My medicine uses the power of nature and natural healing. But what else is out there in the rest of the world? I want to travel and learn from healers around the world. I want to make my medicine the best."

James had seen what his friend had been able to do many times in the past. He had benefited from those very skills. Cantu was talking about a voyage of discovery, he told himself. The truth be known, he had become bored with simply transporting cargo. While it was lucrative, only the challenge of going to sea held his interest anymore. At least in the navy, he was at sea for a purpose greater than just to make money. Would this be a chance to repay his friend for years of friendship? No, it would be collaboration. Together they would sail the world and learn.

"When do you want to leave?"

Cantu looked back in surprise.

"You tell me where you want to go and we shall go there. Of course, Roger and Jim will be angry with both of us."

The surprise turning to mirth, Cantu said, "My guess is they will want to go with us."

"Then so be it, my friend."

Other historical fiction adventure novels by John Schork are available online from Amazon.com.

DESTINY IN THE PACIFIC

Set in the first desperate year of the Pacific War, "Destiny in the Pacific" tells the story of Bryan Michaels, a disgraced Naval Aviator. A promising career in shambles, his time in the Navy drawing to a close, Bryan is given a second chance following the attack on Pearl harbor. Just as that day changed the course of a nation, it did the same for Bryan. Fueled by anger at the loss of friends and inspired by words of Chester Nimitz, Bryan finds his destiny in the vast Pacific.

THE FLAMES OF DELIVERANCE

Terribly burned in the air war over Europe, the wealthy son of a New York banker discovers love, friendship and redemption as he painfully struggles to recover. Eventually returning to the air battle in Europe and the Pacific, Hank Mitchell finds the strength to overcome his scars and the conviction to do what must be done regardless of the personal cost.

THE KING'S COMMANDER

Following a pact between FDR and Churchill, Jack Stewart finds himself an American in the Royal Navy, tasked with learning the secrets of MI-6. Trying desperately to beat the Nazi's technological advancements, he forms an elite team that strikes deep into occupied Europe. From the back roads of France to the

343

windswept English Channel, the young officer takes on the most difficult challenges of the war and builds a team that can defeat the Nazi war machine.

A JOURNEY OF HONOR

A strange series of events results in two men from opposite sides of the war being thrown together. One is a Commander in the Royal Navy, the other a Colonel in the German SS. But they join forces in an attempt to cripple Adolph Hitler's ability to launch a weapon that could change the course of the war. Parachuting into war-torn Europe, the two men not only prevent a devastating attack on England, but realize they have become friends and comrades.

THE FALKENBERG RIDDLE

As the most terrible war in history approaches its bloody conclusion, the allies and Soviet Union are already preparing for the next. But there are secrets within the collapsing capital of the Third Reich that must never become public. A senior German at the highest level possesses knowledge which could devastate the world. Jack Stewart leads his strike team deep into the cataclysmic final battle of Berlin to ensure that information never becomes public.

THE WINDS OF BATTLE
The Journey of James Addington

Sent to sea as a young midshipman, James Addington, is the son of a British Admiral following in his father's footsteps. Born in the colonies, he sails from New York City in 1770 aboard H.M.S. Andromeda. Over the next three years, battling pirates and slavers, the young man matures into a loyal officer of the Royal Navy. But the

344

terrible events of 1776 drag James back to the land of his birth. As a lieutenant in the frigate Challenger, he is a witness to the bloody Battle of Breed's Hill, as the fledging rebel army takes on the pride of the British Army. Stunned by what he sees, he knows the colonies will be forever changed. What he doesn't realize is that he will change along with them.

Falling in love with a young lady from Massachusetts, Addington finds himself immersed in a tangled web of conflicting loyalties and passions. Does he help crush the rebellion or does he fall victim to the lure of independence? His journey takes him from north to south in the colonies and across the Atlantic as captain of his own ship. From the Battles of Saratoga to Yorktown, he learns the price of friendship and loyalty as the fight for America's independence builds to a thundering climax.

Coming soon !!
THE DEADLY SKY

The author's website is located at: http://www.johnschork.com
The author's email is : john@johnschork.com

Format and graphic designs by:
Jupiter Pixel Publishing
18380 SE Lakeside Drive
Jupiter, FL 33469